About the Author

Norah was born in Banbridge in 1935 and was an experienced Nurse Tutor, being responsible for Student Nurses within three major hospitals in Northern Ireland. Her main teaching programme was 'A.I.D.S. and H.I.V.' Education.
She is married with two children and six grandchildren.

Dedication

I wish to dedicate this book to my mother Ellen, who gave me such a love of English literature. She encouraged me to read from an early age and she herself was an avid reader, particularly of crime novels. I believe this book – my first crime one – is an appropriate one to dedicate to her.

Norah Humphreys

THEY'VE TAKEN LEWIS

AUSTIN MACAULEY
PUBLISHERS LTD.

A CIP catalogue record for this title is available from the British Library.

ISBN 9781786124203 (Paperback)
ISBN 9781786124210 (Hardback)

www.austinmacauley.com

First Published (2015)
Austin Macauley Publishers Ltd.
25 Canada Square
Canary Wharf
London
E14 5LQ

Printed and bound in Great Britain

Acknowledgements

I wish to thank all my family for the support and encouragement they have given to me since I started writing. Particularly I want to thank my grandsons Tim and Mark for their invaluable help with cover ideas. Many thanks to all my friends for their continued support and a very special thanks to the Creighton family for their support in the promotion of my work.

Main Characters

Ellen Hampton
Ellen is the widow of Rob Hampton and mother of Matthew, Charles, Thomas and Lucie. She is now married to Tom Greenlees who is Paul's Father.

Tom Greenlees
Second husband of Ellen and stepfather to her children. Also Lucie's father-in-law.

Rob Hampton
Shot dead by I.R.A. Father of Matthew, Thomas, Charles and Lucie.

Matthew Hampton
Detective Inspector in R.U.C. Married to Julie. Has son Jason and daughter Emily.

Julie Hampton
Julie is married to Matthew.

Thomas Hampton
Is Ellen's son. Is married to Jenny.

Charles Hampton
Is Ellen's son. Married to Sheila.

Lucie Hampton/ Greenlees

She is Ellen's daughter. Was married to Patrick Mullan who was involved in I.R.A. Now married to Paul Greenlees.

Maggie nee Hampton

Is a widow and sister of Rob. Returned from Canada with daughter Rachel and granddaughter Lynn.

Rachel Finlay

Daughter of Maggie. Was divorced when in Canada. Adopted Lynn following Lynn's parent's death in Canada. Rachel is now married to Gavin Finlay and is Lewis' grandmother.

Lynn Hampton

Is Rachel's daughter and mother to Lewis, her son to Arnold Simpson.

Arnold Simpson

Married Lynn bigamously while married to Iris. Is the biological father of Lewis.

Iris Simpson

Wife of Arnold.

John Finlay

Widower. Was married to Dorrie, sister of Rob, Maggie and Eve.

Gavin Finlay

Nephew of John Finlay. Married to Rachel.

Patrick Mullan

Ex-Husband of Lucie. Served a prison sentence for involvement in murder of Rob Hampton.

Helena
Now married to Patrick Mullan.

Lewis Hampton
Son of Lynn and adopted son of Jason.

Emily Hampton
Daughter of Matthew and Julie. Sister of Jason.

Chapter 1

May 1983

The first building Patrick Mullan saw as he stepped out through the gates of the prison and into freedom was the courthouse, where he had been found guilty all those years ago of the most foul of crimes – betrayal of family. The building, with its cream coloured walls and imposing façade, was a stark reminder of that day eight years ago when he had pleaded guilty to collaborating with the IRA. Since that time, he'd had many hours to relive the events, which had eventually led to his incarceration in a prison cell for so many years. Over time, he had come to believe that some kind of temporary madness on his part had made him a participant of a foul crime, which had led to the horrific murder of a totally innocent man. When he had first agreed to collaborate with the McCaughey brothers in the pub that fateful evening, he had never envisaged the murder of anyone, much less a family member. Now, as he stood relishing his freedom, with the May sunshine on his face and warming his body, he vowed that no matter what, he would never be party to such subversive activities ever again.

Even as he walked down the steps of the prison onto the footpath, he saw the real, true reason why he was so resolved to overcome his past and become the honourable man his family had originally believed him to be. She was standing on the pavement across the street and the pale blue dress she was wearing complimented her slim figure and highlighted her fair hair and complexion; Helena, his friend, his confidante during the last two years, the girl who had given him such hope for the future. She alone had managed to lift him from that deep pit of depression and hopelessness he had been in since his committal to prison. And now, to add to his happiness, she had promised to marry him on his release.

He had first noticed the fresh-faced girl during one of the prison visiting sessions; she had been visiting her father, who had been committed for some minor mishap or other, which Patrick could not remember much about. His mother had been visiting him on one of her many loyal visits; during these visits she always insisted he should continue to pray to God for his forgiveness and even equally as important, that of the Hampton family. Patrick reckoned that he was highly unlikely to ever receive forgiveness from that particular family. As his mother talked to him, he noticed the girl smiling at him in a friendly manner even as she talked to her father and somewhat vaguely, Patrick smiled back, too preoccupied with his mother's presence to take much notice of other visitors.

Then, he had received an official notification from one of the prison officers that a young lady by the name of Helena Swain – daughter of Mr Edward Swain, an inmate of the prison – would like to visit him on a regular basis. More intrigued than flattered, Patrick agreed she could talk to him for five minutes during next visiting day. Perhaps she was yet another nosy journalist, eager to quiz him in order to find out something of his motives for assisting – albeit indirectly – in the murder of his father-in-law. But on the afternoon of her visit and her obvious sincerity in his

2

welfare, he quickly realised, this pretty, sensitive, intelligent girl was not really interested in how he had ended up where he was; she just seemed genuinely interested in his well-being and she soon made it clear she was there on a purely personal level.

Helena Swain knew the whole circumstances of Patrick's sentence and imprisonment, and she fervently believed he had never considered the possibility of anyone getting hurt. He had understood buildings would be demolished and cars stolen and blown up., but it had never crossed his mind that anything more sinister was ever planned. He had even admitted to Helena that he had come to hate his brother-in-law, Matthew Hampton, but would never have contemplated actually carrying out any vile, barbaric act against him or indeed, against any of the Hampton family.

Now, Helena was confident Patrick and she could soon put all that behind them and look forward to the future. Besides, Patrick Mullan would soon have disappeared completely as he had been given a new identity on his discharge; he was now Philip Mercer and in a month's time, Helena thought happily, she would become Mrs. Philip Mercer.

The security services had decided some six months before Patrick's release that he needed a new identity, because he was an ex-policeman and having also been involved in an attack on one of his own colleagues, he was considered to be at high risk from paramilitaries, or indeed other forces intent on revenge. Not only had the security services given him a new name, but they had also found him a new occupation, which although it only offered Patrick a modest wage, he believed it was a role he would enjoy. When he had told Helena on her last visit to him, that the social worker had informed him that very morning he had been accepted as a clerk in the council offices in the city of Armagh and would be commencing work there two weeks after his discharge, she was overjoyed. Those who had been responsible for Patrick's welfare must surely have known that Helena lived and worked in Portadown, which was within easy commuting distance of Armagh city.

Now, as Helena stood in the arms of Patrick, the man she would soon marry, and whose new name, Philip Mercer, she must keep repeating over and over again until she did not know him by any other, she believed they were about to embark on a safe, happy future.

Chapter 2

November 1984

Matthew Hampton looked at the message some well-meaning colleague had placed on his office desk earlier that day. Although Matthew read the words, his brain could not bear to register the reality and meaning of those words. He lifted the page from where it lay under his paper and, although keen to throw it into his waste paper bin, he felt compelled to read on. The message was all quite detailed and obviously, whichever one of his colleagues had left it there, they had no idea how Matthew really felt. His colleague no doubt had felt that he needed to know from a professional point of view, but when Matthew read that Philip Mercer and Helena Swain had had their daughter Alice baptised in the Presbyterian Church in Armagh, he felt an awful rage fill his chest. How could the man dare to enter a Protestant Church of any kind to say any vows before God, when he had so resolutely refused to do so all those years ago in order to marry Matthew's sister? Yes, Matthew found all the information he had learnt about Patrick Mullan over the last eighteen months hard to deal with. The knowledge that security had found it necessary to give the man a new identity and a new job had been hard enough to deal with, although a new identity came with its own serious disadvantages. He did wonder how Mrs. Mullan, Patrick's mother, would deal with the knowledge of her granddaughter's birth; she would be happy for them, Matthew was sure, but then, how would she deal with never seeing her grandchild, it would be so very hard for her. But she would be sensible, Matthew was convinced she would never put her son's life at risk. She was the only person in the family he had any feelings for, he had rather liked Mrs. Mullan and he did feel sorry for her but she would need all her self-discipline to cope with not getting in touch with her son and his family.

Matthew knew he'd had a lot to deal with in the last year; all the revelations about Patrick Mullan and then he had learned of the assassination of the Chief of the Shankill Butchers. He recalled how keen his sense of disappointment had been when he learned that Devlin was dead. He would have much preferred to see that monster in the dock and receive his nemesis, and it seemed the murder had been the work of the IRA, even though they were likely acting with loyalist paramilitaries who had come to realise Devlin was a threat to their own credibility. The whole case of the Shankill Butchers had, without doubt, been one of the most frustrating of Matthew's career, and even though most of the gang had been eventually caught and received long prison sentences, he found his inability to produce sufficient evidence to find the ring leader guilty, a huge disappointment.

It was some consolation to Matthew when his colleagues were keen to tell him and reassure him that it was thanks to him, that the country was now rid of a monster, who had terrified the Catholic community and left nothing, only horror and grief in its wake. His colleagues were convinced that the fact that Matthew had even managed to bring Devlin to trial was brilliant work, and the whole publicity had ensured notoriety for Devlin, which eventually led to his assassination. Although Matthew knew his colleagues were probably right, he was still left with the feeling that he had somehow been inefficient in this case.

Matthew did try to remain positive about his work and his life, but the fact that Patrick Mullan had been treated so well by Security was hard to swallow. The fact they had even given him a job when he got out of prison was, he thought, contemptible. Then, the feeling of inadequacy over the Shankill Butchers still gnawed at him and he felt that the relatives of those who had suffered at Devlin's hands had not been given justice, even though the monster was dead. He was beginning to think that he was not performing to the best of his ability and he realised that the more he dwelt on some matters, the less he seemed to be able to deal with others. And all the time, he was aware that his attitude was beginning to affect his home life. Certainly, the presence of Lewis, their adopted grandson, in their lives, was a real source of joy, and then to be blessed with a beautiful granddaughter should, Matthew knew, make him feel complete. But somehow, although he thoroughly enjoyed their visits, when they left, he felt his good humour desert him and he would be drawn back to his desk to face his work, which at times seemed to be more impossible to deal with than before. It was often, during the times when Jason and Lynn came with the grandchildren and after their departure that he thought of Patrick Mullan and his new family, and wondered idly how Mrs. Mullan was coping with the situation.

Chapter 3

'Helena, don't you think that was a bit unwise'? Philip stood quietly in the kitchen of his home as he listened with some disquiet to what his wife was just telling him.

'Patrick, sorry, I mean Philip,' It was only when Helena was very stressed that her memory slipped back to when she had just met her husband and then she would inadvertently use the name she had first became familiar with. She had practised his new name so often that it just seemed to naturally roll off her tongue. That is, until such times as to-day, when she sensed and feared her husband's disapproval of her actions – disapproval which she knew in her heart to be totally justified.

Against her better judgment, she had listened to her mother-in-law's pleading and tears and had, after much soul searching, agreed to meet her in Armagh the following day. She had promised to bring her grandchild with her so that Mrs. Mullan might see her, hold her and kiss her, because no one knew when she might see Alice again. Then, there were also the demands of Philip's two brothers; both desperate to see Philip, and also their new niece. But here, Helena had been very firm and resolved and had explained, once more, the importance of caution. After all, the powers that be had not given her husband a new identity and a new job for nothing, they must believe the threat to her husband was very real and that there were those out there who wanted revenge.

So, Helena had known full well that Philip would not be agreeable to the meeting, but on this one isolated occasion, she was intent on honouring her agreement with Mrs. Mullan. She felt so very sorry for her and believed the woman would never take any risk, which might jeopardise her own son's safety and she had reassured Helena that she would never be so foolish, and intended to cover her tracks very well.

'Philip, dear,' Helena leaned close to her husband. 'I simply found it impossible to refuse your mother on this occasion. She was distraught when she phoned here earlier. She misses you so much but is prepared to endure that, but she is desperate to see Alice, who is, after all, her only grandchild. So, I have arranged to meet with her on this one occasion.' Helena hurried on. 'We have chosen a small shopping mall in Armagh. She is coming by bus and I have arranged to meet her at the bus station and then we'll go to a very discreet small coffee shop in the mall. I do believe everything will be alright.' Helena put her hand on her husband's arm in a conciliatory gesture, anxious for his understanding as to why she had agreed to meet Mrs. Mullan.

Suddenly Philip relented. 'I know it must be very hard for mother – knowing about our daughter and not being able to see her and she has always been so loyal to me, through thick and thin. But please, Helena, you must be insistent that my father or my brothers do not make any contact, whatsoever.' Philip's voice, although it held a note of anxiety, was still firm and strong. 'I know Brian is immigrating to America, but that's all the more reason why he should not make any move to be in touch. The IRA has been watching them both, I'm sure, especially in the public houses my brothers frequent. As for Gerry, tell Mum the same thing applies to him. Gerry probably imagines he and I would have been the best of buddies had I not had to change my identity, but that's as may be, we'll never know

9

now.' Philip went on, 'just tell Mum there can be no leeway, whatsoever. My brothers have to pretend I'm thousands of miles away or better still, dead.'

'Of course I'll tell her, Philip, and I also intend to tell her that any communication between her and I must be very limited.' Helena was so relieved Philip had agreed to let her meet his mother. 'I promise I will stress that our safety depends on it; she will understand that, I know, she is very well aware that you gave information to the IRA, including the names of those you were in collusion with in Crossmaglen, but I intend to stress it all again to her.'

'I'm probably a bit to blame here too, Helena. I never did stress how important secrecy was. I was so anxious not to alarm her, but now I know we must spell it out; no more secrets. Let's not forget, it's not just the IRA who has threatened me; the UDA has also issued threats because I was involved in getting a policeman's father shot dead,' with that, Philip pulled his wife close and they held one another together for a few minutes. Then, Helena spoke. 'Dinner is in the oven, so let's go and get it, sit at the table, relax and enjoy it. Baby Alice is already in bed and no doubt will be up at daybreak, as usual.'

Even though Helena had been reassured by both her own words and those of her husband's, she still found that sleep evaded her for most of that night, with the result that she overslept the next morning. When she woke to the noise of her daughter agitating and complaining from her cot in the nursery, she realised that Philip had already gone to work. Glancing at the clock on her bedside table, she realised it had gone nine o'clock, no wonder Alice was getting tetchy. Still half asleep, she dragged herself out of bed and headed for the nursery. She was glad Mrs. Mullan had decided to meet for lunch after all, and not for early morning coffee. This meant she had plenty of time to feed and dress Alice, make herself a healthy, leisurely breakfast and give herself time to make her way to the bus station. She wanted to be there, waiting for Mrs. Mullan, when she alighted. This, Helena was determined to do – she did not want her mother-in-law hanging around anywhere, waiting for her. She also had about half an hour's drive and she really needed to keep calm and keep her wits about her.

She arrived at the bus station with a good five minutes to spare and as she parked her car, she decided to remain inside the car – that way she would not have to release Alice's straps and then have to buckle her in again. Besides, the child seemed in a deep sleep at the moment. She could watch from where she was parked when the bus would arrive and she would be able to see any passengers disembarking. She had arranged to meet Mrs. Mullan in a nearby car park. Helena felt it might draw less attention to them both, if Helena was not there to greet her as she alighted. Now, she felt that sitting quietly in the car was better still, and as hers was the only car in the park, her mother-in-law would have no difficulty seeing her.

She only had to wait a few minutes when Mrs. Mullan appeared and as Helena started up the car, she made her way towards them.

'No one got off the bus apart from me, Helena.' were her first words.

'Yes, the whole place seems quite quiet and rather deserted, thank goodness.' Helena answered reassuringly.

Immediately Mrs. Mullan got into the car, she turned round in her seat to see her granddaughter and when Helena looked at her, she realised she was in tears.

'I know Mum, it is very difficult for you, but it is very difficult for us too. Philip misses you so much.'

At these words, Mrs. Mullan seemed to become even more agitated and through her tears she managed to speak

'I did not get to your wedding and I did not get to my only granddaughter's christening.'

11

'I know, Mum, but we have managed to meet up this morning, and we must make the most of the short time we have together.' Helena passed a pack of tissues from the side panel of the car to her mother-in-law. 'Come, dry your tears, Mum. We are going to go for coffee, then there's a ladies' boutique and a children's wear shop in the mall. We can have a good browse around and you will have some time with Alice.' Helena had just spotted a parking space close to the entrance to the mall and deftly manoeuvred the car in to it.

Later that evening, Helena told Philip all about her meeting with his mother. She was as truthful to him as she could be, even telling him about his mother's tears on first seeing Alice. She told him all about their private time in the coffee shop, where his mother gave Alice her bottle of milk, and later how they enjoyed browsing in the shops. She showed him the two pretty dresses his mother had bought for her granddaughter, and explained to Patrick how his mother had insisted on buying for a year-old child even though Alice was only four months old. She was also able to reassure him that when she left his mother at the bus station, his mother was very calm and accepting of the whole situation they found themselves in. She was happy enough, she had reassured Helena, to speak to them on the phone from time to time.

Chapter 4

Theresa Mullan was filled with a wonderful sense of contentment and satisfaction as she sat in the bus, taking her home to Belfast. Her meeting with Helena and her beautiful granddaughter had left her with such a wonderful feeling of optimism and hope for their future, that she felt she could face anything. She believed that she could live with the knowledge of having limited contact with her son and his family, as long as she knew they were happy and safe. Besides, who knew what might happen in the future to change things for them all. For now, everything was well for her son and his family. She hadn't needed Helena's reassurances of Patrick and her happiness. The girl exuded contentment and joy at being with the man she loved and that was what mattered most to Theresa. Now, as she alighted from the bus in Royal Avenue and waited for a taxi to come along to take her home, she was quite excited at the thought of telling her husband, Kevin, all about her afternoon out and how she believed their worries about Patrick were over. Kevin had told her not to hurry home to make dinner, he intended to do that and their two other sons could help with the washing up after they came home from work. He had told her, when she left before lunch, that he would want to hear everything in great detail when she returned.

The taxi ride only took ten minutes and the taxi driver always left her at the entrance to her street, as it was a cul-de-sac she lived in and he could just swing his taxi round at the corner and head off to his next appointment. Besides, Theresa had just a few steps to walk round the corner to be close to home, then a few more steps up the path leading to her front door.

But when she rounded the corner, she realised very quickly that something was terribly wrong in her street. She became aware of several police cars parked alongside the pavement. How many were there, she had no idea, and although she always associated police vehicles with noise and sirens, there was a real ominous silence pervading the whole area. An awful foreboding took hold of her and she began to walk as quickly as she could, intent on getting on to her footpath which would take her to her front door and to the comfort and security which lay behind it. Just as she reached the footpath, a dear, familiar voice spoke to her – a familiar voice but with such a good deal of sadness in it.

'Mum, you must not go in there.' It was her son Gerry's voice and he reached out to her, and held her close as he spoke.

'You can't go in, mum. Something terrible has happened. The police are in there.' Her son's voice was pleading. 'Let me take you next door to Mrs. Maguire's.'

'What is it, Gerry? I must know.' Theresa tried to be free of her son's tight grip on her but he held her so firmly she felt she had trouble breathing. 'Please, I must know.' Then the realisation hit her. 'It's Kevin, isn't it? Something has happened to him.' Now, she looked directly at her son's face and saw immeasurable sadness, shock and disbelief written there.

'Yes, Mum.' Now Gerry held her closer to him, almost as if he needed her comfort and familiarity as much as she needed his. 'Please, mum, let me take you next door, away from all this and Brian and I can tell you what we know about what has happened.'

Her son's voice, his whole demeanour, had told Theresa everything, and now she did not care where she went at that moment in time. Her darling husband was dead, that was all she needed to know. It didn't really matter about anything – nothing mattered now and never would again. It didn't matter why the police cars were there or why her sons didn't want her to go into the house. Kevin was dead – her easy-going, loving and thoughtful husband was gone. He would never speak to her again or hold her tight while she cried tears for Patrick and his absence from their lives. She was really alone now and it didn't matter where Gerry wanted her to go. Woodenly, she allowed him to guide her, his arms tightly around her, into her friend and neighbour, Sally Maguire's house. Somewhere in the recesses of her mind, she knew she would soon hear that her husband had met a violent death. That would be why the police were here, she had no doubt about that. But it wouldn't matter what she heard, it wouldn't change anything, her darling Kevin was dead.

Later that evening though, Theresa began to realise that it did matter how Kevin had met his death. The policewoman assigned to help her was so very sympathetic towards her but when actually telling her about her husband's last minutes, she did not go into much detail. She explained that after tying her husband up, they had ransacked the house, and although there was some indication that they had beaten him, there was no sign that he had been shot or stabbed. Then, the policewoman had gone on to tell her, in the most gentle of terms, that they had left a note to say that this was the first stage in their plan of revenge; very soon, they intended to carry out the second stage and their real goal was to find Patrick Mullan. That would happen soon, they said, as they had found details of his whereabouts in Mrs. Mullan's bedroom.

At the mention of her son's name, Theresa stood up, wild-eyed and crying in an inhuman way. The policewoman had great difficulty in placating her, but she gradually settled when the policewoman's calm, slow voice telling her of Patrick's safety and that his family was well looked after, penetrated her thoughts. She also added that they had no idea, at this stage as to who might be responsible for her husband's death. It might be the IRA because Patrick had divulged information about them to the CID. Or was it the UDA, intent on revenge, because a police officer had been targeted all those years ago and it had resulted in the police officer's father being murdered? Then, the policewoman went on to say that they were confident that forensics would soon let them know.

Helena had arrived back from leaving her mother-in-law at the bus station in Armagh some twenty minutes ago. As she entered the kitchen, the first thing she did was switch the oven on for Philip's dinner. She had made sure she had prepared it all the evening before, knowing she would have little time after leaving Mrs. Mullan at the bus stop. She had had a very substantial lunch with her mother-in-law so she was not in the least bit hungry. A cup of tea and a piece of cake was about all she would be able to manage. While she was waiting for the kettle to boil, she prepared some food and a bottle of milk for Alice, who was still asleep in her car seat after Helena had carried her into the house. She was sitting at the kitchen table enjoying her tea when the noise of a car heralded her husband's arrival home from work. Just as he appeared in from work, a broad smile on his face, the telephone rang.

'Mrs. Mercer,' the voice sounded very authoritarian, yet calm and orderly. 'It is Inspector Wright here. A police car will be along in less than ten minutes to collect your husband, yourself and your child'. The voice sounded urgent 'You must not on any account take time to pack. A bottle and perhaps some food for your daughter, your handbag and your husband should bring his wallet. It is an unmarked police car but please take good note of the registration number, so you will know it is the police. You are at grave risk but we intend to ensure your safety.'

Helena set the phone on its cradle, lifted Alice's basket containing her bottles and formula milk which she had not as yet, had time to unpack after returning home. Trying to keep as calm as possible, she spoke urgently. 'That was the police, Philip. It seems we are at grave risk here and we don't have time to pack anything. The inspector says to just bring a bottle and food for Alice, my handbag and your wallet. That is all we have time for, someone will collect us very shortly.'

Just as she finished speaking to Philip, they both became aware of the lights of a car sweeping into their driveway. Woodenly, Helena spelt out the registration number she had written on a slip of paper. Philip nodded then relieved Helena of baby Alice in her chair and her bag with her bottles and milk in it. Putting his arm around his wife's shoulders and reminding her to collect her handbag, they quickly made their way to the car. The back door was opened by a young police officer in uniform. As they settled themselves in the back with Alice between them, the constable closed the door and made his way to the front passenger seat, then they were on their way.

'Constable Harding is in uniform to try to reassure you that we are who we say we are. You will be taken to the ferry for Liverpool and from there to a safe house. In England you will be provided with a new home and a new job where your safety will be more or less guaranteed. But under no circumstances must anyone, not anyone, know where you have gone.' The Inspector driving the car had decided that Patrick Mullan should not know about his father's death until he was safely in England. It would be much better that way.

Listening to the words of the Inspector, Philip and Helena could only cling to one another across their baby daughter and pray they would be safe. Meanwhile, Alice slept soundly in her car seat, blissfully unaware of the events which would shape her whole life.

The light blue Ford Capri which had been stolen from a driveway on the Antrim Road in Belfast earlier in the day, roared into Philip and Helena's driveway approximately twenty minutes after the police car's departure. The driver and passenger seated beside him, the gun on his knee, were delighted to see Philip's car in the drive and the house ablaze with lights. They parked the car right outside confident of success in this, their latest venture. Even though both of them may have thought it strange that the front door was ajar and swung in so easily to accommodate their entry, they still confidently moved on, gun at the ready. It was only when they moved into the kitchen and realised the oven was on and a shepherd's pie beginning to burn there, they began to suspect they had been outwitted in their quest. When they went upstairs and found no evidence of anyone, they realised their quarry was gone and this time they had been thwarted in their thirst for revenge.

Chapter 5

Matthew was just vacating his office around 7.30 p.m. when his telephone rang. He was tempted not to answer it, he was tired and anxious to get home, have something to eat then treat himself to a whiskey and soda, before retiring for the night. But still, one never knew who would wish to speak to him and he automatically reached over and lifted the telephone to his ear.

'Hello, Inspector Hampton here' he said.

'Hello, Matthew, it's Cecil Wright here. I thought you should know that Patrick Mullan's father was found dead a couple of hours ago – around 5.30.p.m. to be precise'. Before Matthew had a chance to reply, not that he was capable of saying anything, he was so shocked to hear such news, the Inspector went on. 'He was found dead in his own home. He had been tied up and beaten, that's as much as we know. Mrs. Mullan was out and one of their sons found him on his return from work.'

Matthew eventually found his voice. 'Thank you for telling me, Cecil, I am truly shocked. The man may have held Republican views, but he was a quiet inoffensive being – that's how I remember him anyway, not involved in anything paramilitary at all.'

'Of course he wasn't, Matthew. We believe it might be someone out for revenge or maybe they did not mean to kill him – just frighten him a bit. We don't know as yet who is responsible but hopefully we soon will.'

'Keep me posted about it, will you, Cecil?'

'I certainly will. I think you should also know that his son Patrick, wife and child were moved out of the country tonight'. Cecil Wright was reluctant to bring Patrick Mullan's name up, but he believed Matthew Hampton should know and be informed from the outset about what was happening.

There was a long silence over the phone 'Are you still there, Matthew?'

'Yes, Cecil, but you know how I feel about all this.'

'I'm sorry, mate, it had to be done and I felt compelled to tell you. He was, after all, an informer for us, so we are now duty bound to protect him.'

'I know, I know. I apologise for my resentment and thank you for telling me everything. If you must know, I'm real sorry about Kevin Mullan; a decent man and Mrs. Mullan will be devastated I'm sure'.

'She is that, Matthew, but perhaps some time later we will be able to help her'.

Matthew thanked his colleague again and in a troubled, preoccupied state of mind, replaced the receiver, left the office and proceeded to head home.

'Matthew, could you please come for dinner, this is my third time to call you.' Julie sounded exasperated as she spoke. Indeed, there was a note of sheer desperation in her voice and the truth was, she was quite desperate. She loved her husband dearly but his behaviour in the last few months reminded her of that awful time after Rob's death, when Matthew had withdrawn from all of them, to live in a world of his own, where no one dare enter. Even in the last few weeks, he had seldom eaten at the same time as she and

Emily did, even if he was home from work, and he was generally uncommunicative and morose most of the time. She had no doubt that the death of Patrick Mullan's father had brought everything back to Matthew. At least they hadn't shot him – it seemed he had died from a heart attack brought on by the shock and violence of his beating. Now though, the only time Matthew seemed to brighten up was when Lynn and Jason called with the children. Then, he did sit at the dining room table with them and he appeared animated enough to play with Lewis and Eva. But always with their departure and goodbyes, Matthew's good spirits seemed to desert him and he became withdrawn and dejected – just as Julie remembered him after his father's brutal murder. This time, Julie found that her tolerance for her husband's depression and ill humour was not something she could cope with so easily second time round. Of course, she and Matthew were both so much older and this time the reason for her husband's state of mind seemed more intangible and obscure, but Julie had no doubt it was linked in some way to the nature of his job with all its triumphs and failings.

Well, this time, Julie was determined that Matthew's form would not rub off onto her and she meant to live life in a more positive light. They could not continue to look back on the past but must, for the sake of their children and their sanity, look to the future. For that reason, Julie had decided to join some club or instruction class or other. She had no idea initially what she would like to do, but felt the need for some diversion from Matthew and his problems. Then the idea of painting classes came to her; she had always had a flair for such work when she had been at school and had received praise on several occasions from her teachers. In particular, she had loved drawing country scenes, birds and animals and believed she might have a talent for it. No doubt, she would find her skill had deserted her when she tried again, but still, it was worth pursuing.

Now that Matthew was still so engrossed in his work, Jason was happy in his marriage and Emily at thirteen was becoming more and more independent, Julie's absence on two evenings a week would scarcely be noticed.

Julie found the first few weeks of her art class quite daunting, but she persevered with it and soon struck up a friendship with two other women of the same age group, who told her that they too had been at a loose end in the evenings. One of them had recently been widowed and the other had told Julie that when her husband came home in the evening, they ate their tea in silence before he disappeared into the television room until bedtime. Julie however, remained discreet about her reason for joining the class, simply telling them both she wanted to brush up on her painting skills. There was no way she could ever divulge the nature of Matthew's work and after hearing the two women and their reason for being there, Julie felt guilty about Matthew, and did contemplate staying home as she had always done. At least she was very blessed that their immediate family was intact – unlike so many others in Northern Ireland, who had suffered bereavement. Matthew was simply working very hard; he was totally dedicated to his profession and what could possibly be wrong with that? Maybe she was being too harsh at the moment, but then on the next evening, when she was leaving to attend her classes and he never made any comment of any kind to her, she became newly determined to continue with her nights out.

Matthew, from his seat in the study, heard the front door close behind Julie, and realised very belatedly that she had just been telling him she was going to her painting class. Guiltily, he realised he had not even answered her, he was so engrossed with the mound of work on his desk. He knew he should make an effort to drag himself away from his papers in the evening and spend more time with Julie and young Emily, but recently, he seemed lacking in any energy to even talk to them and yet at the same time he did not seem to get through his work the way he used to. Some of his unsolved cases seemed to prey heavily on his mind, but without him being able to concentrate on any of them. He still was obsessed with the Shankill Butchers case and believed that Devlin, their psychopathic leader, should have faced his nemesis in court. Instead, he had been assassinated and probably by one of his own. This case alone swamped Matthew's mind and emotions, leaving little room for any concerns about his family and their problems.

Chapter 6

December 1984

'Aren't you going to join us for a drink this evening, Julie? You above any of us ought to be celebrating your success. You did after all, get such a high recommendation for all your paintings from the tutor.' Whilst smiling all the while, Esther nodded her head vigorously as she spoke. 'So, come on, one drink and then we'll all head home, sober and respectable as we ought to be. Besides it's only two weeks to Christmas and that in itself is cause to celebrate.'

Julie smiled and nodded in agreement, even before Esther had finished speaking. Julie admired her new-found friend so much, widowed so tragically, yet still struggling on in a most positive way while she herself seemed to be wallowing in self-pity.

'Of course I'm coming, Esther. I can't think of a nicer way to end our first term together.' Julie replied, 'but please don't put much emphasis on our tutor's assessment of my work, it may not mean very much outside this circle; after all, it is only his opinion.' Julie was yet to be convinced, in spite of her tutor's praise that her work was of much use.

'That remains to be seen, Julie. I believe Mr Semple sees real talent in your work.'

'I love your belief in me, Esther, I really do, but in the meantime, let's join the others and go to the 'Bird's Nest', have a drink with everyone and celebrate the end of our first term together. After all, I'm one of the lucky ones. The bus stop is only a couple of hundred yards from my avenue, so I can safely have a drink.' Although Julie was not keen on alcoholic drink, she was anxious to celebrate with her new colleagues. They had become firm friends in the last three months and had supported one another through all the praise and criticism meted out to them from their tutor. Besides, she was in no hurry home, Matthew had told her he was going to interview some new suspect in yet another one of his cases and Emily had told her she was going to Jason and Lyn's house to play scrabble. So to-night, she need not feel at all guilty, her family were doing their own thing, and so would she.

Later, as Julie sat with her colleagues in the cosy pub with its Christmas tree and lights beckoning everyone to call in and enjoy themselves, she could not help but compare the homeliness of the place with her own home at present. Certainly, the Christmas tree stood in its usual corner beside the fire. The usual holly decorations adorned the pictures on the walls and the Christmas stockings she had made years ago hung from the mantelpiece. But Julie knew her home now lacked the warmth it had once known. Something was lacking and as she sat there sipping her drink with her colleagues, she suddenly realised that it was her own lack of enthusiasm and interest. Matthew's obsession with his work and his withdrawal from his family in the evenings had created an awful apathy in her and there and then, Julie made up her mind that she was going to try to get into the spirit of Christmas, and that she would start this very evening, when she got home. She would put on a couple of carols on her record player and hopefully some of that spirit would rub off onto Matthew, she had to believe it would.

'Julie, are you sure about catching the bus? I can easily drop you off you know, it's not much of a detour, after all'. Her tutor was smiling kindly at Julie as he spoke. They had just vacated the pub and everyone agreed it had been a very pleasant evening and an excellent pre-Christmas celebration.

'Thank you, Mr. Semple but I do know the bus will be along in a few minutes. I use this route daily, so I know it very well, and when I alight from the bus I have a mere two hundred yards walk to my front gate. So please' Julie tentatively touched her tutor's arm, he was a man she admired so much. 'I'll see you in a couple of weeks' time, Mr. Semple and thank you so much for everything'.

'Alright, Julie, if you're sure about that, and remember what I said – you have real talent.'

As Julie boarded the bus which would take her home. The words her tutor had spoken warmed her heart and she hugged them to her. She was determined to tell Matthew what had been said and hopefully, he too would be interested in this, her latest hobby.

Julie had never noticed the brown-haired man seated at the back of the bus, watching her intently as she looked for her familiar bus stop, she was so taken up with seeing Matthew, talking to him about her paintings and intent on getting him more involved in Christmas, with all its necessary preparations. She would do anything to help bring them close again and she knew that Christmas would be just the time to do it. She didn't notice the man getting off at the same bus stop as she did.

"Dad, dad, please wake up.' Matthew was aware of someone shaking him vigorously, and suddenly wide awake, he recognised his daughter's voice.

'Emily, yes, I'm awake. What's wrong?' he said, as he strove to become properly alert.

'It's mum, dad, she hasn't come home. She told me she would get the last bus home, and it's long past that time. Where could she be?' Young Emily sounded distraught and the alarm in her voice penetrated through to Matthew and immediately he was on high alert, aware he had as usual, fallen asleep with his head on his hands on his desk.

'Steady on, Emily, your mum may be getting a lift, it is after all, Christmas time. Luckily, she left me the telephone number for her tutor, in case I ever needed to contact her during lessons, so let's see what he says.'

The tutor's words, when he answered the phone to Matthew that Monday evening, chilled him to the bone. Mr. Semple told him he had personally escorted Julie to the bus stop and she had assured him the bus would be along very shortly, adding that she would be home in fifteen minutes time. Matthew realised, as he stood with the telephone in his hand and Emily waiting expectantly at his side, that it was now over an hour since Mr Semple had left Julie. Something terrible had happened to his Julie, his darling, neglected Julie, on her way home from her painting class.

Chapter 7

The notion of revenge had dominated his thoughts and mind for some time but he had seemed to lack any imagination as to how to go about it. Then, suddenly, he was faced with what seemed to be an ideal way to avenge his brother, when he saw her boarding the bus. It was such a coincidence that he had been using public transport at all, but his car had been in the garage for repairs and he'd had no option but to travel by bus that evening, following a meeting he had had in Belfast.

He would have recognised her anywhere. The images he had seen of her and her husband were, he believed, imprinted on his mind for eternity. Now, as he watched her climb the few steps into the bus and make her way towards the front of it, he felt quite excited that here, at last, was his chance for revenge. For some time now, he had longed to be innovative and seek revenge for his brother. Somehow, he felt he owed it to him. Why he should think so, he had no idea, probably family ties and loyalties, little more than that. Until tonight however, he'd had no idea how to carry out such a mission and then suddenly, it had all become crystal clear to him. He had no easy access to Matthew Hampton, but why not mete out some justice to his nearest and dearest? That would surely cause far more suffering to the man than any physical harm would do. Now, as he silently watched and waited from the back seat of the bus, he began to plan his movements and actions.

As he sat in the back seat quietly watching and waiting for the woman's departure from the bus, he realised he had nothing with him with which to inflict any injury. But still, this was a golden opportunity for him. He had strength and weight to his advantage, good winter gloves in his pocket, and a good scarf to conceal his face. They would considerably diminish the risk of revealing his identity. This was definitely the opportunity he had been waiting for – he might never get another one again. As he became aware of her rising from her seat at the front of the bus, he had to admit she was a most attractive female, even though he imagined she must be around fifty years of age. She was tall and slim and although her hair was streaked with grey, it was thick and glossy and gave her an air of dignity and elegance. For a few moments, her whole appearance of femininity made him ashamed about the violence of his thoughts and feelings. But then, he thought of his brother and Matthew Hampton and resolutely, he too rose from his seat, preparing to alight at the same bus stop as she.

He was disappointed when he first alighted from the bus; the footpath was well lit and he felt thwarted that after all, his chance for revenge was not going to be tonight. But then, as Mrs Hampton walked on, he realised the street lighting was no longer flooding the area and both of them had entered an unlit part of the road. Quickly and quietly, he made his way towards her and he knew she was totally unaware of his presence – then he struck.

Much later that evening, dishevelled and shaken by all that had happened and the realisation of someone approaching as he grappled with the woman Hampton, he sat, with a large whiskey in his hand, in his flat. He was gratified that he had made a clean getaway and the only physical injury he had received was a scratch on his left cheek, when the Hampton woman had been trying to defend herself. The small scratch would be easily explained and could have been done with his razor. He was quite pleased with himself when he heard a woman had been critically injured in an assault on her way home from an art class in the city. He wondered how Mr. Hampton would be feeling now as he sat at his wife's bedside. Now, the man would know what it was really like to suffer. Again, he thought about how lucky he was to make his escape before the person out walking their dog had come across him. He was fairly confident there would be nothing at all to link him to the crime and he was the last person the police would suspect – he had never been in trouble with the law before.

Chapter 8

'I cannot bear it, Thomas – Charles.' Matthew's voice was no more than a whisper, so that his two brothers had to bend low to hear him.

'I cannot bear to see my Julie like this. How can it have happened? Who could have done this?'

'There, Matthew. Be consoled that Julie is going to be alright. The surgeon has been most reassuring'. Charles spoke in his usual calm, reassuring voice. 'And be assured, Matthew, we will soon find the man responsible for Julie's injuries.' Even as Charles spoke to his brother he knew Matthew was beyond hearing any mundane words of reassurance and who could blame him? When he himself had first seen Julie lying in the hospital bed in Intensive Care, her face and head battered beyond recognition, he too had found it difficult to believe the Consultant's words that Julie would be alright. How could she possibly survive the assault she had suffered at the hands of some fiend? But then, the Consultant had reiterated that her facial injuries were, in the main, superficial. He did stress he was more concerned about her leg injuries but that was something they would not know about for a few days.

Julie was dimly aware of a dear, familiar voice floating towards her as she tried to establish where exactly she was and what could possibly have happened to her to account for this agonising, excruciating pain in her leg. A pain which was so severe, she felt she must lose her reason and scream aloud for help to relieve her agony. But then, she found she was incapable of screaming and could only emit soft, agonising moans. These must have been sufficient to bring help to her, as she became aware of a presence at her side and someone whispering that they were giving her something to ease her pain. She felt movement of her arm and in a matter of minutes, her agony was eased and she was being transported into a deep sleep, where the pain she felt or what might have happened to her did not matter anymore.

'Your wife will rest now for some time, Mr. Hampton, and you must use this opportunity to rest too.' Ward sister was kind, but her words rang with authority as she spoke to Matthew. 'We will know better tomorrow how he r leg is. The most important thing now, is to keep Mrs Hampton pain free and to prevent any further shock to her system.' Sister paused, as she looked at Matthew, 'I'll bring another easy chair for one of your brothers, if they wish to stay with you.'

Thomas, anxious about Matthew's state of mind, was quick to say he would remain with his brother and Charles could call with the rest of the family and let them know Julie had been found and was receiving the best care possible.

'I also need to let you know, Mr. Hampton, that your superior has organised a guard to be with Mrs. Hampton on a twenty-four-hour basis.' Sister's voice was so low, Matthew had to bend close in order to hear her. 'Your Superintendent believes that this may not be some sort of random attack on your wife, but may be a means of targeting you. Now please.' Sister's voice had mellowed considerably, 'you must try to get some sleep – we can assure you, we will take care of your wife.'

In response to the Sister's words, Matthew just shook his head numbly, he felt he would never be able to sleep again, not ever. His mind was so alert, and he felt his body had been bound up with strings and they might snap at any time. Now, as he looked at Julie and her grotesquely swollen face, he realised Sister's words from the Superintendent had just confirmed his greatest fear; someone was desperate to do him unimaginable injury and hurt, and must intend to do so through his beloved family. Well, it was up to him to be one-step ahead of whoever it was, he had to ensure they were caught before anyone else was hurt because of him. Now, he felt his Superior must come to the hospital to see for himself the injuries inflicted on Julie and what plans they must make to prevent any more attacks.

Chapter 9

After leaving the hospital, Charles drove straight to Jason and Lynn's annexe, anxious to give Jason some news of his mother. When Julie had been found by a man out walking his dog, the man had quickly raced to a nearby house and raised the alarm. An ambulance was quickly on the scene and Julie was taken to hospital, where she was admitted to intensive care straight away. Here, her identity was quickly established and her husband was informed of what had happened.

Charles had learned all this from Matthew, when he had rang him in a distraught state from the hospital, to let him know what had happened. He asked him to go to his house to collect Emily and take her to stay with Jason and Lynn, but he also said that, for now, although he wanted Charles to come to the hospital, he thought it best if Emily and Jason kept in touch by telephone. Charles was glad, after he had taken Emily to her brother's house and explained to her that the hospital were looking after her mother, that he had gone to support his brother and after seeing Julie and hearing what the Ward Sister had said he felt reassured that Julie would survive the assault on her. That was all that mattered and he intended to reassure her son and daughter, that even though she had a long fight ahead, with all their support, she would recover from such a horrific ordeal.

Before he'd even parked his car outside the annexe, Jason had the door open wide and one look at his nephew's face told Charles Jason had feared the worst. Quickly, he reached out his hand to the young man, 'Your mum will be alright, so let's go inside and I will tell you what I know over a cup of tea.'

Jason led the way into the sitting room where Emily, Lewis and Lynn, with little Eve close beside her, were seated. He could see that keeping Julie's family from her, had led them to believe the worst. Anxious now to explain why Charles wished to spare them seeing their mother as she was, he hastened to explain to Jason. 'Your dad intends to keep you up to date about your mother, but he wants you to carry on as usual – as best you can – and look after Lynn, Emily and the children. I assured your father you would have no problems with that.'

'If that's what Dad wants, I'll stick to it, as long as we are kept up to date with mum's progress.' Jason was anxious to see his mother, but saw the wisdom in only his father being there. He knew, he was all his mother would want or need, to be with her.

Charles could see Jason was resigned to staying away from the hospital in the meantime, and Charles decided it was best he said nothing about Matthew's supervisors and his suspicions, that the assault might be linked to Matthew himself. There was no need to add to Jason's worry and distress at the moment.

'Mr. Hampton, Mr. Gregson would like to speak to you after the ward round today.' Sister Reid spoke in her usual soft, but somehow authoritarian manner. It was a voice which Matthew had somehow found very reassuring over the last four days. 'Could you have lunch in the canteen and be back here around one o'clock.'

'Of course, Sister, but is there something wrong?' Panic rose in Matthew's chest and he whispered the words. 'Julie seems so much better – at least I thought so during the last day or so. She is talking to me, even though her mouth and tongue still appear very swollen.'

Sister was anxious to reassure him. 'Certainly, Mrs. Hampton has improved, but there are a couple of details Mr. Gregson needs to speak to you about. But please.' And the authoritarian note was back in her voice. 'You must not worry, all will be well.'

Despite Sister's attempts at reassuring him, Matthew still felt there was something she was keeping from him. There had been something in her manner, a slight evasiveness as she spoke. Were they worried about how Julie might be, psychologically, on her return home? Matthew had thought a lot about how this trauma would affect his wife mentally. It was something he was prepared for and was already making plans to help her deal with the trauma. Now, as he waited for one o'clock to come round, he bought sandwiches and a pot of tea in the hospital canteen, but found he had no appetite for the sandwiches, so he just sat quietly drinking his tea until it was almost one o'clock and he must return to the ward.

As he left the lift and began to walk the corridor, he kept a watch for the door marked 'Mr. Gregson, Private'. Coming upon it, he tentatively knocked at the door, which was opened at once by a spotlessly clean young woman in a navy two-piece suit.

'Mr. Hampton, just go on through, Mr. Gregson is expecting you.'

An hour later, Matthew left the hospital, and after ringing his Uncle John, he was on his way to see him. After his conference with the Consultant, he had gone back to see Julie, but she was fast asleep and the staff nurse in charge advised him to go home and return later that evening. But Matthew felt he could not face his children at the moment and needed to talk to someone who might understand what he was going through. He could only think that John Finlay would understand – if anyone had suffered loss and trauma in his life, Uncle John had. Matthew knew that what he was enduring now, paled into insignificance beside what John Finlay had gone through. His youngest son had been murdered, his other son had been wrongly convicted of murdering his brother, and his wife had suffered a breakdown, from which she had never recovered. Yet now, everyone marvelled at his Uncle's calmness and acceptance of all that had happened, and his capacity to work and help his niece Rachel, in the Nursing Home. Now, as Matthew spotted the Nursing Home in the distance, he knew he wanted to draw on some of that strength of spirit John had. As he parked his car, he began to relive the words Mr. Gregson had told him in the privacy of his office some time earlier.

'I'm afraid we must amputate Mrs. Hampton's leg above the knee, Mr. Hampton.' The words were spoken gently, and even in his despair, Matthew had appreciated how compassionate this surgeon was. 'We did hope it wouldn't come to this, but your wife was subject to a ferocious and sustained attack. We believe the man who assaulted her was a fit, heavy man and he subjected her leg to his full weight for a sustained length of time, no doubt in an effort to control and terrify her. In doing, so the blood supply to her right limb was irrevocably impaired.' The surgeon paused and then, when Matthew made no reply, he went on, 'I'm so sorry, Mr. Hampton. I have not informed your wife yet. I thought it would be best if you were present when I told her.'

Matthew nodded dumbly, knowing that he would desperately want to be with Julie when she heard such news. He wanted to hold her and tell her he loved her, no matter what.

Matthew was so preoccupied with his thoughts as he parked his car, he did not at first see his Uncle standing in the doorway, then begin to make his way, his arms outstretched, to meet Matthew. As Matthew felt the comfort emanating from the familiar figure holding him, he believed all would be well. This man had survived so much and surely, God willing, Julie and he could overcome this ordeal. Then, without even asking any questions, John quietly led his nephew into the large, comfortable lounge of the Home, and when Matthew saw his Aunts, Eva and Maggie seated there, he felt at once drawn into their circle of love, warmth and compassion.

Chapter 10

1985

'Julie and you moving in here is only temporary, you know, Matthew. You would think by the armfuls of clothes and bed linen you have there, it was going to be permanent'. Even though Lucie's words sounded almost like a reprimand, her voice and soft, loving expression belied her words.

'I know, Lucie, but I want the place to feel like home to her. I thought by having her own familiar belongings with her, it might help to make her feel good'.

'You don't regret agreeing to you both coming here to the annexe for a time, do you, Matthew?' Lucie looked searchingly at her brother, 'It's just with Paul and I being in the field of medicine, we felt we might be of some help to you both and we are only a few steps away.'

'I think it was a marvellous idea and so does Julie. I believe the thought of going back to our cottage, so close to where it all happened, was unbearable for her.'

'I did think that might be the case, so I'm really glad I thought of it.' Lucie looked relieved as she went on, 'and Jason and Lynn, never mind Lewis and Eve, absolutely love your bungalow. There is so much more room there for them all than there was here. And I believe Monty, Jason's collie is delighted too, to be back on home ground.'

'I knew they'd all love it, Lucie, but apart from anything else, this is much more compact for Julie. Our bungalow is a bit too spread out at the moment for Julie to manage to get about.'

'Let's get her belongings unpacked and into some sort of order for her. Then, we'll have a cup of tea, before we set out to bring dear Julie home.' Since the terrible assault on her sister-in-law and the knowledge that she was to lose her leg, Lucie had been determined to do everything she could to make things as easy as possible for her and Matthew. She felt in some strange way she owed Matthew all her love and support since that awful time, when she had so readily forgiven her ex-husband for his involvement in their father's murder. She believed, Matthew had never fully understood how readily she had forgiven Patrick Mullan. It was for this reason that Lucie felt the need to demonstrate, in spite of all they had gone through, that her love for all her family remained constant.

Matthew looked at the mountain of mail on his desk in the office and found the prospect of opening all those envelopes, piled up in front of him, quite daunting. He had not been prepared for such a backlog of work, which had sat there, waiting for him to deal with it. Certainly he should have known better, but during the last three months since Julie had been almost taken from him, work, with all its permutations, had been the last thing on his mind. There was only Julie, darling Julie, whom he had so wantonly neglected over the last couple of years, so that she had sought some companionship elsewhere. And all because of his work, which now seemed to hold so little interest for him. He was done with it all; the worry, trying to find proof where there seemed to be none, getting the proof to convict someone believed to be guilty but impossible to convict without the evidence. Then, there was the agony of learning of yet another gruesome death.

He was done with it all, let some young, enthusiastic man – a less emotional and sensitive one than he was – take over. He was determined to quit, he had almost lost everything in his efforts to bring justice to all those other people out there who had lost loved ones during this conflict. He believed it was through the grace of God that Julie was coping with her ordeal and now they were really close, closer than they had ever been. Indeed, he had even hated leaving her this morning, so early, to come here, but Lucie had popped in and assured him she would be there for a time. Julie had insisted she had become used to her wheelchair and could manipulate it very efficiently around the annexe, but he had never left her for a whole day since she had been discharged from hospital and he would be here until six o'clock. So here he was, preparing to give his notice of early retirement and to leave everything up to date for his successor, whoever it might be. But first, he must deal with the dratted mail taking up space on his desk.

As he leafed through the envelopes, one by one, an unfamiliar, childish writing seemed to leap out at him and there was something about it and the crumpled state of the envelope, which seemed to chill him. With some disquiet, he slit open the brown envelope and a yellow page of a jotter fluttered onto his desk top. Slowly, Matthew unfolded the page and the printed words – written in the same childish way the address on the envelope had been – were few and had been underlined with red pen. As Matthew read them, he was in little doubt that his Superintendent's belief about Julie's attacker and his words of caution to them were well justified.

'I DID NOT GET TIME TO DO A GOOD ENOUGH JOB'

'BUT MY NEXT JOB WILL BE PERFECT'

'I OWE IT TO MY BROTHER'

As Matthew read and re-read the words before him, he wondered how he could possibly walk away from his occupation and his position, to leave someone else to discover his wife's attacker.

'Uncle John, I'm sorry to bother you, but as I was passing on my way home from work, I thought I would call and see you.' Matthew had felt compelled to confide in someone about this latest development in his and Julie's life, and had immediately thought of John. 'Emily and Lucie are with Julie, so I know she is in good hands until I get back.' Matthew was anxious to reassure John that everything was alright with Julie. 'Are you still working here, helping Rachel and Gavin?'

'Yes, I do like to keep busy, Matthew. Would you like a cup of tea?' Before Matthew answered him, John added, 'Let's go to my quarters and we can have some peace for a few minutes. It can be a bit noisy in here, especially coming up to tea-time,' and John indicated that Matthew should follow him upstairs to the suite he had shared with his wife, Dorrie, until her death.

On entering the suite, John indicated a chair at the window, and in spite of his own troubles, Matthew remembered that it was his Aunt Dorrie's favourite place to sit. It was here she had watched the traffic wending its way through the streets and looked out on the pedestrians, purposely walking on the pavement as they did their shopping.

'Matthew, there has been some development, am I right?' John spoke directly to his nephew, immediately they were seated.

In response Matthew nodded dumbly, and produced the envelope containing the page, from his pocket. Silently, he handed it to John, who immediately began to scan the writing. He looked steadfastly at Matthew.

'You know what you must do with this, don't you?' John sounded quite authoritarian, almost angry.

'So you don't think it is a hoax?'

'Well, it might be, Matthew, but it isn't something you can take a chance on. So please,' John was adamant. 'Give both the jotter page and the envelope to your forensic expert first thing in the morning.' And John handed the offending note and envelope back to Matthew.

'Now, let's have a good strong cup of tea before you go home, and I'm sure you don't need me to tell you to keep this information strictly between the two of us and the experts. Better not to worry anyone else in the family at the moment.'

Chapter 11

'Lewis, we are going to see granny Julie today after school but don't forget she's had an accident and has a sore leg, so you must be quiet and gentle because she has a bit of difficulty getting around the annexe'. Lynn was unsure how much information she should give her son regarding his grandmother, but she knew she could not put off their visit much longer. Lewis was always asking when they were going to see granny Julie and granddaddy Matthew, so Jason and she had decided that Lynn would take him today after school. Lynn had told Julie, and she was delighted to hear that her grandchildren were at last being allowed to visit. Lynn had explained to her mother-in-law that Jason and she just wanted to make sure Julie was ready for such a visit. Julie was managing her prosthetic limb very well, and remained cheerful in spite of everything she had been through. Everyone in the family had been so very attentive during her spell in hospital and had always done so much to encourage her. Sheila, Charles's wife, and Jenny, Thomas's wife, were very attentive to her every need. They were the ones who washed her hair for her, painted her nails and brought her the most expensive face creams for her skin. It was her two sisters-in-law who did so much, Julie knew, to boost her morale and help her to realise her disability was not the end of the world, but just more an inconvenience than anything else. She knew she would always remember their kindness and their optimistic approach to her during her time in hospital. Then there was Lucie, with all her expertise about surgical and medical matters, it was her who had encouraged Julie to regain her physical strength, and helped her to cope so well with her prosthesis. Indeed, Julie knew that without all the support from all of her family, from the youngest to the oldest, there were many times when she had felt she must go under. Then there was her darling Matthew, who had just been there with his 'no nonsense' approach at all times which had gone a long way to ensuring her survival. Some members of the family where quite surprised to hear Julie say how calm Matthew had been, they had only seen Matthew in despair and on the verge of tears on many occasions. He must always have made sure Julie did not see him in such a state as they did, but kept up a cheerful appearance in his wife's presence and that was a real recommendation.

'Now, Lewis, I need you to watch Eve and take care of her when we call at the annexe. She can be a bit boisterous, as you know.'

'I'll keep her right beside me, I promise, mum. Will cousin Emily be there, mum? I'd love to see her, too.'

'Of course darling, Emily looks after grandma until your grandfather comes home from work, not that Julie needs much looking after, she is so independent.' Julie knew that Lewis and Emily, in spite of the age difference, had become very close when Emily had gone to stay with them during her mother's stay in hospital. The two young cousins had shared a room due to limited space in the annexe. She hoped that meeting up with Emily today would lessen the shock he might have at seeing the change in his grandmother. As for Jason and herself, they had visited Julie most days, so had seen the improvement, slow though it was in Julie but this would be Lewis's first time in about four months so he was bound to see her altered. Lynn and Jason had been very appreciative of Arnold Simpson during Jason's mother's time in hospital. Lewis's father was always more than willing to look after both Lewis and Eve for them any time they wished to go to Julie. Mrs. Simpson had always accompanied her husband any time he came to visit Lewis or collect him from school, and Lynn knew the woman idolised the boy and helped as best she could to look after him.

Julie was looking forward to seeing Lewis and Eve again; it seemed so long since she had hugged and kissed them, listened to their voices, high and excited, relating to something or other about their playtime or their school times. She was grateful Lynn had told her when to expect them to call, she was determined to look her best and intended to wear trousers today, something which she invariably did now. That way she hoped Lewis would not ask her any awkward questions about her prosthesis. It wasn't that she minded it so much, but it might be difficult to explain to an eight-year old boy what had happened and that it was an artificial limb. Besides, deep down, she was still rather embarrassed by it and felt humiliated. She knew she should be ashamed of herself for feeling like this – she had mastered it so well, had recovered well both physically and mentally and she knew it was thanks to her family and all the understanding and support she had received from them all, which had enabled her to deal with the fear and terror of what had happened to her that night. Still, there were some 'bad' days when she had to admit that because she still had her feminine vanity and had always tried to look her best, she resented the prosthesis and how it looked on her body. And that was the only reason she had trouble accepting it all. As for Matthew, he always seemed to sense when she was having one of her 'off' days, and would be particularly attentive to her.

It was only after continuous persuasion from her, after they had moved into the annexe, that he agreed to return to work on a part-time basis. Lucie and Paul had reassured him too, that one or other of them would be there to help Julie if she needed anything. Yes, she was very well looked after, Rachel, Jason's mother-in-law and her husband Gavin called very regularly since her discharge from hospital – usually two or three times a week – and brought magazines and fruit on every visit. Then, Rachel offered her some physiotherapy in her Nursing Home, free of charge, this Julie readily accepted and Gavin picked her up each Monday afternoon and brought her back to the annexe. Those eight sessions of physiotherapy had been invaluable to her and had helped her deal so well with her disability.

Everyone was very supportive and comforting, but the one subject Julie longed to talk about seemed of little interest to anyone else, or perhaps they were trying to protect her. But it was something Julie could not understand; of course her physical well-being was important, but did no-one, not even Matthew, understand her overwhelming need to find out who was responsible for the assault? In the early days, she had been questioned on several occasions about her attacker, when her interviewers would urge her to try and remember something, anything at all about that night. But Julie could only recall the dreadful weight of someone bearing down on her, the excruciating pain in her legs, her face and her abdomen. Then, worst of all, the abject fear she felt that she was going to die. The police reassured her that they would be looking for a big, heavy man, no doubt about that. They also told her they had established he had been wearing trainers, treads on the grass verge told them that. They did not tell Julie that the trainers were an extremely common brand, worn by a large cross=section of the community. It was only when they questioned Julie further about the likelihood of her recognising him in an identity parade that Julie remembered before she lost consciousness, that she had only had a fleeting glimpse of the dark head of a man, his face blotted out by an enormous thick scarf. So she knew she was faced with the reality that she would never be able to identify her assailant in any identity parade.

Chapter 12

Perhaps it had been a very risky thing to do, to go in the middle of the night to that police station, take the risk of being spotted, then to shove the envelope into the letterbox situated at the side of the front door. Even now, in the warmth and security of his room, the sweat broke out on his forehead and he began to shake at the prospect of being caught. He had taken what precautions he could; he had dressed himself in black from head to foot, worn the quietest footwear he possessed and gone at the time of night when everything was beginning to quieten down and shut down. In spite of the risks, he did not regret what he had done, some awful compulsion had overwhelmed him so that he had to remind Inspector Hampton that he was still thinking of him – he was still out for revenge for his brother. He had been so frustrated during the last weeks when he had heard nothing of how the woman was. He had even gone to the outskirts of the cottage where he had known Matthew Hampton lived and where his wife was heading for, when he accosted her. But here, he found no sign of Inspector Hampton or his wife; he had only seen a couple of kids playing in the garden at the side of the house. It wasn't until a young man appeared in the doorway calling the children that he realised he was looking at Matthew Hampton's son. He remembered him so well, the night he appeared on television with his father appealing for information about the assailant. It was then that an awful, but very clever idea began to form in his mind. He knew just the way to get back at Hampton and this time he must not fail, but he was going to need help – he could never manage such a project on his own. To ensure complete success, he would certainly need help on this, his second attempt to avenge his brother. He was glad now he had taken the risk to deliver that letter, he needed to let that cop know he meant business and was still going to make him suffer. Now, he had wonderful plans as to how to make that happen; all he had to do was to confide in some of his buddies, enlist their help with a promise of good payment for them.

Before retiring for bed that same evening, he made several phone calls to friends he had not seen for a time. When he outlined his plan, he was shocked when a couple of them laughed aloud at the idea of him carrying out such a scheme. Two others he rang were equally scathing, insisting he would never get away with it. They said they would need to see some money up front before they would consider getting involved in such a thing. He simply did not have any money but undaunted by his mates' attitudes, he was determined to carry on with his plan. He was first of all, going to have to get money.

The young man in the off licence on the Lisburn Road was anxious to make a good impression with his new employers. He had been here now for three weeks, he enjoyed his job – it was after all, just a means of some very necessary income to allow him to continue with his university studies. Every customer who had come in, he had treated with the utmost politeness and had always ensured they were informed of all the special offers which were available at that time. Now tonight, he knew his boss would be delighted with the takings for the evening. It was Friday evening and they always did well on Friday he believed, but this evening he knew was exceptional. He was just beginning to count the money from the till and transfer it into one of the black bank bags they used to transport it to the safe at Mr. Longley's house when the doorbell went and a black hooded figure, brandishing a knife, rushed in.

'Right, mate, if you don't want to get hurt, hand that money over now.' The voice was rough, threatening.

Quickly and suddenly, Simon Taggart reacted. He flung the bag containing some money from the till across the counter where it slithered onto the floor.

'That's it, mate. That's the takings.' At the same time, Simon came round the counter as the intruder bent down to pick up the bag. Simon's intent had been to tackle the intruder, but he had been so preoccupied in thinking about his employer's money, he had forgotten about the fact that the intruder had a knife. Just as he tried to pin the intruder down as he reached for the bag, Simon felt an agonising pain in his thigh and had to release his grip. In agony and despair, he watched the hooded figure make his escape, the money bag securely under his arm.

"A young man in his late teens, who was employed in an off licence on the Lisburn Road, was injured when he was stabbed by an intruder around eleven o'clock yesterday evening. The intruder escaped with some money but thanks to the presence of mind of the sales assistant, it is understood the majority of the takings were still in the till. The intruder only got a small percentage, which the assistant had transferred to a bag. Although the young man was injured, he made his way to the phone at the rear of the premises and raised the alarm. He was taken by ambulance to hospital where his condition is described as stable"

The 8 a.m. news relayed the incident so accurately, he could scarcely believe it. The only thing they hadn't said, was how much money was still in the till. He would never know that now. He only knew he had only managed to take

£150 from the place. Whether he could bribe anyone to help him with that amount, he did not know. He knew too, that to any one of his mates, it would seem a meagre payment. But it was all he had and it was better than nothing. He could always sign an IOU for a further thousand pounds, to whoever would help him. Now he knew for certain he could only afford one accomplice, but if they kept their wits about them, they would be alright, and his brother and indeed their whole family would then be avenged.

Chapter 13

April 1985

Philip looked across at the expanse of green grass which sprawled across the whole area in front of the row of terrace houses with all their immaculate, shining front doors and windows. It was truly lovely in England and especially here in Hailsham, a small market town situated a few miles from Gatwick. It was here that Helena, Philip and Alice found themselves after their sudden departure from Northern Ireland, and it was here they were shown one of the terrace houses as being their new home. It was a neat, attractive house, identical from the outside to all the others in the terrace, but inside, during the last few months, Helena had worked hard to put her own identity on the place. She had started downstairs in the living room, firstly stripping old, discoloured wallpaper from the walls and redecorating the whole room in shades of soft pink and green. The house had already been furnished, though sparsely, when they arrived there, approximately thirty-six hours after leaving Northern Ireland.

Helena had soon gone shopping in Hailsham market for small pieces of occasional furniture which, in her experience, and remembering her parent's comfortable but stylish home, was what was needed to make a house a home. After she had finished the living room to her satisfaction, she began to update the bedrooms upstairs. Here, there were three average sized rooms and a bathroom. The bathroom was good, having been decorated in a blue and white scheme, which were Helena's favourite colours for such a room, but the bedrooms although adequate, were dull and inspiring. She set about to convert the smallest room into a nursery for Alice. Their daughter was now eleven months old, slept all night, and Helena and Philip both felt it was time she had a room of her own. She did not wish to introduce pink into the scheme, as she would like to have more children and hopefully a son, so she decided on a pale cream and aqua as her colour scheme.

The other two bedrooms, Philip and hers and the guest room, would have to do in the meantime, because she felt she needed a break. Besides, Philip and her did not mind the beige coloured walls and carpet. As for the guest room, it was most unlikely they would need it for anyone, given their position.

Many times during their days in England and when Alice was safely tucked up in bed, Philip and her would talk about their relatives and how much they missed them. On the very first night of their stay in Hailsham, Inspector Wright had called personally to see them, to tell them that Philip's father was dead. He told Philip he had died on the evening they had moved Philip and his family from Armagh. It was shocking news to learn, more especially, when the Inspector told them that he had died of a heart attack, following an assault in his home. The good news the Inspector was thrilled with was the fact that whoever had broken into the Mullan's home, had left numerous finger prints, and the Inspector assured them, it was only a matter of time until they were caught. What Cecil Wright did not tell them, was the fact that the assailants had found information in Philip's parents' house, which would have led them directly to Philip and Helena, although he did stress that they thought it best to get him out of the country, in light of what had happened to his father.

Although Philip was grief-stricken about his father, he was now deeply concerned about his mother's welfare and emotional state. The Inspector told him that someone would keep in contact with Mrs. Mullan and her two other sons, and he would also keep in touch with Philip and let him know how everything was. Cecil Wright's words brought some reassurance to Philip and he was determined to try and make the best of his new environment. After all, he had Helena, the love of his life, and their beautiful daughter. He had been given a job on his arrival here doing security for a large pharmaceutical firm a few miles from his new home. It was a job he felt he might start to like as it suited him so much better than the one in Armagh. So, just as long as he was kept informed about his mother and brothers, he felt he would be able to cope without any direct contact with any of them.

He knew that Helena too, must think about her father. Since his short spell in prison when Philip had been there, he had managed to keep out of trouble, as far as Helena and he both knew. He lived with his other daughter, who was ten years older than Helena and was single. Helena's mother had died from cancer when Helena was sixteen years old. The Inspector had told them he had visited them on one occasion and assured Helena all was well there. The Inspector probably believed there would be little, if any, threat to their well-being. They were not viewed as a target it seemed, by any paramilitary organisation.

'Helena, I have some interesting news for you.' Philip had just arrived in from work a few minutes before, and was in the process of helping Alice feed herself with her mashed potatoes and mince, a great favourite of hers. 'I'll tell you all about it when Alice is in bed and we're having dinner.'

'If you remember love, Brian, my older brother, had applied to immigrate to Canada. Well, according to Cecil Wright, he leaves in a month's time.' Philip had insisted that he would not tell Helena what his news was until they were both well seated at the dining room table, he felt it was too serious a topic to endure many interruptions. 'He has already got a job out there, in the building trade, I believe. But now it seems, Gerry has also got a job as a lorry driver and wants to move into a flat of his own. It seems he cannot bear living at home anymore. The memory of dad and seeing him in that room is just too much for him.' Philip regarded his wife earnestly as he continued. 'It seems Mum too is having trouble coping with it all and soon she will be in that house totally on her own.' Philip hesitated, unsure how to explain what he must say. 'The Inspector thinks that the very best thing for mum would be for her to join us here, but this has to be your decision, my love, and your decision only.'

'The Inspector thinks your mother should come here, Philip, but what about the risk of someone finding out our plans?'

'It would all be in absolute secrecy. It would all happen in the middle of the night, more or less how it happened with us. The Inspector has guaranteed all that, so that's not the problem.' Philip went on, 'It's you who will be with my mother all the time, not me. I will be at work, so you must think seriously about it.'

'Philip, as long as our safety is guaranteed, your mother is so very welcome here. I would love to have her and it is only right she should be with us. What else is there for her? Tell the Inspector, yes, yes.'

And as Philip looked at Helena's face and how it was lit up at the thought of his mother joining them, he marvelled again at the good fortune he'd had when he met her.

Chapter 14

Gerry Mullan was at a complete loss as to what to think of his life or his future anymore. Here he was still living in Bryan Street with his mother, but according to one of the most heavily guarded secrets, it would not be for much longer. He had been so looking forward to his job as a lorry driver, he would be earning some much needed money and moving into an apartment in an inconspicuous area in Belfast. But now that he was aware that his mother would probably not be here in this house that he and his brothers had lived in since childhood, and perversely, now that the opportunity had arisen for him to cut his motherly ties and become independent, he found he did not want to go anywhere. He wanted to come home in the evenings and find her here, his dinner on the table, the place spotless and all his washing and ironing done. But he knew it was all too late to turn back now; if he did not strike out now for his independence, he never would. Besides, he needed a lot of privacy; somewhere he could bring his mates without being disturbed. Then again, he would be able to sleep better without lying listening to his mother roaming the floors, whimpering and calling out names, sometimes Kevin her husband, and sometimes Patrick her son. How he longed to help her, to make recompense in some way for all she had suffered.

Then, suddenly, Gerry was left alone in the house, his mother had gone. He was told she had gone to join her son, Patrick, but he was not told where, by the authorities. It was his mother, swearing him to secrecy, who told him briefly where she was going, explaining to him that at least he might have some idea of where she was. He was so glad that at least his mother trusted him, because, he was informed by some Inspector that it was best he did not know, or ask any questions. They made it very obvious they could not rely on him not to tell someone. As if he would ever tell anyone in this country about how things were for his brother and mother; that they had to go into hiding. No, apart from the risks, he was too ashamed of how things were for them all – he would never talk about that. It was a disgrace that any of his family should have had to move away, incognito. It was just a horrible sequence of events which had led to this. If Patrick had not been sent to Crossmaglen all those years ago, he never would have become involved with the IRA. He was also sent there at a very vulnerable time in his life, when his marriage had just broken up. And now, because of it all, their whole family had been split up and he would probably never see his mother or Patrick again. He tried to become reconciled to the whole situation, but always, he was left with a bitter, frustrated feeling of injustice. Perhaps he should have gone with his other brother, Brian, to Canada. Brian had done his best to coax him to come with him.

'Why don't you come with me, Gerry? This place here, well, I can't see people sorting their problems out a hundred years from now. Everybody's stuck in a time warp and I want none of it, and neither should you. You're a young man; strong and capable – forget all 'the goings on' – they are just perpetual.'

But something held Gerry back, some vague hope for the future and a better place for everyone here. Also, he felt the need to live independently with just a couple of his pals calling into his flat from time to time, and then of course, there was always his fear of travel. On the road he was fine, but the thought of travelling by air or sea was a nightmare for him, and he did not think he could master those fears. Also, he reminded Brian frequently, right up until he set sail for Canada, that someone should stay until the police found out who was responsible for the assault on his father. He was disappointed when Brian's attitude to this was that their father was dead and nothing could bring him back, and identifying the assailants would never do that. It was a very sobering thought, Gerry knew, but he intended to stay here in the hope the culprits would be found and committed for trial.

Chapter 15

'I have to tell you, Matthew, we are not much further on than we were two or three months ago.'

Matthew's superior, Superintendent McAllister had telephoned Matthew to call into his office as soon as he arrived into work.

Matthew nodded dumbly and produced a duff coloured envelope from the inside pocket of his jacket. 'I was coming to see you this morning anyway Sir.' Matthew handed the envelope over to the Superintendent. 'I received this in this morning's mail.' He pointed to the stamp on the envelope. 'This one's been posted, Sir – it is franked as you can see.'

Ernest McAllister nodded as he looked at the envelope and then withdrew the single page of jotter. Delicately, he smoothed the page in order to read the words written there. Then he raised his head and addressed Matthew.

'These words are identical to the last two messages you received, are they not?'

'Yes, Sir, they are.'

'That leads me to think we may be dealing with someone with limited writing skills. This is the third message and the print and the wording is always the same, is it not?'

'That does seem to be the case. It is what I have observed too, Sir.'

'What I feel you must do, Matthew, is to research in depth, the criminals you have found to be guilty of some crime or other – no matter how trivial or serious it might have been – and try to establish what family they have. Have they brothers? ' The Inspector hesitated and then sensitively added 'I know without a doubt we are looking for a man for your wife's assault, so we must assume at this moment that it is a man we are looking for regarding the letters and that he is probably acting alone.'

Ernest McAllister put the page back in the envelope and placed it in a tray on his desk. 'We'll let forensics have another go to find something, I know nothing has been established from the last two notes, but I feel he's bound to slip up sooner or later.' He smiled reassuringly at Matthew. 'Please be assured Matthew, we'll do all we can to find this man. In the meantime, let's have that list of suspects as soon as you can.'

'Thank you, Sir, for all your support and understanding.'

'Matthew, there is something else I need to let you know – nothing to do with this case – but I think you do need to know. A young man belonging to the UDA has been arrested in connection with the death of Patrick Mullan's father. There is not much doubt about his guilt; the fingerprints found in the house match his but we know there were two of them, so we are hopeful of very soon identifying the other one. So, we have some success there, Matthew, and we must remain positive about finding Julie's assailant. We will catch up with him, I'm sure of it.'

'This UDA man, is he known to us? What do you think his motive was?' Matthew found he was interested to hear more about Patrick Mullan's case, besides, for a brief moment, it took his mind of his own worries.

'Yes, Matthew, he has been in trouble before.' The Superintendent hesitated then went on. 'It seems it was in revenge for your father's death.'

Matthew nodded slowly as his superior talked; at the moment he could not find it in his heart to condemn the man. He knew that was very wrong of him; he was a criminal and had caused the death of a man he himself had a great deal of respect for. But he could understand his motive so very well, he had felt just the same way over the last few years, since the death of his father. But then, his professionalism always came to the fore. Now, he held out his hand to his superior.

'Good work Superintendent. He'll probably be charged with manslaughter, don't you think?'

'Yes, I believe that will be the case, Matthew.'

Ernie McAllister rose from his desk, and shaking Matthew's hand, smiled warmly at him as he made his exit. Only when his colleague had gone, did the Superintendent allow himself to consider the likelihood of identifying Julie Hampton's attacker and bringing him to justice; they had no forensic evidence worth talking about, unlike the Kevin Mullan case, and Julie herself had said she doubted if she would be able to identify him. Now, as he lifted the offending letter in order to send it to forensics, he thought again of Julie Hampton and how she had survived her ordeal. If no one was caught, at least she was alive but still, after all she had been through, she deserved justice. He was glad too, that he had arranged a guard to and from school for Matthew's family in case the perpetrator would strike again, as he had threatened to do.

He was glad he had not succumbed to the temptation to go under cover of darkness to deliver his letter into the police station. He felt that he might be tempting providence if he attempted to do so again – he felt he might not get away with it on his third attempt. So he had put a stamp on it and taken it to a roadside post box on the Newtownards Road and posted it there. He felt it safer if he sought out a post box three or four miles from where he lived and he made sure he wore gloves when he was posting it. He was beginning to feel more confident with each day that passed and tomorrow he had arranged to meet his old pal in their favourite haunt. He had outlined his plans briefly over the phone and told him the amount of money he could give him as a down payment. He also promised him an IOU for a further thousand pounds after the success of their mission. He was delighted when his friend didn't laugh at him but told him he might be interested and actually thought the whole thing exciting and challenging.

The very next day, after carefully handing over the money in a secluded corner of his favourite bar, he knew everything seemed to be in order. His pal had consented to do the driving and he himself would play the main part in it all. And his helper had assured him he knew exactly where to go, so he had no worries there. But they were in no hurry, they could bide their time, until they were both absolutely certain it was fool proof. Then, he knew Matthew Hampton would really suffer, as he should, just the way his family had. But not only would Matthew Hampton suffer emotionally, he would also suffer financially. This time he must succeed in avenging his brother.

Chapter 16

'Inspector Hampton, I'm afraid we have found no prints apart from your own and the Superintendent's on the letter or envelope.'

Matthew had been impatient to hear what forensics had to say about the latest message he had received. He had clung to the hope that the assailant would slip up sometime soon, and he knew his Superintendent had been optimistic about that too, but once more they were disappointed.

'There is one thing, Sir,' the young trainee forensics officer sounded most respectful as he spoke. 'I think it might be worth trying to trace the culprit by the type of jotter and envelope he seems to be using all the time. It's a very unusual jotter, both in colour and the thickness of the pages, different from the usual run of jotters found in newsagents. I think too, that the envelope was printed to match the jotter – the colour and texture are identical.'

'Do you know, I never noticed that, Nevin.' Matthew felt he had been most unobservant here.

'But of course you wouldn't. Sir, you would only have seen what was written on the page. No doubt about that.'

'I'll come over and pick up one of the letters again and talk to my superior about your suggestion, Nevin. See if he thinks it worth pursuing.'

'I'll keep it here. Just ask for me when you arrive.'

'Thank you, Nevin and thanks a lot for hopefully giving me some sort of opening.'

'It might not come to anything and it might involve a lot of work trying to trace the original printers and then try to establish which stationers might stock such notelets. So don't get your hopes up too much.'

'Of course not Nevin, but still it might be something.'

'I'll see you later.'

'Leave this with me, Matthew. I intend to get a couple of young constables on to this right away. They can contact a few well established printers, see if this type of notepaper is familiar to any of them and then perhaps, see which stationers they supply.' Ernie McAllister set the note to one side. 'But this is going to be quite time-consuming and labour intensive, so you will have to be patient. In the meantime, you and your family must be very vigilant, Matthew.'

'Yes Sir. We check our cars daily and the children I know, are well guarded to and from school each day and indeed, wherever they are going, someone always accompanies them. We are taking no chances.'

'Good, that's reassuring' his Superior smiled encouragingly. 'I'll keep you informed of any developments as soon as I know.'

Later that evening, Matthew longed to confide in Julie about the threatening letters. His wife was so very much improved now, trying her best to discard the wheelchair altogether and managing to walk normally with her prosthesis most of the time. She even insisted on making the evening meal for them both and had it heating in the oven on his return from work. But improved though she might be, he knew he could not tell her anything about the letters. It would be a very selfish gesture on his part, wishing to share the burden with Julie. It was much better if she remained in ignorance of the threat.

'Lynn brought the children to see me after school again today.' Julie's voice sounded so alive and vital when she spoke, that he was glad he had decided to keep things to himself. 'That's the second time they've been here and do you know, they've yet to notice anything different about my legs and my walking. I find that quite amazing.'

Matthew rose from his seat by the fire and crossed the room to his wife. 'It is you who are amazing, darling. You have mastered your walking and your whole posture so very well. I am so proud of you.'

'I am rather proud of myself, dear.'

'So you should be, you are a strong woman.' Matthew kissed her fervently as he spoke.

'Let's have dinner now, Matthew, and a quiet read of the papers. Then I want to hear all about your day. That is, as much as you can tell me. Then we'll have an early night.' Gently, Julie pushed her husband from her and led the way into the dining room. 'The children do tire me a little, you know, but it is a rather worthwhile tiredness I have after seeing them. By the way, Emily said she would stay the night with Lynn and Jason but would be here first thing in the morning.'

'Good, that's good, as it is Saturday, I am off work and although I have a bit of a backlog of work in my study it can wait. We will have a lovely day out together and have tea in some fine restaurant.' Matthew felt the urge to indulge himself and his family a little at the moment and tomorrow seemed the ideal time to do so.

Chapter 17

'I believe we may have a bit of a break-through here at last, Matthew. There is still a lot of work to be done but this is the only lead we have, so we have to make the most of it,' and although the Superintendent's voice was solemn, he had a smile for his colleague.

'What is it, Sir?' Matthew was impatient to hear what his superior had to say and felt he was very slow in telling him what information he had.

'We have managed to trace the printers for our notepads and envelopes, but I just wanted to warn you first that we have still a long way to go.' Ernie McAllister held up one of the threatening letters Matthew had received over the last couple of months. Then he went on. 'The printers are a firm in County Fermanagh and they have informed us that there are a few stationers who have an outlet for this particular type of letter.' The Superintendent did not miss the look of hope and optimism on Matthew Hampton's face and prayed he was not giving this man false hope of success. He had been through enough. 'Robinson's is the name of the printers and they have listed eight outlets throughout Northern Ireland who order and stock these notelets. I have the list here, Matthew.' and he handed the sheet of paper with the names on it.

'Thanks, Sir. I see one is in Limavady, one in Ballymena, three in Newtownards and the remaining three in Belfast. I notice Sir, one of the outlets in Belfast is a small newsagents come stationers on the Shankill Road.' Matthew looked across at his Superintendent. 'It's just a hunch but that outlet sounds more low key and nondescript than the others.'

'I agree, plus the fact that it is close to paramilitary quarters, so you never know.' Also, Newtownards is not renowned for any paramilitary activity, Limavady is rather remote. So that leaves Ballymena and the Shankill Road. So I say, start closest to home with the Shankill Road.'

'I agree, Sir. So what would you like me to do?'

'That's the thing, Matthew, what will we do? We can approach the owner of the newsagents and try to enlist his help in identifying who buys the jotters and envelopes.' Here, Inspector McAllister hesitated 'But can we depend on this newsagent? You know as well as I do that he's just as likely to warn whoever made the purchase that we have been making enquiries. We must be careful, Matthew, really careful.'

'Of course, Sir, of course we must.' Matthew's initial reaction to this information was to identify the newsagents concerned and to ask the proprietor to try to remember who had bought the jotters and envelopes from him. But now, common sense and his professional training came to the fore and he knew his Superior was right. No one was to be trusted. All around, lay suspicion and danger and no one must be prepared to put their lives at risk by indiscreetly and randomly going and asking questions from someone who might well be under suspicion themselves.

So what was to be done? What could Matthew do? The newsagents would have to be watched, but that would not be the easiest thing to do and might also arouse suspicion. How much easier would it actually be to be investigating a newsagent in Newtownards, but this was different, the UDA lurked everywhere in the Shankill and if one of them was responsible for the attack on Julie, they would be ruthless and vicious.

'I know we need to be careful, Sir. The first thing I'll do is drive that way – in an unmarked car of course – and try to get the layout of the place; where exactly it is situated, what streets lie off it. Then I'll think about where best to put some surveillance on the place. '

'Good man, Matthew. If we did manage to isolate a good strong suspect, we might well have good evidence against him, after all. But we have to catch him first'.

'How do you mean, Sir? What evidence?'

'That new young forensics trainee who came up with the idea of tracing the jotters, decided to fingerprint the stamp on that last letter. It seems they had not done so because they were anxious to see the area of posting, but young Nevin decided it was worth a try, and he discovered a fingerprint. Our culprit must have absentmindedly checked the stamp was on properly before putting on his gloves to post it.' Ernest McAllister was delighted to see Matthew Hampton's careworn face light up for the first time in weeks. 'That young man Nevin, whatever his name is will go far. Mark my words'.

'And so he should Sir. He, above anyone, has given us hope and I do not intend to forget it.'

'Now go and see what you can find out about the newsagents, its layout etc., Matthew. I hope to see you sometime in the morning.'

'Thanks Sir, I'll do that and I'll be in touch.'

It was a somewhat different Matthew Hampton who left the police station; he seemed a man who had some great purpose in life.

As Matthew drove along the Shankill Road – a road he knew very well – he tried to recall where the newsagents in question might be but he could not remember ever noticing one because he would have been looking for something else entirely then – quite possibly some UDA hide out. Then, suddenly, he noticed it situated right on a corner where a side street ran off the main street. The side street was Ivan Street, Matthew realised as he drove slowly past, and Ivan Street was well known as a street that call girls frequented on a nightly basis. He turned the car and proceeded back along the Shankill Road and then turned left into Ivan Street and drove slowly along. It was around six o'clock in the evening, the place was deserted and the streetlights which had just come on a short time before, seemed to give the area a sense of eeriness and mystery almost. Slowly, he turned the car once more and drove past the newsagents in an attempt to gauge the respectability of the shop. To his disappointment, it too, looked eerie and unkempt, which left Matthew feeling, as he headed for home that it was highly possible that the owner of the establishment might well be embroiled in some illegal pursuit or other.

'Rachel, it's only a thought at the moment, nothing more. I wondered if you might know anyone involved in an escort agency that might be prepared to help me.' On impulse, Matthew had decided to call with his cousin Rachel, before going home. He had thought of talking to Uncle John, who was so wise, and would give him good sound advice. But then he remembered the role Rachel had played when Mr. King had confessed to Leo's murder and decided to talk to her first.

'It's just – well, you had so much success in obtaining a confession for Leo's murder, I wondered if you might have any ideas at all as to how to nail Julie's assailant. And I did wonder if you had any contacts whatsoever, with anyone who would act as decoy in a street I would like put under surveillance. We might, just might have a suspect who frequents a newsagent on the corner, but we have to be careful not to go stumbling in and asking suspicious questions.' Matthew hesitated then went on, 'But if you have no contacts, Rachel, worry no more about it. I'll think of something else.'

Rachel was silent for so long that Matthew began to think she was annoyed with him for bringing anything up about her past. No doubt, she would not like being reminded of it, she was after all, now happily married to Gavin who had, it seemed, so easily overlooked the fact that Rachel had been a call girl at that time in her life. And then she spoke.

'I'll have to think seriously about all this, Matthew. It is such a grave matter we are dealing with here.

'I'll need to talk to Gavin and he has gone to Banbridge to give an estimate to a couple who want an extension built and I don't expect him home for at least another hour.' Rachel seemed preoccupied with her thoughts. 'I was in a different situation when Gerald King came to see me with his confession. It is all so very different now, as you know, Matthew.' She hesitated, 'Still, if I can help in any way I will, Matthew. Are you still getting all the security you need?'

'Yes, indeed, Rachel, My superior has insisted on it. The children and Julie are supervised when they go out anywhere. But the worrying thing is, Rachel, I know from my experience, that if someone wants desperately enough to do something, they will find a way.'

'Please don't say that. All our family's lives are involved here. They are your grandchildren and they are mine, so we have to be vigilant. If I can do anything I will, believe me. But surely no one would be interested in harming the children?'

'I hope you're right, Rachel, but we are beginning to feel a sense of urgency in finding this person. And as I've said, we feel we might be getting somewhere and we are concentrating round the Ivan Street area. I am also going to go over my past convictions of criminals from the Shankill area. I will try to establish if they have any brothers, then try to eliminate or incriminate one. It is a painstaking task but one I must do.' Matthew sighed, 'Just when I intended to give up my wretched job and retire, I now find myself busier than ever.'

'What? You retire, Matthew, with all your talents and experience. Please, you must not do that, especially now when there is so much at stake.' Rachel sounded quite panic-stricken at the thought of Matthew leaving his profession and someone else being appointed to find Julie's attacker.

Chapter 18

'You're what, Rachel? I can't believe what I'm hearing.' Gavin's voice sounded hoarse and rough as he spoke. 'You're saying you want to help Matthew and the only way you know how is by assuming the role of a street-walker.

'I simply don't know of any other way I might be of help to him. He seems to think, because Mr. King confessed to me of his cousin's murder that somehow or other, I can help find Julie's attacker before someone else in the family is hurt.' Rachel looked at her husband beseechingly as she spoke. 'Gavin, I need you to try to understand how much I want to help Matthew and Julie. After all, they are my only daughter's parents-in-law and I feel a strong sense of commitment to them.'

'Does offering your help to Lynn's in-laws mean you and I must suffer?' Gavin's voice now sounded scathing as he looked at Rachel.

'I promise you, Gavin, I would never, ever break the vows I made with you at our wedding. Never again do I intend to have sex with any other man, no matter what. I promise.' Rachel struggled to keep her voice low and calm – she must convince her husband of her fidelity.

Rachel's words were followed by a long silence, only punctuated by the tick of the clock on the wall. Eventually, Gavin spoke.

'Oh, come on Rachel, if you intend to do a bit of street walking you must know what the men's expectations will be.'

'Gavin, there are other ways of gaining a man's confidence and obtaining information. I don't have to have sex with any of them'. Now, Rachel realised that Gavin was withdrawing from the conversation more and more. 'Look darling, let's leave this conversation for now. I'm sure Matthew will find other ways of catching and charging the culprits.' Rachel hesitated, uncertain whether to stress anything more about their dilemma. 'I just felt I might be of some help. Also, Matthew's superior feels the offender is preparing to strike again at any time.'

Momentarily, Gavin relented as he listened to what Rachel was saying, but then the implications for their relationship hit him anew and he rose from his seat and began pacing the room.

'Let's just hope and pray that the police apprehend this monster before anyone else in the family suffers. Matthew is a very clever man and I believe he will soon come up with a plan of his own to trap the culprit. And while I know you would do anything to help, I don't want our marriage to be put to the test. That's the last thing I want and as long as you know my limits for tolerance in how you help Matthew and Julie, Rachel, we'll be fine.'

Alfie and he had been observing the school now for over three weeks just to establish how the land lay. For those three weeks, the two of them had watched and waited to find some loophole in the security that surrounded Matthew Hampton's grandson as he made his way to school on a daily basis. Either Alfie or himself had been there every morning from 8.15a.m.to 9.a.m. Then, one or other of them were there every afternoon from 3.p.m. to 4.p.m. to watch for any lapse in the security that surrounded the boy but there was none. Not one opportunity ever presented itself to them and the task now seemed much more daunting than he had first thought. Perhaps some of his friends who had sneered so heartily at him when he had first suggested doing it had been right, perhaps he would never get away with it. But now it was no longer just a taste for revenge he had, it was also the idea of coming into some money. Revenge would be sweet but the money would make life so much more comfortable and so much easier.

He simply had to find another way to carry out his plan but it was not going to be easy. Now he regretted sending off those stupid notes – that had not been a good idea and had simply alerted everyone of the need for security.

The cottage lay somewhat back from the road, its front door and latticed windows placed at an easily accessible angle to the front garden and path. The back door however, was situated at the long side of the house, no doubt because this was where the main expanse of the garden lay and was where Jason Hampton's son and daughter played ball games so happily and always a black and white collie dog scampered round their feet in an attempt to catch the ball himself. It was here, there was a side driveway, possibly used for visitors' cars, and off this drive, a side gate led into the garden.

From the relative safety of the overhanging trees in a field on the other side of the road, and for the past week, he had watched the garden and the two children playing in it, most afternoons. As he watched and studied the place, he knew his mission was indeed achievable. The only drawback he could see was the dratted dog continually at the children's feet and he hoped that the mongrel would not raise a hue and outcry when he attempted to take the boy. He had contemplated taking the young girl with the blonde curls and smiling face, but she only looked to be around two or three years old and he knew he would find it difficult to cope with any child of that age. It would have been different if he had a girlfriend who might have helped him, but he didn't. All he had, was a rough drinking mate, who probably both ate and drank too much which was probably the reason why he was a bit slow to react to anything he said to him. So, after much discussion with Alfie, it was decided it had to be the young, blonde boy they must take.

It was all so easy after all. To think he had waited and pondered for weeks about his plan, but then, perhaps because he had pondered so much, that alone ensured his success. Now, they drove up the road, turned into the side driveway and he instructed Alfie to park outside the gate and to keep the engine of the car running. He himself stepped down from the passenger side of the car and on the pretext of asking where a Mr. Aubrey Gregg lived, approached the young slender boy, the collie dog attentive and alert at his side. He asked the boy a low mumbled question mentioning the name Gregg, which he knew the boy would know as people of that name lived further up the road from Jason Hampton's cottage. Before the boy could make answer he hauled him through the gate and as the dog started to growl and made to come too, he delivered a fierce kick to it and closed it firmly in the garden. Quickly he placed the sticky tape he had with him over the child's mouth and with the help of Alfie, managed to bundle him into the back seat of the car. As they sped away they were relieved to see that there was still only the little girl and the collie in the garden. She was running screaming towards the back door, the dog at her heels, yelping piteously.

'Just be quiet, boy. That's all we want. We won't hurt you, I promise you that.'

He had removed the tape from the young boy's mouth when they were a safe distance from the cottage. The boy looked terrified, which was something he had not considered might be how it would be. He had only thought of informing his parents and grandparents and telling them the amount of money he wanted. Never once had he thought about how it might affect the child. How stupid had he been? And now, faced with the look of fear on the young lad's face, he did not know how to respond. He only wanted the young boy to know he meant him no harm. Now he spoke as softly to him as he knew how.

'You'll be alright, son. Just keep your head down, don't move and we'll get you something to drink shortly. There's a petrol station along here, we'll get you a drink. Do you want anything to eat? A chocolate bar, maybe?

The boy just replied with a wild shake of his head. At the same time, his mate, the driver, muttered, 'What's wrong with you, mate? We've just kidnapped somebody – act like we have, for God's sake. Or we'll end up just being a laughing stock in the community.' His mate then muttered words under his breath, words which Jimmy Devlin knew he was not supposed to hear, but the words. 'You are certainly not the same elk as your brother was – he was ruthless,' did not escape him, but he decided to ignore them.

Just the same, in spite of Alfie's scathing words, he insisted they would stop for a bar of chocolate and a drink for their hostage. Later, as they approached their destination they both agreed that Lewis Hampton must be seen to go into the flat willingly, although it was around seven o'clock in the evening and beginning to get dark they still needed to be careful. So it was made clear to the young boy he must take both their hands when they parked the van and proceeded to enter the flat.

'It is vital you remain quiet, Lewis. If you cry out you might come to harm. Do you understand this?

Lewis nodded silently, his face white and his body stiff and unyielding, all the time seeming to wait patiently for his captors to make the next move. Both men were impressed at the young boy's acquiescence and acceptance of his fate as they brought him into the flat. After insisting he eat a beef burger and take another drink, he was led to the small room, where he would remain until everything was sorted out. It was a tiny box room with only a single barred window high on the wall letting in a tiny glimmer of light. There was a mattress on the floor, a single chair and a bucket close by and there was no other furniture in the room. Before he left him, his captor reassured him. 'As soon as we make contact with your dad, Jason Hampton, we will be able to release you soon after.'

The boy spoke in quizzical tones. 'What about my other dad, Arnold? Will you let him know where I am?'

'What do you mean, your other dad?'

'My real dad, he's my real dad.'

'I have no idea what you're talking about. There's a mattress, a blanket and a bucket if you need the toilet. I'll talk to you in the morning.'

As he joined Alfie in the living room, he pondered on what the lad had said. Another daddy must be a figment of his imagination, but that was children for you, they could conjure up other people into their lives so easily. Perhaps his imaginary daddy would keep him from being too lonely in that room he was in.

Chapter 19

When Arnold Simpson opened his front door in answer to the bell ringing he scarcely recognised the face of the young man standing before him, it was so altered, and then he spoke.

'It's me – Arnold – it's me, Jason Hampton.' Jason did wonder, in spite of the nightmare he found himself in, why Arnold was not letting him in the door.

'Oh, I'm so sorry, Jason. I just did not recognise you.' What on earth was wrong? This dishevelled, pale and shaking man was not the Jason he knew so well. He opened the door, gripped Jason's hand and pulled him towards him. 'Please, follow me through here,' indicating his sitting room. 'Iris is in here too.' He felt the need to let Jason know of Iris's presence so sure he was that something was terribly wrong and perhaps Iris ought not to be told.

Jason made no comment to Arnold's words, indeed, he did not seem to hear him, but just followed him into the room. Now, he stood just inside the doorway. 'It's Lewis, they've taken Lewis.' Jason spoke incoherently then began to pace backwards and forwards, his hands clasped tightly together, his face so tormented and anguished looking. 'It was little Eve who alerted us, she came crying to the back door with Monty barking and growling in her wake. Eve was incoherent, just shouting 'Bad man, bad man, I want Lewis, I want Lewis.' Imagine Arnold, they took him from our garden, almost in front of our noses.' Jason's voice held such disbelief that such a thing could have happened. 'I raced out immediately, of course, and saw the fresh tyre marks close beside the side gate.'

Arnold could scarcely hear some of Jason's words but tried to be as patient as possible until the young man gained a measure of control. Then, after he had asked him to repeat what had happened, he asked him, rather unnecessarily he imagined, if the police had been informed?

'Yes, Arnold, Dad was on the scene very shortly after I rang him and the police are combing the area as we speak and they have also set up road blocks.'

Now the knowledge that his precious son had been kidnapped swamped Arnold Simpson's mind. His son was gone, abducted it seemed from the garden he loved so much. How would such a young boy cope? Those were his father's first thoughts. Would he be terrified? Would he be crying continually? Or would he be struck dumb with fear? They must find him immediately. Somehow they must find him safe and bring the offenders to justice at once.

'What are we to do, Jason? What do the police recommend we do?'

'The police advise us to remain as calm as possible until we hear from the kidnappers. They believe the offenders simply want money and have no desire to harm the boy. The police believe it would not do the culprits' cause – whatever their cause might be -much good if they were to harm the boy. No one likes to think of a child being hurt.' Jason strove to keep control of his voice. 'Dad also says if we have heard nothing by tomorrow evening, they will arrange an interview and appeal on television from both of us, for his safe return. The police also reckon, Arnold, that when they hear you are Lewis's biological father, and not me, they will be even less anxious to do him harm and will be glad to have a quick closure here.'

'I would like to have an appeal as soon as possible, Jason. I would feel at least I was doing something to help bring Lewis home. It would certainly be preferable to sitting around in despair and torment, wondering where he is and what he is going through.'

'News of his abduction will be on the evening news bulletin, so at least people will be alerted to a young boy's disappearance and be on the look-out for anything unusual in their area.' Jason went over to the older man. 'We're in this together, don't forget that. Arnold,' and put his arms round his shoulders and held him tightly. Then, he turned to Iris who had been sitting quietly in her favourite chair by the window, her expression, as always, unreadable. He put his arms round her and hugged her passionately. In response, Iris looked directly at him and then patting his arm said in a comforting voice. 'It'll be alright, we'll get Lewis home. We'll go and look for him tomorrow when its daylight, and we'll all go together.'

In response, Jason tightened his hold on her, and overcome by the innocence of her words, wished for a time, that he could be like her.

Before he went back home, Jason knew he must find the courage to inform his Uncles, Charles and Thomas, and their wives as to what had happened to his son. He knew that Matthew and Julie were going to let his aunt Lucie and his Uncle Paul know, but they had decided not to tell the older members of the family until the following morning, but certainly, if it came to a television appeal, they would have to be told before they saw it on the screen. There was also one other, very important couple that Jason wanted to tell. And that was Tracey and her husband Timothy, now living in England. If only Tracey had been here. Jason thought, she would have been wonderful support for Lynn, but Tim had obtained a post in a very creditable finance centre in Bath about a year ago and they had moved over there. Now, with two young children under the age of three, Tracey's visits back to Northern Ireland had been put on hold, but the two girls were still in touch by telephone. So Jason would not want Tracey or Timothy to see the appeal on television without having been told by her friends beforehand of the nightmare they were in.

Chapter 20

The message, when it came, was not by telephone. Either the kidnapper had no easy access to a telephone or was too afraid of any call being traced. The notelet arrived by post on the second day of Lewis's disappearance and the words were written on the now familiar beige paper and inserted into its matching envelope.

It was a clear message, the writer said he did not want to appear greedy but if Matthew Hampton wished for the safe return of his grandson, he would need to pay a ransom of £100,000. When Matthew's superior read the words out to Matthew, his initial reaction was one of relief. His grandson was alive, the kidnapper meant him no harm. He was, after all, not out for any kind of revenge for something or other Matthew had done to his brother. He was only after money.

'This is not too bad, sir. I expected much more threatening words and perhaps a demand for a huge amount of money – money which I would not possibly be able to raise.'

Superintendent McAllister nodded silently, then, in a firm voice, went on, 'I appreciate how you feel, Matthew, but on no account must you rush in and pay this money. This man or men have committed a major crime and it is our duty to get your grandson safely home, but at the same time we must trace these men and bring them to justice.'

'Sir, Sir.' Suddenly Matthew broke down in tears. 'This is my grandson we are talking about here' he said through his tears. 'Of course, I'll raise the money to pay for his safe return. The message does say he will give us time to raise it, then he'll let us know where he wants us to leave it. So we have a few days in which to get the money and try to find Lewis. I am also still going over some of my past cases, where I knew someone I had been responsible for sending to prison has at least one brother, but it is a slow process, I can tell you. However,' Matthew managed to control himself as he continued, 'I do feel that we have narrowed the field of suspects considerably by identifying the source of the letter pads and envelopes. At least it is with some relief that I can discount Patrick Mullan's brother. I had done a bit of research on him you know, Mr. McAllister. Because he had left the family home and moved into a flat on his own where a couple of men were in the habit of calling. I thought perhaps they were the conspirators and that Patrick's brother held me responsible for him and his mother having no contact with Patrick. Then, I discovered that Gerry Mullan is just a hardworking man who likes to go to his local for the odd drink or two, but we found no evidence whatsoever that he was linked to any organisation, so I have removed him from my list. I am convinced the culprit is in the UDA – or at least his brother was, but who they are, I don't know – I have no leads whatsoever at present. I intend to put a couple of my men on duty outside the newsagents to watch the comings and goings of the customers. That, I feel might be tricky enough, as any strangers knocking about there will be very obvious, Sir.'

'Yes, we need to be very careful how we go here. We don't want to put any lives at risk and we have to remember how brutal the UDA has been in the past, so it is vital we act as undercover as possible.'

'I will bear that in mind, Sir, but when I receive the next message from the offender I will act on it at once.' Matthew's voice sounded strident to his Supervisor's ears. 'I won't let my grandson down, not at any cost.'

The Superintendent rose from his seat and coming round to where Matthew stood, so quiet now and resolved, he put an arm around his shoulders. 'I would never expect you to let your grandson down if it is in your power to do otherwise, Matthew. We'll make the most of the next couple of days to try and trace Lewis, but we must have a television appeal with Jason, yourself and Arnold Simpson, the boy's natural father, present.' His Superior now seemed more focused on action rather than talk. 'I'll arrange it all for this evening – just make sure all three of you are in the TV studio. I think it best that the boy's mother is not present, I always believe it is expecting just too much of a mother to go in front of the cameras and try to talk. So it is best if she is spared that. Besides, I'm hopeful, Matthew, that when they realise Arnold Simpson is the boy's natural father, they might panic and leave the boy off somewhere. It does happen you know, Matthew.'

Matthew knew he dare not hope for such a simple ending to this nightmare and after vacating the police headquarters, he made his way to his bank to establish how soon he could access his savings. On being told it would take six to seven days Matthew resolved that he would make it clear to the kidnappers later that evening on television that he would have the money in that time.

In the event Matthew did not need to mention his access to money, Arnold Simpson was the one person during that broadcast that carried most weight in what he was saying. He said he was in a position to meet the kidnappers' demands within the next couple of days, that he was Lewis's biological father and that Jason had adopted Lewis, with Arnold's consent, on marrying the boy's mother.

Arnold Simpson's entreaty for his five-year old son's safety was a highly emotional one and when he had finished, the commentator was visibly moved. There was a poignant silence for a moment as Jason was asked to speak, but he was so overcome with emotion, he wept uncontrollably in front of the camera. It was his father Matthew, who initially kept a measure of control and begged people to report anything untoward, no matter how trivial it may seem to be, to the police. But when he held up the photograph of his grandson in his school uniform, his face became an ocean of grief and he could not say another word.

Chapter 21

The broadcast appeal for Lewis Hampton was on the main evening news at 6 p.m., in order to capture the attention of the majority of people who were always keen to hear the latest news on their arrival home from work. As the masses listened to the voices of those three men appealing for the young boy's safe return, the hearts of so many were deeply touched by the ordeal of the family involved.

As Patrick Mullan sat in his living room, a glass of whisky in his hand, intent on watching the television, he was alerted immediately when he heard the name Hampton. He remembered the name only too well and then he saw his ex-brother-in-law, Matthew, on the screen in front of him, appealing for the safe return of his grandson. Suddenly, any remaining bitterness Patrick felt towards this man and any part he might or might not have played in his being sent to Crossmaglen all those years ago dissipated and all he felt was uttermost sympathy and horror for what had now befallen Matthew Hampton and his family.

Who on earth had done this? Why had they done it? He hoped to God it was not an attempt by anyone to avenge Patrick's imprisonment. The IRA had threatened for years now to avenge his arrest and also the arrest of the two brothers who had fired the shot which killed Matthew Hampton's father. Might it be someone else entirely? Matthew Hampton must have made more than a few enemies during his time in the RUC, Patrick thought it was very likely that he had but since Patrick had come to live in England, he was so out of touch with anything that was going on in Northern Ireland, he could not even begin to speculate.

Since Helena and him with their daughter Alice had arrived here in Hailsham, a small market town in East Sussex, Patrick had thrown himself into his work in an attempt to wipe out the past and his part in that awful crime. But he had found it difficult, and having to take on a new name and to lose touch with friends and family and have no contact with them was hard to bear. And he knew Helena was desperate at times to contact her father and sister but he knew she never would. His mother coming here to live with them had been such a godsend, she was a wonderful grandmother to Alice, and she and Helena were firm friends. They were a wonderful support to one another, because if Helena missed her family, so too did his mother miss his younger brother, and he knew she worried about him a lot. To have no contact whatsoever, was so very difficult for them all. But that, it seemed, was how it must be; Patrick and his family must remain safe.

Now he rose from his seat and went in search of the two women who were, no doubt, in the kitchen preparing the evening meal with Alice's presence being heard coming from the dining room.

'Matthew Hampton's grandson has been kidnapped.' He announced as he joined them. His voice sounded sharp and strident in the narrow confines of the kitchen.

'Oh, no, please God!' His mother was the first to speak as she set down the saucepan of potatoes she had just been preparing to mash. She quickly crossed herself and muttered some words to herself. No doubt words of prayer, Patrick thought.

It was Helena who came to him, white faced and shaking, and put her arms around him. 'His grandson, you say, love? Why on earth? What age is he?'

'I don't know, Helena. I missed that part. I was so shocked, I suppose. But I think,' Patrick tried to recall the photograph of the young boy as it as flashed on the screen. 'I think he looked maybe around five or six maybe, I think.' He shook his head, uncertain now what he had seen or heard, and reached for the whiskey bottle where it sat on the kitchen shelf and poured himself another drink.

'Come, Patrick.' In the privacy of their own home, Helena had resorted to calling her husband by his original name, not Philip, as she had been educated to do before they left Northern Ireland. When they were out together, she always tried to remember to call him Philip, but usually ended up not giving him any first name. But anyway, they so rarely socialised with others, they felt safe enough and were content and safe in their own home. 'Let's go in to the dining room and have something to eat. Alice is there in her high chair and she is beginning to get impatient.' Helena made to guide her husband towards the small room off the kitchen, which served as their dining room. 'Leave your drink for now and have it as a nightcap perhaps. What do you say?'

'I'll have a few sips of this with my dinner. I can fill up later as a nightcap. But don't worry, Helena, I'm all right.'

Helena sighed as they entered the dining room, how she wished it would only be a few sips Patrick would have, but she knew that is not how it would be. He would probably drink steadily for most of the evening as he usually did now, and this latest horrible, haunting news from Northern Ireland would not help Patrick's frame of mind.

'I hope to goodness that young brother of mine is not mixed up with this in any way. Some time ago Gerry and Brian talked constantly about taking revenge on Matthew

Hampton. At least with Brian in Canada, Gerry is less likely to have the courage to do anything. But I never understood him leaving mum's house to go into a flat on his own, you know I was a bit suspicious about that.' Patrick took another drink from his glass then went on, 'When I worked with Matthew Hampton I liked the man, you know. He taught me a lot in the police and for a time we were good friends. So I feel this is terrible for him.'

'Of course it is. So we must concentrate on praying for the young lad's safe return.' It was Patrick's mother who spoke. 'We are so very fortunate, we are all safe here. I know we have no contact with any of our loved ones but we have each other. But what it must be like for the small boy's parents, we can't even begin to imagine.' Theresa Mullan rose from the table 'I shall fetch my rosary beads and say a prayer at the table, if you don't mind.'

'Of course not, mother.' Helena was quick to reassure her mother-in-law. 'Of course we must pray.'

As she left the dining room to go in search of her beads, Patrick's mother said to Patrick, in a reassuring voice.' I don't think you need worry anything about Gerry being mixed up in this. He promised me way back that he would never get involved in any paramilitary action. So please,' she addressed Patrick, 'put that thought out of your head.'

'Well, if he promised you that mother, I'm just so glad; that is something I never knew.' And Patrick rose from the table and began to move towards their sitting room. 'Bring your beads in here, mother.' indicating the room. As Patrick settled himself in his favourite chair, he marvelled at his mother's unwavering faith in God and her belief in the power of prayer. How often had he, Patrick, prayed in his lifetime, but now tonight he prayed earnestly that his mother's heartfelt pleas for Matthew Hampton's young grandson's safe return would be answered. How could anyone, no matter what their grievance, wish for any other outcome?

'Who is this Arnold Simpson? I have to know, young man. Is he your real father? Is Jason Hampton not your dad, then? You must tell me.'

Lewis looked fearfully at the man who was speaking to him and knew, even as the man talked so frantically to him that he, Lewis, had not many answers to his questions. He just knew he seemed to have been locked in this dark room for ages, although the man had told him he had only been there for a day and a night. Now the man was telling him that he might soon let him go home if he would tell him all about this man, Simpson. Indeed, the man who had taken him from his garden had been quite kind to him, bringing him plenty to eat and drink since he had brought him here and put him in this room, which hadn't even a window for him to see out of. And, he had been quietly spoken until now, when he had come in to him and in a raised, agitated voice had asked questions which Lewis was unsure of any of the answers to.

'Arnold Simpson says he is my real daddy but I live with my other daddy all the time. My grandfather is always telling me I am lucky to have two daddies.' Lewis's voice trembled as he spoke.

God, the boy seemed frightened now, and he had gone to such lengths to reassure him that he would do him no harm – In truth, the boy had such appeal about him that he was beginning to wonder about the wisdom of this venture. And now, according to the broadcast on television and the young boy's answers to his questions, it was turning out to be a complicated affair and he wondered if he would be able to handle it all. Who was going to fork out the ransom money? It did look as if it was going to be the man Simpson, not Matthew Hampton. But his whole campaign had originally been to make Hampton suffer for what had happened to his dear brother and now, it looked as if Matthew Hampton was not to suffer financially. But still, by the look of him during the television broadcast he was suffering greatly. He had seemed barely able to talk; his face was ashen and wracked with lines of worry and despair. So perhaps emotional suffering was far better than any financial suffering might be.

But where did Arnold Simpson fit into this family? Was the young boy the result of an affair between him and Jason Hampton's wife? It would seem so and suddenly he felt thwarted. Now his mission to avenge his brother seemed such a hollow, empty pursuit regarding the Hamptons. And suddenly, he felt the need to get out of his flat and perhaps seek a bit of feminine company, as he did from time to time, feeling the warmth of a female body might bring him a measure of relief. It had been a harrowing couple of days and he needed to hold on to the idea of the money he and Alfie would soon share. He had been expecting Alfie to call this evening, but so far, there was no sign of him. Perhaps he meant to stay under cover until the money had changed hands and the episode was behind them. It wasn't really like him, he liked to be in the middle of everything and stick with the job until it was finished.

But the boy would be fine on his own while he went out for a couple of hours and he knew the boy could not go anywhere. And he would make sure he had food and something to drink until he returned in a couple of hours. Doubly checking that the door of his apartment was securely locked before he departed, he made his way to his car, intent on enjoying a couple of hours light relief. Besides, he had just remembered he needed to purchase more of his favourite notelets and envelopes from his newsagents and that in itself was reason enough to go out.

Now, whatever else transpired, he believed it was in the lap of the Gods.

Chapter 22

'Gavin, I am so sorry you feel you can't trust me here, You don't really believe me when I tell you I will be true to you, no matter what it takes. But we are now in the middle of a nightmare the whole family dreaded would happen. And if I can do anything to help find Lewis, my darling grandson, safe and unharmed, I must do it.' Rachel tried to keep her voice firm and to sound reasonable. Surely Gavin would understand why she was prepared to take such desperate measures to try and find Lewis.

'It is a police matter, Rachel, not something you should be getting involved in. And if only I could believe that you were not already resolved to help, even before Lewis's disappearance, I would be more accepting of what you want to do to help.' Gavin's voice was ice cold and not once during their conversation had he looked directly at her, and Rachel had no reassuring answer for him, because she really did not know the true answer to that herself. She only knew that darling Lewis's kidnapping had given her resolve to help in any way she knew how, and if it was by going street walking then that was how it was.

Now it seemed to Rachel, as she tried to make some eye contact with Gavin, that he was already viewing her with the utmost distaste and displeasure, and her blood ran cold at the thought of her husband leaving her. How could she bear it? Surely she must abandon her idea of helping Matthew? He would understand so well her dilemma. But then there was Lewis, locked up God knows where, and there was her daughter, Lynn, now beset with grief and worry over her son. No, this was something she must do – she would do. Gavin and her feelings for one another must be shelved for now. What the future held for them both she did not know, but then she did not know what it held for her beloved grandson. Now she kept telling Gavin how sorry she was, but she was going to do it.

'Whatever my decision might have been before Lewis's disappearance is irrelevant, I now feel totally justified in helping find Julie's attacker and my grandson's kidnapper. So I am so sorry, Gavin.' Even before Rachel had finished speaking Gavin had made his way towards the door of the living room and Rachel could hear him climbing the stairs and moving around in their bedroom. She sat down wearily and waited in dread for the sound of him going out of the front door.

But later, in spite of Gavin's absence from their home and possibly her life, Rachel contacted Matthew, not committing herself to anything but just listening carefully to what he knew about the street he had named. He did say it seemed a good site to watch out for any suspicious persons who might answer the description of Julie's assailant. Certainly, Matthew believed the area might have possible links to the attacker. Then, after preparing herself as best she could and confident she at least knew what to wear to attract a man who would be interested in an escort for the evening, she made her way towards the Shankill Road. And as she drove along, she was relieved to realise that she now had a real sense of purpose. This was much better than sitting, imagining all kinds of torture and torment Lewis was going through – she was now doing something about the whole situation. If she could keep her head and keep her wits about her, she might have a measure of success in her mission, and she knew she was, in spite of everything, looking her best. She had decided to wear a smart black jacket and skirt and her favourite pair of red high heels. When she had owned the brothel in Canada, all those years ago, everyone knew an escort girl by the colour of her shoes. Hopefully men still saw red shoes as an indication of a call girl's attire. She was well aware she was no longer a young, voluptuous girl, but hopefully she would give off an air of experience and maturity to some men. Indeed, Rachel knew that an awful lot depended on just that.

She had left her car some distance from where she intended to do her walking and had travelled by bus for the remaining distance, just alighting across the road from where the newsagents Matthew had told her about was situated. Matthew had also shown her the notelets and envelopes, which had been used to send the threatening messages. On the pretext of buying an evening paper and some sweets, Rachel entered the shop. It was coming up to 8 p.m. and the shop was deserted. After exchanging some pleasantries with the grey haired assistant behind the counter, Rachel enquired if the shop stocked writing pads and envelopes, the assistant said that they did and indicated a rack in a corner of the shop which held all manner of cards, an assortment of pads, envelopes, spools of thread and small boxes containing safety pins. Rachel spent a few minutes in selecting a nondescript white notepad and envelopes, but noted with satisfaction that the buff notelets and envelopes were occupying one of the slots in the rack. After paying for her purchases, she slipped everything into her handbag and left the shop, very pleased with what she had discovered. But even though Rachel's initial find seemed worthwhile, she spent the next two hours on the street which Matthew had told her was one of the streetwalkers' favourites for business, without seeing any man who even remotely looked as if he wished to meet any escort that evening. But Rachel was not to be easily daunted and she made her way home around ten-thirty, resolved to return the following evening, because always the picture of Lewis, her darling grandson, was uppermost in her mind. What was he going through? Where was he? Were his captors being kind to him? Now, as she made her way to the bus which would take her to her car, she was tempted to go back to the shop and demand to know the name of the person who bought those notepads but then she remembered Matthew's warning about being very careful and resolutely, she made her way home. A home, which she knew would not have Gavin there when she reached it, unless he had had a great change of heart. This she knew was very unlikely, he had been so bitter towards her the last time they spoke. But surely now that he knew of Lewis's disappearance, he would have had second thoughts. But even before she turned into their driveway, she knew the house was deserted; no lights burned there and there was no car in the drive. He had really meant what he said, but then she knew that her husband was convinced she meant to help Matthew even before the horror of Lewis's disappearance. And Rachel was well aware that Gavin would have great difficulty coming to terms with that knowledge. But as she entered the hall of her home, she knew she dare not dwell on Gavin at this moment in time, there was only Lewis to consider. Gavin was well and he was still with them. Whereas, none of them knew anything about Lewis, whether he was even alive and if he was, where was he? How was he? This was something she must do, she really had no choice, nor did she want one. If she lost Gavin because of her actions, she would be heartbroken but still she knew she must do it. Each and everyone in the family were desperate after all, desperate for help, desperate for someone to do something. She must consign her thoughts and feelings for her husband into the future. That was how it must be if she were to have any chance of success. Lewis was all-important and she thought again of the fear and terror he must have suffered when he was taken from his home. Lewis was the present and she would do all in her power to help him.

The following morning, Rachel rose early in order to go to her nursing home as usual, and to get the report from the night nurses on duty. Matthew had hoped to keep the news of his grandson's disappearance from his Aunts, Eva and Maggie, and his mother Ellen, in the meantime. But the media coverage was going to be so intensive that Rachel and he thought it best to tell them, and that Matthew ought to be the one to do it. Although they were distraught at such terrifying news, they were a wonderful support to one another and to Matthew's Uncle John and his stepfather, Tom.

Now, this morning, as Rachel sat drinking tea with them all in the drawing room of the home, she stressed to them all how important it was to remain optimistic, and that she believed they had good leads. Never once did she contemplate telling any of them the role she intended playing while trying to apprehend the abductor.

Chapter 23

Rachel's senses were suddenly alerted to a car pulling up on the other side of the pavement. It was not so much the car, it looked quite a respectable, clean looking one, it was the man who was clambering out of it. He was a huge man in every way – Rachel quickly reckoned he must be at least six foot, four inches in height. Certainly he was much taller than Gavin who stood at six foot. But it was not only his height which was so significant, he was big in every way and must weigh at least twenty stones. And suddenly, Julie's description of her assailant came to Rachel, her heart quickened and her breath caught in her throat. Julie had always insisted her attacker was a huge man, those were her words, and she had always maintained she got the impression of a great head of dark brown hair.

Was this Julie's assailant? Slowly, Rachel moved along the pavement a little away from the shop, keeping her head high and her step as firm as she could, still watching the man's movements. She noted that he entered the shop, seeming to check money he had in his hand as he went. When he disappeared into the darkness of the premises, Rachel turned and began to walk back onto the pavement in front of the newsagents.

In spite of dusk beginning to fall and the inadequacy of the street lighting, he noticed the woman walking purposely along the pavement even before he had parked his car. By God, she was an attractive one all right. She was tall and slim and held herself very proudly as she walked along. She had a mass of thick blond hair framing high cheekbones and she had a very aristocratic appearance about her. Certainly she was not in the first flush of youth – he reckoned she was a woman in her forties. But so much the better, he did not want a young inexperienced girl who would wait on his every move and say so. No, this woman looked exactly what he needed tonight; someone who would be in charge of everything and lead the way towards satisfaction and fulfilment for him.

Rachel walked a little way past the shop and was rewarded to hear footsteps behind her.

'Are you out on business ma'am?' His voice was rough and uncultured. She turned to face him, striving to remain as professional as she always had been all those years ago.

'Yes sir, I am.' Afterwards Rachel was amazed at how she had kept her emotions in control, because the man in front of her was in the process of putting a pack of notelets, identical to the ones Mathews had shown her, into his jacket pocket.

'Yes indeed I am, sir, out on business.' She said, keeping her voice and expression calm and serene. She knew now so much depended on her behaviour and her reactions to this man who stood in front of her.

'Good, my car is just across the street.' Indicating the vehicle Rachel had seen him in earlier.

Rachel looked over at the car, although she was already aware of which vehicle he meant. Besides, there were only two other vehicles parked in the street. Then she looked at the man standing beside her and suddenly she felt a real fear course through her body. How could she possibly carry this liaison off? She did not know. Had she the courage to get into that car and be taken to God knows where? Could she even begin to satisfy this man with her empty embraces and kisses and all that that might entail?

Then she thought of her darling grandson Lewis and knew her fear would never equal the abject terror he must have felt when he was taken out of his beloved garden and favourite playing area. Now he was holed up only God knows where, alone, without his parents, his sister and his much loved dog, Monty. Suddenly Rachel was resolute, she could act the part; she was experienced with men and she knew how to humour them and meet their needs both emotionally and sexually. She would see tonight through and she intended to learn as much as she could about him. Everything tonight depended on her behaviour; she was going to make sure she gave no cause to arouse any suspicions in this man now walking beside her towards the car he had indicated to her.

Now, she turned to him and smiled brightly, 'You lead the way to open up your car sir.' Then she added, 'It's such a pity I gave up the rooms I had here in Belfast. They were so comfortable and so relaxing but unfortunately the police were onto me or so I was led to believe and I left them. So this is a new venture for me.' She hesitated, had she said too much? He must never know the rooms she was talking about now formed part of her beloved nursing home. She must keep her wits about her at all costs. 'I am not much used to doing much in cars. There is not much room; you do know what I mean?'

As he opened the car door for her, the man seemed preoccupied for a moment and then hastily said. 'I have a very comfortable bedroom not far from here. But we would need to be very quiet – my young brother lives with me. He must know nothing about what I do on some occasions.'

'I understand, sir. I need the utmost of secrecy too sir.'

Now Rachel knew as she travelled along the Shankill Road, everything was more of less out of her hands.

Although she must at all costs keep her wits about her, she also needed to pray for some divine guidance and intervention over the next couple of hours.

Chapter 24

The flat her companion drew up alongside was one of at least fifty in a huge complex in an area of Belfast totally unfamiliar to Rachel. Now, as the man switched off the engine beside her, she could have kicked herself for not having paid at least some attention to where they were going. What had she been thinking of? She was useless in this game, she reckoned, but she had been so absorbed in how she was going to handle everything that lay ahead of her, that she had not given a thought to where she might be heading. Quickly now, as she climbed out of the passenger side of the car at her companion's say so, she briefly tried to memorise the area around her, and some of the street lights glowing in the dusk managed to highlight a couple of side streets leading off the road they were on.

'Now remember,' as he took her arm, gently enough, Rachel thought as she stood at the door of the apartment. 'Remember, not a word; we must be silent when we go in here. My young brother will be asleep and he knows nothing about my private life, nor must he.' The voice was harsh and emphatic. Rachel simply nodded in assent and followed the man into a dimly lit hall, off which doors seemed to lead to various rooms. Silently, her escort opened the first door on the right of the hallway, switched on a light and indicated she should go in.

It was obviously the living room of the flat, with a couple of comfortable enough looking chairs, a sofa and a couple of small tables with a television nestling in the far corner of the room. Remembering the warning for silence, Rachel turned to her companion and simply smiled and nodded in appreciation, by way of showing her liking for the room and its contents. Quietly, he reached for her jacket, and helped her remove it before going over to the corner of the room and opening a door of a unit which Rachel saw served as his drinks cabinet. In a whisper to her, he asked what her choice of drink would be, indicating a row of bottles in the cupboard. She pointed to a bottle of rose wine and with a smile, he removed the bottle and poured some into two glasses which were sitting on top of the cupboard, obviously in readiness for such an occasion. Then, placing the glasses on one of the small tables Rachel had seen when she first entered the room, he led her to the easy chair she had noticed earlier.

Was this where it was all going to happen? Rachel was puzzled, he had seemed quite emphatic about his rather nice bedroom and had mentioned it a couple of times on the way here. But as she sat silently sipping the wine he had presented her with, he soon enlightened her, explaining that he felt she was something of a lady and he felt the need to treat her as such. But when they finished their drink, he would take her to his bedroom, where he had very high expectations of their evening together. Rachel's heart was heavy as she listened to this man's words, at the same time, remembering her promise to Gavin. How on earth, in the circumstances, could she possibly avoid having sex with this man, without suffering at his hands? She did not know, but she needed some delaying tactics and suddenly, she whispered very quietly that she needed to use the bathroom.

Should she flush the toilet? He had intimated to her that she must be so very quiet in the bathroom and Rachel began to wonder that if his young brother was such a light sleeper, perhaps she should not perform such a simple hygienic act as flushing the toilet after she had used it. But

Rachel could not bear to leave the toilet unclean after her use and decided to be her usual self and leave the place as she would like to find it.

'Mr, Mr. I need my bucket emptied. Please Mr, can you empty it for me? I need to use it and I need a drink too, please, Mr.' A voice sounded somewhere in the flat, a voice which seemed young and very frightened and desperate. Rachel knew immediately it was not the voice of her companion's younger brother she was hearing. No, it was not his brother but oh dear God, it was the voice of her grandson.

Almost in a trance, with a feeling all this could not be happening, she opened the bathroom door and stepped out into the corridor. Just as she realised her grandson's voice was coming from a room immediately facing the bathroom, her escort appeared in the corridor beside her. Without even considering the consequences of her actions, Rachel crossed to the door where Lewis's voice had come from and began desperately trying to open the door, all the time sobbing and shouting. 'Lewis, Lewis it is your grandma Rachel here. I'm here darling, I'm here!'

Her escort immediately grasped her by both arms and led her back along the short corridor to the living room, where the remains of the two glasses of rose wine still sat.

'Who exactly are you?' He demanded, but Rachel quickly realised that his voice held a rather frightened note rather than a threatening or aggressive tone.

'I am who I told you I was earlier. I owned a brothel in Canada and in Belfast but because of the police I had to give my houses up'. Rachel kept her voice low and persuasive. 'The only thing I didn't tell you was that my grandson had been abducted, but I never believed you could possibly have anything to do with that. I came with you to your home because I wanted to.' Rachel was desperate to sound most convincing, but she knew everything now was fraught with danger and she had possibly now put both Lewis's and her own life at risk. What was she to do? What appeal could she make to this man? Yet she still felt a glimmer of hope when she looked at his face, he seemed to believe her when she had said she had come to his house simply for his company and for no other reason.

'Please, please just release my arms?' she asked looking directly at Lewis's captor's face.

'You must know I cannot allow you to leave here.' Her companion said as he realised his hold. 'I must keep you here until I decide what to do.' He hesitated, and then went on, 'I'm expecting my mate later this evening and he'll know what to do for the best. In the meantime you'll share the box room with your precious grandson, my dear.'

On hearing he was expecting some accomplice later, Rachel's blood ran cold. Sometimes, all an evil act needed to be carried out, was active encouragement from one evil human being to another. Rachel prayed silently, as he took her by the arm and brought her to the door of the room she now knew was Lewis's cell, and where she could hear his quiet sobbing echoing into the corridor. Time seemed to stand still for Rachel when her captor opened the door and she saw her darling grandson sitting on a wooden chair, sobbing.

'Lewis, my darling, my darling, I'm here with you, there is nothing more to be frightened of. No one can harm you now.' At her words, her grandson looked up and around him like one in a trance, and seemed to peer in disbelief through his well of tears. Then, he was on his feet and in her arms; his soft warm familiar body wrapped in hers. Then Rachel heard the sound of the door closing and the key being turned in the lock.

Chapter 25

Although Rachel's disappearance made the headlines in the next morning's television news, the police were very circumspect as to the events surrounding her disappearance, saying only that they believed she had gone out last evening determined to find her grandson. They added that if anyone had seen a lady in their area answering her description, to immediately be in touch.

Ironically, Iris Simpson too, was determined to find Lewis, her beloved stepson, and had managed to slip out of her home in Helen's Bay sometime in the early hours of the morning. When Arnold awoke and discovered he was alone in bed he initially thought his wife had simply gone to the bathroom, though normally she would wake him and let him know she needed to go. This was always an indication for him to switch on their bedroom and the landing light, in order to show Iris the way. But this morning, she hadn't wakened him, and he doubted very much that in the horrific circumstances they found themselves in at the moment, he would have been in a very deep sleep. He soon discovered that Iris was not in the house or the grounds surrounding their home, and soon he was telling the police that not only was his cherished son missing, but now too was his wife.

As Patrick Mullan listened to the evening news on his return from work and after having a couple of strong whiskeys, he found himself very confused about all the events surrounding Mathew Hampton's grandson. Who on earth was this woman Rachel? It seemed, she was the child's other grandmother, but now she too was missing. What sort of conspiracy was going on against the Hampton's? For God's sake, was it not time all the ill will and the feuds were ended once and for all? What was to be gained now, by totally wrecking that family circle? As he listened in disbelief, the commentator was saying that yet another member of their family; the boy's stepmother, who had been injured in a bomb explosion in Belfast, had wandered off. The commentator stressed that she was sometimes confused, and keen to help find the boy, had simply wandered away. At no time did the police believe that she too, might have been abducted.

Patrick pondered at length on all he had heard on the television, he must try to memorise it all in order to be able to tell Helena when she came back from visiting her friend in Eastbourne. She'd had a day off from work and had organised the day for Alice, his mother and herself, and told him not to expect them back early. She would leave him something to eat in the fridge, that he would be able to reheat himself. When he had come home from work, the first thing he had done was to reheat the shepherd's pie, Helena knew it was one of his favourite meals and he had enjoyed it very much with his whiskeys. Now though, it was his time to set out for his usual evening stroll, which included calling in to the off licence to purchase some whiskey for himself; he did not like his stock to become too low. This was his usual routine; have dinner after arriving home, then no matter what the weather was like, he would always go out for a walk and then purchase a bottle of his favourite tipple on the way home.

It was a very mild night for a leisurely walk but strangely this evening Patrick scarcely noticed, his mind was in turmoil about Matthew Hampton's family and the truth was, his conscience was bothering him because of his role in their tragedy. He was also thinking about his young brother and hoped his mother was right about him. She maintained that he could never have anything to do with the abduction of Lewis Hampton. She was indeed quite adamant that Gerry had never been embroiled in any criminal activity of any kind. As he walked along the familiar footpaths of Hailsham village, which would lead him to the off licence, he wondered again, why he was so concerned for the Hamptons. Then he reminded himself that after all, he had been married to Matthew Hampton's sister, Lucie at one time, and he had been a member of the family. Now, as he made his way along the footpath, he found he had great difficultly sorting out all the connections in the family. Certainly, this boy's grandmother and mother had not been around during his time with Lucie. He knew he was somewhat preoccupied as he walked along. But just the same, he was very careful as he walked towards the off licence, the traffic was always very heavy here and drivers just seemed to ignore the speed limit. It was on his return from the off licence that he was hit by a driver who mounted the pavement, crushing Patrick against some concrete posts which bordered the footpath. The driver who failed to stop, just sped on through a red traffic light, was travelling at least sixty miles per hour in a thirty mile zone. Patrick had done all the right things that night, both when he was going for his drink and returning with it in his favourite canvas bag.

For two days and two nights, Helena and Patrick's mother took it in turns to sit beside him, holding his hand, stroking his forehead, talking to him, willing him to make some sign that he could hear them, he could understand them. But he lay so very still and silent in that hospital bed, that the women despaired of getting any response. On the fourth afternoon when both women were with him and Alice was being looked after by a neighbour, he suddenly opened his eyes and looked, firstly at Helena and then his mother. 'I'm sorry, mother. I'm sorry, darling. Tell them all I'm sorry.'

Quickly, Helena moved closer to her husband and wrapping her arms around him whispered 'It's all right, Patrick. You have nothing more to be sorry about.'

Her husband turned his head slightly to look at her and gave a small smile, then giving a long sigh, passed away in her arms.

Chapter 26

'If you let me out of this dark room just for a little time I would like to talk to you.' Rachel had spent what she reckoned was the last six hours, alternatively sitting thinking in the small box room Lewis and she were locked in, and going over to hug her grandson, and wrap the blanket round him where he rested on the mattress on the floor. 'I think Sir you should listen to what I have to say.' Rachel felt more confident this morning in how she might handle the nightmare situation she now found herself in, but she would need to be very careful how she spoke to her captor. Everything depended on her persuading him that her idea was a good one.

'Please, this won't take long. Just let me out to speak to you for a few moments.' There was no reply to her entreaties, but just as Rachel was giving up hope of him wanting to hear anything of what she had to say, she heard the sound of his step in the corridor and then the grate of the key as he turned it in the door. He opened the door wide and indicated she follow him back into the corridor. Then, turning to Lewis, he told him he would bring him breakfast shortly, then he locked the door again and headed towards his living room.

When they reached the living room, he indicated the chair in the corner of the room away, Rachel observed from the only window in the room. He then went to the kitchen area and pouring two coffees into thick breakfast mugs, offered Rachel one. Eagerly, Rachel took it, she was very glad of it, she was so very parched after being cooped up in such a small airless room. After taking a few mouthfuls of the liquid and when her thirst was somewhat quenched, she spoke.

'Please let my grandson go, he is only five years old, and I will stay here with you in Lewis's place.' Rachel spoke quickly, before her courage deserted her. 'I will stay here with you until the ransom is met, whatever the ransom is sir. I'm sure my family will meet your demands as much for my sake as they would have for Lewis's. Until then, I'll do whatever you want of me but please just let my darling Lewis go.'

Rachel dare not let her mind dwell on Gavin or what he might be thinking or feeling now. Lewis's safety and life was all that was important, and now as she watched this great hulk of a man pour another coffee for himself, she prayed he would at least consider what she had just said.

'Why should I think your family will pay the same amount for you as I want for your grandson? Besides, this man Arnold Simpson who says he is Lewis's father is the one who is going to pay the ransom.'

'But don't you see, Mr Simpson will be so grateful to have Lewis back safely, he will willingly pay for me too. Besides, I have a lot of family who love me very much and will be prepared to raise the money. I know they will.'

He did not answer at first, just sat sipping his coffee and then looking into the dregs of his mug. Then he eventually remarked, when he realised Rachel had nothing to add. 'I'll think about what you've just said, but I need to be careful where I'll leave the boy – that is, if I give him up.' Now, he rose to his feet. 'I have to put you back in the box room I'm afraid, this street gets very busy and I don't want you tempted to try to raise the alarm until I have decided what to do with the two of you. So let's go back to your grandson. If you need the bathroom, I'll wait outside it for you. I don't expect you to use a bucket as the boy has had to do.'

'Thank you, yes I do need it.' Rachel made her way to the bathroom, as dignified as she could, knowing he was waiting for her out on the corridor before returning her to the box room, where Lewis had just finished eating toast and drinking milk.

Matthew had not gone to bed at all that night after learning of Rachel's disappearance. He was wracked with guilt. How could he possibly have allowed her to put herself at such risk as she obviously had done? What had he been thinking of? He had been thinking of nothing, only the safety of his grandson. That's what he had been doing, thinking only of his own family, but now, Rachel was at risk too. He should just have let Arnold get the money, and arranged to deliver it in exchange for Lewis's safe return. That way, everyone would have been safe, but now he believed that two of the family were living in fear of their lives. He should never have listened to Superintendent McAllister when he had stressed the importance of finding the culprits and not handing money over too soon. He knew that now, now, when it was too late.

Now he felt he would have to seek Gavin out, but no one seemed to have any idea where he was. He had not been at Rachel's and his home when he had called that last evening, nor had he called at the nursing home as he usually did. Well, at least he knew where Gavin was working at present. He would go there in the hope of speaking to him, though what he wished to achieve, he did not know. But perhaps he could shed some light on Rachel's very last movements and if she had contacted her husband in any way.

'Rachel – missing you say.' Gavin's voice shook as he addressed Matthew. 'Since when may I ask?'

'She has not been home since yesterday evening some time, Gavin, and she did not call at her usual time in the nursing home to get an update on anything that was happening there. I thought you might know something about her movements.' Matthew's voice tailed off when he saw the expression on Gavin's face and suddenly, he realised that Rachel and her husband had a major difference of some kind and it did not take Matthew long to realise that Rachel must have gone in pursuit of her grandson. She must have made her final decision after speaking to him.

'My goodness, Gavin, did she go to the streets of the Shankill Road in order to find Lewis?' Matthew continued and his voice held some disbelief. 'Of course she has done exactly that. I am so sorry. I am totally responsible I believe, for this.'

'I am convinced she intended to try to find Julie's attacker. She had made her mind up to help you even before Lewis was abducted.' Gavin's voice held a note of bitterness.

'Gavin you must believe me when I tell you that I only wondered how Rachel might help before someone else was hurt. She was so instrumental in bringing young Leo Finlay's murderer to justice and I was desperate because of the threatening letters I was receiving. I would have turned to anyone for help and somehow or other, Rachel came to mind, but never in my wildest dreams did I think she would take to the streets in order to help.' Matthew's voice held a depth of admiration. 'It must have taken a lot of courage and determination to do so. She must also have trust in you Gavin, when she felt you would understand and accept her motives for doing so.' Matthew knew he was rambling on now but somehow he knew he must try to make Gavin understand why Rachel was doing what she was doing. He was somewhat rewarded by a certain softening of Gavin's features, and his brilliant blue eyes softened and became less steel like.

'I told her if she went street walking I would not be able to bear it and I would not be around.' Gavin looked steadily at Matthew now, an uncertain look on his face. 'Perhaps if she had decided to do this after Lewis's disappearance I would have understood but she had decided to do this before Lewis disappeared. She went simply to help you.'

'I think Gavin, her real reason for going was because she felt there was a real threat to other members of the family, and so it has proved to be.' Matthew's voice was now no more than a little whisper and he realised he was losing control.

'I need to think about everything Matthew. I hope that both she and Lewis are found safe and well. In the meantime, I will spend my nights here in the shed over there.' As he spoke, he pointed to a wooden hut at the far corner of the building site. 'I have so much to come to terms with – luckily I have an easy chair and a kettle to make some tea. It's all I want at the moment.' Gavin shifted uneasily, 'I'm sorry I cannot promise to be of any help to you here Matthew. I just feel so lost.'

Those words 'I feel so lost' tore at Matthew's heart as he made his way to his son's house to let him and Lynn know the latest developments, hoping they would not have heard anything on television. How did he ever imagine Rachel might be able to help? But Rachel, brave, kind Rachel had decided on her own to assist him and now, dear Lord, she too was missing.

'Oh Matthew, we are so glad to see you.' It was Lynn who opened the door to him and he was surprised to see some semblance of a smile as she greeted him. 'Come right through. Jason is having a nap at present and Eve is in the garden with Emily and Monty.' Again, that half smile which seemed to transform her weary face into something resembling normality. Immediately Matthew reached forward and enveloped her in his embrace.

'How can you bear this, Lynn, and try to keep going in such a positive way?'

'Don't you see Matthew, for Jason, Eve's and Emily's sake, I must believe, I have to believe that everything will be alright.'

'You are a gem in all this, Lynn.' And Matthew tightened his hold on her,

'Do we need to waken Jason?' Lynn asked him, then again 'Do I need to waken Jason? I will only waken him if you have anything to tell us. Is there any news at all?'

'I have no immediate news of Lewis, but it is too early for that, we all know that. But yes, I would like you to wake Jason.' Matthew was anxious not to alarm Lynn, but he knew it was vital that Jason was with Lynn when she heard of her mother's disappearance. That would be very hard for her and Matthew doubted if Lynn would be able to keep up such a brave front when she heard of her mother's disappearance coupled now with that of her first born child.

After Matthew's departure some time later, Lynn could not begin to function. She was prostrate with grief and Jason realised that their son's abduction had been unreal to her. Perhaps she had never really believed it had happened. It might have been better if she had joined himself, Arnold and Matthew for the appeal on television. Certainly, that was when the reality of it all had hit Jason, when his son's disappearance had been broadcast worldwide. Now, Lynn seemed incapable of functioning, and it was left to Jason to see to all the normal everyday occurrences, not that he believed anything could ever be normal again.

After Jason said his goodbyes to Matthew, he did wonder what on earth could be done to ensure both his adopted son and his mother-in-law were safely returned to their families. The most worrying aspect of it all was that the police efforts during the last couple of months to try to find his mother Julie's attacker had failed miserably and the thought of that failed mission made Jason's blood run cold as he tried to maintain some normality in his daughter Eve's and his wife's life. Then, when he remembered the abductor's demand for a ransom and Arnold's insistence he would provide all that, Jason knew the man would be true to his word and his heart lightened as he went into the bedroom where Lynn lay staring silently at the ceiling. Very quietly, after putting his arms round her slim body and holding her close, he whispered, 'everything is going to be alright darling, Arnold has guaranteed that for us, and I have no doubt, whoever has Lewis, has your mum too and they will let them go together. Arnold will see to it, I am convinced.'

Chapter 27

'What do you suggest I do with your grandson? I can see that to keep both of you here might not be such a good idea. If I do decide to release your grandson, I would need to be convinced that your family would be as willing to pay the ransom for you as they would be for the boy. I have almost convinced myself that indeed they would be willing to pay up, simply because by letting the boy go, they will realise that you are making an enormous sacrifice for the lad.' Her captor's eyes never left Rachel's face as he talked, but Rachel was determined to show resolve and commitment in what she had said.

'I believe you should release Lewis as soon as possible. If you don't, I believe it is only a matter of time before every police force in the country is searching for you. By letting my grandson go home, my family will believe you are a reasonable man and will be prepared to negotiate with you regarding my release.' Rachel knew she was appealing to this man's better nature – if he had one – but she believed it was her best chance to obtain Lewis's release. 'I can also assure you wholeheartedly; if you take Lewis home I shall make no attempt whatsoever to escape. I realise too, that you must put me under lock and key until your return. Then, you must decide what you must do with me.' Rachel believed she would be safe enough here while a new ransom was renegotiated between him and her family. She could only pray that things might move pretty quickly but at the same time, there was no doubt she was at her abductor's mercy.

'Well, let's not get away from the reason we met up in Ivan Street in the first place, and that reason for our meeting still remains. And I am expecting you to service my needs after my return from leaving the boy off. That is, if I do decide to let him go.'

Rachel had been preparing herself all day to hear those words from her captor. After all, by stating quite clearly, she was prepared to stay with him and offer him comfort what else did she expect? Now he was telling her he would make a decision shortly about Lewis Hampton but he must now lock her back in the box room. Once he had turned the key in the lock she lay down on the mattress beside Lewis who was fast asleep, no doubt her presence here must have been very reassuring for him and he was probably now catching up on any sleep he had lost when he had been first deposited in this box room. As she lay with her arms around her grandson, she spared a thought for Gavin. Where was he at this moment? How was he coping with her behaviour? Did he realise she was missing? Perhaps he didn't even know, if no one had told him then he would be in the dark about her absence. Did he know she had not returned to their beautiful home? Or had he not returned to it either following their disagreement? She loved her husband so very much but even so, she could not possibly regret any of her actions during the last twenty-four hours. How could she? Wonder of wonders, she was with her grandson and he was safe and maybe, just maybe, if she had played her cards right with their captor, he would soon be home.

What celebrations would there be then, when Lewis, beautiful, sensitive Lewis, was home safe and sound. Jason and Lynn – his parents – and his grandparents would be beyond happiness. And of course his great grandparents – her mother Maggie and Matthew's parents, Ellen and Tom, would be beside themselves with relief and joy at his safe return. As Rachel lay there in that dark, dank room with only the warmth of her grandson's body to sustain her, she did not care what happened to her. It did not matter – Lewis would be safe, back in the folds of his family. For herself, it did not matter. After all, she had scarcely been a respectable, upright member of society either in Canada or Northern Ireland for quite some time. The only good thing, ironically, Rachel thought, was the fact that her skills in brothels had led her to the discovery of Lewis. So, she was quite prepared to accept her fate with this man, who was, she believed, sitting in the next room, contemplating what he would do with her. She did not have to wait very long, she heard his step in the corridor and then he unlocked the door and indicated quietly that he wished Rachel to join him in the living room. She rose from the mattress where Lewis still slept, the sleep of a young child who had temporarily forgotten anything that was happening around him.

Now, as she sat facing her captor in his living room, nervously she wondered what he had decided to do. What plans had he decided on, regarding Lewis and herself? She had no idea, and could read nothing from his demeanour, but she was surprised when he spoke to her in quite a moderate voice. 'I need a drink before I go anywhere. It will take some nerve to go out there with your grandson. That is if I can do it at all.' He sounded unsure and Rachel's spirits dropped. But then he went on 'One drink will be alright, and I want you to have one with me.' And he looked at her appraisingly. Rachel was glad then, that her appearance and presence were not lost on him. Thankfully though, he made no move to come close to her or to touch her.

'Of course I will, your wine is really good.' She knew she must keep humouring him.

At Rachel's remarks, he seemed to brighten considerably and then he smiled, more to himself, Rachel thought, than at her. 'I have decided to keep you here, my dear.' And now he was looking at her in such an eager, leering way that Rachel wondered what she would actually have to face with this bear of a man. Certainly, she knew she would never be able to defend herself in any way, but his next words to her made all his leering and all her worries about him seem quite trivial.

'I am going to put the boy in my car shortly and leave him somewhere, somewhere he will be familiar with and will be able to find his way home from. Where I will leave him, I haven't quite decided yet, but I will have to tell your family, whoever they are, that I want the same ransom amount for you as I was asking for the boy. I would like to think that by letting him go home, they will appreciate my generosity of spirit and will pay up for you when I say so.'

Now, as Rachel watched him, she realised his expression had quickly changed from one of sexual desire to one of greed, and relief washed through her as she realised his ultimate goal was money. If only he would become totally obsessed about the ransom she might yet escape his sexual advances. Her captor had indeed, suddenly remembered that his main mission in all this had been to obtain money from the Hamptons. And part of him wished that this man, Arnold Simpson, who was purported to be the boy's father, would not wish to part with any ransom money once he knew his son was safe. Then it would fall on the Hampton family to cough up, and that was what his aim had been all along, to make Matthew Hampton suffer both financially and emotionally. Once Hampton realised that his son was free because this woman had instigated the boy's release, he would be more than happy to pay up, but he was in no hurry to get the ransom for this woman, he intended over the next few days, to have some enjoyment and relaxation from her. It was what he really needed, he had been deprived of a woman for too long and he needed some light-hearted relief from all the tension he had been under since the boy's capture. If he had still had Alfie's company on occasion, he believed that would have helped him. Alfie's gruff, basic ways had always helped him from becoming too morose and downcast about things. But now he scarcely knew anything about Alfie, he had promised to call as soon as possible with him, but there was no sign of him and it was getting rather late in the evening. On reflection, perhaps it was no bad thing that Alfie wasn't around at the moment. He would have been furious to learn that he had brought a woman to the flat and that it was the lad's grandmother. He would have called him all sorts of names, he knew that. No, he needed to get rid of one of them and it must be the boy. The woman would be much better company.

Chapter 28

'Please Sir, my name is Lewis Hampton.'

The policeman on duty behind the desk roused himself from his reverie. He had just been thinking how nice it would have been to have had the night off tonight, and to be sitting in front of the fire with his wife. He realised he had been almost asleep when he was suddenly alerted by the sound of a young voice speaking to him from the other side of the desk.

'Please, please, sir, will you let my daddy know I'm here and I want to go home.' The voice was very plaintive and apprehensive to the ears of the constable. Then suddenly he was alerted to the reality of the situation and who exactly the young boy was now standing before him, pleading so earnestly, and excitement and anticipation rose in his chest as he spoke now to the boy.

'Oh, my goodness me, you have been freed my boy! Lewis Hampton, did you say?' With that, the constable came round to the other side of the counter and putting his arms around the young, vulnerable, scared boy standing there said, 'You're safe now, lad. Let's go into the back here and we'll soon have your dad round here to bring you home.' With that, Constable Johnston led Lewis, his arms still tightly round him, into the office which during the day would be buzzing with policemen and women all reporting on their latest incidents and having endless cups of tea and biscuits. Tonight, as it was on most nights, it was deserted.

'You have a seat right here, young man.' The constable indicated a chair close to a two bar electric fire set into the wall, a fire which he now switched on. The boy looked as if he might never feel warm ever again. 'I'm going to fetch you some milk and biscuits. You wait there.'

Now the boy became frantic. 'Please, sir, I must have my daddy here. That man has my granny, Rachel, with him.' The boy's voice shook. 'I want my granny home, sir. We need to get her home, Sir.'

'Right son, I'll ring your daddy right this minute.' And so it was with a new air of importance that Constable Johnston headed to the telephone. He was the man now who had all this information to impart to this boy's father. To think that such a short time ago he had wished he was home at his fireside, when in fact he wouldn't have missed all this for the world. To think he was going to be the one to tell his superior such wonderful news about this boy. But then of course, he would have to tell him that the boy had said that the man had his Granny Rachel. Of course, everyone knew of Rachel Finlay's disappearance but few people had actually thought there was any connection between her and young Lewis. But, according to the young boy, and he had no reason to disbelieve him, the abductor now had the child's grandmother. It was such a pity that he actually had to tell his superior all this news, it was such a pity he had no way of contacting the boy's parents, but he had no idea who they were. Besides, he was duty bound to tell his superior first.

'You say you have Lewis Hampton sitting in the barracks. Man dear, do you not know who this boy is? Who his father is?' Without waiting for an answer the Sergeant thundered down the phone 'That's Detective Inspector Hampton's grandson you have sitting there. Do you hear me? Matthew Hampton's grandson.' And the booming voice of the Sergeant emphasised to Derek Johnston the words 'Detective Inspector' in a most sarcastic voice. A voice that inferred that Derek was a fool of the first order for not knowing this.

'Sorry, Sergeant. I was not aware of that.' Perhaps all the publicity and all the posters displayed round the place, not least in this very barracks should have indicated some connection but not once had it entered his head. Some detective he would make, thank goodness he had no aspirations for such a role. All he wanted was to be a community policeman, to try to make his community a safer and happier place for everyone.

'Sergeant, the lad seems very distressed about his grandma. He says the man has her locked up.'

'Oh, I see.' Suddenly his constable's ignorance of who the boy was did not matter. After all, he was new to the barracks and was not that familiar with the staff. Now this information Constable Johnston was giving him was big stuff, important stuff. 'I'll get on to the family straight away. Make sure the boy has a drink and something to eat.'

'Yes, Sarg. I promised him something after I rang you.'

'Make sure it's the chocolate biscuits that everybody tries to keep hidden in that tin on the top shelf that he gets. We want his grandfather to know we treated him well.'

'Of course, Sarg. I'll do that.' Derek Johnston answered. No point in telling his superior he had intended to give the child those very biscuits, even before he knew he was any Detective's grandson.

Derek Johnston knew he would never forget the look on Jason and Lynn Hampton's face when they saw their son, waiting in that bleak barrack room, in such anticipation for them. In truth, he felt he was an intruder in their private world of love, gratitude and joy. All three were wrapped in each other's arms weeping sheer tears of joy, and Derek

Johnston's heart was overcome with emotion at the scene before him. His eyes filled with tears and he felt humbled by it all. Yet in spite of all their joy, these young people were aware that their happiness at their son's release was so diminished by the knowledge the boy's grandmother was now missing. In spite of all their happiness, a happiness so very touching to anyone who witnessed it, Derek Johnston knew that Lynn Hampton must be frantic with worry about her mother, who they now knew was being held captive. One horrifying nightmare had just been replaced by another, and Derek Johnston thought it was the cruellest trick to play on these young people. How do you possibly choose between a much-loved son and a very much-loved mother and grandparent? But thankfully, and at least temporarily, that decision had been taken from each and every one of them.

Just as the young family were beginning to regain some control over their emotions, the door of the office opened and Derek realised, even before the man spoke or was introduced to him that this was Matthew Hampton, the child's grandfather. He went immediately to his grandson and held him tightly, kissing him and stroking his hair continuously, all the time muttering endearments to him.

Then, turning to his son, Jason, he said. 'Let us get the boy home to his own house and his own bed. We'll try to get all the details first thing in the morning.' Then, he turned to Lewis. 'Daddy Arnold is on his way from Helens Bay to your house, so we need to get moving.' When he released his grandson, he went over to Lynn and putting his arm round her shoulders, said, 'Enjoy and appreciate these moments, Lynn. We'll soon have Rachel home and you and I know she is very strong mentally. She'll be able to cope. I believe that and so too must you.'

Lynn nodded in reply and her face seemed to have lost the gaunt, anxious look which had been such a part of her over the last few days. Then she whispered, 'I will depend on you, Matthew, to keep her safe and we will I hope, hear everything from Lewis in the morning. For now, I relish bringing Lewis home and wrapping him up in his warm bed once more. I am pretty confident too, that Lewis will be able to give us some clues as to where mum is. He's a bright boy, you know.' Then, by way of a good night, she leaned over and kissed her father-in-law on the cheek.

Chapter 29

He had left Lewis Hampton as close to the local police station as he dared without running the risk of being seen. While he had no wish for the boy to get lost if he did not know the way – that would really complicate things for him – equally, he had no desire to be caught at this stage in the whole procedure. He had also made sure he put a blindfold on the lad before he left the flat, he did not want the boy remembering the way and bringing the police to his door.

Well, now he had done what the woman had beseeched him to do – let the boy go and hold on to her instead. He smiled to himself as he drove back to his apartment. The arrangement suited him so very well. He would be in no great rush to demand a ransom for her. That might be something he would contact Matthew Hampton about in a day or two. In the meantime, he intended to enjoy himself with her and he was sure looking forward to that. The last twenty-four hours had not worked out the way he had intended, but he was not complaining about that because he meant to change all that very shortly. Now, the thought of her lying on that mattress on the floor of the box room, her attractive body folding into it was enough to arouse him and he was really looking forward to the remainder of the evening. He would bring her out of that room and lead her to his bedroom, where the bed would be able to accommodate them both and her curvaceous body and his manly one would just sink into it.

As he turned the corner of the avenue leading to his driveway, he noticed a familiar car parked outside his flat, and as he drove towards it, he saw someone was sitting in the driver's seat. As he parked his own car in the driveway, a man who looked vaguely familiar, proceeded to get out of the car and walk towards him. Then, he realised it was one of Alfie's mates and as he approached him he saw he was carrying a holdall.

'Can I come in for a minute? I have a message from Alfie.'

'Sure you can.' Secretly, he cursed the man standing before him, the street light emphasizing his rough appearance, but he needed to know where on earth Alfie had got to. He had been beginning to think he had met with an accident or was lying blind drunk somewhere, having forgotten all about their mission.

'Right, come on through, mate.' As he led the way to the door, inserted the key in the lock, opened up and indicated the way into his living room. 'Right, what is it, mate? Alfie was to be here last night but never showed up. What's the message from him then?'

'It's not good news, I'm afraid. Alfie's been arrested. He told me to come and tell you quick. He says you're to forget all about some mission or other, he says you would know what he meant. He says to be rid of it quick, or they'll soon be on to you too.' The man hesitated for a moment, then he unzipped open the canvas holdall he had been carrying and produced a metal object from it. For a second, Jimmy Devlin could not focus on what it was, then, he realised it was a handgun Alfie's pal was holding out to him.

'He wants you to take care of this for him until he gets out of prison. He did say you might be glad of it yourself.'

'I'm not familiar with guns. What did Alfie think I might need it for?'

'Search me, mister. I'm just delivering the message – and at great risk to myself I might add. You have to take this gun – I don't want it – and Alfie specifically said you were to have it.' Alfie's mate was beginning to sound quite agitated.

'Well, I'll put it away safely.' It was best he took the weapon, if for no other reason than to placate Alfie's friend. But he must hide it away before his female friend noticed it sitting around, he instinctively knew she would be terrified at the idea he had arms in his flat.

'What exactly is Alfie charged with?' he had almost forgotten to ask about that, he had been so taken aback at seeing the gun.

'Actually it was on the news earlier, mate. Mind, it didn't give his name, they just said they had arrested a second man in connection with the manslaughter of Kevin Mullan – Patrick Mullan's father. The other man was arrested, I think, two or three weeks ago.'

'In the name of God, was Alfie responsible for the raid on the Mullan house in the Falls Road district? 'What on earth was he thinking of? We just don't go there. Why on earth did he do that? Has he told you anything about it?'

'He said it was all to do with avenging the death of Rob Hampton – Matthew Hampton's father.'

Now Jimmy Devlin was stunned into silence, on the one hand Alfie had sought to avenge the death of Matthew Hampton's father, then on the other hand he had been happy to avenge what had happened to Jimmy's brother, by kidnapping Hampton's grandson. Alfie must be very mixed up indeed and probably was not, and was never going to be, the most loyal, staunch person to involve in the mission he had become involved in.

Suddenly it dawned on him that he was now in grave danger of being identified by none other than Alfie himself, as the abductor of Lewis Hampton. No doubt alcoholic consumption over time had taken its toll, so he was probably not always responsible for his actions or what he told people. Now, he knew it was imperative he acted quickly to be rid of Lewis Hampton's grandmother and claim the ransom. He had no intention, after putting himself at such risk, to end up with nothing. So, as soon as he could arrange a rendezvous to have the money handed over, so much the better.

Now, he took the gun from Alfie's pal and carried it over to a small cabinet, which contained his car insurance papers and his rent book, and placing the gun carefully inside, he closed the door and locked it. Then he took the key to his bedroom and placed it in the drawer of his bedside cabinet. Returning to his living room, he spoke to the man standing waiting there.

'Tell Alfie I'll do as he says. I'll keep the gun safe for him. I know I shouldn't but I will. Tell him that, will you? Also, tell him I'll be along soon to see him.'

After Alfie's friend's departure from the flat, he sat for quite some time with his head in his hands – thinking about all that had happened in the last forty-eight hours, and the dilemma he felt himself to be in. But he had got rid of the boy which he believed now was a good thing, but the woman was here and he still wanted her, and he intended to have her, but above all, he still wanted the ransom money. So the sooner he made contact, the sooner he would have the ransom money and the sooner he would be rid of her. He was concerned that sooner or later, Alfie might talk to someone in the prison, talk about their triumph in abducting young Lewis Hampton.

He was going to have to take a chance and deliver the note to the police barracks; hopefully the ones in there would have been really busy and engrossed with the arrival of the boy. They would have endless phone calls to deal with from the media and all its reporters, so he was hopeful he might go unobserved.

Thank goodness he had bought some notelets and envelopes the evening he had met the young lad's grandmother. Now, he would write down the time, date and rendezvous for the exchange of the ransom money and her. It would not matter if some of the words were wrongly spelt – spelling had never been his strong point in school. On the message, he would also insist that Matthew Hampton would deliver the money to the appointed place and at the appointed time. Only Matthew Hampton. If any others came, he could not guarantee the lady's safety. As he printed the message on the notepad, he began to feel really excited and confident about the whole venture. He realised this evening, that he must have the upper hand in this whole affair. After all, he had a gun, to carry some extra weight in what he was saying and doing. He was in a much stronger position now, to negotiate with the relatives of the woman in his box room, especially Matthew Hampton. He was in a better position now to wield some power over him.

Chapter 30

The police doctor had assured the family after a thorough examination of Lewis, that he had not been physically harmed in any way. Indeed, he was in good physical shape considering his ordeal, although the doctor stressed that a great deal of emotional trauma might be the case as a result of his being kidnapped.

Meanwhile, Matthew had decided to go back through his records from ten years ago, when he might have sent someone or other's brother to prison for some crime. He had managed to highlight four or five possible leads within the UDA. At least, having the knowledge now that the notelets had originated in a Shankill Road newsagents, had narrowed down his search considerably. There did not seem to be much doubt that this was not the work of the IRA on this occasion, but rather the Ulster Defence Association and its associates.

Early the next morning, as Matthew prepared to go into the office, he reflected back on the previous evening and everyone's joy at seeing Lewis tucked up in his own bed and requesting that his Aunt Emily be allowed to sleep with him and that Monty might lie at the bottom of his bed; requests which were agreed to very readily. Although the doctor who examined his grandson had asked him a few questions relating to how he had been treated and how he was feeling, very few other questions had been asked of Lewis that evening, everyone agreed that could all keep until the next day. It was much later that evening, when the question of Rachel's abduction was addressed. Lynn and Jason's feelings, while overjoyed at their son's safe homecoming, were tempered by deep concern and worry for Rachel. Arnold, who had travelled from Helen's Bay earlier that evening, bringing Iris along with him, were both overwhelmed and overcome with emotion at the enormity of what Rachel had done to ensure Lewis's release.

'I fully intend to honour my agreement with the abductor and pay the ransom, after all, my son would not be lying in his own bed tonight if Rachel had not helped secure his release. So I, for one, am indebted to her forever. Besides, I can actually well afford the £100,000 he is demanding. So please, none of you worry on that score.' And Arnold smiled at the family seated around the room.

'I just want to say that I insist on being there, wherever the meeting is taking place. I wish to hand the money over personally and the sooner that is done, the better, and we have Rachel back with us.'

'I agree, Arnold. Let's hope it won't be long before we hear from them again. We desperately need to have Rachel back as quickly as possible.' Matthew replied and he knew the family in the room were wondering what Rachel might be enduring right at that very moment. 'But we just have to wait until we hear from them and what their plans are. That's the thing about kidnappers – they're the ones so very much in control. They're the ones who issue the demands, I'm sorry to say. But just the same, I'll be at my desk first thing in the morning to try and identify these men. In the meantime, let's go home and try to get some sleep, it may refresh our minds.'

'Arnold – Lynn and myself would like you and Iris to stay here tonight, we don't want you driving back to

Helen's Bay in your mobility car at this time of night. So please stay.'

'Why, thank you, Jason. Iris and I will be pleased to stay with you.' Secretly, Arnold was delighted to be staying, knowing his son was tucked up in this house, safe and sound. It was like a miracle; he had been abducted and then suddenly, he was safely home and it was all down to Rachel. They all knew that Matthew had told him in the strictest confidence that she had gone into a street off the Shankill Road renowned for street walkers, and she had taken on the role of one. Such ingenuity and courage she had shown, and at what cost to herself? How did she think she would cope with any of these men who, according to media reports, might resort to cruelty? And what might even be happening to her at this time? He could not dwell on that aspect of this whole nightmare, but must concentrate on making sure he had the money by tomorrow, even though they had heard nothing from the captors about meeting up.

Perhaps in the morning his son might be able to give them a lot of information but tonight, they had limited the questions to how he had been treated by his captors. They were reassured when he told them he had been really kind to him and at times Lewis thought he even regretted he had ever thought of kidnapping Lewis. But of course, having a boy in your keeping was totally different from having an attractive, intelligent woman like Rachel.

Now Matthew was intent on trying to leave for the office, making as little noise as possible. He doubted if Julie would have slept very well with all the uncertainty of what might be happening to Rachel. Julie and he had insisted on going home from Lynn and Jason's, although his son had asked him and Julie to stay. Matthew had explained, he must be in early to work. Besides, Julie and he felt Arnold and Iris should have the spare room. Jason had suggested Arnold and Iris would be comfortable on the sofa bed in the lounge, but Matthew reckoned Iris might easily find the front door if they were in the living room, and make her way out of it. So, Julie and he had made their way home around one o'clock in the morning. He especially did not want to wake Julie, he knew she was reliving her own nightmare of the vicious assault on her and wondering if Rachel would suffer as she had. He was just in the process of picking up his car keys from their bowl on the kitchen sideboard, when the telephone rang in the lounge.

'What is it, Matthew?' Julie appeared in the doorway.

'That was the barracks, darling. We didn't have too long to wait. Our captor wants to meet up to get his ransom and to return Rachel,' Matthew was smiling now. 'You go back to bed, love, it's only six o'clock. I'll let you know everything later and I'll inform Jason, Lynn and Arnold as soon as I go into the office.'

As he drove to his office, his mind was reeling with the news he had just heard. It seemed the captor had the audacity to go once again to the police station and put his message into the letter box right beside the main doors. Either the man was very clever and timed his movements to perfection, or else he was very stupid indeed. Certainly, the words on the messages they had been receiving from him would indicate he was uneducated, but Matthew had learned over the years in the police force not to underestimate any criminal. They themselves now needed to watch their every move and proceed with the utmost caution. It was Rachel now, not his darling grandson, who was depending on them to ensure her safety and as far as he was concerned the stakes were the same. Rachel had been brave enough to ensure Lewis's freedom, but at what cost to herself? He still believed the money was still the major catalyst between them and surely that was good reason for hope.

As he parked his car, he wondered where the rendezvous was that the captor wished them to meet, and who did he want to bring the money to him? Would he want to come face-to-face with Matthew himself? Or what of Arnold? He was the one who was paying out the money so readily. Arnold had not once wavered in his determination to pay whatever the abductor demanded. His reasons were two-fold; he owed a debt of gratitude to Rachel of such magnitude that no money could ever pay for what she had done, but he also believed he owed the police a debt of gratitude for finding Iris so quickly the morning he realised she had disappeared. He knew their appeals from their police cars as they drove around Crawfordsburn and Helen's bay had led to the two young girls coming forward and reporting seeing a lady of her description sitting on a park bench in Crawfordsburn Park. They had been observant enough to see that she only seemed to be wearing a coat over her nightdress, and on her feet she just had slippers.

After that episode, Arnold had employed a nurse to look after Iris all the time. Last evening it was the first time they had been out together on their own, since that episode. Knowing that she was going to Jason and Lynn's house, where she would see for herself that Lewis was home, must surely settle Iris and she might not have the same desire to wander off. Certainly, Arnold could see that she was much more content, even though, Arnold realised she was very aware that Rachel was missing.

Chapter 31

Rachel had lost track of time since her captor had taken Lewis from beside her, the warmth of her grandson's body had given her such comfort when she felt she most needed it. Now she was alone – alone in this darkened room with just the dire choice of lying on the mattress on the floor, or sitting on the wooden chair over at the wall. And for some reason, she preferred sitting on the chair, she did not feel as vulnerable as she did when she lay on the mattress. When she was sitting on the chair, she might manage to have some control over what was going to happen to her. During the last hour, or what Rachel imagined must be an hour – it seemed such an interminable length of time – she had heard no sound or seen no sign of her captor and that was so unnerving for her, not knowing where he was or what his intentions were.

She knew he had returned to the flat after he had taken Lewis away, and wondering where he had left Lewis and indeed had he left him safely somewhere, had flooded her mind for such a time when she sat there on that wooden kitchen seat. Yet she knew he had returned, for someone else was with him, and Rachel's blood ran cold as she listened to the low voices talking in the living room. Was this his accomplice? It probably was, who else might it be at this hour? Soon, she heard the front door open and close, then a car drive away, and the ensuing silence in the flat gave Rachel some hope that if it was his accomplice then perhaps he had gone. That much was such a huge relief to her that she could have cried as she sat there in the dark. Trying to deal with one criminal was a monumental task in itself but having to face two of them – well she did believe she would have very little chance of survival with the two of them. After all, they were bound to begin to feel somewhat cheated, their original prize had been handed back, at least Rachel believed that was how they would feel. Now they were left with the boy's grandmother, and anything might go wrong for them now. After all, Rachel figured, the two abductors had no knowledge of her family and perhaps the abductors would feel that none of her own people would think she was worth the ransom. So, with the two of these men involved, Rachel had reckoned her risk of never seeing her loved ones again was considerable. But now, on hearing the front door closing and a car starting up, she believed only her original capture was present. Indeed, because of the fear and anxiety she had faced during the last couple of hours, she knew she was prepared to meet any of her captor's demands. It didn't really matter what she had to do to get out of here, she was now desperate to see her family, to feel their arms round her and just be with them. As for Gavin, she could not bear to think about him, but she knew he would find it difficult to hold her in the same regard as he had always done. She believed her husband was lost to her, but she just prayed that at least her grandson was safe with his family, and when she thought about Lewis, once more, he was all that mattered. This was what this was all about and Rachel found she had renewed courage to face whatever the next few hours had in store for her.

She had not much longer to wait when she heard his heavy step in the corridor, then the key was turned in the door and he was standing before her; a great hulk of a man.

'Right my dear; I want you to know it is payback time now. Before I deliver you back to whoever your nearest and dearest are, you and I need a little time to enjoy ourselves. I haven't even had time to show you my comfortable bed and my cosy bedroom, but that is all about to change my dear.' His tone was low and Rachel felt he was attempting to be seductive but his voice just seemed threatening to her. Even as he regarded her, he continued to talk in the same monotone.

'I have delivered the boy to safety and I have also arranged to collect my ransom in a particular place and at a particular time. So I feel before we part company, when I take you to the designated place on my note, that you owe me quite a bit for ensuring your grandson was safely returned to his parents. Don't you think so? And don't you agree?'

Initially, as she rose from the chair in the box room, Rachel could only nod dumbly in response to the questions her captor was throwing at her. Then she realised she must have some level of conversation with him; her life probably depended on it because now, as she looked at him, she saw a new air of assurance, of aggression that she had not seen before. In truth, until now, she felt she might have some power to manipulate the situation between him and her to her advantage. But now, as he took her arm and led her away from the dark box room where Lewis and she had been holed up, she sensed a new controlling manner emanating from him. Suddenly, she was truly terrified for her own safety; she must do whatever he commanded of her. As she entered the living room of the flat and sat down once more on the sofa, she allowed herself another private loving thought for Gavin − he would never be able to forgive her for the situation she found herself in. He had after all, taken her on and married her, loving her unconditionally, in spite of knowing about her chequered past. To expect him to have any regard or respect for her after this, even if she was fortunate enough to come out of it all alive, would just be too much. But happily, now she did believe that Lewis was safely home with his family, otherwise no further arrangement to deliver the ransom hopefully in exchange for her, would have been made. And she allowed herself another ray of hope.

'I have poured drinks for us both, but I think rather than sit here with them, we'll have them in the comfort of my bedroom.' Somehow or other, Jimmy felt insecure in his own living room, he'd had so many disruptions in the last few hours, but before he left the room to escort the woman upstairs, he went to the small cabinet in the corner, and removing the gun, took it over and showed it to Rachel.

'I will be taking this with me tomorrow my love.' Once again, he sounded assured and quite excited. 'I must take it you see, I originally thought I only wanted our Mr. Hampton to deliver the money but now, I have asked that Mr Simpson be there with the money. It's his money after all. But you see, I don't believe that's how it will be. I believe my friend Hampton will be quite insistent that he is present too – more fool he, might I add.' He must have noticed Rachel's stunned reaction to the gun lying in the palm of his hand as he talked. But now quickly, he spoke in a more muted tone, in an attempt to reassure her.

'You've absolutely nothing to fear my dear. You will come to no harm, you've just to accompany me to the forest and do exactly what I ask.' Having access to this gun had totally changed his outlook on life or so he believed. It had certainly changed his way of thinking about a lot of things. No wonder Alfie had sneered at him when he had insisted on buying Lewis Hampton chocolate and a drink. What had he been thinking of? Now he realised, when he had a gun in his possession, people would jump to his commands. How stupid had he been, thinking to bribe that boy Hampton into submission? As for the woman sitting beside him, a drink in her hand, he had no intentions of being 'soft in the head' when he took her upstairs. She would do as he asked; he intended to make sure of that. There was no doubt having a gun made all the difference.

Now Rachel, because of the presence of the gun, knew so very well she was no longer in control of what would happen when they reached his bedroom. She must go along with each and every demand he made of her. It was not how it might have been in her small brothel in Waring Street, where she dictated the terms. This was something very different, outside her control and she was totally out of her depth.

She realised that the presence of the gun changed everything and must account for her captor's whole change of attitude regarding the situation they were in.

Chapter 32

When Matthew received the message that an inmate in Crumlin Road Gaol wished to speak to him urgently, he was exasperated by the demand to go there as soon as possible. He had so much to deal with right here. He was trying to decide if they might need a police presence at the rendezvous where Rachel was to be handed over in exchange for the ransom money and also if it were safe for Arnold to be the one to leave it at the tree as requested. They had still no idea who this abductor was. Would he be armed? Would he suspect a police presence there? Matthew had no answer to any of his own questions.

'Who is this man in Crumlin Road? Alfie, did you say?' he asked the constable who had just delivered the message.

'Yes, Sir. He had pleaded guilty to being involved in the assault on Kevin Mullan some time ago, Sir. You know, Patrick Mullan's father.'

On hearing then what the charges were which were being brought against this man by the name of Alfie, Matthew decided he better go and find out what the man had to say. No doubt, it would be some sob story or other and the prisoner was probably hoping that because of the murder of Matthew's father and Patrick Mullan's involvement in it, he would think Matthew might lend a sympathetic ear. Then the constable continued to speak and Matthew was instantly alerted.

'He alleges he can tell you about your grandson, who has him and where he is.'

'He says what? But my grandson is safely home as you know, constable. He's been home since late yesterday evening.'

'I know that, Sir.' And the constable stressed the words, 'but our inmate could not possibly know that. He was arrested some time before your grandson was released.' The constable went on earnestly 'He seems genuine and is adamant he knows where he is. He was able to tell us how the boy was and that he talked a lot about his two fathers – he seemed to know a lot about him, Sir.'

Even before the constable had finished speaking, Matthew was on his feet, retrieving his notebook and pen from his desk and indicated to the constable to lead the way out of the barracks.

'A woman there, you say. There was no way there was a woman in his flat.' The man, Alfie shook his head in disbelief at such a suggestion. 'We kidnapped a boy – a mere slip of a boy I can tell you.' Again, that same shake of the head and a look of puzzlement on his face. 'A woman you say, I had no idea he had a woman.'

This man facing Matthew in the interview room in the prison must have been in his early to late forties. But he certainly was not a good specimen of a man for that age, he was overweight, his cheeks were flaccid and under his eyes were sacs of fluid. His hair was thin and had been combed forward towards his face, no doubt to hide his baldness. He looked as if he was on the verge of being an alcoholic, for excessive drinking was written all over him. Now, as Matthew listened to him answering his questions, the man's lack of knowledge about any woman being in his flat was a solace to him. Did it mean her captor had gone out of his way to keep her presence a secret in order to hold on to her for as long as he might dare? Some instinct told Matthew that Rachel's captor desired her company, simply for himself. If that was the case, he felt Rachel might be free from any physical harm – at least in the meantime.

'Who is this man, this henchman then? We need some details from you.'

'Oh, dear, Sir.' Alfie wanted to taunt this man sitting before him in his all-powerful role as detective inspector. 'Have you no idea who he is then?'

'I'm not at liberty to say.' Matthew felt the need to be circumspect. Certainly, he had no desire to let this man know that they had no idea who Lewis's captor had been.

'We don't divulge any confidential information we have acquired. Really we just need some confirmation from you as to this man's identity, and as you are probably aware, anything you do tell us will be looked on very favourably by the prosecutors when your case is called. They will likely be more lenient when you explain you had no intention of killing Kevin Mullan and were shocked when he died from a heart attack. Although of course, he took the heart attack as a result of the beating he got.' Now Matthew wondered if he had been too accusing and waited with bated breath for the man's answer. He was rewarded when the prisoner leaned forward and whispered through the mesh which divided them.

'Sure, mister, he's a brother of the leader of the Shankill Road butchers, Sir. You know Andy Devlin – him that was gunned down by the IRA in one of our very own back streets. Well, my friend has always blamed you for all the publicity his brother got over all those killings, he has always said, sir, that you pointed the finger. He knows you did not send him to prison, but he says you pointed the finger.'

As Matthew sat on the edge of the seat at the opposite end of the table from where this man Alfie sat, so confident, yet so naive in his story telling, he was stunned by what he was hearing. In all his research and his frantic search for evidence, never once had he even considered looking at Andy Devlin's file, the leader of the Shankill Butchers. After all, the evidence he had presented had utterly failed to convict him, with the result that he was free to go back to his evil ways. It was true however, that not long after his release, other forces decided to rid society of this evil man and officially, it was recorded, he was gunned down by the IRA But the authorities had never been in much doubt that his own UDA members had colluded to get rid of him. Even they were beginning to fear him, and Matthew's blood ran cold when he realised that he had just been told that this evil man's brother was the person who was holed up with Rachel and who had initially abducted Lewis.

Now Matthew had great difficulty controlling his emotions and longed to reach over and grab this particular prisoner by the throat and demand he tell him every last detail about their warped evil plans when they first thought of abducting his grandson. But he knew he must remain calm if he were to obtain as much information as possible from this weak looking, inferior image of a man. And now, he did not disappoint Matthew, knowing he had his undivided attention, Alfie made the most of what he knew about his mate. He even told him that it was he who had robbed the off licence a few weeks ago, stabbing the young employee, before he made off with some of the takings. He even explained to Matthew that the money from that robbery was to pay him so he would help his mate.

Once Matthew heard Alfie relate the events of that evening and the amount of money his mate had managed to steal, Matthew knew this inmate, vague and uneducated though he seemed to be, was telling him the truth about the whole criminal action the two of them had embarked upon.

Chapter 33

How had it all come to this? Here he was in his dead brother's lock up shed, come garage, with this woman whom he was beginning to realise he knew very little about and now had also discovered he had very little feelings for. Certainly, when he had first seen her in Ivan Street, her fair hair shining even through the dusk which was beginning to settle and her immaculate clothes emphasizing her sleek figure, his emotions and his sexual appetite had been aroused. But during the last forty-eight hours, his desire for sex had diminished and he now knew so well, it was initially because he had discovered she was Lewis Hampton's grandmother. That had certainly brought things into perspective when he had discovered that. What sort of trick had fate played on him? Then he had thought about his moment of weakness, when he had suggested bringing her to his flat. What had he been thinking of? Him knowing full well he should not let anyone near it while he had the boy. So, what had possessed him to make such a suggestion? He knew now that it was the woman herself with her talk of her bedrooms who had made him think it was quite a good idea. Then, to discover in his apartment who she really was; Lewis Hampton's grandmother. The whole situation was so very unreal to him, yet here he was with this woman, in his brother's lock up garage, and he asked himself again, how had it all happened?

The last few hours had been very eventful for him, first he had delivered the boy close to the barracks and then he had also delivered the ransom demand some time later. At that stage, he had been so very confident of his success. Nothing, he felt, could possibly go wrong. Then of course there was the initial visit from Alfie's friend telling him of Alfie's arrest and predicament. Then, a few hours later, a second visit from the man, to inform him that an urgent message from Alfie had arrived, to tell him that the police knew who he was and where he lived. Alfie's message to his friend was very clear, he needed to vacate his flat at once and go undercover. His brother's lock up shed was the only place he could think of, he had a key to it and he knew that it had always had a kettle and a fire if they were needed. God knows, he hated that garage, even though he himself had rarely frequented it but according to police reports, this place had witnessed many horrific tortures and murders at the hands of his brother and his gang. But this was the only place he knew where he could bring his car in and lock himself and his captive in to. This dump of a place they were now in, did not compare well with the flat they had been in barely forty minutes ago. Then, he had been on his way into the bedroom with her, when the doorbell had rung and he had felt compelled to answer it after everything he had heard about Alfie. As he sat now, on a low chair beside a table facing this woman he had brought home and whom he had now lost all sexual interest in, he could only imagine the horrors which must have gone on in this place, and he found it very difficult to come to terms with the knowledge that his brother had been responsible for them all. He knew now he must not dwell on all of that, he had to keep his head and concentrate on getting the ransom money in exchange for her. Now, looking at her, he could see she was really terrified.

'You have nothing to be afraid of my dear, we are in this together. We are in here and here we must stay until tomorrow evening. Then I'll happily bring you to your destination in exchange for my ransom. I know I have the gun here but it has nothing to do with you, it is merely for my own safety.'

Rachel longed to say, if it had nothing to do with her, why had he threatened her with it if she did not go quietly to his car to be taken to this bleak, filthy place? But she said nothing. Indeed, when she first realised they were leaving the flat, she was elated. Did that mean he was running scared and that the police were on to him? She did not know, but she was thankful she had got another reprieve from having to go to bed with him and being forced into some kind of sexual activity or other. She was, in spite of her fear, thankful for that, and she could sense now that her captor's only thought at present was for the ransom money and his own safety. She just hoped that in itself was not a dangerous thing for her, for probably while he found her attractive and the thought of sex with her was something he looked forward to, she was safe. Now that urge had left him, would he begin to look on her as just a burden to him and then if that happened would the ransom money also lose its appeal and would he only think of his own safety? Still, he appeared concerned about her at present, and was reaching her a bottle of water and a rug he had just retrieved from his car. 'We'll need to drink something while we're here and we need to keep warm, It's only two o'clock in the morning, so we have quite a few hours to put in before tomorrow evening. So, put that rug around you and try to sleep. I want you to look well when you meet your folk tomorrow, I want my ransom money.'

Rachel did as he told her to, although she wondered vaguely how her looking well or not would affect him claiming the money.

'Our abductor has been tipped off, Sir. His flat was empty, but there were signs he may well have been entertaining someone.' The constable who had been sent by Detective Inspector Hampton had been well trained by him. "Miss nothing." He had always told him. "Take note of everything, no matter how trivial it might seem to be. Believe me," his boss had always said, "It might prove invaluable to us," And that was why the young constable had been so meticulous after he had broken down the front door of the flat he and his colleague had been sent to, and entered the place. He was more than ready to give the place a thorough going over. But apart from two empty wine glasses sitting side by side in the living room and a tissue which smelt strongly of a woman's perfume, there was little else to report, apart from the single mattress on the floor in a small windowless box room and a bucket which smelt strongly of urine. Obviously someone had been in there, but then his superior had known that when he sent him there, but it was good to more or less have it confirmed.

'There are no signs of life whatsoever, Sir. I think our man must have left in a hurry. How his mate got word to him so quickly is a mystery isn't it Sir? I believe he must have had some good contact in the prison, sir. Someone who was going to act immediately and get the message to our captor, Sir.' It was not like the young policeman to be so presumptuous to his superior but this case intrigued him, simply because he had been told it had all to do with Matthew Hampton's relatives. That was as much as he knew, everyone was so very secretive about it all, as if he would dare go and talk about it, he knew better than that, besides, he respected his boss big time.

'Don't worry, constable. In the meantime, be in my office at eight-thirty a.m. in the morning. We have quite a big day's work scheduled.' Perhaps, Matthew thought as he listened to his constable, it was all for the best that Jimmy Devlin had been tipped off. He personally had been very concerned about his officers storming into a flat which might prove to have limited means of escape for either the offender or his captor. And the knowledge they now had that their captor had a gun was an added anguish to Matthew, it only added to the vulnerable position Rachel was already in and put her at such increased risk in such a surprise situation. Matthew realised he was quite prepared to have patience here, he believed it might well pay off, he was quite prepared to sit this culprit out because he believed the ransom money was still of immense interest to him.

'Let's wrap up our search for the night and we will arrange everything in the morning, to ensure we have success in our work tomorrow.'

Chapter 34

'Arnold, I think it might be best if I and some of my comrades go to the designated meeting place to hand over the ransom money to this man Devlin, in exchange for Rachel.' Even as he spoke, Matthew felt some relief that now at least, they were able to put a name to Lewis and Rachel's abductor. They were no longer dealing with some unidentified person, but someone who now had a name. 'It's not that I think you could not cope with the whole setting but we have to be realistic, Arnold – we know nothing much about this man, what he might be capable of. His henchman tried to tell me that he's just a big softie, the exact opposite to how his brother, the leader of the Shankill Butchers was. But I doubt that description so very much considering the assault on Julie. Besides, we don't know what he might do if he felt he was cornered.' And Matthew's voice was bitter. 'Maybe, just maybe, he has a soft spot for children – he was quick to release Lewis, but I doubt if that is the case regarding women. I do believe Rachel to be at serious risk from his brutality and,' here Matthew hesitated, apprehensive about the need to let Arnold know so much. 'We do know he has a gun, so I think it best if I deliver the ransom money and we will ensure there are some undercover police there in case we have any trouble from him.'

'I'm sorry, Matthew, I simply don't want any other presence there, only you and I. It is much better if we obey this man's commands. He did say he wished me to be there, to have the money in a black attaché case and to leave it at the foot of the tree nearest the duck pond in Drumvanagh forest. I think we would be advised to do what he asks – to the letter – to ensure Rachel's release.'

The tone of Arnold's voice did not invite any argument. 'After all, Matthew, you've just said he has a gun and I have no doubt he would use it if he felt he was walking into a trap. My being there will convince him we are following his instructions to the letter.'

Matthew felt very humbled as he listened to the wisdom of Arnold Simpson and his argument for going to that desolate park at ten o'clock at night. He knew the man was so right in what he was saying; if Jimmy Devlin suspected anything was wrong and a trap had been set for him, he would be capable of becoming trigger happy very quickly. Once again, Matthew was remembering Julie's awful assault. In his present frame of mind, trapping this man had become uppermost in his mind and now he knew that was so wrong, he must concentrate on Rachel's freedom and safety; that was what mattered most of all. Now he found he was most agreeable to go along with all Arnold was saying.

'We'll go in my disabled car, Matthew. I think that would be most reassuring to our friend, the kidnapper. It seats four very comfortably and we will be able to return Rachel to her family once we have left the attaché case with the money in it where he has asked us to. I do agree with you on one point, Matthew, we must make sure Rachel is there before we leave that case with the money in it at the tree. No doubt, he'll be there somewhere, among those trees and hedgerows, watching our every move. So let's make sure we don't make a wrong one'. Arnold looked at Matthew, his expression unreadable. 'I know there are risks, Matthew, but there are risks for you too as well as me. Whether one is a policeman or one a civilian in this case, the risks are all the same. You do know that – I know you do. So we are in this venture tomorrow evening together, Matthew. In the meantime' Arnold went on, 'I am going back to Helen's Bay tonight and will return in good time to collect you tomorrow evening. I want you to take good care of the attaché case which I have with me today. You can then hand it over to me tomorrow evening when I collect you.' Arnold was smiling at him with as much reassurance as he could muster. 'When I pick you up tomorrow evening we'll make it look as if we are just going for a nice drive. Whatever you and your superiors decide to do about undercover work, I won't ask and I don't expect you to tell me. Just remember, all we want is Rachel's safety, nothing else matters.' Arnold rose from his seat beside the window in the annexe. 'Now please try to get some sleep, as I shall be doing – Iris and I. Do you intend to go to your desk as usual in the morning?'

'Yes, I have a few things needing sorting out. I want to find out if we have any record of our abductor having been in any kind of trouble before, or was it his brother's murder which was the impetus for his change in behaviour? That should not prove too difficult now that we have his details. We also have a fingerprint from one of the threatening letters, which should prove that he sent them. If we are fortunate enough to arrest this man, we should be able to tie him in with Julie's assault, the threatening letters and Lewis and Rachel's abduction. I don't often give my opinion to anyone Arnold, but I am now giving it to you. There is no doubt, the same man is responsible for everything I have just mentioned.'

'I believe so too, Matthew, but if he eludes us tomorrow night, I doubt if he will get too far. I would imagine you will have a few blocks and a few high alerts out for him.'

'Please, Lewis, you must go to bed. It is long past your bedtime darling. I promise you that soon, very soon, you will see Grandma Rachel.' Since their son's safe return some thirty six hours ago, the boy had spent some considerable time looking out through the window, watching, he said, for his grandma to return home. Nothing either Lynn or Jason said to try to reassure him seemed to make any difference to him. It was almost as if the boy knew that he had been returned home safely because his grandma had to stay, not that any of them had voiced those words to Lewis since his return. In fact, as a family, they had insisted on celebrating his safe return. Every one of the family had joined in the celebrations; Lynn and Jason having insisted on his own grandparents Ellen and Tom Greenlees being there, also Lewis's great Aunt Eva, Lynn's grandmother Maggie and of course, dear Uncle John who was always so supportive to each and every one of them through any crisis. They all, collectively, had come to embrace Lewis and to celebrate his safe return into the heart of the family, and to thank God for his safety. But certainly, the celebration was tempered by Rachel's absence and although everyone tried to be optimistic in believing the ransom money was all that mattered to the captor, if some of the members of the family thought about Julie and the horrendous attack on her, they kept those thoughts to themselves, determined too, to be optimistic. And certainly, young Lewis's insistence that the big man had been very kind to him was reassuring.

'Lewis, we will see Grandma Rachel tomorrow night, and when she comes home, we will let you stay up ever so late. How would you like that then?' Lynn held her son close, he was so dear to her, and she could scarcely believe she was actually holding him safe in her arms. During the awful hours when he had been missing, she had despaired of ever holding him like this again. And how well she knew that she had her mother to thank for her son's safety. And she desperately needed to know that Arnold Simpson and Matthew must make sure that nothing, absolutely nothing happened the following evening.

'But now, Lewis, we must all go to bed, else by tomorrow evening, we'll all be too tired to talk to grandma. Why Eve was in bed two or three hours ago, go and crawl in beside her, but don't wake her, like a good boy.' On occasion Lewis sometimes liked to sleep with his young sister, but then at other times, he preferred his own bedroom. But tonight, the idea of sleeping with his little sister had really appealed to him.

'Right, mum, I'll sleep beside Eve tonight and in the morning I'll tell her all about grandma coming home.'

By way of answer, Lynn hugged her son tightly, she believed that Eve had scarcely noticed that her grandmother was absent from her life, she was so overwhelmed by Lewis's presence back with his family. She had only once mentioned – since Lewis's homecoming – about the bad man taking him out of the garden. As for Monty, Jason's collie, he had scarcely left Lewis's side, only going out to the garden to relieve himself, then crying loudly at the back door to be readmitted. Then, he would search frantically for Lewis until he found him and wherever Lewis slept, whether it was Eve's bed or his own, Monty slept at the foot of the bed.

It was with relief that Lynn helped Lewis undress and get him into his pyjamas and with endless kisses and hugs and reminders to be quiet, she was able to re-join Jason, Arnold and Matthew in the living room.

'We are well organised for tomorrow evening, Lynn. We know exactly the time and place for the exchange of money for your mum. Arnold has already given me the money, so it is safely here. So please try not to worry, everything will be alright.' Matthew did not divulge and

157

thought he ought not, that his superior had insisted that there must be some police presence in the forest. Superintendent McAllister was determined, he told Matthew, that the kidnapper be given no chance of escape. They had to make it difficult for him, he could not be handed the sum of £100,000 and hope to get away with it. Although Matthew agreed in principle to what Ernest McAllister was saying, he would have much preferred to let the transaction happen and then seek to arrest him. After all, with all the roadblocks they intended to set up, he could not get far. But Matthew's argument fell on deaf ears; his superior was adamant that an undercover police presence must be there. Besides, they must be very sure indeed that he was going to hand Rachel back to her family, and that he did not decide to keep her for his own pleasure. Now when his boss talked like that, he was actually voicing Matthew's own fears and he decided his boss's orders were for the best. But he did not intend to let anyone in the family know about it – that must remain confidential.

He had not told anyone in the family, apart from Arnold, that they now knew who the abductor was. If any of them knew he was the brother of the leader of the Shankill Road butchers, they would agonise over Rachel's safety, believing her to be in the hands of a monster. He had not even confided in his Uncle John, whom he normally told most of his problems and woes to. He had had great difficulty in coming to terms with the reality of who had kidnapped his grandson and now held Rachel. And to think he had even considered Patrick Mullan's brother as a possible suspect, a man who had never been in any trouble in his life. He felt ashamed when he thought about it. True, over the years, he had received numerous threats from the IRA for Patrick and his henchmen's arrests. And then of course, Patrick Mullan had to take on a whole new identity, leave his mother and brothers and go to another country. So at the time, Matthew had reasoned, it was quite plausible for someone to be tempted to take revenge for such a situation. But he experienced a great sense of relief when he proved Gerry Mullan – Patrick's brother – was totally innocent. But the worst of it all was, he had never dreamt who the real abductor might be, and he knew now that the brother of someone much more sinister than Patrick Mullan was holding his cousin Rachel hostage.

Chapter 35

Gerry Mullan rose around six a.m. on the day his brother's body was being brought back to Belfast. He was very glad the night was over – he believed he had not slept at all, the whole night. His mind had been so active through those dark hours, that it was just a relief for him to see daybreak beginning to come through the window of his bedroom, and to prepare himself and try to come to terms with the ordeal in the days that lay ahead.

It was Helena who had rung him, to tell him that Patrick had had an accident. He had multiple injuries she told him, and asked him to pray for his brother. Initially, when Gerry had heard Helena's voice on the telephone and she had told him who she was, he knew it must be something serious, to give Patrick's wife cause to take the risk and ring him. He immediately thought his mother must have been taken ill, when his sister-in-law went on to explain about the hit and run driver and that Patrick had simply been walking along the pavement. Gerry heard all Helena said, but somehow, it did not seem to register with him. Multiple injuries, Helena had said, but surely Patrick would survive it all. He was a young, strong, resilient man – surely he would be alright.

When Helena rang three days later to tell him that his brother was dead and that they would be bringing his body back to Belfast for burial, Gerry was beside himself with grief. For the first time in his life, Gerry drank himself into a real stupor that same evening. He liked the odd drink or two, liked going to his local pub and relaxing with a couple of friends over a pint, but he had never consumed the quantity he did that night. The following morning, he had just felt so helpless and hopeless, that he wanted only to lie in that darkened room and think about Patrick and what might have been.

It was the persistent ringing of the doorbell, which forced him to haul himself out of bed and reluctantly make his way to the door. It was the young local parish priest who stood there. Gerry recognised him immediately, even though he himself was an infrequent attendant at chapel. But he remembered all this man's kindness and attention he gave to his mother, his brother and himself after his father's death.

'Sorry, father, I'm so sorry. Please do come in.' Gerry opened the front door wide. 'I'm afraid I'm a bit under the weather this morning, father.' Gerry knew there was no use pretending to this man, he was much too astute.

'That's very understandable, Gerry. Very understandable indeed.'

Something in Father John's voice, a sympathy, a tenderness there, was too much for Gerry, and for the first time in the two days since Helena had rang to tell him his brother was dead, he burst into tears; loud, gulping sobs which almost seemed to be choking him.

Tenderly, the priest put his arms around Gerry's shoulders and guided him into the living room. A room which Gerry was normally very proud of but this morning was littered with empty beer bottles and smelt strongly of alcohol.

'Sorry, father. About the state of the place, I mean.' Gerry managed to say through his sobs.

'Why, it's fine, just fine, Gerry. We'll clear up these bottles, then we'll have a cup of tea and a good chat. Where will I get a bin bag for these empties?' and Father John was already beginning to lift the empty bottles and place them on the table beside some others lying there. Quickly, Gerry went into the kitchen, retrieved a black bin bag from a cupboard and at the same time, put the kettle on to boil. He was mortified that the priest had seen both him and his apartment in such a state. Would he ever live it down? He did believe he might, because Father John was so very understanding.

Soon they were seated in a much tidier room, the window had been opened to allow some fresh air to waft through and they were each drinking a good strong cup of tea. Father John began to speak.

'I want to say, I am truly sorry about Patrick. I also want to say that your brother had well and truly paid his debt to society, both by being in prison and by being isolated from his family. His widow wishes you to know, Gerry, that his last words to her were 'Tell them, I'm sorry.' So I have no worry over Patrick's soul, and neither must you have, Gerry.'

'Thank you, Father, for telling me this. You have always been of great comfort to me.'

'Now as you know, Patrick's body will arrive at the airport around ten o'clock in the morning. I thought I might accompany you there, Gerry. That is, if you are agreeable to that, of course.'

'Oh, would you, Father? I never dreamt of such generosity. It is so very kind of you.'

'If you feel you and your mother and Patrick's widow would benefit in any way from my presence, I would be pleased to accompany you.'

'I do know myself and my mother would feel blessed if you were there and although I cannot speak for my sister-in-law, I do believe she too would appreciate it.'

'That's that settled then, Gerry. Now let's look at the room you have thought of for your brother when he returns here.' Although Father John suspected Gerry Mullan had not thought about anything much since he had received the news of his brother's death, he thought it would be best if he did so. 'Then we'll look at the order of service.'

'Patrick will be in my bedroom with me. Mum, Helena and Alice will be in the spare room.' Gerry was rather proud of his bedrooms, he had brought his own and Brian's two single beds from home when he had moved here and they fitted well into the spare bedroom. He had plenty of room for his visitors.

His own bedroom was quite spacious and there would be plenty of room for Patrick when he came here and Gerry was very happy to stay with him throughout the night.

'Brian is flying out from Canada tomorrow, but he says we must not worry about him. He has booked a room for a couple of nights in one of the hotels. I'll show you my room now, Father. I hope you think it will be alright.' Gerry led the way down the corridor to his own bedroom and although there was a slight smell of alcohol and the bed was unmade, the room looked rather inviting and was clean and tidy.

Father John went out of his way to reassure Gerry that his bedroom was ideal and that the top of Gerry's chest of drawers would be an ideal place for the Mass cards and all the candles. After agreeing on the order of service which Father John said Helena had already discussed with him over the telephone, then with promises to be at Gerry's flat around nine a.m. the following morning, and after saying a short prayer, the priest made his departure.

Chapter 36

Gerry was so very grateful for the priest's presence at the airport the following morning, when he met his mother once again, and his sister-in-law and his niece Alice – neither of whom he had ever set eyes on before. He would have recognised Helena anywhere from her wedding photographs, his mother had always been so proud to bring them out from her sideboard and show them to him from time to time. But – oh, such circumstances under which they were all now meeting he thought, as he hugged and kissed his niece Alice and saw how she grasped her mother's hand tightly, unsure and uncertain in this new world she was now in. And as Gerry saw the little girl, so shy and awkward in his presence, he thought about her future. This was Patrick's daughter – a daughter Patrick would never see mature into a young woman. He would never witness her achievements in school or in her work. He would never be there to approve or disapprove of her boyfriends, never see her married or enjoy her children. Now, as he hugged his mother and then embraced Helena in that airport, he felt his heart must break, not only because of his own grief, but the knowledge of what the two women before him must be suffering. As Gerry waited with his family, Father John held on to his arm while they were all together there, in that airport foyer waiting, they all knew, to hear that their beloved husband, son and brother, was ready for the next stage of his final journey. The funeral director spoke directly to them when he approached, but he spoke so very respectfully and reverently, that Gerry knew they had chosen well with their funeral furnishers, simply because his brother deserved that utmost respect and reverence the funeral director was portraying. 'We are ready to bring your husband home, Mrs. Mullan.' as he addressed Helena, whom, Matthew realised, he must have assumed to be Patrick's widow. Again, in spite of his anguish and grief, Matthew was grateful for such a display of intelligence and respect.

On the journey back to Gerry's apartment, the conversation between the family was very sparse and Father John too, was silent, respecting that each one of the passengers in his car wished for a respectful silence, no doubt to think of the loss of Patrick. Gerry wanted on one hand, to ask Helena more about where they had lived in Hailsham, how Patrick had settled in to his new life over there. Most of all, he wished desperately to know about the accident which had robbed Patrick of his life, but he lacked any courage whatsoever, to address any of these questions to Helena or his mother, so he remained silent, haunted only by the bare facts that he and his brother had no contact whatsoever for so long, in order to try to protect Patrick and keep him safe. Yet his body was even now being carried in a hearse from the airport to his apartment. He was the victim, they said, of a hit and run driver. And for Gerry, the fact that he had had no contact whatsoever with Patrick for so long in order to keep him safe, had all been so futile and he found that so difficult to bear; a simple phone call would not have made any difference to Patrick's safety, as was now so apparent.

Later that evening, his mother, Helena and Alice did manage to eat something and to drink endless cups of tea – he had no intention of even mentioning alcohol, he was still trying to come to terms with the state he must have been in when Father John had called, not that Father John had referred to it at any time, something Gerry was so very grateful for. When his mother said she was tired and would like to go to bed, Helena immediately agreed and the two women retired to the bedroom, where Alice was already fast asleep in one of the beds. Sometime later, Gerry went to his bedroom and sat beside his brother's coffin. He talked to him throughout the entire night and he kissed his cold brow so many times. He lit several candles, which were sitting on the small table in a corner of the room, even though he did not know why he was doing it. He thought a lot about Helena throughout that night and how grateful he was that even though she was a Protestant and Patrick had married her in a church and their daughter had been christened in a church, she wished her husband to have a Catholic service in a chapel. He knew without a doubt, it would give his mother a certain peace to know he had been a Catholic to the end. For himself, he no longer knew what he believed. Where was God? Was there a God at all? Was this Patrick's final retribution for his wrongdoing all those years ago? If that was so, he was a cruel God, because Patrick had paid for what he had done and had been trying to lead a normal, honourable life, but that life had been taken from him. His belief in his Catholic faith he believed had been sorely shattered.

'Hallo, Lucie, how are you?' Matthew had been trying to decide when would be the best time to seek out Lucie and Paul, in order to let Lucie know that her ex-husband, Patrick Mullan was dead. So he was surprised to see her this evening, on the eve of the night of Arnold's and his rendezvous with Rachel's abductor. Even when she said she wanted his advice about something, he did not consider it had anything to do with Patrick Mullan. So he was quite shocked when she spoke.

'Matthew, what I am going to say to you may seem so very wrong at this agonising time in our lives, and I want you to know that I think and pray for Rachel all the time. She has made the most wonderful sacrifice for her grandson and I hope her captor is not being cruel to her – whoever he is and why he has done all this. But sometimes, events happen outside our control and I needed to let you know that I intend to go to Patrick Mullan's funeral tomorrow afternoon. I mean, to just go to the service and you need to know it is with Paul's blessing that I am going.' Lucie looked at her brother, craving his understanding. 'Matthew, he was my husband. I loved him once, you know. I feel it is appropriate that I pay my respects. Patrick has paid dearly for any wrong he did in the past, but why I'm telling you this is because I need to know how you feel about my going.'

Matthew was silent for a moment, then turning to Lucie, he hugged her warmly, 'Of course you must go, Lucie, and of course you loved him and you loved his mother very much. And when you see her, tell her how sorry I am for the loss of her husband and her son. It is so very hard for her. And Lucie, I forgave Patrick a long time ago for his betrayal to us. So don't worry on that score. As for our own crisis, I am confident it will be resolved very satisfactorily tomorrow night. Everything is organised and we just have to wait until the time of the rendezvous to come round,' Matthew went on. 'You will be back from the funeral quite a few hours before Arnold and I have to go to our meeting with Rachel's captor. So I'll see you then. Going to Patrick's funeral is quite an ordeal for you, so please, do take care.'

'I will, Matthew, and I will see you back here to-morrow, late afternoon, I would imagine.'

The chapel was surprisingly full, Gerry thought, as he greeted the mourners as they filed past him in the foyer and took their seats where Brian, his brother who had just flown in from Canada, earlier that morning, was showing them to. Most of Patrick's old friends had made their way there, which was very pleasing for Gerry and no doubt, he thought his mother would appreciate it too, in spite of her grief. Later, just as the service started, Gerry noted a couple of very professional looking men quietly enter and take their seats at the back, and Gerry's instincts were immediately aroused, these men were detectives, he had no doubt about it. He remembered Helena's words yesterday, when he had finally managed to pick up courage and ask her about the car which had knocked Patrick down; she had told him then that the police had told her they needed to rule out any terrorist involvement, so that was why they were here. If it proved to be not just a simple hit and run accident, someone from here would have to be involved and have tipped off someone in England, that was how they worked their evil ways, or so Gerry had heard. And now, as he listened to the priest, he just hoped that it was a simple hit and run, perhaps the driver had too much to drink, but he longed now for no terrorist involvement. As to why he hoped there was none, he could not explain that to anyone. Maybe he believed everyone had had enough, where was it all going to end? Peace, just peace was what everyone here needed, just peace.

Now, as they filed down the aisle carrying the coffin of his brother, Gerry noticed a young woman standing at the back of the chapel and as the cortege approached her, he thought she looked rather familiar. It was only when they were standing, waiting to shake hands with the mourners and also to invite them into the chapel's recreation room for tea and sandwiches, that she made herself known to him.

'I want to say how sorry I am about Patrick.' It was so obvious Patrick's brothers did not know who she was. 'I am Lucie, Gerry. I was Patrick's first wife. I just wanted to pay my respects to him – I was after all, his wife.'

For a moment Gerry was speechless, then, remembering his manners, Gerry grasped her hand. 'Lucie, how kind of you to come. Are you alone?'

'Yes, I am quite alone. Gerry. I do believe that, under different circumstances, Matthew might have been here too. Patrick was a colleague of his, after all. But you may have heard, we have a family crisis at home, so even for Matthew to consider coming was out of the question. I, myself, must leave shortly in order to re-join my family in their vigil.'

'Oh, please, Lucie, you must come into the hall, meet up again with my mother and be introduced to Helena.' As he spoke, Gerry looked over at his mother, who was staring curiously at Lucie. 'Mother is wondering where she has seen you before, not that you've changed, but we never expected such a generous gesture of forgiveness. Here, she is coming over now.'

Suddenly, Lucie was engulfed in Mrs. Mullan's arms, so tightly, she could scarcely breathe. 'My dear, my dear. How kind of you, how very kind of you.' and she began to sob loudly and unashamedly.

'Helena,' she called now to her daughter-in-law. 'Helena, this is Lucie. She is here today in spite of the family trauma. I am so very touched by you coming here, Lucie.'

'Mrs. Mullan, there is nothing I can do to help with our family crisis at present, so don't be concerned on that point. Besides, we know it will all be resolved in a few hours' time. With Lewis already safely back with his family, we are confident his grandmother will soon be too, and I really wanted to be here, you know.'

'Please, please, Lucie, you must join us for a quick cup of tea before you leave. I shall always remember you with much love and affection.' And again, the tears welled up in Mrs. Mullan's eyes and Lucie reached over and cradled her in her arms until she became more controlled. She knew her ex mother-in-law had still a lot to face as she watched the body of her son being interred in his final resting place. That was something Lucie would not be able to attend and she reckoned it was for the best if she wasn't.

Chapter 37

'You have never asked me yet what my reasons were for abducting your grandson.' During the last few hours in the confines of his brother's dilapidated, dirty, lock up shed, this woman was strangely silent as she sat there, so immobile. It was as if she had accepted her fate, whatever it might be. 'Are you not at all interested in why I did it?' He felt driven to talk about something, anything would be better than her silence.

'You did it for the money, did you not?' How Rachel longed for the next few hours to fly in until they left this filthy shack and drove to this forest he talked so much about. But the likelihood of those hours "flying in" was unlikely to happen.

'No. No.' He sounded quite emphatic. 'That was really an afterthought. It was not in my original plan.' He must let her know all about it. Who he was and why he had done it. 'I did it to avenge my brother. Matthew Hampton, who I know is Lewis Hampton's grandfather brought my brother to court, on very slim evidence, might I add. He had him tried before a judge and jury and – wait for it – he was found "Not Guilty" because, as I have just said, Matthew Hampton had no real evidence against him. But it was thanks to our dear Detective Inspector Hampton that my brother's trial made big, big headlines, and the finger was pointed at him for being responsible for all those murders around the Shankill. So after his acquittal, some people took the law into their own hands and shot him dead. So as far as I'm concerned, Hampton was to blame for my brother's death.'

'I see.' Was all Rachel said, although her mind was reeling as to who this man possibly was and indeed who his brother was. But Rachel knew she must be very careful with what she said. She dare not let this man know her real reason for being in Ivan Street that fateful evening; that she knew all about his messages to Matthew and that it must have been he who assaulted Julie that evening. He must never know that it was all that information which had led her to Ivan Street that night in the hope of identifying the culprit, which by the look of things, was exactly what had happened

Then her kidnapper continued in the same monotone voice, which, in spite of her position, annoyed Rachel so much. 'I thought I would take out my revenge on his wife, but then, I found out she was back home from hospital and seemed as fit as a fiddle. Then I turned my attention to others in his family – but I did send messages to warn him I was going to do something. They just weren't careful enough. They made it easy for Alfie and me.' A proud note had entered his voice, a fact that did not escape Rachel.

Rachel decided that it might be best that she admit to knowing something, after all, she was a close member of the family and it might seem strange if she had known nothing.

'I certainly knew of Matthew's wife assault, why, everyone did, but certainly, Matthew Hampton never spoke of any connection between his wife's assault and his grandson's kidnapping. But then of course, he wouldn't, he would be duty bound to keep that confidential.'

'I daresay.' That was good news to hear, Hampton must have been too scared of the consequences if he told anyone about the messages, so that was real good to know.

'Do you know who my brother was, at least who they said he was?'

'I would have no idea. I don't follow any of that. I'm just intent on earning a living and trying to keep my true profession a secret from both my family and the police.' Now Rachel felt like she was going back in time, before her marriage to Gavin, when secrecy was all-important to her, when she had the brothel.

'My brother was Andy Devlin, reputedly the leader of the Shankill Butchers. Surely you've heard of them?'

'Oh, I've heard of them, but then of course your brother, you say, was acquitted.' Much better to show some knowledge. Rachel thought, although she could not believe that this man sitting just a few feet from her was actually a brother of that monster. She tried to reassure herself that her mother had always taught her that no one is responsible for someone else's behaviour in a family, but her mother's words now were meaningless to her – she was terrified as to what was going to happen to her. She sincerely hoped that no extra police presence would be anywhere near that forest tomorrow evening, when the ransom money would be handed over. That, she believed, was her only chance, that it would be peaceful enough and uneventful, but she felt very strongly that if her captor was thwarted, things might become very dangerous for anyone who was present. It was simply the extent of Julie's injuries which led Rachel to think this – her captor had not ill-treated her in any way, but Julie was proof that he was capable of great violence, and probably, the police had no way of knowing he was armed. Still, they would be sure to come prepared for such an eventuality and that should be of some solace to her. But as she sat in that shed, a rug around her knees, she felt so cold and isolated from her loved ones, and the prospect of ever seeing them again became more remote, she felt her heart must stop beating at any minute.

Chapter 38

'Iris darling, would you not prefer to stay in here with Nurse Maureen and have a quiet evening in as we usually do?' Arnold was shocked to hear his wife's demand that she accompany him to Belfast. She said she wanted to see Lewis and would stay with him and Jason and Lynn until Arnold and Matthew returned from their liaison.

'I want to go with you Arnold. You are my husband and I want to be with you. I want to keep you company in the car until you meet with Matthew, then you will have him for company.'

'As long as you do know that you must not come with me to meet Rachel's captor, Iris. That would be out of the question. You can only be with me until we meet Matthew, that is, if I consent to you coming with me at all.' Arnold spoke very firmly, Matthew and himself could not afford any last minute mishaps or complications arising. This venture was for Matthew and himself to cope with – no one else must be anywhere near Rachel and her captor.

'No, no. I don't want to do that. I just want to see Lewis and stay at the cottage with them all until you come back.'

Now Arnold could think of no valid reason why Iris should not come back to Belfast with him and spend some time with Lewis. Besides, his wife seemed to have settled down really well with no sign of the old agitation or distress she had been prone to. He believed it was the calming influence of her nurse, Maureen Dawson, which had made such a difference to her.

'Maureen, I'm going to take Iris with me for the drive and to see my son Lewis. She'll be fine with Lewis's mum and dad and then we'll be back here tonight as soon as possible. Please pray that everything will go well and that Lewis's grandmother is returned safely to her family.' Arnold had decided right from the beginning when the nurse had first come to look after Iris, that he would be truthful regarding the family's ordeal and how he believed it had contributed to Iris's instability. It was then that Maureen told him frankly that she knew all about it, as she had seen him on television when he was lodging the appeal for his son. But she assured him that she was bound by her code of confidentiality not to discuss any patient with anyone, so he need not worry on that score. Now she told Arnold that she thought Iris going with him to see Lewis was a good idea.

'She'll come to no harm with you, Arnold, and I'll catch up with some ironing while you're away. I'll fetch her coat, while you start the car, then I'll bring her out to you.'

Later, as they travelled along the road from Helen's Bay to Belfast, Iris seemed so happy and well adjusted, that he was glad he had agreed to bring her with him. However, when they reached the cottage which had originally been Matthew's and Julie's – but was now Lynn and Jason's – it was obvious no one was at home. The house was in darkness and their car was not in the driveway. It was obvious no one was there. So Arnold drove on into Malone Place, to the annexe where he had arranged to meet Matthew, before driving to their destination to hand over the ransom money. Matthew must have been watching for him coming, because he had the front door open before

Arnold had parked his car. When Matthew saw that Iris was in the car, he looked immeasurably shocked and worried, and Arnold hastened to explain.

'Iris wanted to see Lewis, Lynn and Jason, but there doesn't appear to be anyone at home.'

'I know. Arnold, they were being inundated from all sides with reporters and the media in general, so they decided to go into hiding until this whole nightmare is over.'

'I see, I'll leave Iris with Julie and Emily if I may.'

'I'm sorry, Arnold, Lewis wanted his other grandma with him, and Emily too, of course, He was most adamant about that.'

'I can't leave her alone, Matthew. It looks as if she has to come with us, we don't have time to take her anywhere else, not even over to the home. We can't afford to be the least bit late, because it might have serious repercussions on Rachel. But Iris has been very calm and logical and if I tell her to stay in the car and wait for me I have no doubt that she will.'

'That should be all right. Besides, I'll be parking the car quite a distance from our meeting place, so our captor will not see her. As for myself, I have found a very suitable hiding place, but don't worry, Arnold, I won't be far from you. Now let's get going, we have about thirty five minutes to get there.'

Chapter 39

The hours had seemed interminable since he had first arrived here with this woman and it was with some relief that he watched the first streaks of dawn begin to filter through the narrow windows of his late brother's garage. Surely the place would soon warm up a bit – he certainly hoped so because the woman beside him seemed so cold and still he began to fear that she would not survive until the appointed hour, when he would hand her over in exchange for the £100,000 this man Simpson seemed happy enough to pay. Throughout the long night, the woman's unresponsiveness had worried him quite a bit, she had refused any of the food he had brought and had – apart from a few sips of the water he had given her – barely touched her drink. Now, she just sat motionless with the rug he had brought from the car around her knees. It had been in the early hours of the morning, when he had begun to think the woman must be suffering from the cold and he might have her body on his hands before any rendezvous took place, that he remembered seeing a small electric fire on one of the rare occasions when he came here. Then, with something approaching desperation, he had begun to search the place and was rewarded when he found the fire lodged in at the back of one of the cupboards. He was delighted when he then found it was still in working order, that was the thing about the electrics in here, he had been amazed when he had discovered the lights were all still in working order. Obviously, the electricity board had not switched it off for non-payment of bills, but then he remembered how his brother used to boast to him about never paying electricity for years. He told him he'd had his electric circuited to someone else's meter and they must be good pay because never once had he been cut off for non-payment. Jimmy had then placed the fire as close to his captive as the lead would allow him and was rewarded with some sign of movement – she began to rub her hands together – and he knew she was coming round from the near stupor she had been in.

'Please, what time is it now?' she eventually spoke, another sign she must be feeling warmer and better.

'It's gone nine a.m. We have a few more hours left here, so you must really eat some of this bread and cheese I brought and drink some of this tea out of the flask.'

She nodded dumbly and agreed she would eat a piece of bread and drink some tea. But the first couple of bites of the bread seemed to be enough, although she drank the tea eagerly enough. He was glad now he'd had the presence of mind to look for the fire, otherwise, he believed he would have had a very ill woman on his hands. He intended to burn the fire all day and he would continue to insist she drank fluids. He needed her to be able to walk towards Arnold Simpson, seemingly fit and well, not someone he might have to half carry or support in the forest.

How he wished Alfie was still part of this venture, he would not have minded in the least giving him some of the ransom money, if he'd had him for a bit of company. He would soon have told him exactly what to do in that gruff manner of his but it was impossible for Alfie to be here, he was locked up in Crumlin Road Gaol as a result of trying to track down Patrick Mullan, Matthew Hampton's ex brother-in-law. So Alfie was out of the equation, it all depended on him now, and then the money would be all his.

Languishing in Crumlin Road Goal, Alfie had many long hours to think about his mate and the latest racket they had become embroiled in. He knew now he would not be getting any ransom money for the young Hampton boy. None of that would be coming his way, but that did not bother him in the least. He had earned quite a wee bit of money because of his knowledge of Patrick Mullan's and his family's whereabouts. He had been asked to try to keep track of that supposed policeman, Patrick Mullan, ever since his release from prison and the money he had been offered was pretty good. So, unfortunately they had just missed him one night – the night Kevin Mullan, Patrick Mullan's father had died and wasn't that the reason why he was here in this damned prison? To think they must have only been a matter of minutes late that evening, he must have had a good tip-off to get away so easily. So, he had received no money at that time but since then because he had a determination to find out more, he had begun frequenting the mainly Catholic bars, and during the last few months, he had overheard many things about numerous events. Whether he would ever use the information in the future, he did not know. But still, he took good notes and filed everything away carefully. Then, he struck lucky one night when he entered a public house at the lower end of the Falls Road and recognised Patrick Mullan's brother, Gerry, from a newspaper photograph taken after his father had died and the police and the family were appealing for witnesses. It was an interesting conversation he overheard between Gerry and a couple of friends he had with him. He was confiding, in a low voice, to one of his friends, about his brother and his family and how well looked after they were by the authorities and the good job and the good house he had somewhere in England. Somewhere in England he understood, where no one minded what your religious beliefs were, just so long as you were a respected member of the community, which Gerry believed his brother was. He had even added that evening that he knew his brother was in a small hamlet in the South of England – a hamlet which had a name sounding like Hailstone, he thought, but surely no one in England would give a village such a name. Alfie realised that Gerry Mullan was quite inebriated that evening, otherwise, he surely would not have been talking the way he was.

Well, now Alfie was in the position that he could inform his contact that it was only a matter of time until Patrick Mullan was traced.

Now, just this very evening, he had learned Patrick Mullan was dead and he knew he would soon be in receipt of his final payment of a few hundred pounds. So truly, the lack of payment from his mate over the Hampton boy did not trouble him very much. After all, he had only driven the car that had taken the child to his mate's flat. So he had not merited payment because he had been arrested and locked up here in this cell. But he was confident now that he would get a short enough sentence for his role in the initial raid of the Mullan house because of all the information he had told police about his mate and the boy, Lewis Hampton. He had told them where he lived, who he was and the fact that he had a gun.

But he intended to draw the line there in what information he told the police. He had no intention of telling anyone that he had any hand in informing others where Patrick Mullan had moved to. After all, when he had given that information, he did not know, nor wish to know what they intended to do with the information. He did not care, he only knew he was going to be rewarded big time and it seemed likely it was going to be very soon. He had just received a message from one of the prison officers that someone wished to visit him, and bring him something to eat.

And he believed that he would soon have the money handed to him, surely that was what the visit would be all about.

Alfie was delighted when, a few hours later, a prison officer announced that he had a visitor and he must come to the visitors' room and the prison officer was to escort him to the room. He was soon shown a seat facing the grilled barrier, by the officer. A man Alfie did not recognise at first, no doubt because he had gone out of his way to make sure he was not going to be easily identified, was seated on the other side of the grill. He wore dark glasses and a black peaked cap on his head, and although it was a good disguise, Alfie realised who he was straight away.

'Charlie!' he whispered.

Charlie shook his head quickly and then spoke equally quietly. 'I brought something for tea – a food parcel with a good cake in it. The prison officer has it. No doubt checking there are no razor blades or knives in it.' While he was talking to Alfie, he was slipping him an envelope from his inside pocket with a knowing look on his face. Alfie quickly slipped the envelope into the pocket of his trousers, out of sight of any officer. He knew the man who had brought him the money would have had to bring him something to eat to make the staff believe that was all he had brought. He was going to enjoy the cake later this evening, the food here was not the best and certainly a luxury like a cake was unheard of. Later tonight when all was quiet, he would count what was in the envelope then he would know what they had thought his information had been worth.

Charlie made his exit from the prison and from his friend, Alfie, as inconspicuous as possible after delivering the cake to him and the envelope. Poor Alfie, he thought to himself, as he walked towards his car parked out on the roadway. Poor Alfie, it was such a shame he had been arrested and was now in prison where he was certainly going to be interrogated by the security forces. And knowing Alfie, he would soon crack up, Charlie believed, and tell all he knew. So Charlie was not prepared to take that risk. There was no way he wanted to end up where Alfie was. As for the money he had been given to hand over to Alfie, it was safely in his safe at home. Alfie would be disappointed when he opened the envelope and found it empty but then Alfie was certainly not going to need it any more – he had made sure of that. And he would never be able to tell anything about him to those police.

He was most appreciative of the person who handed him the money so readily and believed he intended to take it to Alfie, and he was very confident that they would never grass on him – he had no concerns about them, they never could report anything about him without implicating themselves and they were far too grand to ever let that happen.

Later, when the prison officer came back with the cake for Alfie, he suggested that he might think of sharing it with some of the other inmates. Alfie was indignant at this idea, pointing out it was such a small cake, one he could finish at two sittings. Then, not wishing to appear too greedy he added, 'I'll keep you a piece, officer.' When the officer left him and Alfie was sitting with his weak, prison issue cup of tea and his slice of cake in his hand and the knowledge of his reward safely tucked into the envelope in his pocket, he spared a thought for his mate and the young lad he had kidnapped. How was that all going for Jimmy? He hoped it would all go well for him, as well as it was going for him.

Chapter 40

Rachel was only dimly aware that the man sitting beside her was speaking to her. His voice seemed such a long way off. Who was the great hulk of a man sitting beside her? Where was she? She had no idea – she only knew she had never felt so cold in all her life. And then, even as she sat there, she felt some glimmer of warmth radiating towards her and she did her best to stretch forward towards this wonderful source of heat.

'Look, you must take something, eat this biscuit and drink this hot tea.' The man was reaching her a cup with one hand and feeling the need to assure her that it was just a biscuit he had in his other hand. Eagerly, she reached for the tea and although it almost scalded her lips, she drank the entire cup quickly. But the first mouthful of the biscuit seemed like sawdust and just clung to her parched lips and tongue and with a shake of her head, she handed it back to him, this stranger at her side.

Gradually though, as the heat from the fire warmed her limbs, her body and her skin and the warm tea seemed to warm her blood, her memory returned and she knew exactly who this man was, where she was and why she was here. But it did not matter anymore where she was or what happened to her and how her family might feel if she never returned home, she had brought this all on herself – she had no doubt about that. As for her grandson, now in the mists of her mind, she believed he would have been released anyway by his captor. She'd had no need to intervene and cause Gavin, her dear husband, such anguish. All the family had needed was a bit of patience but patience was not something Rachel had any great reserves of and obviously Matthew, her cousin, did not have either. That would account for him approaching her in the hope she might know of any street walker who might be of help to them. Not that Matthew – in his wildest dreams – had expected her to take on the role of street walker. No, he had just sincerely hoped she might have had some contact with some of them. But Rachel had always believed, since coming to Belfast and working in isolation in her particular profession, she'd had absolutely no contacts that might have helped Matthew snare the captor. That was why she knew she had to help him herself.

'If you're not going to eat, you have to drink plenty, should it be just hot water. I've found an electric kettle and there's a water tap over there, across the room. So, I'll keep boiling water on the go. I don't want you looking ill when I hand you over. They'll think I've been ill-treating you.'

Somewhere in the recesses of her mind, Rachel acknowledged that this man had not ill-treated her, nor did he seem to have done so to Lewis. No, she could never say that, but that did not stop her feeling terrified, simply because she always remembered Julie and the assault on her. So, very obviously, he was quite capable of violence when he felt it was well justified. She could only continue to pray that soon it would all be over. Now, she spoke to him 'What is the time, please?'

'It is coming round to eight o'clock. We will leave here in an hour's time, around nine p.m. I need to check everything out, make sure no one else, like the police, are lurking in the forest.'

Although Rachel made no answer, she was amazed to hear what time it was, she had thought it was around ten o'clock in the morning. She had actually lost a whole day. She must have been asleep and then suddenly she realised that the coldness of this place must have put her into some kind of a stupor, which she had just woken from. Eagerly now, she grasped the cup of tea her captor was handing to her, she had just realised the importance of keeping her wits about her. That was crucial, if she was to have any chance of surviving this ordeal.

'The appointed time for meeting is actually 10.15p.m. Arnold, but I always believe in giving myself some leeway. So when we arrive, we'll check the place out carefully. I don't know why really. I don't suspect him to try to outwit us in any way. He just wants the money. I suppose it's just my police training has made me so cautious.'

'I think it's no bad thing, Matthew. Our very first priority is Rachel's safety, after that, I don't really care that much about apprehending the culprit. I know for you it is very different, it is your job and I hope you succeed in tracking him down. For me, well the money is so irrelevant in comparison to Rachel's life.'

Matthew just nodded as he negotiated the car into the forest designated by the abductor, as the place they were to meet. He was glad Arnold was unaware of the identity of the culprit, although for Arnold, knowing their captor was the brother of the leader of the Shankill Road butchers might mean very little to him. But what worried Matthew now, was that this man now knew the police had identified him, having been tipped off by his friend, Alfie. Alfie who, when this ordeal was over, Matthew intended to interview very soon about his possible involvement in other crimes he had reason to believe he might be involved in.

Where is prisoner, Alfred Reid, Cell Number 22? Why has he not reported for his cleaning duties?'

'Sir, he was still asleep when I put his breakfast tray in to him. I called him, Sir, to let him know his breakfast was there. I'll go check that he is awake, Sir.'

'Be quick about it, man, the cleaning round has started. And remember, the prisoner has to receive just punishment for this serious lapse in his punctuality. Let him know that, officer, before you bring him here.'

Prison Officer Dempsey had only been recruited into the prison service a mere six months ago and he had just realised from the tone of his senior officer's voice that he should have made absolutely sure that the prisoner in Cell 22 was awake and ready to participate in today's chores. Well, no one had made that clear to him – in fact no one had made anything in this job he found himself in, absolutely clear. It had all been assumed that he ought to know, but how could he possibly know about anything to do with the prison service? He had no experience of such an occupation, such a life. He had seen the job advertised, had applied for it and had been accepted. It had been so easy. And now, well, it was just so boring. He was bored with being the watchman at the gate, checking every single person in and out of that prison. He was bored with walking endlessly round that perimeter wall and the perimeter fence so continually during his shift. But nothing so far had prepared him for what he discovered when he went back to Cell 22. The man lying on the bed, his head turned towards the wall was, Paul Dempsey believed, dead. He knew by the stillness of the body and the fact it was in the same position as when he called in earlier. He knew by the terrible silence of the place when he spoke to him. And when he turned him over, his worst suspicions were concerned, Alfie Reid, the prisoner in Cell 22, was dead. Now he must go and inform his senior officer and unfortunately, it was not the fate of the prisoner, which worried Officer Dempsey. Uppermost in his mind was the knowledge that he would be severely reprimanded for not checking on his prisoner properly at breakfast time. But surely, to Officer Dempsey's mind, finding one of your prisoners dead in his cell must be a very rare occurrence indeed? But no doubt, he would not get a chance to voice that thought.

Chapter 41

'We are just coming into Drumvanagh forest, where our rendezvous with our Mr. Simpson and his money will be. You have absolutely nothing to fear from me, my dear. All I want is to get the money from this man, in return for me handing you over safely to him. I'm just sorry that the circumstances were such that we could not get to know one another better, we might have enjoyed ourselves. But things changed for me and everything became rather frantic and urgent, I'm afraid.'

Rachel knew exactly what he was referring to when he said he was sorry they had not got to know one another better. He was referring to them going into his bedroom and how that had all been thwarted by the arrival of some man. After that, it had all become an emergency to vacate his flat and Rachel had felt rather blessed, even though it might only be temporary, that another sexual contact with her had failed. At least she had been spared all that, even though she felt her ordeal was far from over. She did not trust him and she knew he still had the gun and who knew what might happen here in this forest where the birds sang so heartily and the wild flowers flourished and bloomed all summer long.

Now he was continuing to speak to her.

'I just want you to get out of the car and at all times, you must stand in front of me, even when I go over to the tree beside the pond, you must be in front of me'

Rachel simply nodded, indicating she understood what he was saying and would comply with his wishes. Indeed, she understood only too well, she was to be his shield in case of any trouble here in this forest. And although she prayed earnestly that no one would be hurt, she believed that Matthew Hampton, being the detective he was, would not like to see her captor walk away so easily with any ransom money. She had no doubt that even while he would do his utmost to ensure her safety, his instinct and quest for justice would, of necessity, make him do whatever would be necessary to trap this abductor.

Now, as she walked over the uneven grass of the forest and approached a clear area, she realised, she knew the place so well. This was the same forest Gavin and she had walked leisurely through on many summer evenings since they had married. But her captor had brought her in at the opposite end of the forest, an area which was unfamiliar to her and of course, she had never heard of the forest's proper name – Drumvanagh – it had only ever been referred to as 'the forest' by the locals. The knowledge that she was so close to home was both heart-breaking and yet hopeful because so many people knew the place; that its very familiarity seemed to reassure her and uplift her. And certainly, as she continued to walk along, careful of the uneven mounds of grass, and always in front of her captor, she realised that anyone could be lulled into a calm, peaceful frame of mind here. The atmosphere was so tranquil and soothing, the silence only broken by the harmonious sound of birdsong. But suddenly, as she was stepping out into the clearing on the approach to the pond, the silence was broken. It was a woman's voice which was now penetrating the silence and she was calling Rachel at the top of her voice. And to Rachel's horror, she recognised

Arnold's wife, Iris, and she was now racing towards Rachel. With a strength born out of sheer desperation, Rachel wrenched herself free from the arm of the man who walked closely behind her and raced towards Iris. She had only one thought in mind – she must find cover for Iris before she was hurt.

'He has a gun, Iris. Please, please, I'm all right. Get over to the hedge, he has a gun.'

Suddenly, the air was rent with some awesome noise, similar to and reminding Rachel of hailstones beating against the windows of her home. Then, even as she heard the noise she felt a searing pain in her chest and then she wondered vaguely, before she tripped and fell how she was to reach Iris before she got hurt. As she fell forward, she was aware Iris was now lying on the ground. Had she realised she would be safer from all the noise if she lay down? Rachel thought Iris was lying so very still and quiet that she thought she had been hurt, but Rachel did not seem to have the energy to move any closer to try and help her. As for all the noise – how she longed for some quietness. She just wanted to go to sleep and then gradually the noises faded out of her consciousness.

Gerry Mullan, after a very sleepless night, decided it was pointless lying in bed any longer, just looking at the ceiling, thinking about Patrick. He knew he was dwelling on what he might have been able to do to help his brother over the years. But in his more rational moments, he acknowledged there was little he could have done to change the course of his brother's life. As he climbed out of bed and quietly put on his dressing gown and pushed his feet into his slippers, he tried to be as quiet as he possibly could. He was anxious not to disturb his mother, or Helena and his niece, they had been through such an ordeal since Patrick was killed. Returning his body back to Northern Ireland had been a very sad journey for them, then his funeral yesterday and burying him with his father, before saying a last good-bye to a loving husband, father and son. Gerry was so thankful that at least his family had decided to stay with him for a few days, he would be so glad of their companionship and perhaps, he dared to hope, they needed his.

After making a mug of hot tea and carrying it into the living room, Gerry decided, just for something to keep him occupied, to put on the seven a.m. news on the television. He would keep it very low and it would be a bit of company for him, until his mum or his sister-in-law joined him. When he switched the set on and adjusted the volume to a low setting, he was immediately alerted when the newsreader announced that there had been a serious shooting in a forest known as Drumvanagh forest last evening. It was understood that a woman had been shot dead and a man and a woman had been critically injured. The newscaster added that when further information became available it would be reported, but they had no further details at present. The next news was equally dire, Gerry thought, as he listened to the newscaster reporting that an inmate in Crumlin Road Goal had been found dead in his cell and the police were investigating the cause of death.

Chapter 42

The surgeon could not have been more sympathetic to Arnold, explaining very gently, how he and his team had fought hard to save his wife. The bullet had ripped through her pulmonary artery and although they had done everything they could to repair it, it had proved impossible and Iris had died on the operating table.

The surgeon had been told very little about the circumstances of the shooting but somehow this lady who had died and the other one who lay in a coma in intensive care had been caught up in it. He thought it particularly sad about Mrs. Simpson, as she already had a history of having been involved in a bomb blast in Belfast some time before and according to her medical records, this had left her confused and suffering from memory loss. Now, her husband – who had been involved in the same bombing and had suffered the loss of both a lower limb and an upper limb – was alone and a widower. And as the surgeon offered his condolences, he wondered how this man was going to cope with this latest, most awful tragedy in his life. He was very thankful that Mr. Simpson had not been alone when he broke the news of his wife's death to him. Another gentleman was there, who the consultant believed was a Detective Inspector. Now the detective spoke.

'What of Mrs. Finlay, how is she?' Matthew had needed to call on his reserves of courage to even ask about Rachel. Some awful fear had come over him so that he could not bear to listen to any more bad news, not after what the last twelve hours had brought to them. He was in some awful deep, black pit and he seemed incapable of climbing out of it.

'Mrs. Finlay is out of theatre and is in intensive care. She seems to have taken the brunt of the gunfire, Detective. We have removed three bullets; one from her chest, from her abdomen and another from her neck. Mrs. Finlay has been critically injured, we are keeping her in a coma and she will be having round-the-clock medical care and observation. I'm afraid that is all we can tell you at the moment, Detective, but if there is any change we will contact her husband. We have his telephone number.' Then the surgeon added, 'The man who was shot in the legs has been placed in a single ward at your request. I understand this man is under police guard now, so a single ward is essential, to allow the security forces to carry out their duties discreetly.'

'Thank you, Sir.' Matthew was glad that their abductor had survived the shooting and although injured, they had been assured he should recover. Matthew intended to interrogate this man just as often as the hospital staff allowed him. To do that successfully and skilfully, he certainly needed privacy to do so, and a single room should prove to be satisfactory regarding secrecy and confidentiality.

Matthew had known from the very first moment when their offender had opened fire on Iris, that Rachel had taken what he thought to be a hail of bullets. She had raced towards Iris in an attempt to shield her and had been hit it seemed three times. It was one of the policemen hiding undercover in the shrubbery who had shot Rachel's captor in both legs. Whoever the policeman had been – and Matthew had yet to establish that – Matthew had acknowledged he had certainly been an excellent shot. He had obviously remembered Matthew stressing that he wanted their captor alive, at all costs. Although everything that had happened in the forest last evening had an atmosphere of such terror and unreality about it, Matthew knew it was he who had alerted the emergency services and had the injured immediately taken to hospital. And now to hear, as he stood beside Arnold, that Iris was dead, seemed just too much to endure. Now, he touched Arnold's arm, he did not add they were no longer of any use in that hospital, so bleak and desolate at two o'clock in the morning. They would now have so much to do and he could not bear to think on it. A funeral had to be arranged, relatives informed and he had to seek Gavin out and let him know about Rachel.

'Matthew, I want to stay with Jason and Lynn. I do hope that will be all right. I need to stay close to Lewis, he is all I have now.' And now, Arnold began to sob as he let Matthew lead him out of that place where death and illness seemed to lurk in every corner. Matthew knew then he must put his own guilt, worry and grief to the back of his mind and help this broken man make some sense of what had happened.

'Of course you must stay, Arnold. I will take you wherever you want to go and I will stay with you as long as you need me.'

'Perhaps you would let Iris's nurse know what has happened. She can stay at my house as long as she wishes. I shall of course reimburse her. '

'Of course, Arnold, I'll sort everything out for you.' Matthew held tightly to him as they made their way out of the hospital and across to the car park.

'Give me the keys; I intend to do the driving Arnold.' Matthew was deeply concerned not only for Arnold's emotional state, but also for his physical state. Most times, everyone forgot Arnold had a prosthesis fitted both in his leg and arm, he was so adept at walking and using his limbs quite normally. But now, Matthew knew Arnold was feeling the weight of those two structures, he was so weakened by the tragedy of the last few hours. This was a broken man, Matthew realised, as he helped him into the passenger seat of his car and he prayed that somehow Lewis, his beautiful, sensitive son would give him hope for the future. For Matthew believed that at this moment, Arnold had lost all reason for living. What regrets he must have, Matthew thought, as they began their sad journey to Jason's house, by indulging Iris and agreeing to her accompanying him to Belfast. What a cruel twist of fate then that she had to accompany them on their awful mission. Yet when both men had left her in the car, as far as Matthew could recall, although everything became so blurred in the aftermath of what happened, she seemed happy to wait in the car for their return. But now, Matthew believed – he had thought about Iris's actions a lot as they sat in that bleak waiting room in the hospital – she deliberately deceived them and had every intention of following them to make sure Rachel was safe. Certainly, in the car on the drive to the forest, she had stressed on two or three occasions they must make sure Rachel was safe. They must do that, she had told the two men, and they had assured her each time, that they would. To think that her concern over Rachel's safety had cost her her life, and worst of all, even now, they did not know if Rachel was going to be safe. But Matthew could not bear to think on that, but rather like Arnold, he longed to be at Jason and Lynn's house, where he knew Jason had taken Julie and Emily earlier in the evening, so that they might all be together. Like Arnold, he craved their love, their comfort and their understanding. As soon as the morning would be here he knew he must go to see his aunt Maggie and tell her that her daughter Rachel was critically ill and in a coma in hospital. He would try to ensure his own mother and step-father, Tom, were present when he gave her the awful news. He also hoped that the senior nurse in Rachel's nursing home, who was in charge since Rachel's disappearance, would agree to aunt Eve and uncle John being there. Then, he must face the prospect of seeking out Rachel's husband, Gavin, and telling him how it was. That, he dreaded more than anything because he believed, deep down that Gavin held him responsible for what Rachel had done and now he would blame him for the consequences of her actions. He even dreaded meeting Gavin more than helping Arnold to make funeral arrangements and he acknowledged to himself, that was because Gavin was right in his accusations – Matthew had planted the idea in Rachel's mind. And often, Matthew had wondered if he had secretly hoped Rachel would take up the challenge of going street walking in order to track down Julie's attacker. He did not know but initially, he had just sincerely hoped that she did know of someone who went out on the streets. Thinking now of Julie's attacker, Matthew knew he would never forget the look of shock on the abductor's face when he saw Iris race across that forest in an effort to protect Rachel, and the fear that became etched on his face as the man realised he was cornered. It was then that he had opened fire, randomly shooting at the air around him and obviously, he had very little experience of fire-arms. Tragically though, his random shooting had killed Iris Simpson and critically injured Rachel.

Now, all Matthew wanted was to forget everything for a few hours and be with Julie, Lynn and Jason and try to support them through their grief for Iris and their deep distress for Lynn's mother, so ill in hospital.

Chapter 43

'Matthew, I'm so sorry to disturb you at such a tragic, sad time in your life, but I do need to talk to you.' Matthew recognised the voice on the other end of the telephone as being Superintendent McAllister. Initially, Matthew was taken aback by his superior, referring to him by his first name; it was something he rarely did over the telephone. Certainly, he had done it earlier in the day, when he had commiserated with him on the tragedy, but then he had been speaking to him as a friend, not as his superior. But now he felt, judging by the tone of Ernest McAllister's voice, this was business once again.

'Yes Sir, do you need me to come into the office or can you tell me over the phone?'

'I think it best if you could come in, Matthew, I do need you to see something.' Ernest McAllister continued, 'I want to stress that what I want to see you about has no bearing on your horrendous situation. This is something different Matthew.'

'I'll come straight away, Sir. Arnold and I have just returned from the funeral furnishers. I'll make sure Lynn and Jason are going to be with him and I'll be there in about twenty minutes.'

As he drove towards the barracks, Matthew wondered what on earth the Superintendent wanted to talk to him about at such a time. Could it not possibly have waited? But then, Ernest McAllister was the consummate professional, putting his job before absolutely anything else and expecting everyone else to do likewise. And as he drove along, Matthew became more and more annoyed at the very idea of his superior expecting him to drop everything and come to hear what he had to stay.

So, as he parked his car, then entered the police building where his superior's office was, he had worked himself into a right state of resentment. His attitude was evident to Ernest McAllister, as he rose to greet his detective inspector, an attitude he fully understood and was prepared to ignore. As he looked at Matthew, taking in his gaunt haunted appearance, perhaps he should not have sent for him, but he felt this latest information was too important to ignore. Without preamble he said, 'I need you to read this, detective.' As he handed Matthew a rough piece of paper.

As Matthew unfolded the page, he recognised prison issue writing paper with "On her Majesty's service" boldly emblazoned across the top. Intrigued and more subdued now, Matthew opened the page and what he read there was a shock to him.

'What is this Superintendent? Who is this man?'

'The man who, it would seem wrote this note, is dead. He was found dead in his cell in Crumlin Road Gaol early yesterday morning. His name was Alfie – Alfie Reid.' The Superintendent looked at Matthew, sharply, 'You know this man? I can see his name is familiar to you.'

'Yes Sir, it was he who gave me Julie's attacker and Lewis's kidnappers name and address Sir.' Matthews's voice registered shock at what he had just read. 'He says he is dying. He thinks it was the cake – that he had been poisoned. Then, he writes – it is almost illegible Sir, the last couple of lines, that is. He says he wished he had told me earlier that they were on to Patrick Mullan and knew all about him.' Matthew looked up, 'The last words are just a squiggle Sir, totally illegible.'

'I know Matthew; it is of no help to us whatsoever in finding out what our friend Alfie was talking about. But there is no doubt he was poisoned. The cake has been taken away for analysis, but who came and gave such a present to our friend, we have no idea. I wondered if perhaps, when he was telling you about Julie's attacker, did he give you any hint of any kind what he knew about Patrick Mullan's whereabouts?'

'Certainly he said nothing about Patrick Mullan, I would have remembered that. Not even a hint and I was most meticulous in my note taking when I was with him.'

'Just as I thought, Matthew, but I felt it was important that you knew this. I believe Patrick Mullan was murdered, that it wasn't just a hit and run by a dangerous driver. I believe it was a deliberate act of murder, and this note supports my theory, I do believe.'

'I believe so too, Sir, and when I return for duty, I intend to try and resolve this case. Patrick had paid his debt to society and I believe he probably deserved another chance. I think he had learnt his lesson. So justice should be done for him too, Sir.'

'I'm glad you agree Matthew.' Ernest McAllister felt as he listened to Matthew Hampton, that his detective had finally forgiven his ex-brother-in-law for his involvement in his father's death, and surely that could only be a good thing.

'I'm sorry if it seemed inappropriate for me to tell you all this at this time, but I was hopeful you might throw some light on this name, Alfie, and what he was obviously trying to tell us. And do remember Matthew, in spite of my workload, I think about what you are all going through, and I pray for Rachel's recovery.' He rose from his desk, came round to Matthew and put an arm round his shoulders. Matthew felt his resolve not to be emotional in front of his boss dissolve and he broke down into tears.

'Matthew, if there is anything I can do to help, please call me night or day, it doesn't matter. Financially or emotionally, it doesn't matter, just remember that.'

As Matthew travelled back home, he amazed himself at his line of thinking. He was not thinking about the prisoner, Alfie Reid, and his letter. He was not thinking- just for that moment – of Arnold and his grief, nor was he thinking of Rachel in intensive care. No, he had suddenly remembered, when Ernest McAllister had mentioned finance, seeing Arnold prop that attaché case up against the tree beside the pond. Who had retrieved the case? Certainly, it was not the abductor; he was lying in hospital under police guard, so who was it who had retrieved it? He would have to, out of necessity, find that out. It had been so unprofessional of him not to have established who had lifted the attaché case. He certainly owed it to Arnold to retrieve the case as soon as possible from whoever had taken charge of it. Although he knew any talk about attaché cases or money would be quite meaningless to Arnold at this time in his life, but it was on Matthew's mind and he knew it was just something else which had to be sorted out.

Chapter 44

The night before Iris's funeral, Arnold did not go to bed at any time, even though Lynn had insisted on giving him a nightcap of hot whiskey and a couple of aspirins. She told him, ever so gently, that he needed them; he had so much to face the following day. She told him too, that she had placed a hot water bottle in the bed in the spare room for him; even though it wasn't a cold night it might be of some comfort to him.

Arnold thanked Lynn for all her attention and assured her he would try to get some sleep at some stage during the night, but for now he just wanted to sit with Iris where she lay, so cold and still in Jason's study. He sat quietly in Jason's leather armchair and listened to the noises of the family as they prepared for bed. Rightly or wrongly, he had felt it best if his son Lewis did not see his stepmother's body. He had told him the truth as far as possible, explaining that Iris was dead and that she had been shot. He told him she had been shot dead by the man who had abducted Lewis. He had also told him that his stepmother had been intent on rescuing Rachel, and the captor had panicked on seeing Iris there and had opened fire randomly. He had also to tell his son that Rachel had also been shot and was in hospital, but he did not say anything about how critical Rachel was.

Now, in the solitude of Jason's study, he could think about Iris and their last few years together, and in spite of their injuries and disabilities, how happy they had been And the presence of Lewis in both their lives had been a source of great happiness. That happiness, Arnold knew, was thanks to both women who had featured in his life; Iris for her forgiveness when he had lived with Lynn for those months in Scotland and Lynn's forgiveness of him then having pretended to be divorced and going through a sham wedding service with her. Not only had the girl forgiven him for that, she also wholeheartedly forgave him for coming to Belfast on that fateful day of the bomb explosion, seeking out a solicitor and threatening to take their son from her. Iris and he were both overwhelmed when in spite of all that he had done, Lynn made it clear she wanted him to have a pivotal role in Lewis's upbringing.

Yes, Iris's last few years of her life had been happy, they had spent considerable time with Lewis and at least his wife had died knowing Lewis was safely back home in the care of his family. He had to thank God for that, at least, even though his heart was breaking and he was shattered by her loss.

He did not think he would ever eradicate the scene in that forest when the two women fell, so horrifically wounded, just a few feet from Matthew and himself. Shock and disbelief, he knew had left him initially unable to move, then at the sound of more shooting, he raced over to his wife, shouting at Matthew to get help. His wife lay curled on her side, quite peaceful looking, he thought even in his distraught frame of mind. He could see blood was seeping from a wound in her side and yet more coming from her mouth. He lay down on the rough grass beside her, wiping her mouth with his handkerchief, talking to her and begging her to speak to him.

It was only when some kind hands helped him up and told him they were taking his wife to hospital and he should follow with Detective Hampton in his car, that Arnold thought he had been quite selfish in not checking on Rachel too, where she lay a few feet from Iris. He had thought at the time that If Iris knew he had not seen to Rachel she was going to be very annoyed at him.

And now, as he sat quietly beside his wife, the tears flowing unheeded, in the solitude of that room he spared a thought for Rachel. Rachel, who they had all been intent on saving, keeping her free from harm at the hands of her captor. Now, he knew that Rachel's life lay in the balance, she had been shot three times, in the head, the chest and the abdomen. All of her family, who had been so anxious about her safety, had failed to keep her safe, Iris was dead, and their assailant lay under police guard in the same hospital as Rachel lay. Arnold wondered what sort of an upbringing this man Devlin and his brother must have had. His brother had committed such violent atrocities on innocent people that the judge had said they were the very worst he had heard of in his long career. Yet the amazing thing was, their mother seemed so unaware of how evil they were, for according to the media, she had maintained they were incapable of violence of any kind. Yet the whole evidence told a very different story and perhaps that was where their mother had gone wrong, perhaps from their very early years, she had refused to believe they were capable of any wrong-doing.

As the dawn began to break and Arnold still sat beside the coffin, inwardly, he thanked Lynn again for making them realise the wrong they would have been doing to her by trying to get custody of his son. Only for Lynn's generosity, everything might have been so different. Perhaps if someone had told the mother of those two monsters how wrong she was and had she opened her heart to the possibility they needed correction, perhaps their lives might have been different. Wasn't he himself proof that people can go down the wrong track in life? And yet there is always the ability to change, he believed that. It was much too late for the Devlin brothers. One of them had already had to face his maker with the blood of so many innocent people on his hands and the other, he understood from Matthew, had shown little remorse for what he had done. As for Iris, he knew she would meet her God with the innocence of childhood with her and her kindness always in doing her best to help others. Yes, Iris would be with her God, and that knowledge gave him great solace and comfort in the midst of his grief in the early hours of the day they would take her to her final resting place. He could only hope that his belief that she was happy, would sustain him during her burial and his final good-bye to her. Perhaps it would help him bear the unbearable.

Matthew knew he must seek Gavin Finlay out before Iris's funeral took place. Surely, the man must have heard about the shooting which had occurred two nights ago? Did he never listen to the news at all? But of course, the media had not as yet disclosed the identity of those dead or injured. The newscasters stated that the names of those involved in the shooting would not be disclosed until the next of kin had been informed, and Gavin was Rachel's next of kin. It fell to Matthew on this, the second day since the tragedy, to try to locate him and let him know that his wife lay critically ill and in a coma in hospital. He knew he must tell Gavin everything – he owed it to him – from the moment Lewis was safely home and their plans to rescue Rachel and how it had all gone so tragically wrong because Iris had tried, in her naivety, to help ensure Rachel's safety.

Matthew intended to leave the annexe early, because he wished to visit Arnold to see how he was bearing up on this very sad day for him. He was surprised to find both Julie and Emily up and about in the kitchen when he entered it. Emily was having breakfast and Julie turned from the stove as she spoke to him. 'Matthew, I have some of your favourite coffee brewing and there is bacon and toast in the oven. Please take a good breakfast -you need it to sustain you today.' Julie went over to the table to fetch a cup and plate, but Matthew quickly reached her and held her closely. 'I'll get my own breakfast and I promise to eat up if you do the same, and Emily too, of course'

Matthew had noticed how drawn and pale Julie looked, and even though Lewis was safely with his family, his safety had come at an awful price to everyone, with the loss of Iris and Rachel's condition, which weighed so heavily on everyone.

Now, Emily was speaking to him. 'I'm enjoying my breakfast, dad, I didn't realise I was so hungry.' And his daughter smiled warmly at him. Matthew, as he looked at his daughter, marvelled at the resilience of children and their ability to overcome grief and quickly become optimistic. Emily and later, Lewis too, he realised there and then, would be all right; other interests and even the joy of just growing up would enable them to cope, but what of the adults? He knew all the family faced a harrowing time and he prayed that Rachel might be spared and they would only have to cope with the loss of one from their family circle. Any other outcome was unbearable to think of.

Chapter 45

It had just gone ten a.m. when Matthew drove into the building site where he had last spoken to Gavin, and where he had told him he would be spending his days and nights in the near future. There was no sign of him around the grounds and Matthew made his way over to the wooden shed, which Gavin had told Matthew on his last visit he intended to make very comfortable for himself. All was very quiet as Matthew made his way towards the door, then after knocking, he waited a few moments for some response. When none was forthcoming, he decided he must go in, indeed he had to. He could not leave the place without seeking him out, speaking to him and telling him all about Rachel. He was surprised to find him fast asleep in the easy chair he had told Matthew about, he had his feet up on a stool and a thick multi coloured blanket wrapped round him. And for a whole second, Matthew envied the sleep Rachel's husband was in; he himself felt he had not slept for weeks. Unfortunately now, Gavin's sleep was going to be so horribly disrupted, and by Matthew. It was then he realised Gavin must have been drinking, the smell of alcohol pervaded the small hut and Matthew knew Gavin must have been fighting his demons in his own way. He was just about to shake him awake, when he opened his eyes and realising Matthew was there, deftly swung his legs off the stool and stood up.

'Sorry, Matthew, I have overslept it seems, but I wasn't expecting any company. I've been away you see, I just got back late last night and had a few drinks to help me sleep – and boy, did they work.'

'Good, that's good, Gavin.' Matthew wanted to add. 'And you'll need more, Gavin,' but instead he asked. 'Did you say you've been away?'

'Aye, I was away down South. Got an offer for these special bricks the woman I'm working for needs for her extension. I had to take the lorry and I had to stay overnight as the weight of the bricks made for a very slow journey.'

'So when did you go?' Matthew was beginning to realise that Gavin may not have heard anything about any shooting.

'Two mornings ago.' Suddenly, Gavin was alerted. 'There's something wrong, isn't there? It's Rachel, isn't it? You better tell me, man. Take that seat. I'll have to make coffee if I'm to understand anything of what you are telling me.'

Then, while Gavin made coffee at the small folding table in the hut, Matthew told him all that had happened on that fateful night. He did not spare any detail. And when he had finished, Gavin, who had had his head bowed low while listening intently looked up at Matthew and Matthew was shocked at how Rachel's husband was. He seemed to have aged ten years since Matthew had last seen him, his face was gaunt, his cheekbones prominent in his thin face. Now his mouth was working as if he wanted to speak but he was incapable of it.

Now, Matthew went over to him and led him to the chair Matthew himself had just vacated.

'If you put your jacket on, Gavin, I'll take you with me, Tom – my stepdad will stay with you until you begin to feel better. I'll take you to their house and I know my mum will also look after you. You look ghastly, Gavin.' Matthew knew he could not walk out of this hut and leave Gavin, who was obviously in deep shock. Silently, Matthew helped him on with his jacket then led him to his car and still in silence, Matthew drove him to his own mother and stepfather's house. Tom Greenlees was the nearest relative Matthew could think of at present who might be of some support to him.

When Matthew left the gate lodge where his mother and stepfather still lived, having explained briefly to them why Gavin was in such a state of shock, he was thankful he had thought to bring Gavin to them. When Ellen had listened to what her son was saying she went straight into the kitchen and reappeared shortly with a mug of steaming hot coffee in her hand. 'Drink this, Gavin. You have had a great shock – this might make you feel better.' Ellen looked at her son 'Matthew, Tom and I will look after Gavin here until he starts to feel a little better so don't worry about him.' And Ellen smiled her reassuring smile. As he drove on towards his office, he thought a lot about Gavin and he was suddenly struck by his lack of interest in going to the hospital to see his wife. Where Matthew had expected it to be his first instinct, he had simply allowed Matthew to bring him to Tom who Matthew knew would no doubt support him. No doubt the shock of such news would have been very severe, but still Matthew wondered at his reaction. He just hoped that when the shock wore off, Gavin would be anxious to see Rachel. Rachel, who had sustained such awful injuries and was so critically ill but perhaps he had not conveyed to Gavin just how critical things were. But Matthew knew there was little he could do to help Gavin who probably had believed that Rachel, with all her years of experience, would have been able to look after herself and keep herself safe. No doubt, he had felt that with all her past experience and dealing with so many differing personalities, any man would succumb to her charms. Certainly, Gavin would never believe that any man would wish to harm her. But now everything had turned out so differently for her because, in spite of her allure, she had been very vulnerable, and whether because of a deliberate or accidental act, she was now at death's door.

All that, Matthew believed, would have a profound effect on Gavin and now he regretted leaving his parents' home in such a hurry. He should have stayed with Gavin for a while and explained how he understood his thoughts because he too, had thought Rachel to be immune to anything happening to her and how wrong they had been proven to be.

Matthew was immensely relieved when his office phone rang some two hours later and his stepfather said that Gavin would like to go to the hospital and hoped that Matthew would be able to drive him there. Matthew tidied up his desk before leaving his office and was soon in his car to collect Gavin from his parents' house. In comparative silence, the two men drove to the hospital and Matthew gave Gavin some directions as to how to get to the Intensive Care unit. He felt it best if Gavin was by himself when he first visited Rachel. Later, Matthew learned that Gavin sat in a chair beside Rachel for the next two days and nights, refusing food and just drinking water. He just sat transfixed, looking at the still, pale face of his wife. Never once during his vigil did Gavin enquire of any member of staff how his wife was. Probably, everyone believed, because he could not bear to hear, in the initial stages, what the staff would tell him about her injuries or her prognosis. So the staff in intensive care respected Rachel Finlay's husband, aware that he was in some world they were incapable of reaching and knowing that his suffering was beyond their comprehension.

Chapter 46

'I intend to sell my house in Helen's Bay.' Arnold was speaking to Jason and Lynn over breakfast. It was three days now since Iris's funeral, three days in which Arnold, apart from appearing for meals, sought no one's company, instead just returning to the guest room which Lynn had insisted he must have until he had decided to return home. He had even surprised Lynn by not actively seeking out his son, instead of which Lewis had always had to go to the room to seek Arnold out. But now, as he spoke, his son entered the kitchen and going over to Arnold, hugged him and said 'Does that mean you will be living here with us, with mummy and daddy Hampton?'

Arnold seemed to suddenly notice Lewis's presence beside him and holding him close, he gave a glimmer of a smile – the first anyone had seen in the last few days. 'I'm not sure about living right here, son, but I fully intend to go and live somewhere not far from you, so I will see you all the time. What do you think, Lewis?'

'Great, daddy Arnold. Can we start to look soon for a new home for you and I'll come very often and stay with you. Then you won't be lonely, never again.' And Lewis looked at Arnold with such an expression of young devotion that Arnold suddenly felt the black clouds of the last few days, which had enveloped him so that he was incapable of any coherent thoughts, begin to evaporate.

'That's a very good idea and maybe if daddy Jason is free, he will come too. Then, when we have sorted out a new house for me, we have to get you organised to go back to school. How will you feel about that, love?' Arnold hastened on. 'Someone will always take you and bring you home. You have nothing to be afraid of, not ever again Lewis. But we must get you to school to learn, because if you don't learn, you won't be able to get a job and with no job you would have no money, Lewis.' Arnold was determined that his son must not know that it did not matter if he never got a job, because all of Arnold's wealth would pass to his son. Arnold believed it was important that his son was taught to have a good work ethic, especially in light of what had happened to him. He needed to make his own way in the world. It would be so easy to indulge his every whim and Arnold was resolved that that must not happen. As Arnold sat at the breakfast table with Lewis and the others he knew that guiding him on a decent, respectable path in life would be his – Arnold's salvation – and help raise him out of this black pit he found himself in.

'Let's go and get ready, young man and we'll go and visit a few estate agents and look at what properties they have for sale. What about you, Jason? And Lynn, are you coming with me?'

Lynn and Jason, now very relieved indeed to see some spark of life in Arnold, rose hastily from the breakfast table and began carrying the dishes over to the sink for washing, Lynn remarking that they were ready to go anywhere, just as long as she was back in time to visit her mother in hospital.

'Gavin is still sitting with mum but I have insisted that when I come in later, he goes home and has a rest and something to eat. The staff say that while mum is in this induced coma, they can't really tell very much, only that this induced rest is essential to give her any hope of

211

recovery.' Lynn continued 'Are you sure about selling your home in Helen's Bay? I know you loved it there, all that peace and tranquillity.'

'Of course I did, Lynn, but anything I have is here now – Lewis, yourself and Jason, not to mention little Eve. So, yes, I am quite sure, my dear.'

'Well of course then, we'll go with you and as you say look at a few estate agents' windows – see what's on offer and no harm will be done if you don't see anything that appeals to you.'

Meantime, Jason was calling for Eve, who had gone outside with Monty. 'We'll have Miss Eve with us too, Arnold. There is no play-group on Saturday mornings, but she's a good, obedient child.'

'Sorry, Jason, although I included her in my conversation just now, I had actually forgotten about her this morning. I'm not myself at all at the minute, I believe.'

'Well, of course you aren't, Arnold, and Lynn and I would like to make it clear, we don't expect you to be yourself. We still think you are remarkable and if you want to stay with us for some time, we would be more than happy to have you here.'

'How kind of you. I might well take you up on that until I find somewhere satisfactory, and that might well take a little while. But I know I could not bear to go back to live in Helen's Bay, too many memories.'

'Well, I too, really want you to stay here, Arnold, until you are really ready to move.' Lynn remarked.

The family spent quite an informative morning visiting estate agents and looking at so many different brochures and although Rachel was uppermost in Lynn's mind as she trudged round Belfast, she tried to give little indication of it. She knew Arnold needed their support too, anything that might help lift his spirits, even a little, was well worth trying. But during their visits to the estate agents' premises, while Lynn and Jason would have guided Arnold towards small, compact properties suitable for one or two people and in close proximity to where they themselves lived, Arnold only seemed interested in the most opulent, spacious mansions on the market. As they tried to show some enthusiasm for the mansions, Jason observed that probably the man would find it very difficult to downsize and they would find it equally difficult to give him advice as to what to do. In the end, they left it to Arnold to decide which brochures to bring home with him and as Jason had suspected, it was only the ones with information about the large houses he had under his arm. As Lynn remarked to Jason later that Arnold was so grief stricken he could not possibly make rational decisions and they would be better to indulge him and go along with what he felt at this moment in his life.

As she drove to the hospital later that afternoon, Lynn was distraught, although she was marginally less worried about Arnold and his frame of mind – he had seemed bright enough when they had been with him earlier. She was very worried about her mother, still critically ill in the induced coma. She had enquired of the doctor the previous evening when they might be considering withdrawing some of the coma inducing drugs, but the doctor on duty had told her it was much too soon to think in those terms. Her injuries were such and her condition so critical that they believed it was to Rachel's advantage to continue to anaesthetise her

Gavin was still sitting in the chair beside Rachel's bed when Lynn entered the ward and she was struck by how much he too was suffering and how utterly selfish she had been regarding her stepfather. She had been so wrapped up in her own agony and suffering that not once had she considered how Gavin must have felt when Rachel first disappeared. Then, to be told she was critically ill because of how wrong everything had gone in that forest.

Now, she threw her arms round him and kissed him fiercely on the cheek. 'Gavin, I'm so very sorry. I have totally ignored how you were feeling in all this but I was so wrapped up in my own emotions that I never looked beyond them.'

'No, please don't even think like that, Lynn, I in turn was so wrapped up in my selfish, prudish feelings, I did not spare many thoughts of you in your anguish; firstly over Lewis and secondly your mother. It is I who owe you an apology, dear' and Gavin returned her kiss and hug there and then.

'There is no real change in Rachel, but the staff say her vital signs remain steady and that it's encouraging, but they don't expect to see much change until they start withdrawing the drugs and see how she responds. They have advised me to return in the evening and perhaps again in the morning. What do you think, Lynn?'

'I think you should do what they advise you to do, Gavin. You have sat here for the last forty-eight hours and you certainly need a proper rest – not just a doze in an armchair. You also need something more substantial to eat than what the nurses have here and I'm sure you would feel better if you were freshened up. I mean to stay here for a time, Gavin, and then some of the family members said they would relieve me. I think either Sheila or Jenny will be here later, they know I like to get back to Jason and the children and Arnold too, of course.'

Chapter 47

June 1985

Matthew knew he had to go and talk to Arnold sooner rather than later, he had been putting it off for a week now and this was something he could not understand in himself. Usually, he faced things head on no matter how difficult they seemed to be. But this was different, he had deluded Arnold and now this evening, he intended to be honest with him and tell the truth. He would go to Jason and Lynn's house after he'd had his tea and tell Arnold what he had done. He knew Lynn would be at the hospital to see her mother who was – the very next morning – going to start to have her coma inducing drugs reduced to see how she would respond. So there would only be Jason and the children there, and he would try to time his going to the cottage with the children being in bed. It would be better, in the meantime, if only Arnold knew what he had done.

'Hello, Matthew, come in.' it was Arnold himself who opened the door in response to Matthew's ringing of the doorbell. 'There is only me here – apart from the children – Jason decided he would go with Lynn to the hospital to see Rachel.'

'It's yourself I came to see, Arnold.' Matthew spoke quietly as he followed Arnold into the sitting room – he had no desire to wake the children this particular evening.

'Would you like a drink – a beer – or perhaps tea or coffee, Matthew?'

'Coffee would be lovely, Arnold.' Matthew was glad to see Arnold seemed to be coping with the loss of Iris somewhat better. He seemed brighter somehow and that reluctance to even move out of his chair had gone. In fact, as Matthew watched him it would have been difficult for anyone to know that Arnold had any artificial limbs anywhere, never mind one in his leg and one in his arm. No doubt, the presence of his son and Lynn and Jason in his life was of great support to him.

'How have you been, Arnold? This coffee looks good.' As Matthew took the coffee from him and set it on the table beside his chair.

'Well, I've been busy, Matthew. I am in the process of selling my house in Helen's Bay and I hope to move to Belfast to be closer to Lewis and you all. Lynn insists I stay here until I find somewhere suitable, which is of course, so kind of them.'

Matthew was surprised to hear this, to make such a major decision so soon was, he hoped for Arnold's sake, going to be a wise decision. 'That will be so beneficial for you, Arnold, just to be near your son. But make sure you find somewhere suitable for you.'

'I have two or three places in mind. Perhaps in a day or two you'll come with me to have a look and help me decide.' Arnold suddenly decided that he would ask Matthew's advice about what he was thinking of doing. After all, he was Jason's father and might have some thoughts about how Jason would feel about it.

'I would love to do that. But firstly, Arnold, I have to tell you how I have deceived you.' Matthew waited to see Arnold's initial reaction to what he had just said.

'You – deceive me? Never, Matthew. What do you mean?'

'I want to explain about the missing attaché case that was left at the tree.'

'You mean the case the money was in? Has it been found?'

'No. No. It hasn't, Arnold. But it doesn't really matter if it never is. You see I took a real risk before Iris, yourself and I went to the forest. I took your money out of the wallet and replaced it with wads of paper; paper which was wrapped in genuine £50 notes. I did use I think, six £50 notes to wrap the paper in. I could not bear to see you parting with all that money and to be honest I felt it was a reasonably safe thing to do. I reckoned our abductor was unlikely to hang around long enough to count it all but might just give the contents a perfunctory check. In the event, he never got a chance to go near the case but someone else must have lifted it that night in the midst of the chaos that ensued. Unfortunately, so far we have no idea who lifted it but at least they only got £300 instead of £100,000.' Matthew felt so very much better since he had told Arnold what he had done.

But even though he now had the ransom money, would it mean anything to him? He had suffered so much more than any money could possibly compensate for. The whole business was such a tragedy, but they must try and continue to go on. They must try to remain optimistic about Rachel. Rachel, whom Arnold had been prepared to part with all that money for.

'I do know this is all so hard for you to take in, and I do hope you don't look on it as blood money. It is your money, I have it in my safe at home, and I intend to bring it to you tomorrow.'

'Why didn't you tell me sooner about this, Matthew? It has been quite a few days now, I would have understood your reasons for taking such a chance. Let's just say I'm sure I would not have approved at the time but I certainly approve now and I know you were trying to help me.' Arnold hesitated then his voice shook as he went on. 'And the fact that there was no money in that case made no difference to what ultimately happened in that forest. So I thank you, Matthew.' And Arnold gave him such a warm smile that, for the first time since Matthew had removed the money, he was glad he had had the courage to do so.

'£100,000 is quite a bit of money and I know I can put it to good use at the moment instead of putting it back into my bank. Perhaps, when you bring the money tomorrow, you would have a little spare time to come and look at some of the properties with me. You might be able to help me decide.'

'Of course. I'll arrange something. It will probably be the afternoon but I'll ring you in the morning to confirm the time, Arnold. Now, I must be going, it's getting late. Give my love to Lynn and Jason and I'll be in touch tomorrow regarding Rachel, as well. '

As he drove back to the annexe, Matthew was relieved to have the burden of the money lifted from his mind. He had meant to tell Arnold to let Lynn and Jason know about it, but then thinking about Rachel and what she might have to go through tomorrow had put anything else out of his mind.

Chapter 48

'There is nothing to worry about at this stage, Mr. Finlay. It does sometimes happen that the patient needs to be sedated again. Your wife became very distressed and her blood pressure very unstable, so really, we had not much choice, only to reintroduce the coma inducing drugs.' The Consultant's voice was steady and reassuring as he spoke to Gavin and Lynn, who had joined her stepfather in the interview room just a few moments ago.

'Is my wife stable now? May I go in to see her?

'Yes, her pulse and blood pressure have settled and she seems fairly stable at present. We have also commenced her on antibiotics as her chest was giving us some cause for concern. I see from her notes that she was caught up in a fire some years ago, which left her with some problems. So that has complicated our ability, in her present situation, to keep her lungs free from infection, and that might have accounted for her distressed state earlier.' The Consultant then added. 'So that should see an improvement in her condition within the next twenty-four to thirty-six hours, If that is the case, we can consider withdrawing some of the sedative drugs again, and certainly Mr. Finlay, you may go in and see your wife.'

Lynn accompanied Gavin into the side ward where Rachel lay, so calm and peaceful looking and although she did not say anything to Gavin, she thought her mother's colour had changed. Whereas before she had had a rosy hue to her cheeks, they now looked quite grey and waxen. But Lynn realised her stepfather had not noticed her colour but was just thankful she was so calm and peaceful after witnessing her distress and agitation earlier in the day. Now, Lynn watched Gavin as he took his usual seat at the side of Rachel's bed and marvelled at the inner strength of the man who could sit there for such long periods of time without a word of complaint. Whereas Lynn found that she quickly became exhausted after two or three hours. Now she knew Gavin just wished to sit alone with Rachel, his whole body language was telling Lynn this, so with a whisper to him that she would relieve him later on that day, and giving him a warm kiss on the cheek, she left him with her mother, knowing he would devotedly sit there watching for any change which he would immediately report to a member of staff.

'No, Arnold, mum did not respond very well to the withdrawal of the drugs, but the Consultant has assured us that this is very common, especially that she now has a chest infection, which they are now treating with antibiotics. They say they will attempt to withdraw the sedation again in a few days' time and they do keep telling us that her vital signs are fairly normal. I left Gavin with her and I think he doesn't really want anyone else there when he's there. So I told him I would relieve him later in the day.' Lynn felt rather uncomfortable talking about her mother to Arnold. At least her mother had been given a chance of life and was receiving the highest level of medical care. Arnold's wife, dear Iris, had been given no such chance, and yet Lynn knew that if Arnold knew Lynn would be upset talking about Rachel, he in turn would be very upset. There was no one who wished Rachel a speedier return to health than Arnold did.

'Are you going out, Arnold?' Lynn noticed that Arnold was all dressed and had his best walking stick in his hand.

'Yes, Matthew has agreed to accompany me in my new house search, so he should be here in about fifteen minutes Lynn. I have switched the kettle on, and I want you to look at the brochures I brought home and tell me which of them would be your favourite.' With that remark, Arnold disappeared into the kitchen but returned balancing very expertly, a cup of tea in his good hand, which he handed promptly to Lynn, returned to the kitchen and retrieved a couple of biscuits for her.

'It's hard to say, Arnold, although I think something less palatial and grand would suit you very well.' Although Lynn had originally been determined to say nothing to Arnold about the grandeur of the houses he was looking at, now since he had asked her, she seized her opportunity. Arnold seemed about to reply but the ring of the doorbell heralded Matthew's arrival. He entered the living room and held out a large brown container to Arnold. 'Make sure you put that somewhere safe, Arnold. Did you tell Lynn and Jason about it?'

Lynn knew immediately that it was the ransom money that was in the container. Arnold had told Jason and her all about it last night. 'I think it is wonderful that you changed the money over, Matthew. I'm sure Arnold does too.'

'Indeed I do.' And Arnold took the container and disappeared into his room with it, reappearing a few minutes later and after a hurried farewell, the two men made their way out of the cottage and into the car. Then, as Matthew started up the car, he asked Arnold to give him directions to where the first stop was. As they drove along, Matthew listening intently to Arnold's directions, he was thankful that, in spite of Arnold's grief and the constant worry of Rachel's likely recovery, Arnold seemed to have developed a very eager interest in this house hunting. It was something Matthew could not understand, the urgency of it all, but then grief made people act in the most peculiar way. He himself had been through it all with the murder of his father, and if moving house from Helen's Bay to Belfast was keeping him occupied and sane, Matthew for one, would support that. Even though, as the morning wore on, and the three properties they looked at all seemed so grand and palatial, Matthew began to wonder how serious Arnold really was about moving. These houses were so unsuitable for a man who was so essentially alone, even though he might, on many occasions, have Lewis to stay. But Matthew said nothing, he felt very justified in humouring Arnold. After all, why not after what the man had been through?

'Matthew, you must wonder, although you haven't said anything, why I am looking at such large mansion type houses, or perhaps you think I'm just passing time to fill my empty hours but I can assure you it is not so.'

The two men had just returned to the car after viewing a beautiful property just off the Malone Road, with beautiful grounds planted with the most beautiful flowers and shrubs.

'I need to talk to you, Matthew. Let's go somewhere for coffee and I'll tell you something about my plan.'

'Of course, I would have my own private quarters in the house and my own front door, so there would be no question of my intrusion into Lynn and Jason's life. I would never do that Matthew, but just to know that they and Lewis were close to me, that they had a place of their very own and their future was assured, would mean everything to me. Certainly, it would be preferable to me than going and sitting alone in my grand house in Helen's Bay, so you see I have my own selfish reasons for doing this.' Arnold paused for a moment as he took another sip of his coffee and then went on, 'Don't get me wrong, Matthew, they have a fine place in your cottage, but it is yours, and I think if I can help Lynn and Jason with their future, then so I should. I can never forget that only for Lynn's generosity of heart, and indeed Jason's too, I would never have known my beloved son and even much more importantly, neither would Iris. Lewis gave Iris much love and happiness in the time they had together. So you see, Matthew, I owe them so much and this idea I have is a mere gesture in an attempt to thank them for their kindness.'

Throughout Arnold's telling of his reasons for wanting to purchase such a mansion like the type he and Matthew had viewed earlier in the day, Matthew had sat dumbfounded at this man's generosity and thoughtfulness. He thought back to those dark days when Lynn had discovered that she was not married to Arnold – that he had a wife. Then, when he had discovered Lynn was pregnant with his son, how he had threatened her with taking her to court to obtain custody of their Lewis. Now, in spite of sending Lewis to a private school and paying all his fees and providing so generously for him in every way, his dearest wish was to provide a mansion for Lynn and her husband. Matthew marvelled at the frailties – the strengths and weakness – of human nature, how anyone can be led on to a wrong, immoral path and yet through the kindness of one person, see the error of their ways and have the capacity to make atonement for them.

Now, Arnold was continuing to speak and Matthew saw that Arnold was quite animated. 'That money which you so bravely held on to, Matthew, in spite of the risks, will go a long way towards the costs of any changes I might need to make to ensure my privacy. So, in the most unexpected way, you have contributed to the security of your son's and his family's future and I personally am extremely grateful for your presence of mind and ingenuity in the midst of the awful ordeal we all found ourselves in.

You are certainly to be commended for that alone, Matthew.'

Now for the first time, Matthew felt a glow of pride for what he had achieved. But It had taken Arnold to help him see that indeed it had taken some presence of mind and an innate sense of justice to try to ensure that Lewis and Rachel's captor did not carry off £100,000 from that forest; and for the first time in this ordeal, Matthew felt better about himself and how the whole incident had been handled. For the first time, he realised that the ensuing tragedy that had happened had been down, he believed, to Iris's presence there. It had been her presence in the forest that had changed everything, it was not how the police had organised everything or indeed his or Arnold's presence. It was seeing this female running towards him, which had dictated how the captor behaved. Certainly, from the interviews Matthew had had with him in the hospital ward, it was all Jimmy Devlin could talk about. 'That bloody woman.' He had just kept repeating. 'She made me panic – it was her that done it. It was her.'

Matthew knew that Iris's death, essentially brought about by her insistence that she accompany Arnold from Helen's Bay back to Belfast, was something Arnold now had to live with and over time try to accept. No wonder he was desperately seeking constant companionship in his life and he wished that companionship to be his own son and his family. Matthew decided there and then that he would actively encourage Jason and Lynn to go along with Arnold's wishes, and before they left the coffee shop that morning, he told Arnold that that was exactly what he intended doing.

Chapter 49

'We have reason to be cautiously optimistic about your wife Mr. Finlay. As you know, we started to withdraw her sedation early this morning and so far the signs are good. There is little agitation or distress and it is important that we begin to monitor how your wife is when she is conscious, so it is still very early days. As I am sure you understand, the drugs are given to try and maximise rest for her body, as we believe this aids recovery. Also, she responded well to the antibiotics for her chest infection – it has cleared up.'

'I do understand, but as you've just said, the signs are good for my wife.' Gavin looked hopefully at the consultant who had been taking care of Rachel during the last three weeks and half weeks. During that time there was great cause for concern on two different occasions; firstly, Rachel had suffered a very serious pneumonia, then, a serious infection in one of the bullet entry sites had necessitated a return to theatre for a deep incision to remove debris, pus and any lingering infection. Surely now, Gavin thought – although he did not voice it – surely nothing else could go wrong.

With yet another thank you to the surgeon for all the attention he had administered to his wife during her time in Intensive Care, Gavin made his way into the ward and was amazed to see Rachel, her eyes wide open, trying to focus on him as he made his way towards the chair where he had sat in despair, but praying desperately for his wife's recovery.

'Rachel, Rachel,' and he leaned forward, looking earnestly into her eyes. 'It's me, Gavin, Rachel.'

But although Rachel paused for a second in her eye sweeping motions, she continued to gaze all-round the room in what, Gavin thought, seemed to be in some kind of wonder. So Gavin sat quietly in his usual place, watching his wife trying, he thought, to focus back into this strange world she found herself in, until finally, she slipped into a quiet natural sleep. A sleep which, Gavin felt looked as if it was the first real one his wife had had in almost four weeks.

Even after Rachel had fallen asleep Gavin still sat in the same chair he had sat in since the shooting and wondered, as he had so many times during her critical state, what the future held for them both. How would he cope if she were suddenly to have another relapse and die? How would he feel? He would be grief-stricken, he knew that. But would he have forgiven her whole-heartedly for what she had done to him, even with her knowledge of how he felt about what she intended to do. He loved her, he knew that, and he admired her bravery and the sacrifice she had made for her grandson and his safety. All those things he loved and respected and admired about her. But still, he was weighed down by resentment at her, for putting their marriage at such stake, and worse, for ignoring how passionately he felt about what she wished to do. Yes, in spite of her total acceptance of his unwillingness for her to become involved, she had still done it all. Surely, someone else in the professional world could have been called on to do what she had done? He was sure they could have. But it was Rachel who now lay there, still so seriously ill and it was he, Gavin, who was sitting here wondering just how far-reaching forgiveness could be.

He did not know the answer to this searing question which penetrated his brain as he sat with Rachel day after day, simply because he still loved her. He believed he must shelve this question until his wife was recovered and then perhaps it might all be resolved. He was very conscious too that the rest of the family who came to visit – her mother, Maggie, Lynn and some of her other elderly aunts – thought his devotion such a wonderful, thing. And because Gavin knew he had not yet forgiven Rachel for what she had done, even in her critical state, he was weighed down with all the guilt of his complex feelings and emotions.

'Mum darling, you'll never believe what Arnold Simpson has done for us. Please mum, try to concentrate while I tell you. It is unbelievable, really unbelievable.' Lynn, always on her visits to Rachel during the last week and indeed during her whole time in the coma, had insisted on keeping her up to date with everything that was happening in their lives. Unlike myself, Gavin thought, who had sat silently day after day, mostly engrossed in his own thoughts, watching her so slow stages of recovery.

'Mum, he has bought a mansion – that's the only way I can describe this house – a mansion and he wants Jason, me, Lewis and Eve to live in it with him. I can't believe his generosity and kindness. And to think we dreaded him coming to Northern Ireland to find Lewis and me. What do you think of that mum?'

In response Rachel turned to her daughter and smiled happily. 'I think it is so lovely for you, my dear. And remember you were so very forgiving of him always, my love. So I'm just glad he has obviously never forgotten that.'

At his wife's reaction, Gavin's breath caught in his throat and for the first time since the shooting, he now believed Rachel was on the road to recovery. And if she could remember so much about Arnold and Lynn in the past, surely she would soon be able to remember all that had happened to her. Now he got to his feet, and going over to Rachel, kissed her warm cheek and told her how strong she was getting and how the sound of her voice was like music to his ears. Rachel responded by turning to look at her husband and reaching for his hand, she squeezed his hand and smiled lovingly at him.

Three weeks later, Rachel was discharged from hospital, on the understanding she was going to a room in her own nursing home as part of her convalescence. Rachel, although she had no memory of how she had ended up in hospital in the first place, was only too glad to go to her own nursing home, where all her relatives who she did remember and loved so much, dwelt. Lynn had made a point of talking to the consultant and staff at length about the reasons for her mother's memory loss. She was reassured when they told her that the shock of the shooting and her horrendous injuries, coupled with her time in the induced coma, would account for her amnesia. They did stress that if and when her memory did return, she might be subject to serious mood swings, night terrors and the like. So it was important she was well cared for.

Chapter 50

Rachel loved her room in the home. Uncle John, who had been in charge of the place since Rachel's absence, had been in charge of ensuring everything ran smoothly, had insisted she must have the one with its very own sitting room, kitchen and bathroom, where he and Dorrie had spent many quiet, contented times there. After all, he told Rachel, she owned the place and it would be a strange thing if she couldn't have the best room in the house, would it not?

Rachel had been told by her consultant that as her memory returned, she might have nightmares about what had happened to her, but she had been in the home for two weeks now and so far she could not remember anything about what had happened, but neither had she had any nightmares. Gavin called most days to see her and on each occasion stayed for a couple of hours, and although Rachel asked him on a couple of occasions if he would stay with her at night, he said that just at present, he thought it best if he did not. After all, he said, she still needed monitoring by the nurses at night and he would be sure to be in the way of them carrying out their duties. Rachel accepted what her husband was telling her but somewhere in her subconscious mind, she felt things were not right between them. She was aware that there was some obscure reason for this, something she had done, something she had said which displeased him. It was there, just on the edges of her mind but somehow no matter how she tried, that reason always slipped away from her. And in her weakened, frail state, she found it impossible to dwell on anything much. It entailed far too much effort to think about. She was much too tired. She simply had to let things be as they were, perhaps Gavin would tell her what she had done or indeed if she had done anything. In the meantime, she was glad of his company, enjoying simple pleasures like having tea and cake which her mother Maggie, frail now but still sprightly enough, would bring to her room every afternoon, telling her she needed to eat up in order to put on some weight.

Then, Lynn visited often, sometimes with Jason and the children, other times she would come alone. Always, Lynn would ask her mother gently, if she could remember anything about what had happened, and so far, Rachel did remember Lewis being kidnapped and she even remembered talking to Matthew and telling him she would like to help find her grandson. After that, she had to admit to Lynn, she could remember nothing until the day in the ward, when she realised Gavin was sitting beside her and she was in a strange place and in a strange bed. The consultant had told her, on that same day, that she had been involved in a serious shooting incident and she had been critically injured, He had gone on to tell her that another lady, by the name of Iris Simpson, had tried to help her but had been shot dead. The consultant had explained that it was the shock of her ordeal, which had given her such severe amnesia of those events but that as she recovered physically, hopefully her memory would return.

After that, even in her weakened state, Rachel grieved deeply for Iris, although she was at a total loss as to why Iris was trying to save her and from what had she been trying to save her. She felt for Arnold's loss and when he came to visit her – when he learned she had recovered consciousness – she was touched by his kindness. When she confided in him about her total bewilderment as to all that had happened and the awful mist and fog in her mind regarding it all, Arnold was the one who listened so carefully to what she said. He was never dismissive of her despair but he told her that perhaps by talking things over that she did remember, she might begin to remember other snippets. He always stressed to her that she had been such a brave woman to do what she had done. Then, smiling at her he stressed, 'No matter about anything else, what you remember and what you don't remember, just always remember that, my dear. That you were so very brave.' And because of his quiet, unassuming ways, Rachel looked forward to his visits.

Sometimes, when he came, he talked about losing Iris and how she had believed she could help Rachel. He always stressed to Rachel, the happiness her daughter Lynn had given both Arnold and Iris by giving them such access to Lewis and allowing them to be such a part of their lives. He praised Lynn, on many of his visits, for all she had done in spite of Arnold's deceit in the early days, leading her to believe he was free to marry her, even though he was still married to Iris and intended to remain so. He reminded Rachel of that awful time when he had threatened to fight for custody of Lewis and wondered how Lynn had even tolerated him anywhere in her life, never mind her generosity of spirit towards him. There was no doubt, he told Rachel on many of his visits, how her daughter had totally changed both his and Iris's moral attitudes and their whole way of life. And when Rachel tried to remind him of his present generosity regarding the home he was purchasing, Arnold stressed how he was simply trying to show some appreciation.

Always after Arnold's visits, Rachel's injuries somehow seemed more trivial compared to what Arnold had suffered in the past. She had all her limbs and faculties, whereas he had lost an arm and a leg but had overcome his disabilities, and resolved no doubt, to lead as normal life a life as possible.

Since Rachel's discharge from hospital and now safely ensconced in her lovely room in the Nursing Home, Arnold's visits were not so frequent. No doubt, everyone was beginning to feel she was well out of danger and as such, there was not the same pressure to visit. But Rachel missed Arnold's visits and her ability to talk over, as he had suggested, all she could remember. But no doubt, he believed that as she was on the road to recovery and he had given her such useful advice, he did not feel it was necessary to come so often to the home, where of course, she was surrounded by her relatives So, Rachel was determined to follow Arnold's advice and talk about what she did remember and at what stage did she believe her memory failed her. When Gavin called in the evening after his day's work, she insisted on talking to him about what her last memories had been when they were told Lewis had been taken and they were all as a family, at a loss how best to help find him. Rachel found Gavin very non-committal about what might have happened after that. Even when she questioned him about Lewis's homecoming and how that had all come about, he reminded her that the consultant had advised them all not to give Rachel much information. The consultant had stipulated that she might well delude herself into believing that she actually remembered the incidents someone told her about. Much better, the advice was that something unexpectedly triggered her mind to recall something more naturally. Yet, always at the edges of her mind and through the frustrating mists which never seemed to clear, Rachel felt she had done something, something may be to do with her grandson, which had annoyed her husband. But how could that be? How could anything, anything at all to do with Lewis possibly upset Gavin? Why he loved the boy, idolised him, she believed, almost as much as she did. Then, when Gavin left her in the evenings, alone in her nursing home, she wept tears of frustration. She did not know anything of her recent past, nor did she know what the future held. She did not even know if Gavin still loved her, still wanted her, or was he simply doing his duty to his wife, who had been so gravely ill.

Chapter 51

Matthew visited Rachel as often as he could, even though he was still working full time in the police force and his workload at present was extremely big. There was considerable pressure on him to obtain results sooner rather than later. But he still remained very concerned about Rachel and her future, so he made a point of trying to go and see her at least twice a week and he was always rewarded by her obvious joy in seeing him coming into her room. On one particular evening, he realised he had disturbed her a little when he started to talk about Arnold. They had been discussing Arnold's generosity in providing such a beautiful home for their children and grandchildren and how happy he was at the thought that Jason, Lynn and the children would soon be joining him. During the conversation as Matthew thought of Arnold and all he had been through and now his obvious renewed enthusiasm about the property he had purchased, Matthew inadvertently mentioned how beneficial Arnold had said the ransom money would be. Ransom money Arnold had always maintained he was very prepared to spend, as it was still his, and would go a long way in helping to fund the renovations for the whole project. Not that Arnold needed the money, Matthew stressed to Rachel, but it was still right that he had not had to part with it. Even as he spoke, Matthew realised his mistake, Rachel's face paled and her eyes became huge and focused on his face.

'What do you mean, Matthew? Ransom money, I should know something about that, shouldn't I?'

Cursing himself for forgetting about Rachel's condition and her amnesia, Matthew answered quietly.

'Yes, Rachel, my dear it is something you should know about and I have no doubt it will come back to you. But in the meantime, please don't be alarmed, perhaps my saying something about certain things might trigger something in your brain eventually, and you will start to remember. Even now, I believe what I have just said has alerted you to knowing something about the ransom money.'

Rachel nodded solemnly and already Matthew knew she was striving to get through those mists in her head in an effort to recall something from her recent past. Before he left her that evening, he did his best to reassure her. 'Try to remember, Rachel, but don't strive too hard because it may only distress you. Let everything take its course.' And before he left, Matthew kissed her warmly, assuring her he would be back in a couple of days' time to see her and they would have a further chat.

As he drove home, Matthew felt he had no real regrets about trying to trigger Rachel's memory, not that he had purposely done so this afternoon. It was just that he was beginning to feel very strongly that the odd trigger or two to jolt her memory might be no bad thing. Maybe pussyfooting around her was not the answer. It would be interesting to hear the next time he visited her if she would be able to recall anything else of her ordeal.

Now though, as he steered his car into the driveway at the side of the annexe, he knew he must put Rachel and her loss of memory aside in the meantime. He had, in his study, a box full of notes from the dead prisoner, Alfie Reid's flat, and he must concentrate on those notes, to try to establish if there was any evidence, anything at all, which might help him in his search for his ex-brother-in-law – Patrick Mullan's killer.

After a wonderful dinner of roast lamb and potatoes followed by homemade chocolate cake, all made by Julie, Matthew, with promises to his wife that he did not intend to work too late, made his way to his study, to start to try to make some sense of the notes this man, Alfie, had left in his apartment. It was such a painstaking task, between the unkempt, rumpled state of most of the papers, papers, which the dead man had kept so very carefully, and the illegible scrawl of his words on the papers. Matthew, as the night wore on, became more and more despairing of gleaning anything from the contents of the boxes. It was obvious from the contents of each and every one of those boxes, that Alfie had not had much intention of making things simple for anyone who looked at his writing. In fact, as the evening wore on, Matthew began to believe that this man had quite deliberately left these notes in order to make it exceedingly difficult for anyone to find out anything and in order to taunt them. He was tempted to give up his perusal, after all, it was one o'clock in the morning and he was becoming more and more frustrated the longer he looked at the papers strewn across his desk. It was only the recurring theme of two initials – MH – which kept him seated at his desk, initials he reckoned must form some sort of a code or other. If it was a code, it was a most unfamiliar one to Matthew; in all his time in dealing with paramilitary organisations, this was a new one. This intrigued him, besides, it had been fairly well established that poor dead Alfie, had not been a member of any organisation as such, but was just a petty criminal, working in isolation and mainly for reward. He had worked, Matthew suspected, regardless of any political or religious organisation; it was quite obvious it had not mattered to Alfie. That was obvious in the fact he had become embroiled in trying to track down Patrick Mullan, to avenge Matthew's father and on the other hand, he had been prepared to help kidnap Matthew's grandson in revenge for something or other and hold him to ransom. When it boiled down to it in Alfie's case, it was all about money and little or anything to do with any beliefs of any kind. In Matthew's opinion, this was highly dangerous, because leaders in either organisation could use a petty criminal and then discard them without a thought. And so, he believed, had been the case here and he had paid with his life.

But who had offered prisoner Alfie money for finding out Patrick Mullan's whereabouts? The abduction of Lewis was a different venture, Alfie's help had been enlisted by Jimmy Devlin and he had been given a deposit with the firm promise of much more when the ransom money had been handed over. The police knew all that, but they had no ideas as to who had offered him money for finding out about Patrick. Matthew did not know, but he intended to find out, if not tonight then tomorrow night, If not tomorrow night, then the next or the next. He only knew that he was determined to track down the person responsible for his ex-brother-in-law's death.

Later, as he crept quietly into the bedroom and silently slipped into bed beside Julie, he realised the only recurring theme throughout prisoner Alfie's notes, had been the letters MH, and before Matthew fell asleep, he found himself wondering what that code stood for. He believed MH was the crux of the whole enquiry, and if he knew what it meant, he might be on the way to finding out more, much more. Which organisation was it, Matthew wondered; surely it had to be either the IRA or the UDA, but it was going to be difficult to ascertain which. It would have been irrelevant to Alfie who it was, he would not have minded in the least where they came from, as long as they brought the money. He saw no point in returning to interview Alfie Reid's accomplice in the raid on the Mullan's home, the accomplice had already admitted that he was the one who had beaten up Kevin Mullan while Alfie searched the house for clues to Patrick Mullan's whereabouts. When he found some information in his mother's bedroom, they had left the house and anxious not to have their car traced had decided to steal one for the purpose of going to Armagh to seek out Patrick Mullan and give him a beating up as, according to Alfie, that was their instructions. Although, Alfie's accomplice said, he had taken a gun just in case Patrick Mullan might have been supplied with one for his own safety. But when they arrived at their destination, the Mullans had gone and he understood Alfie Reid had lost interest after that, certainly he had heard nothing at all from Alfie Reid since that evening. But then he had been arrested shortly after and probably Alfie had decided to steer clear of him.

Chapter 53

Matthew had had a poor night's sleep and appreciated the fact that it was a Saturday, and he did not need to make any appearance in his office. Instead Julie and he together with Lynn and Jason, Arnold and the children were going to look at last minute changes to the house Arnold had purchased. Matthew found he was really looking forward to his day out, he loved looking at properties, loved the prospects of renovating, commenting on and upgrading them. And although he could never aspire to purchasing the type of properties Arnold had been viewing with the aim of buying one of them, he still very much enjoyed looking at them and thinking how he himself would convert such a property, given he had the money to do so. After some time spent browsing around Arnold's prospective new home, the family intended to go later on in the day to the nursing home and visit not only Rachel, but all his other relatives. Then, they intended to go on from the home to the lodge, to see Matthew's mother, Ellen, and his stepfather, Tom. Matthew felt very guilty that he had not seen his parents in over a week, but they always assured him that they saw as much of him as they did of either Thomas or Charles. They always assured him that Lucie, their daughter, and their daughters-in-law, were very faithful visitors, and called on a regular basis and certainly kept them up to date about everything. They knew, they said, from what Julie told them, that he was a very busy man. Indeed, since they had first heard of Patrick Mullan's death, his mother, Ellen, had been very disturbed by it all. Matthew understood her feelings only too well, after all, Patrick had been her son-in-law, someone her daughter, Lucie, had had strong feelings for. Someone, who then was involved in the murder of Rob, her husband, so it was only natural that his mother would be upset.

When Matthew visited later on that day, he decided that he would not mention he was involved in any way in the investigation into Patrick Mullan's death. It might be a cruel thing to do even after all these years, to talk about Matthew now trying to solve the mystery of Patrick's murder, when Patrick had been embroiled in Matthew's father's murder. Besides, he wanted to unwind this weekend and enjoy his time with his family, then, on Monday, he would start all over again, going over everything again and again.

When Arnold and Matthew finally arrived at the nursing home they were a good two hours behind schedule so much so that Julie and the others said it was much too late for all of them to troop into the home. Then Lynn suggested that Julie and Emily must come to her house, help her make dinner and then Arnold and Matthew join them after they had visited Rachel and they could all dine together. Both men agreed, more than willingly, that it seemed a very good idea.

When Matthew and Arnold arrived at the nursing home and made their way to the private quarters where Rachel was, Matthew was delighted to see Gavin seated beside Rachel on the couch she had brought over to the window just the previous week. She had told Matthew she delighted in watching all the passers-by and trying to imagine what their lives were like beside hers. Rachel welcomed the two men with open arms and then disappeared into the kitchen to make tea.

'My goodness, Gavin, Rachel seems very sprightly. Is she as well as she appears to be?' It was Arnold who had spoken.

'Yes, she seems very well, but her memory for the events of her ordeal have not returned yet, so I think it is recommended that she stays here for another few days until she may recall something of that time.' Gavin replied, quite evasively, Arnold thought.

'Why is Gavin so anxious that Rachel's memory returns before she goes home to their home, Matthew?'

Matthew was quite taken aback when Arnold asked him the question about Rachel and Gavin's attitude towards her. He had been pondering about the very same thing himself and now Arnold was voicing the question that was on Matthew's mind so much. Why indeed was Gavin so reluctant to bring Rachel home? In the last week, he told Matthew that he had employed someone for two whole days to clean the house from top to bottom and to do all the washing and ironing which had been left untouched for so long. He had even told Matthew that the place was shining brightly and looked like home once more. And although Gavin had said nothing at all about it being in preparation for Rachel's homecoming, Matthew had made the assumption that it was. Matthew just hoped, although he said very little to Arnold on the way home, that Gavin was not going to hold any grudges against Rachel, for what she had done, after all she had gone through. Indeed, what they had all gone through. Perhaps there was a much more simple explanation for Gavin's behaviour, perhaps he was getting over-anxious about her recovery and feared she might have a setback when she did return home. Now he voiced these thoughts to Arnold 'I think Gavin can't wait to have things back the way they were for Rachel and him, and unfortunately, he may have to learn to be patient,

Arnold. We all have to give Rachel time and perhaps plenty of it.'

Arnold thought for a moment before answering 'I hope you're right, Matthew. I hope that's all it is, but since you told me about their differences when Lewis was kidnapped, I just trust Gavin is not taking the moral high ground here. After all that has happened, none of us can waste time on issues like that. We have all suffered enough so let's hope Gavin doesn't want to bring any more upset on either Rachel or himself. She is a beautiful, brave woman, whom many men would wish to cherish and look after. Perhaps our Gavin might need reminding of that, no matter about Rachel's memory loss.'

Later that evening, after an enjoyable dinner made by the women of the house, Julie, Emily and Matthew made their way home. As he drove back to the annexe, he made up his mind that he would visit Rachel more often and give her some other clue as to what had happened. He believed something soon must trigger some deep memory within her brain.

Chapter 53

November 1985

Lucie And Paul were very disappointed when Matthew and Julie told them they would be returning to their cottage within the next few weeks as Lynn and Jason would shortly be moving out to go to their new, beautiful home on the outskirts of Belfast with Arnold. Julie had described Arnold's new home in detail to Lucie, and how Arnold had ensured he had his own private quarters and entrance, but within a stone's throw of his son and his family. She thought it sounded wonderful and seemed the ideal solution for Arnold, who would not have that awful feeling of loneliness, which he would inevitably have if he was living alone.

But it would be the first time in years that the annexe would be empty. Her father-in-law, Tom, had been the first to occupy it and then, when he was marrying her mother, Ellen, he had moved out. On Aunt Maggie's arrival from Canada with Rachel and Lynn, they had been most appreciative of the quarters, as of course had Lynn and Jason, when they had first got married. Lastly, it had proved an ideal place for Julie after her amputation, but now, she was so very well recovered, it was only natural they would return to their cottage, rather than putting it on the market. They had loved the annexe, they told Lucie, but

Emily was now at the age when she wanted to bring some of her friends to her home and they felt that perhaps she needed more room. Besides, they had always loved their garden and Jason had spent considerable money recently by making sure the side garden was no longer in the least accessible from the side driveway. The double gates had been removed and a tall fence erected from one end of the garden to the other. Lucie, now as the conversation flowed on, was determined that the annexe of her and Paul's property would be kept alive as it had always been. It would be an ideal place for her and Paul's own two children to bring their friends, to have birthday parties in and indeed, many various celebrations could be held in it.

When Julie had first seen the property Arnold had set his heart on since that very first day he had viewed it with Matthew, she was stunned by the large proportions of all the rooms and the brightness and airiness of the whole place. The front door was beautiful with its stained glass windows at the top and the ornate pillars framing the entrance. There was also a side entrance, which Arnold told Julie, proudly, he had had this installed as his own private entrance. This entrance led into a small hall, where a door to the right, led into a bright sitting room with a marble fireplace.

A door to the left, led to a spacious bedroom and bathroom. At the back of the hall, Arnold had had a small breakfast room converted into a kitchen, with all the amenities he was likely to need. It was certainly an excellent self-contained unit, which had been created for Arnold.

The grounds outside consisted of almost two acres. Here there were two stables and a paddock, beautiful shrubs and flower beds set off the flat, green immaculate lawns. Julie and Matthew felt so blessed and so thankful to Arnold for what he was doing for Lynn and Jason after what everyone had been through. Not that it took a big, grand house to make them happy, but rather, the generosity of young Lewis's father, which gave such joy and the knowledge that he must appreciate having them in his life.

Lucie and Paul were expecting Matthew and Julie to come through from the annexe for an evening meal with them. There would just be the four of them as their children had gone to spend the night with their Uncle Charles and Aunt Sheila, something they did on occasions. Emily was staying with Lynn and Jason at the cottage. Emily had told her parents, she was going to help pack some things in preparation for their move to 'Springburn House', which was the official name for the house which was now Arnold's. Paul, home from work early, had helped set the table in the dining room and he had put out their best glasses, cutlery and napkins, insisting it was a farewell dinner for the time Matthew and Julie had spent in the annexe.

When Julie realised the trouble her sister-in-law had gone to, she protested loudly, saying it should have been Matthew and her who were doing the entertaining. They should be thanking Paul and Lucie for all the care they had given Julie after the assault and her amputation but Paul insisted they had done nothing, only offer free advice from time to time.

During the evening, it was Paul who brought up the subject of Patrick Mullan's death and asked Matthew how Mrs. Mullan, his mother, was. 'She must be so heartbroken, losing her husband in those awful circumstances, then one of her sons in such a horrible way, too. Does anyone ever see her?' he asked Matthew.

'I did call personally one day, simply to offer my condolences,' Matthew answered. 'Then I called on another occasion by appointment to see her son, Gerry. I must admit, I was rather surprised that Mrs. Mullan, Patrick's widow and daughter are still with him but it seems they intend to move back here. I suppose that is only natural, and they are no longer at any risk, I would imagine. Also, any family they have are here' Matthew continued, 'They hope to move into rented accommodation quite soon and I understand it is only a few streets away from Gerry's apartment, which will, I am sure, be of some comfort to Mrs. Mullan.'

'It seems so ironic. Don't you think, Matthew, that after moving to England to try to keep safe that Patrick's life should have been taken from him by a hit and run driver?'

'I am sorry I have to tell you, Paul – and Lucie – that we believe Patrick's death was not an accident. There is strong evidence to lead us to believe he was murdered.' Matthew had been keen to tell Lucie what was suspected about her ex-husband's death – he felt she should know – and now was an opportune moment. 'It has not been reported in an official capacity yet, Lucie. We want to keep it under wraps until we have much more evidence and can tie a few things together.'

Lucie and Paul were very upset and horrified to hear Matthew telling them of yet another murder of someone they had known well. Lucie was the first to speak. 'Really, I suppose that, deep down, I have wondered about Patrick's death. The raid on his home which resulted in the death of his father, then him and his family having to move, as you told me, on two occasions. I suppose it is quite obvious that whoever was trailing him, was not going to give up too easily.'

'I am so sorry to be the bearer of yet more bad news, but we do suspect that a crime has been committed. Confidentiality is absolutely essential, but I do know this information will be safe with you both. Now,' Matthew reached for the wine bottle and began to pour wine into the glasses sitting on the table. 'That's enough of shop talk from me – let us drink to Arnold and his future', as he steered the conversation away from the ongoing investigation in the Patrick Mullan case. It was enough that Lucie knew Patrick had been murdered, but he could not begin to even contemplate their serious lack of progress in the case and their lack of knowledge about who might be responsible. But Matthew was as determined to get justice for Patrick Mullan, as he would be for anyone who had been murdered, and he would not rest until he found out who was responsible.

Chapter 54

They had managed to trace the car. The detective in charge had rang Matthew, to tell him an elderly passer-by in the street in Hailsham, had witnessed Patrick being knocked down and, in spite of his age, had the presence of mind to take a note of the registration number of the car. The passer-by had not come to the police station for several days, it was only when he had heard the appeal on the radio and on television that he thought of the number he had written down on a meagre scrap of paper he had found in his pocket. When he had written the number down, he told the constable behind the desk in the police barracks, he had slipped it into his back pocket and then promptly forgot all about it.

The car, according to Detective Forde, had been found in Eastbourne, in a garage where it had some repairs to the body following a car accident – the garage owner had informed Detective Forde. It had been a good six weeks ago since the car had been left, and no one had ever returned for it. But the puzzle was, why had the driver not returned for his car? On more questioning, Detective Forde was able to elaborate about the damage to the car. There had been rather a large dent on the driver's side and the right headlamp had been smashed. This description of the damage to the car and the number plate tallying with that written down by the passer-by was good enough proof,

Matthew reckoned, that it was the car involved in the hit and run incident.

The name of the owner of the car was registered as being a Mr. Nigel Hanna, with an address just on the outskirts of Hailsham, but the Detective informed Matthew that when two of his men had gone to the house it was deserted and all locked up. On enquiring from a neighbour who lived nearby they were told Mr. Hanna hadn't been seen about for three or four weeks and that there had been no sign of life about the place.

As Matthew listened to Eric Forde and all the details of how they had traced the car but as yet had no idea of its owner's whereabouts, he was filled with frustration and impatience. 'What about a search warrant for the man's home? Have you applied for one?

'I was just coming to that. My men will go back tomorrow with hopefully a search warrant, and try to find any evidence of this car owner's involvement in this hit and run incident.'

'Let me know as soon as possible. I may need to reschedule my work and go over for a couple of days if you find anything at all you might feel would be of use to us here. Because I have no doubt that there is a link between Patrick Mullan's death and someone here – the death of a prisoner in gaol and the enigmatic notes he left are reasonable proof, I would have thought, Detective Forde.'

Detective Forde said that he did agree it looked that way, but Matthew sensed some reluctance in his tone of voice. Did he have doubts about it being murder even when faced with the evidence of Alfie? His prison letters and then his death. Perhaps, Matthew thought, he preferred to believe it to be a hit and run incident. That would make everything so much easier, the case could be closed and they could all move on to other cases. But Matthew, with all his old determination and vigour, was determined to get to the bottom of this mystery and who was the informant here, who had such easy access and such power over someone in England.

It was three days before Matthew heard anything more from Detective Forde, and during that time, he did his best to be patient. After all, no one knew better than he did, how painstaking, going through someone's belongings in someone else's home could be. While he waited for an update from England, he called in one particular evening to see Rachel and was glad, though still somewhat bemused, to see Gavin still visiting Rachel but seemingly under no pressure to bring her home. He asked Rachel how she was progressing regarding her memory loss, but she just shook her head sadly.

'I still can't remember much after Lewis's kidnap and I think – and I was just saying this to Gavin – I recall something about him and I having a fierce argument in our house, I think in the kitchen, about something. But I can't remember what the argument was about,' And Rachel began to get very distressed. 'I just want to know why we had words and what led to it all, but Gavin thinks it best if he doesn't tell me. The Consultant seems to think I need to recall these things myself.' Now she sounded really agitated.

'Rachel, please don't distress yourself, I am convinced it will come to you. After all, you now do remember something about a difference of words between Gavin and yourself. So that actually is progress. If you make a cup of tea I'll have a think about how we might trigger some other memory for you.' Matthew turned to Gavin. 'What do you think, Gavin?'

'To be truthful Matthew, I feel a bit lost about it all. I don't know that I agree with the Consultant to keep everything from Rachel, she's finding it so frustrating.'

Suddenly, as Matthew looked at Gavin and heard what he was saying, an idea struck him. 'Gavin, Rachel, I think if you both went round to your own house for a couple of hours and went into the kitchen, it might just trigger something, help you in some way. Would you be prepared to try this out? I think it's worth a try,'

'I believe you could be right. Surely it's bound to trigger something, Matthew. It has to be worth trying. Anything is.' Gavin smiled at Matthew, he was as anxious as anyone was, that his wife got her memory back. He wanted to know exactly what had happened during the time Rachel went missing, because he too needed to sort out the horrible thoughts and nightmares he was having, as to what had gone on during her disappearance.

When Rachel appeared with the tea and some biscuits on a tray, it was Gavin who spoke to her about Matthew's suggestion, which pleased Matthew, as he was really beginning to wonder when Gavin might think of taking his wife home, and this idea was at least a step in the right direction.

'Oh, Gavin, that would be so lovely, even if it's only for an hour or two. 'Just to see my lovely house again, my lovely kitchen. I remember it all so well but absolutely nothing of what we quarrelled about.'

'Right, that's settled then, Rachel. We'll go early tomorrow evening and spend a little time there. It's getting too late now to think about it. Anyway, you have made such a lovely cup of tea and by the time we have it, it will definitely be too late.'

Rachel sounded so happy when she answered Gavin, that the two men were left in no doubt that Rachel was looking forward so much to seeing her own home, and Matthew hoped that her happiness was not lost on Gavin. Rachel Finlay needed to go home – there was no doubt in Matthew's mind about that, memory loss or no memory loss. Now, she spoke very earnestly to Gavin. 'I'll be ready and waiting for you, love. Can you come here about six o'clock?'

'Of course I can.' Gavin answered. 'Six o'clock it is then. But let's enjoy our tea and biscuits, and Matthew – thanks so much for your suggestion.'

'That's all it is, Gavin – and Rachel – so please, don't get your hopes up too much. Your visit may come to nothing, so do please be prepared for anything.' Matthew realised that Rachel, and Gavin also, may now have pinned their hopes on his idea being the trigger that Rachel needed. The last thing he wanted to see was Rachel being disappointed yet one more time. After he had finished his cup of tea, he wished them both the very best on the next evening, and asked them to let him know if there were any developments. He did tell them that he would possibly not be around for a couple of days, as he was investigating Patrick Mullan's death and might have to go to England. Although Rachel had never known Patrick Mullan – Lucie's ex-husband – as Lucie was married to Paul when Rachel came from Canada, but she had heard of his involvement in Rob's murder. She was now able to fill Gavin in as to who this Patrick Mullan was, although Gavin had heard snippets over time from his Uncle John who had been married to Rob's sister. He had heard of Patrick's death in the last couple of days, but had understood it to be a hit and run incident, but now Matthew was speaking of ongoing investigations into his death and it all sounded very suspicious to Gavin.

It was three days before Matthew heard anything more from Detective Forde and he was beginning to become exasperated and knew he was on the verge of criticising the English Police Force, which was something Matthew tried to make a point of never doing – criticising other police units. So, he was relieved when the Detective did ring to bring him up to date with how the investigations were going and what they had discovered so far in the house on the edge of Hailsham village. They had found a couple of diaries with some phone numbers in them, which may or may not be relevant to the case. There were also several photographs of Patrick Mullan, still in the padded envelopes postmarked Belfast, so there didn't seem to be much doubt that they had been sent from there. Detective Forde said all this in the same monotone voice Matthew had been aware of the first time he spoke to him. Was this just his 'phone voice' when he spoke to anyone over the telephone, or was it a reflection of his lack of interest in the case? Did he just want it all closed up – over and done with, a simple hit and run incident? After all, Patrick Mullan had been from Ireland, so what had brought him to England to be knocked down by a car and killed? Of course, the Detective had not voiced any of this over the telephone but Matthew was sorely tempted to ask him if this was how he really felt, but then his professionalism came to the fore and instead he simply said. 'I'll book a flight out to Gatwick first thing tomorrow morning. I'll let you know later, Detective, what time to expect my arrival. Would someone be available to pick me up from there or shall I just take a taxi? '

Suddenly, it seemed to Matthew, the Detective's voice held slightly more enthusiasm. Perhaps he had realised himself, he was showing a distinct lack of interest in this case. Or perhaps, he would be more professional now that he knew another Detective Inspector would be coming to help with this investigation. 'Certainly, Detective Hampton, I'll arrange to have you collected at Gatwick airport, just let me know which flight you are on and your expected time of arrival.'

With an acknowledgement that he would do so and a 'Thank you', Matthew replaced the receiver, quite intrigued by this investigation, and found he was looking forward to

253

going over to see if there was anything significant in the house that was being searched, and also to meet the Detective in charge of the investigation.

Chapter 55

Rachel was looking forward to going to her own home – it seemed so very long ago since she had been there. She was looking forward even more, she knew, to the drive to it with Gavin and then going in and seeing again all the renovations they had made to the place with such energy and pride, and how pleased and thrilled they had both been with the results. Now, as she stood in the living room of the nursing home waiting for Gavin, she felt so thwarted by her lack of memory over recent events, yet she could recall so much and in such vivid detail of those first halcyon wonderful days with Gavin after their marriage. Why, oh why could she remember so much from those days five years ago, but could remember nothing about more recent events? Events which had changed not only her body, but her whole life and that of Arnold Simpson, who had lost Iris in the incident she so desperately sought to remember but could not. She would have thought such ordeals would have been engraved in her heart and mind forever. But according to her consultant, things in life were just not as simple as that; the more traumatic and meaningful an incident in one's life might be, the more likely it was to be dampened down and relegated to the recesses of one's mind. He also had explained that it would be best if she remembered spontaneously herself, rather than anyone trying to fill it all in for her, it would be so much less traumatic. So when such explanations had been expounded to her, Rachel felt she had no choice only to accept it. Sometimes, she felt it did not matter if she never did remember being shot or Iris being killed, in fact, perhaps it would be better if she never did. But then, there was Gavin and for his sake, she knew she needed to remember because something in those dark days had happened to change him and she owed it to him and indeed to herself, to try to establish what exactly had happened to cause him such distress and even she felt, to alter his love for her.

For the moment, she must try not to worry about their relationship and contain her thoughts about her memory loss and how Gavin might feel about her. Now she had heard his foot on the stairs and as he opened the door into her quarters, he smiled broadly at her and said 'Your carriage awaits you, Rachel' and Rachel was instantly reassured that all was going to be well between them and so she replied light heartedly, 'Thank you, Sir.' And taking his arm, they both exited the home, explaining to Uncle John on the way out that they would be gone for a couple of hours. John watching them depart, hoped that soon, very soon, the pair would be on their way home together for good. He had no idea why Rachel had not yet gone back to her own home, instead of whiling away the hours here, waiting for visitors and looking out of her window, so obviously deep in thought.

At first glance, the kitchen seemed alien and strange to Rachel, then, as she stood there, she recognised the plain cream tiles on the walls, interspersed here and there with a patterned one of a hen, a cow, a pig and she remembered the fun Gavin and she had in selecting them. These particular tiles had always made Rachel smile and she did so now, as she began to recognise her kitchen, possibly her most favourite room in the house. Now, she turned towards Gavin and smiled openly and hopefully at him. 'I have no problem remembering any of this, love. No problem at all.

And it is just as lovely now as it was then.' Rachel went on. 'I would love a cup of coffee. Would you mind putting the kettle on for me, Gavin? I'll have a seat here and enjoy just the reality of being here, in my own kitchen.'

Gavin was inordinately pleased that Rachel remembered their kitchen so well, that fact alone was promising for the future, and her praise for how lovely everything looked flattered him immensely. He had worked hard all afternoon, having taken time out from his latest building project to come home and give everywhere another clean up. 'That's a good idea, Rachel. I would love a cup myself, so I will indeed put the kettle on.'

It was only when Gavin was turning back from the kettle after filling the two cups which were sitting there on the kitchen shelf, that Rachel recalled their raised voices to each other all those weeks ago, and as she began to remember, word for word, their conversation and the likelihood of who she might meet up with if she persisted in what she was thinking of doing, and the implications of what Gavin had said in response to what she had just told him she would like to do to help find Lewis. She knew and remembered very well why Gavin was keeping her at arm's length. Why he was so reticent about bringing her home from the nursing home. Now she must tell him what she could remember.

'I have just remembered our conversation, Gavin. I remember telling you how desperately I needed to find Lewis. I did emphasize he was my grandson, I remember that. I recall you telling me how you would feel if I were to go street walking but I did stress to you and very emphatically too, that I never would have sex with any other man. I remember all that so vividly now, today, and I know you said I would be of no match for some hulk of a man who I might meet up with, and the fact that I did end up in Intensive Care does mean I must not have been able to cope. But I'm afraid I don't remember much else, only our conversation here, then you going up the stairs and then, the sound of you going out the front door.' Rachel paused now, the tears streaming down her face, and she had to wipe them away before she could continue. 'I recall sitting here for a long time, thinking of you, thinking of my grandson and I think I decided I had to ring someone. It was Matthew I rang, I do remember talking to him about some directions or other. I think I ended up telling him I would do all I could to help, I think I did.' Now Rachel looked beseechingly at Gavin. 'Would you mind taking me back to the home, I need to go back. I must go back and see mum before she goes to bed, I need to talk to her.'

'Yes, Rachel, we'll go back now.' And Gavin lifted the coffee cups from the table, the coffee having gone cold in them, and set them in the sink. Now, Gavin felt very saddened for Rachel and what she was going through. He also felt weighed down with guilt for how he felt for what she had done. But she had brought such needless unhappiness to them both by her attitude and by her behaviour and at present, he felt he was not ready to overlook any of it. He believed Matthew Hampton could have engaged someone else to do what Rachel had done, and probably, whoever it had been, they could equally have negotiated Lewis's release.

Just the same, because of his guilt, he helped dry Rachel's tears and then encouraged her to splash her face with cold water from the tap at the sink and dry herself with a towel from the nearby drainer. Taking her arm, he locked the house, then they made their way back to the car and then on to the nursing home. On arrival at the home and on Rachel's instructions, Gavin did not take her upstairs to her quarters, but took her to her mother's room where they found Maggie sitting contentedly, a book in her hand, and a cup of tea on the table beside her. On seeing her daughter, still so waif like in her appearance but so precious to her after all she had been through, her face lit up and she immediately rose to her feet and offered her and Gavin some tea and biscuits.

'I'm just leaving Rachel off.' Gavin explained hastily, anxious to avoid any questions from his mother-in-law. 'But I'm sure Rachel could do with a cuppa. I'll seek out Uncle John on my way out and tell him to bring Rachel some tea – it will save you making it, Maggie.' And with that, Gavin hugged Rachel, lightly kissed her and his mother-in-law, before bidding them good night with promises to be back to visit Rachel as usual the next evening.

Rachel dreaded going to bed that evening, which was most unusual because since she had come to the home she looked forward to bedtime because she always felt so tired. But tonight, she seemed so alert and wakeful. She had sat with her mother for some time and had confided her concern about Gavin's attitude to her and his distant manner. She told her mother she now remembered the disagreement they had had in their kitchen and Gavin distinctly telling her he could not accept what she was contemplating doing. She recalled it might have had something to do with her thinking of going street walking; something she found hard to believe or that she would even consider. But then, she began to realise it was something to do with Lewis and that she might be able to help him. She also remembered ringing Matthew and him telling her something about a street and a shop. Throughout Rachel relating all this to her mother, she was in floods of tears and had to stop several times to compose herself.

'I'm going to fetch Uncle John, he'll know what to do about Gavin, I know he will, love.' Maggie herself was at a loss as to how to deal with Rachel or console her because she herself had been told so little about Rachel's initial disappearance. She had simply been told that Rachel had disappeared while looking for Lewis. So what was Gavin making such a big deal about then? He ought to be so glad that Rachel was making such a wonderful, if slow, recovery, in spite of her frail appearance. There must be something else about Rachel's disappearance that she did not know about, but if anyone would know, John Finlay would. She knew that Matthew Hampton confided most things in John, indeed a lot of people confided a lot of things in him. So, with this thought in mind, Maggie rang down for John, who very promptly arrived in her room and greeted the two women warmly, choosing to turn a blind eye, for the moment, that Rachel was upset.

It was when Maggie told him where Rachel and Gavin had been, although he already knew that, and what she was now able to remember, that John went to her and holding her closely said in a firm voice,

'Gavin's a fool here, Rachel, Maggie. But perhaps I'm being a bit too hard on him when I say that and he probably feels he has very good reason to be acting as he is.'

'Uncle John.' Rachel's voice sounded firm and quite demanding, 'I want you to tell me, here and now, what I did after I rang Matthew. That is, if you know. I am sick of this.'

'Oh, we can't tell you Rachel, you have to wait and see.'

'Nobody is prepared to tell me anything. I just can't take it any more.' Rachel now sounded quite hysterical.

And John Finlay, remembered so well how his niece, now in such a troubled state, had helped him through his son's murder and his other son's wrongful arrest. Not only that, but she was the one who the murderer finally confessed to. Now, as he sat with her, trying his best to console her, rightly or wrongly, he decided to tell her all he knew.

After Rachel had retired to her own quarters for the night, having reassured both Maggie and John that she was most appreciative of what John had told her and she believed that much more of what had happened was now coming back to her, John decided he needed to let Matthew know of the developments with Rachel. He told Matthew she had remembered her argument with Gavin, and John said he had confirmed she had gone street walking and somehow ended up in the same house as Lewis. He was, he told Matthew, able to tell her about the shooting in the forest, but he did not know anything about her time with the kidnapper, only that it was thanks to her, Lewis had been released.

'I did say, Matthew, you would be able to tell her about those two days she spent alone with the abductor. I assured her you had interviewed the captor at length in hospital and knew all about it.'

Matthew had listened carefully to what John was telling him. He was quite relieved to hear that Rachel had been told the facts, at least, of her ordeal, and with assurances to John that he would call round the next evening to see Rachel, he rang off.

Much later, during that same night, Rachel had to receive some sedation, such were the night terrors and nightmares she was having, and a senior nurse sat with her throughout the remainder of the night.

Chapter 56

Matthew had risen early, his taxi which would take him to the airport would be here in approximately fifteen minutes and he had showered and dressed as quickly as possible in order not to wake Julie or Emily. It was only six a.m., much too early for either of them to be up and about. His flight to Gatwick was at 7.15.a.m. so he needed to be heading off soon in order to catch it. Now, before his taxi arrived, he made himself a strong cup of coffee; he felt he might need it in order to keep him awake. He had had quite a disturbed night's sleep and he knew it was partly due to Uncle John's phone call late last night, telling him that Rachel had come back from her own home in quite a distressed state and had begged John to tell her anything he knew about what had happened to her. And he wanted Matthew to know that he had done just that, believing then it was the right thing to do and still believing it was. The truth was that Matthew felt so very guilty for ever having involved Rachel in the whole mess, and he wondered if she was ever going to recover. It was his fault, he should have tried to get someone else to do some street walking – no doubt he would have soon found someone to do it.

Now, as he boarded the plane, he tried to put all thoughts of Rachel out of his mind, he needed to concentrate on the day ahead of him and what, if anything, he might discover about Patrick Mullan's killer. But still, his mind kept wandering back to Rachel, wondering how she would cope with the knowledge she now had, and would that knowledge ultimately help her remember anything else about her horrific ordeal?

The plane taxied on to the runway, before Matthew found he could actually begin to concentrate on the day ahead and the fact that Detective Forde's men had found some evidence in a house on the outskirts of Hailsham to link the driver of the car, which had killed Patrick. So, perhaps they might be getting somewhere in the case, he did hope they would find some concrete evidence because anything found in Alfie Reid's – the dead prisoner's house, had been pretty useless.

On arrival at the airport, as he only had his briefcase with him and no other baggage to wait for, he was able to make his way through, directly to the arrivals area of the airport. He was pleased and relieved to see two young, very presentable looking men, standing watching, one of whom was holding a placard with Matthew's name written on it. He quickly approached them and extended his hand in greeting. Each of the men in turn shook his hand and introduced themselves by their first name only. The taller, broader one of the two, said his name was Stephen, the younger looking one introduced himself as Barry, then said. 'If you're Matthew, just let's head out of here, we have the car parked in a short stay car park across from the front entrance of the airport.'

'Good, that's fine. I have just my briefcase with me, nothing else and I'm booked for the seven o'clock flight back to Belfast tonight. So I'm looking forward to my day here.' And Matthew fell into step with the two young men, who seemed to him to be consummate professionals, certainly their appearance and manners indicated this. Although they were dressed quite casually in light coloured trousers and blazers, their clothes spoke volumes about style and expense and Matthew was impressed. He had not really been looking forward to coming over to England today, suspecting a real lack of interest in the Patrick Mullan case, this suspicion brought about, he knew, by Detective Forde's monotonous voice and his reticence in telling Matthew anything much. These two men however, as they drove away from the airport and on to the wide roads which would eventually take them to Hailsham, showed an avid interest in Matthew's work over in Northern Ireland and were keen to show Matthew what they had discovered on arrival at this house they were searching, where the car involved in the hit and run had been traced to.

'Yes, that's Patrick Mullan alright. I have no doubt about that. You see, Patrick was my ex-brother-in-law.' The two police officers had brought Matthew directly to the house, where they were conducting their search, in an effort to acquire some evidence. It had been a beautiful house at one time, Matthew thought, as Stephen drove the car into the driveway, but now it had a neglected air about it. It had been built in Tudor style with its wooden eaves and shutters but now, the wood just looked weary and sad, with some of its structures crumbling and large patches of paint missing or flaking off. Inside the house, although it too looked tired, attempts had been made to make it comfortable. The police in charge of the case had set up their investigation unit in the large sitting room which faced east and caught the sun for most of the day.

'Yes, Matthew, I know he was related to you, I was first informed when Patrick and his wife and daughter came here to live. I was told all about his prison sentence and what he had done. So, yes, I did know he was your brother-in-law. So far, we have only found the photographs you have in your hand and they were still in the envelope they were posted in.' And Detective Forde reached Matthew the envelope, which had quite clearly a post mark stamped, Belfast. The envelope had been addressed to Mr. Nigel

Hanna of Glen Road, Hailsham – an address, which had been printed very precisely and meticulously, Matthew noted. The letters were so uniform and neat, it was obvious the addressee was determined not to give anything away, when addressing the envelope.

'I'd like to take these back with me – I would need to take them back.' Matthew addressed the Detective directly. 'I'll try to trace the studio the photographs were taken in and when they were taken. I believe them to be within the last three to four years – after he was released from prison. So someone had access to them and then sent them to our Mr. Hanna. I would like to try and trace whoever sent them, that is if you are in agreement that I take them back.'

'Matthew, let's do away with all the formalities, it's better all round. So please call me Michael – and of course, you must take the photographs as they must have originated in Northern Ireland. I don't relish your task, I really don't, but let's take a break for coffee and then we'll see what else, if anything we can turn up.'

Matthew agreed readily to drinking coffee and realised that Michael Forde was a most pleasant chap and very keen to help, and he felt bad now about misjudging him. It was further proof to him, how people's telephone voices can be so misleading. Over coffee, they went through some letters, postcards, receipts and slips of paper, which the two constables who were involved in the search brought to Michael Forde's desk. But the task seemed insurmountable – Nigel Hanna must never have thrown anything out which he thought he might need in the future. The policemen produced information from every cupboard, every drawer and the pockets of any clothes they found and it was the very boredom and 'sameness' of the task that made Matthew realise that something could be so easily overlooked. So, although he was determined to be meticulous and painstaking, the hands of the clock wore on and all of them realised it was impossible to complete this in one day.

'I don't know what I was thinking of, I should have stayed overnight instead of flying home this evening,' Matthew was disappointed at the box of papers sitting on the desk, still unseen by either Michael or him.

So, his investigation must be put on hold, in the meantime they should concentrate on trying to find Nigel Hanna and he felt that might be easier than finding out who sent the photographs. There were loads of photographs of Nigel Hanna over the house and their next step must be to have these circulated in the newspapers and the media, with the appropriate appeals. As he discussed this part of the investigation, Michael readily agreed with him and assured him that Mr. Hanna's likeness would be in the next evening's papers and also on television.

'Now, Matthew, if you have any room in your briefcase, you could take some of the letters, scraps of paper and postcards with you and see if you come up with anything.'

'A good idea, I should be able to take quite a few as I have very little in my briefcase and I'll let you know if I discover anything and you can do the same, Michael, with what I leave on your desk.'

Just around about four-thirty, Matthew began to gather up all he meant to take home, to scrutinize when he had time. He realised he was really hungry now, as he had only had one small sandwich for lunch, anxious not to waste much time. Now Michael Forde was speaking to him. 'There's a small pub just across the road, Matthew, and it serves great food. Would you like to join Stephen, Barry and myself for something to eat in it?'

'I would love that, Michael.' Matthew thought the idea of eating in a quaint English pub just a wonderful idea, more especially at this time of year, when the log fires would be burning and possibly some Christmas decorations would already be in place. He had always loved the eating places in England, even though it had only been on rare occasions when he would have been in one, when he was on holiday with his parents all those years ago. 'If you give me five minutes, I'll just ring my wife, Julie and tell her not to keep me anything.' And in spite of the rather frustrating day they had all had, it was four, optimistic men who made their way across the road to the Stag's Head.

Chapter 57

It was almost half past ten that evening when the taxi left Matthew at the annexe and he felt exhausted when he entered the living room. But when Julie came to greet him and threw her arms round him, kissing him passionately, his tiredness evaporated and he kissed her back with equal ardour.

'I was just in the process of making myself a nightcap of some warm milk, Matthew, by the look of you, you could do with something as well. I'll go and make a hot whiskey for you. I'm sure after the day you've had, you need something which might help to relax you.'

'Thanks, darling, that would be very nice. Were there any messages for me?' Matthew asked, as he made his way into the bedroom. 'I'll just put my briefcase into the drawer in my desk and I suppose I better lock it until tomorrow. No more work to-night.'

'Uncle John rang to say that Rachel had been very distressed over things she now remembers, but John insisted he had stayed with her most of the night and that she was fine now. But he did say, if you could spare a short time out of your day tomorrow, he would appreciate it.'

'Julie, hopefully it is all good news about Rachel. I'm really glad John told her what he did because I know it was causing her great unhappiness and I do believe Gavin was suffering too. Do you think I ought to ring John?'

'Matthew, he was most insistent that you did not, he wanted you to leave it until tomorrow. So come on, love, sit down, and I'll bring in the nightcaps.'

'Where's our Emily, by the way?'

'She actually went to bed early tonight, the school are involved in a hockey competition with Claremont High School – you know the school Charles and Thomas's girls are at. So tomorrow should be interesting. Emily said she needed to have plenty of rest, because her school are keen to beat the defending champions.'

'Well, I hope Methodist College does well, Emily deserves it, she can play wonderful hockey, as you know, Julie.'

'I know she can and Lucie is coming tomorrow and we are meeting up with Sheila and Jenny and then going for lunch, no matter who wins. My sisters-in-law will be cheering on their daughters and I'll be cheering on mine, so it should be good fun.'

'I'm just so sorry I don't seem to be able to go to many of Emily's school activities these days.' Matthew sounded quite down about it.

'I knew you would be up to your eyes when you came back from England and sure as long as one of us is there to support her, that's what matters. And Emily understands how it is with your job, Matthew, she's very good.'

'I am well and truly bogged down at the minute and I do need to go and see Uncle John and Rachel at some stage tomorrow. So as long as you don't mind, love.'

'I'm fine, Matthew, about it all. Now, let's have that nightcap please.'

Julie rose early the next morning with the intention of making her husband a hearty breakfast. He had told her last evening about the lovely steak and ale pie he'd had with the other chaps from police headquarters, and she decided she would show him that she too could cook well. So she prepared a huge omelette with a filling of cheese, tomato, ham and mushrooms in it. Then, she went to their bedroom and told him firmly that breakfast was ready and he must come at once. Obediently, Matthew climbed out of bed and slipped on his dressing gown and slippers and joined Julie in the kitchen. On seeing the steaming omelette on the plate and the cup of coffee beside it, Matthew was delighted.

'My favourite meal, darling, but what's the occasion? I was only away for one day, you know.'

'Well, the truth is, you raved so much about the Stag's Head food that I felt I needed to show you how well I can actually cook when I put my mind to it.'

In response, Matthew grabbed her tightly and swung her round the kitchen before sitting down to enjoy his breakfast, and watching him, Julie felt blessed that their marriage now was stronger than ever. They had been through so much, such terrible trauma, but had come out the other side and were once again a close knit family and she believed that nothing could come between them ever again, Their ability to talk freely to one another, their love-making in spite of Julie's prosthesis and amputation, was always a wonderful experience for both of them. And to complete their happiness, their grandson was safe and his other grandmother, Rachel, was well on the way to recovery. They had all suffered but hopefully now, they could all put the past behind them and look forward to the future.

When Lucie and Julie entered the spectators' area to watch the schools' hockey match, they were delighted to see Sheila and Jenny already there, and so too, was Charles and Thomas.

'My goodness, it's a treat to see the men here, you don't often find the time. So what's different about today?'

'Evelyn told me it was an all-important match for her.' Charles answered. 'So I did feel I could spare a couple of hours out of my day to cheer her on.'

'Same here,' Thomas remarked. 'Jayne tells me this will likely be her last year to play, so I felt I ought to come, and once I knew Charles felt the same way, I was on my way.'

'What about Matthew, I suppose he has a lot on one way or another, and the chances of him finding any spare time in his day is unlikely, especially at the moment. I mean with that prisoner's death and everything.'

'Yes, indeed. Now let's go and look for good seats, so that we can watch the match properly.'

Julie was anxious to avoid any further conversation about Matthew, with Lucie being present, any talk about her ex-husband's death would be, Julie felt, quite distasteful, and besides in such an open place, no one knew who could overhear anyone's conversation. So Julie would not be encouraging any talk about Matthew and his work.

Between them all, they soon discovered good seats and were able to cheer on their perspective schools more or less uninterrupted. Methodist College girls did their very best, but they were no match for Claremont, who carried off the cup for yet another time. But as the girls all tripped off the field where they had been playing, it was obvious there was no animosity whatsoever between them. Emily was just as close to her cousins as she had always been, that much was obvious, she had her arms round Evelyn as they walked along. They all joined up with their parents and it was Jayne who declared that she was starving and could they go for lunch straight away. Everyone agreed very readily as secretly they too were hungry after watching such an exciting match and they all agreed to meet up in about twenty minutes in Isobel's cafe on the Lisburn Road.

'It is hard to believe we are all here having lunch and actually enjoying ourselves. I must admit there were many, many times during these last weeks when I thought I would never know what it would be like to enjoy myself ever again.' It was Sheila, Charles' wife who spoke when they were relaxed and waiting for the meal they had ordered. 'As for what you've been through, Julie, well, you are truly wonderful. No one would ever suspect you had ever been through anything. You are so lithe and supple. You just look great.'

'Well, Sheila, I know I'm very fortunate to be able to manage so well, but in those dark, early days I don't know what I would have done without Jenny and your support. As for you, Lucie, your knowledge and compassion made everything so much easier, and none of you wavered when Lewis and then Rachel disappeared. It all proved to me, the close knit family we really are, and if I can help any of you in any way, just remember I am very fit to do so and would love to do so. But I must not forget Matthew's role in my recovery, he was just marvellous throughout everything, in spite of his work load.'

'Well, as a close knit member of the family as you say, and as his brother, Julie, I think Matthew works too hard and perhaps he should think of taking it easy for a while, let someone else take over. He seems to me to be just dedicated to his job.' Charles spoke very earnestly.

'I know,' Julie answered, but she was relieved to see the food arriving. She did not know who could coax Matthew to take it easy because she knew she couldn't, nor did she want to. He seemed very happy in his work and that was important. Then she added. 'Let us get tucked in, I see the girls at the other table are enjoying it, by the looks of things.'

Matthew had decided to go and see John and Rachel before he went near the office because he knew that if he went there first, he might have trouble getting away to go and see anybody. Besides, he was curious to know all about what had transpired with Rachel the previous evening. He was surprised to see John looking more sober than he normally did. His uncle was a man who always seemed to be ready to give support to anyone who might need it but this morning he looked like someone who needed some support himself.

He was in the nursing home office when Matthew sought him out, going through some papers in a disinterested way. That in itself was most unusual for the man who would normally at this time of day – or so Matthew had always understood from Rachel – be bustling about, sorting out laundry or supervising bed linen and getting the patients up and about.

'Good morning, John. You've had a tough night, I see.' Matthew had decided to be direct with his Uncle, he needed to know all that had happened with Rachel.

'Does it show that much, Matthew?' and John suddenly seemed to brighten when he saw his nephew. He got up from his seat and threw his arms round his shoulders. 'It's good to see you, I'm glad you're here.' Then John, remembering his manners, remarked. 'I'll organise some coffee before I begin to tell you anything. We'll go to my bedroom, it's more private there and we are less likely to be interrupted. In here in the mornings, there are laundrymen, there are men delivering food and other items and everything must be signed for. So we'd get no peace, I'll organise the coffee to my room. So let's go, Matthew.'

Later, over coffee, John related the previous night's events to Matthew. How he had felt so compelled to tell

Rachel what he knew about her ordeal. At this point, he stressed to Matthew that in spite of how distraught Rachel became, he did not regret telling her.

'I believe I did the right thing, Matthew, Rachel was becoming quite desperate and I felt that her not knowing was having a much more detrimental effect on her than knowing the truth of what had actually happened.'

'John, if it's any consolation to you, I was fast coming to the same conclusion myself. I could see Rachel was becoming more and more frustrated and resentful at times, that we all probably knew what she had endured and she didn't.

'Well, she seems to know the most of what happened to her now. After I told her what I knew, she hugged and thanked me for telling her. She said she appreciated it so much and she believed she would now start to remember some things on her own accord. Then, she said good night to her mother and I, then went to her room. I am sorry to have to tell you that during the night she had dreadful night terrors. She told me, after she had had some sedation and was a lot calmer, that she could now remember her captor, all about him, going to his house and finding Lewis there, then negotiating with him to obtain Lewis's relief. She knew he had never touched her because on two different occasions he was contemplating it, he was disturbed by two callers. It was after the second visitor had left, that he told her he now had a gun. She told John, that was when real fear gripped her and she realised that now that he was armed, he could change everything. Then, when he took her to the lock up shed – she did not know where – she began to feel so ill that she thought she could not possibly survive. The drive to the forest seems to be a bit of a blur to her, Matthew, as she says she just recalls seeing Iris running towards her and then falling. She then felt an agonising pain in her chest and her abdomen and she remembers nothing after that, until she wakes up in hospital and sees

Gavin sitting there. And the strange thing, the memory of Gavin sitting beside her seems to distress her every bit as much as the terrifying ones do.'

'And how is she this morning, John?'

'She woke briefly and drank some tea, then said she just wanted to sleep. But of course, that's because the sedation is still in her system. I have someone staying in the room with her, in case she gets distressed again.'

'I think it best then, if I don't go to see her this morning, John. Would that be your advice?' Matthew asked his Uncle, unsure how he could actually be of any help to Rachel at present.

'I agree with you, most definitely, Matthew. She needs rest and she needs time to come to terms with everything and to digest it all. I'll tell her you called to see her and if she says she wants to see you and talk to you, I'll be in touch.' John replied.

Chapter 58

'I have gone over everything I remember about my ordeal, Gavin. I have told you everything as I now remember it, some of which I told you last evening in our own home. Although I am quite prepared that I might have some nightmares and night terrors for some time to come, I am just so thankful that I now remember it all, and I find it incredible that I am still here to tell the tale, I feel very blessed indeed. Sadly, poor Iris was not so fortunate and was killed by that man.'

Rachel paused and looked at her husband who seemed to her, to be almost in a fixed state of shock as he listened to her.

'The Consultant was here this morning and he brought a Psychiatrist along to see me. The Psychiatrist says he will talk to me any time I wish but he thinks that as long as I am surrounded by my family and loved ones, that eventually, I will be able to accept all that has happened, Gavin,' Rachel's voice held am imploring note. 'I am so glad, that monster did not lay a finger on me at any time, and it is important to me that you believe that, Gavin. He did intend to, but the messengers coming to tell him the police were on his tail, changed all that. Towards the end he just wanted rid of me, he did not violate me, he was thwarted from doing so by his friends. Please believe me, Gavin.'

'I do believe you, that is not where any resentment I have lies.' Gavin said, and Rachel was glad to see that some of the shocked, horrified appearance had left him, but before she could reply to this rather puzzling statement from her husband, the door to her apartment opened and Matthew and Arnold's heads appeared round it.

'Is it all right if we come in Rachel? Oh, hello, Gavin. We didn't know you were here, John did not say.' Matthew hesitated from coming any further into the room as he spoke. 'Oh Matthew, and Arnold, I'm so glad to see you.' and inexplicably Rachel's voice broke and her eyes filled with tears. 'Sorry' she added, as she indicated to them to sit down. 'I think the sedation I had last night is still affecting me, so please excuse me.'

'How are you, Rachel?' It was Arnold who asked. 'I'm sure you must be quite relieved to know everything about what you went through, is that not so.'

'Yes, Arnold, I really am. I do believe I'll be able to cope with the knowing rather than the frustration of trying to push my brain to remember.'

'Look, I'll leave you for now, Rachel.' Gavin had risen to his feet. 'You have Arnold and Matthew for company and I need to go and see about a few orders I am expecting to arrive. I'll call back later.' Gavin with a nod and a smile to the two men, left Rachel's living room quietly.

Matthew and Arnold spent some time with Rachel in her apartment, with Arnold insisting he would make the tea if Matthew would carry it in for him and they would enjoy the cream buns Arnold had bought on his way here

Rachel seemed to want to talk about everything she now remembered and the two men let her talk, and she was able to confirm so much at what had happened with Matthew's interviews with her abductor. The man had been brutally honest in telling Matthew how, initially, he had wanted to take the woman to his bed, but it had never

277

materialised, besides, Matthew had not doubted that Jimmy Devlin was telling him the truth. Indeed, Matthew would have thought it more likely that it would have tried to boast that he'd had sex with her. But there again, perhaps he had thought that by sticking to the truth it would help his case, something which Matthew knew was most unlikely.

'I would really like to go home, you know.' Rachel sounded wistful. 'But Gavin says that the Consultant says I'll have nightmares for a time and because I need sedation for another week or so, Gavin thinks I would be better to stay. I also need someone to stay with me.'

'Stay put for another day or so, Rachel, and then we'll have someone assess how you are. Also, you have easier access to sedation here and there are also trained nurses to help you.' Matthew's voice was warm and sincere. 'Julie says to tell you that Lucie and she will be here tomorrow. You might have Sheila and Jenny as well she says. So you'll have plenty of company, Rachel, and after what you've been through, another couple of days will be nothing to you.'

Rachel visibly brightened. 'I'll look forward to seeing all the girls.' She said, 'and Lynn is calling round later and she says she can't wait to get me home to my own home. She says she will look after me and she means to have a word with my doctor.' But Rachel did not refer to Gavin again and how he obviously felt that she ought to stay, and neither of the two men mentioned him again.

Later, after they had left Rachel and Matthew was driving Arnold back to Lynn and Jason's place, Arnold brought up the subject of Gavin.

'I'm not sure where Gavin's workplace is Matthew, but if it is fairly accessible, I might pop round to see him in the next day or so.'

Matthew was surprised to hear this. 'Gavin's building works are just off the Ormeau Road. It's about a couple of miles. I can give you directions but if you want to talk to him, as I suspect you do, you'll get him in his own home around six o'clock any evening, Arnold, and his house is just off the Belmont Road. It's not far.'

'Yes, I would really like to talk to him. I think we have all overlooked what Gavin has been going through in all this, and I think the man's in turmoil – very mixed up.' Arnold frowned now, 'I might do more harm than good by going to see him and trying to talk to him, but I would like to remind him that I have lost my wife in all this and he still has his. I do think it's worth a shot to have a word or two with him.'

'I think you are a gem, Arnold, and I do believe you are right. We all just left Gavin to get on with it and suffer, although at the same time, Rachel was the one who suffered so much.'

'I know that, Matthew, and I agree wholeheartedly, but I still would like to have a word with him. I'll take a drive over at the time you suggest, perhaps tomorrow evening, and I'll let you know how I get on. Do you want to come in for coffee?' Arnold asked, as Matthew drew his car to a halt outside the cottage.

'No, thank you, Arnold. I really must get back to the office, but give Lynn and them all my love and do let me know how you get on with Gavin.'

'I'll do that, Matthew, and thanks for taking me to see Rachel.'

On the third evening after Arnold and Matthew had visited Rachel, Matthew had just finished his evening meal with Julie and Emily when the telephone rang and when he answered it, he was really surprised to hear Rachel's voice on the other end. It was the first time she had rang him since the kidnap of their grandson and now her voice sounded joyful and happy.

'Matthew.' she began, 'I wanted to let you know that I am going home tomorrow. Gavin is coming in for me around lunch time.' Now she sounded quite breathless. 'Isn't it wonderful? Gavin went and spoke to the doctor and said that he would take charge of my sedation and he would be there at night all the time. Gavin says he never wants me out of his sight again, not ever. He says he means to look after me in every way. He says I deserve it after everything I have been through.' Rachel paused for another breath and then rushed on. 'I thought he didn't want me anymore. Perhaps you never noticed, Matthew, but he was very distant with me at times, but he is just wonderful now. I wanted you to know that everything is so good and I wanted to thank you for everything you've done. I do believe it was your suggestion that Gavin and I went home for that couple of hours, which helped us both, so thank you again.'

Matthew could have said, only for his looking for someone to do a bit of street walking, you would never have been in trouble in the first place but he only said. 'I'm so glad for you, Rachel, I am sure you will go on now in leaps and bounds when you go back home.' And after promises to be in touch, they said their goodbyes. Matthew had purposely avoided replying directly to Rachel's praises for his suggestion and her conviction that that was what had led to the change in Gavin's attitude and behaviour.

After replacing the telephone in its cradle and re-joining Julie and Emily, he related to his wife this latest information. Julie was delighted to hear that Rachel was now going home to her own house and told Matthew she would leave it for a couple of days before ringing her. Matthew agreed with her in an absent minded way, in truth his mind was racing and he thought back to that evening when Arnold had told him he intended to call with Gavin and have a chat. Arnold had promised to contact Matthew and tell him if anything worthwhile had transpired but he had heard nothing from him. So now, he was determined to contact Arnold and he went straight out to the hall again and dialled Jason's number. It was Lynn who answered and after a chat with her father-in-law she went to fetch Arnold.

'Matthew, I was just going to ring you, but you have forestalled me here.' Arnold sounded his usual calm self.

Without preamble, Matthew said. 'What on earth did you say to Gavin? I'd really like to know because whatever it was, I believe it must have worked, because Rachel tells me she is going home tomorrow. So what did you say, man?'

'Oh, is Rachel going home? That's lovely.' Arnold replied. 'Gavin and I just had a little chat about this and that.'

Matthew knew he was not hearing the whole truth here – probably Arnold was reluctant to say much over the telephone and yet every instinct told Matthew he was being just a bit wily with him. He seemed reluctant to share the conversation with him.

'Right, Arnold, I'm interested to hear all about it, how you managed to persuade Gavin, I just don't know, because I know we both thought he was being rather obstinate about everything. Would it suit if I called round to see you about lunch time tomorrow and you can tell me all about it. You did say you would tell me about it, Arnold.'

'Of course, Matthew, I'll tell you, I had every intention of telling you, even though I know you'll think I've been rather naughty and a bit arrogant, but yes, I do intend to tell you.'

'Thanks, Arnold, I'll see you then.'

'You said what, Arnold? You have to be joking.' Matthew had called round to the cottage at lunch time as he had promised Arnold he would; he was intrigued to know if Arnold's and Gavin's conversation had had any bearings on the fact that Rachel was now preparing to go home and was quite euphoric it seemed, at the prospect of doing so.

'You see, Matthew, I knew you would not approve of the content of my conversation with Gavin, but this was something I have been thinking about for the last couple of weeks. You see, Matthew,' Arnold was at great pains to convince him that he was only trying to help by talking to Gavin. 'The way I feel is this; we have all gone through so much both singularly and as a whole family, I believe we have the capacity to either hold one another up and help one another or we drag each other down.' Arnold paused and looked at Matthew with something like appreciation in his expression.

'Only for all of you, Matthew, I would have been down and would have had no will to live but thanks to you all, I felt supported and valued. I felt that life after all was worth living. So then, I felt I owed it to everyone to try to make Gavin, who I believe was a bit misguided for a day or so, see some sense.'

Here, Matthew interrupted. 'I agree with you there, Arnold, I think he was, as you suggested one evening, on his moral high ground, and someone needed to talk to him, but I never dreamt you would have taken the approach you have done.'

'It was a bit extreme, I must agree.' And here Arnold smiled ruefully, indicating the prosthesis on his arm and leg, before continuing. 'Look, I was desperate, and I felt it was desperate times for Rachel, and you know the old saying, 'desperate times call for desperate measures' and that is why I took the approach I did'

'Right, let's have it all from the very beginning of your conversation with Gavin.'

'Well, Gavin was a bit surprised to see me at his front door. I suppose I have been a rather infrequent visitor. But then, he gave me a great welcome and asked me in. He then offered me a drink of whiskey, which I declined because I explained to him, I was driving but told him I would love some coffee. Then without any thought to the matter, I told him I was very concerned about Rachel and how I believed she was yearning for her own home with her husband beside her. Then I asked the question to Gavin quite directly, as to why he did not think it a good idea to have her home in her own house with her husband.'

'I daresay he told you how he felt.' Matthew had reasoned to himself that Gavin would find Arnold – after all he had been through – a good confidante to have.

'Well, he did go through a bit of humming and ha-ing but then he did admit quite readily that he wondered if Rachel still secretly had a yearning to go back to her days of being an escort to men who needed such ladies. That, it seemed, was his main problem; he felt he was being cast aside in search of Rachel's other, more adventurous life.' Here, Arnold paused in his narration. 'I nearly lost my patience here, to be honest. I felt that if he couldn't see that Rachel was only trying to help someone in her family circle, then he himself had no right to be included as part of that family. And I'm afraid I told him so, there and then.'

Matthew was amazed at Arthur's daring but at the same time, he felt humbled by his forthrightness in saying what he believed to be true.

Arnold went on, ' Then – as I've just told you and you seem so shocked about – I told him that his wife was one of the most beautiful women and also one of the bravest I had ever met, and if I thought for one moment that Gavin had fallen out of love with her, that I myself would pursue her.'

Here, Arnold hesitated and looked at Matthew. 'I told him that as I was now a widower and a very lonely one at that, that I would be more than interested in setting my sights on Rachel. I did stress that I would do it even though I had misled her daughter so much and in spite of the fact that I was, in anybody's books, disabled.'

Intrigued and further amazed by Arnold's audacity, Matthew just simply nodded.

'I told him I still had plenty of warmth, compassion and forgiveness in my soul, something I felt that most women still very much appreciated. Not only that, Matthew, I also told him that in the first flush of youth, women may not be all that interested in financial security, but perhaps women who were more mature and had been through a lot of trauma and strife might eventually settle for that.'

Here, Matthew interrupted Arnold. 'Had you been thinking about what you were going to say for some time?'

'To be perfectly honest, from the moment I climbed into my disabled car until I sat in Gavin's so very comfortable sitting room – although I had thought a lot about Rachel and her dilemma – I had no idea in the least how I was going to handle such a sensitive subject. And to be honest with you now, Matthew, I feel really bad about it all, I feel I handled it in a most insensitive manner'

'Insensitive or not, Arnold, I believe that you, and only you, have achieved the results all the family have been wanting to hear and I, on behalf of everybody, thank you so much. It was such a good idea to lead Gavin to believe you might begin to pursue Rachel.'

'But it was no gesture, Matthew, I assure you. I have always admired Rachel, I have admired her for how she forgave me for mistreating Lynn and how she welcomed me into her family, albeit it was for the sake of her grandson. Then, how she changed her whole lifestyle. How could any man not admire her? And in spite of all my love and all my grief over my lovely wife, Iris, I still worried and fretted so much for Rachel and her recovery. So indeed, I was most sincere when I told Gavin I could offer Rachel so much in spite of my disability. So by the sound of things, he has listened, and perhaps at the end of all this, I am the loser here.'

Matthew made an effort to speak but Arnold continued. 'I know I have the everlasting love and companionship of my son Lewis, a love which was so very threatened, but handed back to me by none other than Rachel herself. How could anyone not love her? And no son or daughter's love can ever replace that between a man and a woman. But I want to stress that seeing how close I was to losing my son's love, I am most content with that.'

After Matthew left Arnold and drove back to his office, his mind was filled with all Arnold had told him about his conversation with Gavin Finlay and he knew they were all, as a family, enriched by having Arnold Simpson in their lives. He believed the depth of character, now so evident in the man, was all down to his daughter-in-law, Lynn, who had so willingly stretched out the hand of friendship to her son's father, who had initially threatened to take their son from her. It was Lynn's all-embracing forgiveness, which had made such a difference to all their lives. There was no doubt in Matthew's mind that forgiveness in all areas of life and particularly within families, was essential to enable them all to move forward into the future. He just hoped that if he was ever faced with such a challenge as Lynn had been and at such a young age, he too could rise to the challenge. He sincerely hoped he would.

Chapter 59

'I hate having to ask you to do this, Julie, and only because you have helped me so much in my backlog of work that I can ask you now. I know you know what you are doing, so I feel confident to leave you to it. I do need your help and it will only take a couple of hours, perhaps two hours this week. What do you think? Do you mind?'

'Well, of course I don't mind, dear. Just show me or tell me what exactly you want me to do.'

'It is not the most pleasant of tasks, but I want you to do a bit of sifting of letters and scraps of papers which are in two boxes I have in the study. One box belonged to Alfie, the prisoner who was found dead in Crumlin Road Gaol, and the other box is information I gathered up in England in the house the police were searching, which I stuck in my briefcase and then transferred in to a box in the study. I'll show you exactly where they are and what I want done before I head off to work.' And with that, Matthew rose from the breakfast table and made his way across the living room into his study with Julie behind him.

'I want you to keep whatever is at all legible in one pile for me and mark it as being readable, the other in illegible scraps or letters, put them in another pile for me. But please, please don't throw anything out.' Now, Matthew indicated the two boxes sitting on the top shelf of the unit in his study.

'Anything you or I can't read or make any sense of, I'll be showing to our handwriting experts and let them have a go.'

'It seems simple enough, Matthew and it is a job I can sit down to do, so I don't mind in the least, love.' Julie smiled reassuringly as she spoke. She always liked Matthew asking for her help, it made her feel he trusted her to do it right. 'Go on to work and leave this to me, it seems to be quite a trivial task and one which I hope will be finished by the time you come home.'

'I don't expect you to find anything really helpful but if you do happen to come on something which you think is meaningful, please ring me to the office. Just say something has turned up but please remember, this is all highly confidential.'

'I'll definitely let you know and if I don't ring, you will know I have found nothing of consequence.' Julie said. 'Just set the boxes down on the desk for me, love. They are a bit high up and I would not like to spill them, getting them down.'

Matthew immediately reached for each box in turn and set them on his desk where he could see they would indeed be accessible for Julie. Then they left the study, Matthew locking it as he always did before handing the key to Julie. Before he left for work, Julie said she intended to do the minimum of housework and hoped to get started to the task in the study at about eleven a.m. She felt the sooner the boxes were sorted for him, the better, and she did hope she would be in touch because, she said, she was very excited at the thought of discovering something of consequence to help Matthew. She would feel quite important in that she would be the one to tell him about it. She would feel she was a very important messenger indeed. Matthew smiled lovingly at Julie, recognising that feeling of imparting important information you have just learned about. Now he sincerely hoped that would be the case, and as he kissed her good-bye, he said he hoped she would indeed be in touch.

As the morning wore on and Matthew had not heard from Julie he began to wonder which of the two of them would be the most disappointed that there was nothing of much significance in those boxes. Then of course, Julie might miss something in the boxes, through lack of experience, he was really only expecting her to divide them up into those that were readable and those that weren't. He would be going over every single item himself very soon.

He went out for lunch with one of his colleagues and on his return, asked the two girls in the office if there had been any telephone calls for him and he was assured there had not been. Throughout the entire afternoon, he found himself looking at the clock on the wall or alternatively his watch, on numerous occasions, hoping for a call from Julie, but there was none. And as Matthew cleared his desk around six o'clock, he realised it was Julie he was feeling sorry for, rather than any disappointment he had over nothing of importance being found in those letters and scraps of paper he had brought home. It would, he knew, have given Julie a real lift to be the bearer of important news. The only thing of real consequence was the finding of those photographs in that padded envelope postmarked Belfast, certainly someone from here had sent them to Nigel Hanna, but who? He felt it was not going to be easy, Matthew realised and if those papers in his study held no secrets, where could he go to from here?

When Matthew entered the annexe, Julie came forward to greet him from the kitchen where by the look of her flushed face, she had been bending over the cooker. Her hug and kiss for him was particularly passionate he thought, and for a moment, he felt it was almost an act of desperation. He held her from him and remarked. 'Is everything all right, darling, you seem stressed. Was my task in the study just a trifle too difficult for you?'

Julie smiled at him then, 'Of course not. I'm fine, I may look stressed, but it is just the heat from the cooker I think.' And she patted her flushed face in explanation.

Over dinner, Julie explained how she had separated the two piles of letters as Matthew had asked her to do. She had just wished she had found some information which might be of some help, but she personally had found nothing. But of course, she added quickly, 'That doesn't mean that you won't find something which might help.'

'Well, at least you have sorted the two piles of so called letters for me, Julie, and I do appreciate that very much. It does make things that bit easier for me, when I'm going over everything again. But to be honest, if there are no clues in our friend Alfie's junk, or the information I have brought home from England, I hardly know where to go to from here, unless of course the car driver and owner of the house in Hailsham, which we've been searching, turns up. That's our only hope, I do believe, love.'

Julie made no immediate reply to this but began collecting the dishes and placing them in the sink, turning to Matthew, she said. 'Pour us both a small glass of wine and we'll watch the evening news and try to forget about anything to do with your work and the looking for clues.' As Julie began to pour hot water on the dishes she went on, 'Maybe a rethink and a fresh approach tomorrow might help.'

Matthew thought Julie's voice held little enthusiasm for the subject and no doubt like himself, she was, he reckoned, totally de-motivated, now that she had found nothing of significance in either of those boxes. And Matthew began to feel that it had not been such a good idea to ask Julie for her help. She must be as eager as he was to find the person responsible for Patrick Mullan's death.

Throughout the evening, Matthew noticed that Julie had three glasses of wine, something he had never known her to do before, and when he referred to it, she said she was just enjoying it very much, appreciating him and the quiet time they were having together.

They went to bed later than usual that evening, simply because the time seemed to pass so quickly and Julie maintained, that in spite of having had quite a busy day, she was not particularly tired. When they did retire for the night, Matthew was asleep almost immediately but was disturbed a couple of times because he was aware that Julie was sitting on the side of the bed with her head in her hands.

'Julie, what's wrong? Are you all right?'

'Matthew, I did not mean to disturb you. Please don't worry. I think the wine was not such a good idea. I have a bit of a headache.'

'Can I fetch you anything, love?'

'No. No. I'll be fine.' And Julie slipped back into bed beside him.

The next morning, Matthew quietly climbed out of bed, Julie was fast asleep and he had no desire to wake her. But he intended to talk to her when he came back from work later. He was convinced that something was troubling her and he wondered was it moving from the annexe which she was now so used to, and going back to the cottage with all its reminders of their grandson's kidnap. He believed it could well be that and he was resolved to talk to her about it. Or perhaps it was Emily's behaviour- she had taken to staying with Jason and Lynn a lot so it could be that was upsetting her. Whatever the reason, he intended to sort it out this evening.

Chapter 60

On his arrival home from work that same evening, Matthew was relieved to see that Julie appeared to be in good form and greeted him with a warm smile and a kiss. She told him almost immediately then that Gavin had been on the telephone that morning to say that Rachel and he were celebrating their return home that evening and he would be delighted if Matthew and Julie could join them. Gavin had explained to Julie it would only be for a few drinks and a light buffet and he hoped other members would be free to come. He knew it was short notice but he wanted it to be spontaneous, he said, and he was in the process of ringing round the family at the moment.

'I'll say this; that was quick of Gavin to try and get all that together, but I'm delighted, Julie, and it is certainly something worth celebrating, the return of both Rachel and Lewis to us. It is tinged with a lot of sadness too, with the loss of Iris. I wonder if Gavin has asked Arnold and if so, I wonder if he will come.'

'Yes, actually, he made a point of saying that he had already rang Arnold, Lynn and Jason and that they were indeed coming, Arnold included. He seemed very pleased that Arnold was coming. I suppose Gavin does realise how difficult things are for Arnold – regarding celebrations, I mean. So it is good if he feels up to coming to this one.' Julie answered.

'I think Arnold likes to be involved in any of the family activities and I think that being with all of us or some of us on a regular basis does help him cope.'

'By the way, Gavin says that this party he is having is a small Christmas celebration as well, without any decorations or presents he says. Rachel and he will be going over to the cottage to join Lynn, Jason and Lewis and Eva for a quiet Christmas dinner, but that is all.'

'Yes, Lynn has also asked us, Matthew, and Emily of course, but Lynn just wants a very quiet occasion and I agree, I must say. Jason did say that Arnold says he is going to have a big celebration when they move into their new home, instead of anything lavish at Christmas.'

Julie knew that the family were just so appreciative of everything, after all that had happened, that they were happy simply to be together. Now, she added, 'When does he hope to move into his new home, or rather when do they all at the cottage hope to move? Do you know, Matthew?'

'He told me he hopes to move with Jason and his family about a week after Christmas – he did not want to rush in before Christmas – so then the cottage will be free for us, Julie.' Matthew hesitated and then decided he must establish with Julie how she really felt about moving back. 'Are you quite sure you want to move back? Or after what happened to Lewis would you maybe find it too traumatic?'

'Oh, no, Matthew, Lewis is safe now and besides, Jason has made the side garden and the driveway safe too, so I am looking forward to going back home. I have loved being here too, of course, and being so close to Lucie and Paul, especially when I needed them. Hopefully, we'll still see plenty of them, I certainly mean to see Lucie a couple of times a week as I always have'

'I must say I'm very relieved to hear you say that. I thought yesterday evening and last night when you seemed so stressed and restless that you really did not want to move, that you could not face it.' Matthew thought that just for a fleeting moment, Julie's face clouded over at the mention of last night, but then she quickly smiled at him in a reassuring way.

'Matthew, I was just a bit wakeful last night – that was all. Please don't worry so much. I'm sure I'll sleep better tonight. I'm looking forward to getting out this evening and meeting some of the family. We haven't seen them for a while.' And Julie then added. 'We'll have all the family round to the cottage when we move and have settled in.'

'Good idea, love, but I don't intend to move in until I get the painters in. Lynn and Jason did not do any decorating in the time they were there, they probably felt it wasn't their place and did not know what we would really like. But I want the place looking especially good for you, Julie.' Matthew was just very relieved that Julie was looking forward to moving in to the cottage just as much as he was, and her stressful mood seemed to have lifted.

Julie had been glad to hear Gavin's voice on the other end of the line when he had rang earlier and told her all about the invitation to join them later. At this moment in time, she knew she needed some diversion, something to keep her thoughts in some sort of order and prevent her doing anything rash, which she might live to regret. She had faced a few dilemmas in her life; the murder of Matthew's father and then she had been attacked and assaulted to within an inch of her life. She had suffered the abduction of her grandson and then his glorious return to the family. But this trauma she was now facing, she believed to be the worst. She believed it to be so awful because she could not possibly talk about it to anyone, not even Matthew, especially Matthew. This was something she had to come through on her own, before she made a decision which could and would change the lives of the Hampton family for ever. But for tonight, she was going to dress in her best and enjoy the evening with her darling husband and all the family. She knew she would find it interesting to watch some of the members of Matthew's family, how they seemed to be and wonder if they were as much affected by everything as she was. But there was no real urgency to make any decisions at the moment. Everything was safe with her for the moment.

Gavin had spared no expense in his preparations for the celebration, he had managed to get caterers, at the last moment, to provide a wonderful selection of hot and cold meals all laid out in their dining room, and the most expensive champagne was opened and poured wantonly by him.

'Rachel, you look amazing.' Julie remarked sincerely, as she hugged and kissed Matthew's cousin. 'That blue dress is so flattering and exactly matches the colour of your eyes.' And certainly, Rachel seemed transformed and although she was still waif like, she had a glow about her for the first time since she had been so ill and Julie sensed Rachel was bursting with happiness. To think of all she had been through and to come out the other side and look as she was looking tonight was nothing short of a miracle, Julie thought, forgetting for a moment of her own horrific injuries and what she had endured. And as the evening wore on, Julie noted that without exception, everyone seemed almost euphoric and why wouldn't they? After all they had been through. Even Arnold, Julie noted, seemed quietly content as he talked to Matthew's brothers, Charles and Thomas and their wives, Sheila and Jenny. And everyone in the room, although obviously enjoying themselves, were quietly respectful to Arnold.

At a later stage in the evening, Gavin called on all his guests to drink a toast to remembered friends and family members, especially Iris he said, who had thought to try and help Rachel. When the toast was over, Arnold got to his feet and raising his glass, thanked Gavin for his very kind thoughts. Here, Gavin further added to the conversation by thanking Arnold for his support in the last few days and the very worthwhile conversations they'd had together.

Matthew smiled to himself when he heard those words and he knew he was probably the only one in the room who really knew anything about that worthwhile conversation Arnold had had with Gavin.

'Julie, love, you certainly seem to be enjoying Gavin's champagne, it's not really like you. You always said you didn't really like champagne.' Matthew was quite taken aback by the number of glasses of champagne Julie had consumed since their arrival.

'I am indeed, enjoying it, Matthew, it is beautiful. The best of stuff, I would imagine. And I'm having a lovely evening watching your family and extended family enjoying themselves so much and to be able to put the last horrid few weeks behind them.' Julie knew she had probably drunk far too much champagne but it was really lovely and she still felt as sober as a judge. She knew she just wanted to drink on and as long as she remained comparatively sober, no harm would be done. She would not let her tongue run away with her, not here anyway. She remarked to Matthew how tempting the food in the dining room looked but she did not tell him she had no desire to sample it. She was grateful that although Matthew had noticed her drinking, he had not apparently noticed that she had eaten nothing. She simply could not face it, she had no appetite for it.

Later on the way home in the taxi, Matthew and her in the back seat, and Emily in the front, she leaned in close to her husband and wondered how anyone could destroy all that new found happiness she had just witnessed. How could she possibly do it? She did not believe that she ever could.

Chapter 61

'We've found Mr. Nigel Hanna, Inspector Hampton. '

Matthew recognised Michael Forde's voice immediately. He had switched over once more from the relaxed friendly tones he had heard when he was in Hailsham, to his dry, monotonous telephone voice.

'You were able to trace him then, Michael? Matthew asked lightly. He was determined to keep to the relaxed, friendly interchange the two men had had in Hailsham. 'Where has he been located then?'

'Matthew, I'm afraid our Mr. Hanna is dead.'

'He's what? Not another one surely?' Although he was shocked by this latest news, Matthew noted that Detective Forde had taken the cue from him and resorted to first names. 'He's dead, you say. Don't tell me he has been murdered too. The list goes on and on.'

'No, we believe this to be suicide, Matthew.' Michael Forde sounded convinced of his facts. 'He left a note – it seems genuine to me.'

'Where on earth was he found, Michael?'

'In his apartment in Eastbourne. My men found evidence of this seaside apartment when looking through some of his information, which you decided not to take back with you. As you know, there were quite a lot of letters and cards still to go through. It was an apartment along the sea front, and a beautiful place I might add.' There was a short silence, and then Michael Forde went on. 'Are you still there, Matthew?'

'Oh, yes. I'm just shocked. Please go on.'

'We found him in a back bedroom, an empty bottle of pills and an empty bottle of whiskey beside him. He also left a note which I intend this very morning to send a copy to you for your records if for nothing else.'

'Can't you tell me now what the note says?'

'Right, OK, I will. It says, Matthew, that he did not mean to kill the man in Hailsham village, whom he believed to be Patrick Mullan. He had never killed anyone in his life and he had been told not to, so he thought if he just knocked him down, he could survive. He only meant to injure him and when he heard he was dead, he simply could not live with himself. So I'm sorry, old chap.' He goes on to say that he had never been asked to hurt or injure anyone before. He had always been asked to contact someone else to do that, but this time he was called upon to do it. And he says, Matthew, he needed the money for his mortgage.

'The thing is, Michael.' Matthew knew this would sound callous. 'I know he can't help us anymore and I suspect that he might have been able to tell us a lot.'

'Yes, it is unfortunate, but that's how it is this time, Matthew. Our men are currently searching his holiday apartment for any clues or information that might be helpful but, totally unlike his home, the apartment is very sparse indeed. Indeed, all we've found so far is a small diary with a doctor's number, an electrician's and a plumber, nothing else. So I think anything more that might help is probably in his house in Hailsham, although we have been through almost everything now and we have found nothing else. What about the letters and the other data you took back with you, Matthew? Have you had any luck there?'

'So far, nothing at all and I have only a few more letters and scraps of paper to go through.' Matthew's voice held a note of desperation, he was anxious to wrap up this case but it was becoming increasingly likely that he was to be thwarted. 'I hate unfinished cases, Michael, and loose ends.'

'Look, don't lose heart just yet, old chap.' for the first time since they had spoken to one another, Michael Forde's voice held a touch of humour and Matthew smiled as he listened. 'Matthew, you and I both know that new information can come to us at any time, through any source and sometimes the most unexpected source. So hold on to that, Matthew.'

'I will, Michael, and I look forward to getting a copy of that suicide note and we'll be in touch. If I uncover anything else I'll let you know By the way, I forgot to ask what age Nigel Hanna was, he looked quite a young man by his photographs.'

'We found his birth certificate the day after you returned home, Matthew. He was forty five years of age.'

'Another waste of a comparatively young life.' Matthew answered, then with promises to keep in touch he rang off.

Matthew left his office quite despondent that same evening. Certainly, they were no nearer finding out the person in Belfast or the surrounding district who had been in touch with Nigel Hanna and sent photographs of Patrick Mullan to him. Then, there was the suggestion in the note Mr. Hanna had left, that Patrick was only to be injured, not killed. Was that on the direction of someone in authority or had it just been Nigel Hanna's inability to commit murder? That puzzled Matthew and struck him as someone who did not like violence and did not wish for much to be used. If it was the UDA intent on revenge for Matthew's father, then they had changed irrevocably, they had been renowned for their brutality and violence. Or had it been the IRA, still harbouring a grudge because Patrick had given the names of the killers of Rob Hampton to the police? Perhaps because Patrick had been a Roman Catholic they had decided to show some leniency and unfortunately it had all gone wrong. He did think they were the most likely assailants, certainly he did not think the UDA would have given Patrick much chance, him being a Catholic and having led killers to a policeman's father those years ago. He only hoped the suicide note would tell him more when he received a copy of the note from Michael Forde. Certainly, when he reached home later this evening, he intended to recheck all the data he had brought from England and all he had taken from his friend, Alfie's house. He knew Julie had done so and she was most meticulous and highly alert when checking anything, should it be a simple thing like their monthly bank account. But still, you never knew, the very routine of going over similar letters with all that identical writing might make anyone overlook something. So that was something he had to do and Julie had told him she had left everything there for him in his study – in two completely identical bundles as he had asked her to do – so he could check that she had not missed anything. So there was still some hope that somewhere in those notes on his desk was the clue to who the contact with Nigel Hanna was in Belfast or Northern Ireland.

Chapter 62

'I've just had a telephone call from Michael Forde, Julie.' Matthew was ringing Julie from his office, something he rarely did, but he needed to know if she was in any way interested in Michael's suggestion. 'He would like us to come over to England for a couple of nights and sample the English climate and culture and see how it compares with the Irish.'

'Would that be all there would be to it, Matthew, or would there be any work involved?' Julie sounded quite sceptical.

'Well,' Matthew sounded hesitant. 'He would like me to see the apartment in Eastbourne that Nigel Hanna was found in and also to do a quick search over in the house in Hailsham in case he and his men might have missed something. But he assures me that only one morning would be set aside to do all that, no more than that, he insists.'

'Do you think they might find something yet, Matthew? I thought it had all been gone through, has it not?' Julie tried to keep the anxiety out of her voice.

'Please try not to worry, Julie, I promise it will be a quick once over, the places will get from me. I don't intend to leave you to your own devices for longer than is absolutely necessary. Michael insists it will be essentially a social visit so that you and I can spend some time with him and his wife away from all the mysteries of crime.'

Matthew went on, 'I would really like to go and I think you would love the place; the quaint pubs situated on the roadside, the beautiful shops and the friendliness of the people who live there. It seems to be a very relaxed way of life compared to here. So say you'll go, Julie.'

'Of course I'll go, Matthew. It sounds really lovely and I'm glad you have promised not to spend hours trying to solve the case of Patrick Mullan. I don't think I could stand it, and anyway, perhaps you and Michael are wasting your time, perhaps it was just a hit and run incident.'

Julie sounded really defeatist, Matthew thought, and he believed she must be rather fed up with his work. Perhaps he should not bring any home with him in future. He would have to seriously consider changing all that, it was really unfair to Julie -his disappearing into his study at all times, to try and make sense of any data he might have in there. Then he felt guilty when he remembered how before her assault, he had always brought his work home. There and then, Matthew decided he would not bring another scrap of paper home from his office. He had no doubt now that Julie's stressful mood at times had everything to do with him resorting back to his old ways.

'You might well be right, Julie, about it being a hit and run incident.' Matthew was anxious now to try and humour his wife, he so desperately wanted her to agree to come to England with him. 'We have only some obscure notes from a prisoner in Crumlin Road Gaol to tell us something different, and I would imagine he was no more dependable than a whole lot of others were. So if you are agreeable that a couple of days break in England would be good, I'll ring Michael and tell him we would love to come but I only want to do the very minimum of work when we get there. I will stress to him that I am bringing you on a mini holiday and that he must not waylay me into too much work. The holiday, I'll remind him, was his idea anyway.'

'It does sound a very good idea and I do want to go, love, and I believe that there will be the minimum of work done by you both. So tell your Detective friend that but also say that we don't wish to put them out and we will book into a hotel. It's just with my prosthesis and being in a strange place, it might be a bit awkward and embarrassing I think, Matthew. But as long as you explain all that I'm very keen to go and I know Emily will see it as a good excuse to go and stay with Lynn and Jason in their new home, so we will have no worries there.'

'I think while we are away, now that Lynn and Jason have moved, we should have the painters come in and redecorate some of the rooms in the cottage.' Matthew had been thinking about this for the last few days and now, if Julie was agreeable, he would organise it straight away. 'I'll need you to think of some colour schemes for the room. Will you do that, Julie?'

'Oh, Matthew, please, I would rather leave that to you.' Julie felt in her present frame of mind that looking at any redecorating schemes or indeed anything which might involve looking forward in their lives was just too much for her. Going to England would help her she knew, to feel somewhat removed from the reality of what was actually staring her in the face and which she was still no further on as to what she was going to do about it. But certainly, deciding on colour schemes for their cottage would just be too much at the moment. Would everything have been better had she not discovered what she had?

Of course it would not have been any better because certainly, Matthew would have found it and more than likely everything would be so very much worse for all the Hampton family and indeed, the extended family with their lives changed forever.

Now, as she talked to Matthew, she knew she must make every effort to act normally until she had made an irrevocable decision, one way or another. Now she did her

303

best to smile at her husband. 'I think I would just like you to ask the painters to do all the walls cream and the paintwork white in the meantime, Matthew. Then, when we are well settled in, we can think about different colours for the room. How does that sound?'

Matthew was relieved to hear Julie had made some sort of decision about their cottage.

'Sounds good, I think you've been reading the same article as I have, where the experts recommend to keep everything low key at first and then make other decisions gradually.'

'Well, we do read the same newspapers and magazines, love. So yes, I read that too,' Julie answered.

Matthew, much happier now about Julie's frame of mind, told her he would be home early for tea but he would in the meantime, book the flights and a hotel from the office and that would be that organised.

Matthew and Julie spent two days and nights in Hailsham, in a small hotel on the outskirts of the village. Matthew did make sure he spent a minimal time in Nigel Hanna's house and later his flat, searching for any more clues relating to Patrick Mullan. He was determined to spend as much time as he possibly could with Julie. Besides, the policeman in charge of both of Nigel Hanna's properties had done a marvellous job of clearing them out and assured him they had found nothing at all of consequence. When he returned with Michael Forde to Julie, where she was sitting in the conservatory of the hotel with Marjorie, Michael's wife, drinking coffee, he was quite surprised when Julie showed some interest in his search of the two properties. 'Have you found anything of consequence?' she asked him.

'Not a thing, Julie. I'm surprised at you even asking, after our pledge to have no talk about any mysteries when we were here.'

'I know we did, love, but I suppose I'm still curious about everything.' Julie's voice sounded casual. 'Surely that means you will have little more to do with the case?' Now she turned to Michael Forde. 'Is the case going to be closed, Michael.'

'Certainly it will be put on hold, at the very least, Julie.' And Michael Forde smiled as he spoke.

Julie simply nodded and smiled back at him in response.

Matthew, as he watched his wife, realised that she was anxious about his work load. It was the only explanation for her questions to both him and Michael.

'Unless we get some unexpected breakthrough or other, that will be how it is. I know it is disappointing for you, Matthew, but there is so much more going on, we have to leave this meantime.' Michael Forde turned the conversation to Matthew.

'I too, have a tremendous caseload at present, Michael. I also intend to cut down my work from now on.' Matthew looked over at Julie now. 'Yes, love, I intend to cut my hours to part-time when we move back into the cottage. We will have time for friends and family and perhaps Michael and Marjorie will come and stay and see the wonderful sights in Northern Ireland.'

Julie nodded and smiled at Michael as she spoke. 'When you come you must make sure it is a holiday and no looking for suspects when you are with us, then I will put out the red carpet for you both.' Now Julie smiled happily at the Detective and his wife.

'I guarantee that will be the case, Julie. We will be delighted to come for a couple of days and no work whatsoever involved. Besides, there is only the Patrick

Mullan case with links here, as far as we know, and as we've just said, we have exhausted all avenues there.'

Julie, again just nodded but Matthew noticed that she visibly relaxed when Michael confirmed that their visit to them would just be a simple holiday. Watching her, Matthew now felt very strongly that he was doing the right thing by cutting down on the hours he worked – obviously Julie was finding it all too much.

Chapter 63

January 1986

Julie always waited until she was totally alone in the cottage before going to the dressing table in her bedroom and removing the two notes from the locked drawer. She had found these notes when she was helping Matthew sort out the information he had gathered from the prisoner in Crumlin Road Goal and also the notes he had brought home from England. She studied them once again as she had done in the last two days and knew without a doubt that she recognised the handwriting. After Matthew's return from England and about a week after Gavin's celebration for Rachel's homecoming, Julie had reluctantly taken down the Christmas cards from the top of her wardrobe – cards which she had decided to pack away earlier than she usually did after Christmas. She had been afraid to make any comparisons when Matthew was around between the writings on the notes and that on one particular card. She knew she needed to make the comparisons in total secret. She'd had quite firm intentions to make the comparisons one particular day after the New Year, but her courage had failed her at the last minute. Besides, she reckoned it was much too soon after the wonderful celebrations for Rachel and she could not face the task just then, she did not want clarification of what she suspected, so she returned the cards to their usual place.

But today, she felt strong enough to do it, she believed. Whether that was because she knew Matthew would be home much later from work because he had told her he was going to visit Mrs. Mullan and Patrick's widow, Helena. He wanted to find out if Patrick had ever received any threatening letters or phone calls during his time in England. Emily too, was away from the house, she was away for tea to her cousin Jayne's and, she had told Julie, Evelyn would be there too. The cousins were very close, Julie thought, as with renewed resolve, she opened the drawer and extracted the notes and placed them on the top of the dressing table, smoothing them out as she did so. Once again, she retrieved the Christmas cards from the top of her wardrobe and untying the ribbon which held them together, began to sift through them until she found the card she was looking for. Fearfully, and with a wild hope that she would be proved wrong, she opened the card and read the message before taking it to the dressing table where the notes lay. She saw then, the awful confirmation of all her suspicions. As she sat there in her bedroom, her thoughts in turmoil and despair, she began to hope that Matthew would come home with some worthwhile information from Helena Mullan, and she herself would be spared the agony of making any decision regarding any of this. With that thought in mind, Julie replaced the notes into the drawer, locked it and put the key back in her handbag and then returned the Christmas cards to their usual place.

Matthew returned home around eight o'clock and told her, in response to her questions and her obvious interest, that there had been nothing, nothing at all, in the time Helena and Patrick had lived in Hailsham, to indicate that Patrick might be under any threat. Their time in England, Helena told Matthew tearfully, had been a happy time for them and that happiness had been enhanced by Patrick's mother coming to live with them. So, there had been nothing to indicate Patrick had been at any risk there.

'So, Julie, although it was good seeing them trying to cope, and they did give me a warm welcome, I'm afraid they are not able to provide me with any clues whatsoever.' Matthew was sitting at the table in the kitchen enjoying the steak pie and mashed potatoes Julie had made and kept warm for him in the oven.

'So what do you intend to do now?' Julie asked as she sipped her now nightly glass of wine.

'I intend to take Michael Forde's advice and shelve Patrick's case in the meantime. It will be filed, I hope temporarily, with the other unsolved cases in Northern Ireland. I want to concentrate this weekend on starting to pack up in readiness to move back to the cottage the following weekend. Don't you agree that's a good idea?'

'Matthew, I would love to start packing up here. Lucie told me that Paul and she have lots of boxes in the garage we can use.' Julie, meantime, reminded herself mentally to remember to move the damning notes from their hiding place to her handbag before the removal started. She had an awful dread of them being discovered, she knew they could easily fall out of the back of the drawers during the removal. She must go to the desk later this evening and remove them.

'Then, love, I intend to book caterers just as Gavin did for his party. I don't want you doing any work whatsoever. But first I must speak with Arnold and see when he wants his house warming. I don't want him to think we might be stealing his original idea from him.'

Julie agreed that was only proper, they both also hoped that Arnold might decide to have his party lastly. They both thought it would be the "grand finale" in his beautiful mansion, compared to their humble attempts in their equally humble cottage.

Chapter 64

Julie had surprised herself when she enjoyed herself so much during the couple of days they were in Hailsham. She secretly had not expected to, but was rather dreading what two Detective Inspectors bogged down in crime and the solving of it, might do when they should be taking a break from it all. But surprisingly, there was very little talk about any cases and it looked as if the case of Patrick Mullan was to be filed away – at least in the meantime. When she had been in Hailsham she found she had been able to shelve her worries for the time being. She did feel quite removed from it all when she had been there. Besides, it had been rather easy to forget, because the village was such a delightful place with its quaint shops and pubs and its so friendly, helpful people.

Now, she was back home and the painters had been and gone from the cottage. They had done a remarkable job of the place and Matthew and she had decided to move in the following week-end. Julie was once again, thankful for the diversion, but knew that she soon must make her decision. But she could forget her dilemma when she was packing boxes with a surplus of china and crystal glasses, which Matthew and she had managed to collect over the years, but were reluctant to be separated from. There was one thing she must remember to do, she must remove the notes she had locked away in her dressing table and keep them in her handbag. She had no choice only to keep them with her while they were in the process of moving house, they were likely to fall out of the back of any drawer she might decide to lock them in. Even as she thought of the consequences of anyone finding them, Julie was in despair and she could feel a cold sweat begin to form on her brow. She was beginning to realise that she could not live with the knowledge she had much longer. But what must she do? Should she do the honourable thing and tell all? Could she dare to completely destroy the family and indeed the extended family?

She sincerely believed if she had been a Roman Catholic, she would have gone to a priest for confession. That, she knew, would have been of tremendous help to her – the simple act of telling one other person. She felt such a need to confide in someone and she knew that without a doubt a priest would be confidential and keep the knowledge to himself. At the same time, he would, she felt, advise her in a most sincere way what she ought to do. But she wasn't a Catholic, so to go to a priest would be a sham, and if she told her own minister, she had no doubt he would march her down to the nearest police station and insist she tell all. That was something she was beginning to think, as time went on, that she was never going to be able to do.

One thing was certain, she was going to bury it deep in the recesses of her mind, at least until Matthew and she had their house warming and Arnold, Jason and Lynn theirs. At least those evenings would be wonderful, carefree hours, celebrating so much good that had happened. Julie decided that after all the celebrations were over, that would be when she would make her decision, and not before. The whole family needed to get together, to show their love and solidarity for one another and illustrate the power of family love. But somewhere in all that lightness and optimism, was she going to be called on to shatter that whole family framework?

The first house warming party was, at Arnold's insistence in his rather grand mansion, something Matthew and Julie were initially disappointed about. They would have preferred to have their more modest party before Arnold's extravagant one. But Arnold was insistent that although his would be more lavish, he wanted people to remember Matthew and Julie's, in the cottage where everyone had come through so much. When Arnold said that, Matthew and Julie felt they had no argument to offer in response to what Arnold was saying on the subject.

Arnold's house warming was a memorable occasion for everyone present and Lynn and Jason were particularly pleased that their old friends Tracey and Timothy with their two little girls were able to come and stay for the week-end of the party. Tracey had kept in constant touch with Lynn during her family's ordeal and had promised when she had heard that Lewis and Rachel were safe, that she and Timothy would come and see them as soon as possible. So, the house warming party turned out to be a very suitable venue and a suitable time for them to come.

Arnold had been right after all, Julie reflected, as she looked at all the family and guests now mingling together, in having their house warming in the cottage as the last one. She found that, after all, she preferred it and so it seemed the majority of the family felt the same, telling her that Arnold's sentiments were quite right. Who would have thought a couple of months ago, that such a celebration was ever likely to happen, but here they all were, striving so bravely to forget the terrors and anxieties of the past six months. Now, as Julie watched Arnold talking so earnestly with his son, his son who had been abducted from this very cottage, she felt that no one in the whole group had suffered as much as Arnold had. Over time, he had lost so much but here he was, smiling so broadly at Lewis and then at others as they came forward to greet him. How did he bear the loss of Iris, day in and day out? Some of the family had suffered but at least they were all together again.

Suddenly, it struck Julie as she watched Arnold, that he would be someone she could confide in, he would advise her well, but she knew at the same time he would keep her secret. But the instant the thought entered her head she discounted it. How could she ever think of burdening Arnold with her problems? How utterly selfish that would be of her. This was something that she knew without doubt, she must bear alone.

'Thank you for a lovely evening, Julie.' Then Julie was aware of Charles and Sheila beside her, waiting to say their goodbyes.

'I do hope you have enjoyed it,' Julie said.

'We've had a wonderful evening, Julie, and we would like to say our thank you to Matthew. Is he around?' It was Charles who spoke, with Sheila simply nodding as they stood together. 'We're giving Thomas and Jenny a lift home if only we could find them.' Charles added 'We have to lift our rather rebellious daughter from her friend's house tonight, she wanted to stay overnight but we preferred her to come home, so that's why we must go. I must say Julie, Matthew looks well, he tells me he is reducing his hours and that can only be good.' Then, in a conspiratorial whisper, he went on. 'He tells me the Patrick Mullan case has been put on hold due to lack of evidence. That must be a relief to him I would imagine, it must have been very traumatic for him.'

'Yes indeed Charles,' Julie was grateful to be distracted by Thomas and Jenny who were anxious not to miss their lift. Julie did not want any talk about any crime, least of all the mystery one of Patrick Mullan. She hugged and kissed both Jenny and Sheila in turn, repeating that she hoped they had enjoyed themselves and both the women assured her that they had very much indeed.

Chapter 65

Matthew was going back this morning, to once again interview Julie's attacker and Lewis's abductor, not that there would be anything more to add to Jimmy Devlin's statement. The man had admitted everything during his stay in hospital. He had been discharged from hospital the previous week to Crumlin Road Gaol, still needing to use a pair of crutches following the removal of bullets from the bones of each leg. He was quite incapacitated and was unlikely to try to escape anytime soon. Matthew was going to see him, to get a signed statement from him. He was pleading guilty to the kidnap, to the holding of Rachel, but he still maintained he did not mean or intend to shoot anyone. He told Matthew the gun had only been meant to scare people a bit but he never meant to kill anybody.

But this morning when Matthew visited him in prison, he intended to question him further about his friend, Alfie, and what he knew, if anything, about the connection between Alfie and Patrick Mullan. Surely, if the two men had been working together on the kidnap of Lewis, Rachel's captor must have known something of Alfie's other subversive activities. He was determined to find out this morning, if at all possible.

Later that morning however, Matthew came away from Crumlin Road Gaol, thwarted once again in his efforts to find out the link between Patrick Mullan's accident and someone in Belfast. Jimmy Devlin told him again – even though Matthew had promised him that he would be shown some leniency if he could help them – that he had known nothing about Alfie having anything to do with any other case. Alfie, he told Matthew kept his actions very dark and underhanded. Indeed, he had never dreamt he was doing anything else ever. He thought Alfie depended on him – and him only – for the odd pound or two, and to think he was working away on both sides of the divide, well was it any wonder he was dead, Jimmy Devlin wanted to know? Silently, Matthew had to agree with his prisoner and reminding him his case was being called the following week, he left the prison deep in thought about how people became sucked down into a quagmire of wrong-doing and ended up losing their life because of it. The prisoner he had just left, was a prime example of a misguided quest for revenge for his so evil, brutal brother and now he too would get his just penalty for everything. Matthew had no doubt his prison sentence would be a long one. Surely the jury would find him guilty of murder and attempted murder?

Later, back at his office, Matthew rang Detective Forde to let him know, more out of courtesy than anything else, that he seemed to have exhausted every line of enquiry regarding Patrick Mullan and that he was now agreeable to shelving the case in the meantime. Hopefully, something of significance would turn up at some point. Michael Forde said he was glad that they were both at present in total agreement, but he did promise to keep in touch. He added that although they both had busy lives, he was keen, now that they had forged a friendship, to keep good contact.

'It certainty looks like it has to be put on hold, love.' Julie had been asking Matthew as they sat in the living room after dinner, all about his day. He had told her that morning, that he was going to see Jimmy Devlin in the hope he could throw more light on his friend, Alfie's activities.

'He assures me he knew nothing about anything else Alfie did, and he had never heard Patrick Mullan mentioned, until he was arrested for the raid on Patrick's home and his father's subsequent death.' Matthew replied to Julie's questioning. 'We have certainty hit a dead end just like some other cases in Northern Ireland, but I must say it pains me when that happens. Then again, who knows what turns up in the future.'

'Of course love, and do concentrate on all the successes you've had.'

'Thanks, Julie, I haven't really had many failures I know, and tomorrow I have another interesting but trivial case to investigate and then close.'

'Has it any connection to our cases?'

'It actually is linked to the ransom money, Julie. The empty attaché case was found in one of the hospital bins and there where finger prints on it. Forensics fingerprinted the ambulance men and the paramedic who came to the park, so the missing attaché case has been traced to one of them. I go to interview him tomorrow. I don't expect it will take very long for that, but I thought I would keep you up to date.' Matthew paused and then added as an afterthought, 'The only other person I have informed is Arnold. It was his attaché case after all so I thought he should know. '

Julie was silent when Matthew was relaying the very latest development in the abduction case. He realised she seemed to have lost interest and he reckoned she must have forgotten that there had been four to five hundred pounds still in the case. It was the most trivial of events within all-consuming happenings in their lives, and Julie probably thought that her husband would wrap up the case there and then, so he understood her lack of interest.

Chapter 66

The next morning, Matthew drove into a street off the Ravenhill Road, a street which was lined on either side with neat, spotlessly clean terrace houses. Slowly, Matthew drove along and parked outside number six.

The door was opened promptly in response to his knock, by a tall dark haired man whom Matthew reckoned must be in his mid-twenties. He showed him his identification card and without much change in his expression but just a brief nod, he opened the front door wide and said 'I've been expecting you. Please come in, I know why you're here.'

He led the way into a neatly, if sparsely furnished living room, which looked out on to a small garden with its evergreen hedge surrounding all four sides of it. A child's swing moved slowly back and forward, back and forward, in the light, morning breeze and it had such an abandoned cheerless look about it that Matthew returned his glance quickly back to the man standing beside him.

'I know why you're here,' the man repeated immediately they entered the living room.

'I did not introduce myself, I'm Detective Inspector Hampton and you are, I believe, Harold Davis. Is that correct?'

'Yes, that is my name. Please have a seat. Would you like some tea or coffee perhaps?'

Normally in a situation such as the one he now found himself in, Matthew usually declined drink of any kind, but there was something about this young man – some sadness, a pathos which pulled at his heart-strings. He seemed so lost and vulnerable somehow and Matthew forgot about his professional commitment as he looked at this person standing now in front of him, waiting no doubt to hear what might be going to happen to him.

'Yes, I would love a cup of coffee, please, black with no sugar, Harold.'

While he waited for Harold to return with his coffee, he looked out again at the child's swing in the garden, still swaying in the breeze, and he thought it strange that there was no other sign of a child – no child's shoes or coat or pyjamas were around and he had heard no sound of a child.

'Thank you.' Matthew said as Harold Davis handed him a cup, a very pretty cup, of coffee.

'I know why you're here, Detective. Do you want me to make a statement?'

'That depends, Harold. Let's just keep this quite informal at the moment. If you just tell me the truth you will have little to worry about. So have you anything to tell me?'

'I have the money here sir. I have it all here. I did not touch anything, I swear. I'll fetch it now.' And Harold Davis set his coffee down and made to get up from his seat. Matthew put a restraining hand out to him.

'Why don't you tell me all about it, Harold?'

At those words the young man seemed to shrink in size and holding his head in his hands he burst into tears.

'It is my wife, you see. She is heartbroken. She is upstairs in bed and refuses to get up she is so depressed. And the doctors,' and here he gave a loud sniff in an effort to control his crying. 'They tell me they can do nothing, they say she will come round in time, that's what they tell me.'

'What happened, Harold? Something happened here, didn't it, Harold?

'Our little boy – he was just two. He died four months ago. We are finding it difficult to go on. It will take a miracle to help us forget.' Now Harold Davis's voice was little more than a whisper.

As Matthew listened to this young man trying to explain away his grief, his eyes were drawn back once more to the swing, which at first must have meant so much to the boy's parents but now it seemed only to demonstrate some awful emptiness and despair. And Matthew understood now, his reaction to the little boy's swing and that he had not imagined the abandoned look about it.

'He had cancer you see, and nothing could be done, nothing at all.'

Matthew just continued to nod, at a loss how to help this man cope with his grief and that of his wife's.

Now he was speaking about his wife. 'I thought to take her away, away from her memories here, but of course you can't get away from them, they are with you all the time.' He looked at Matthew, his eyes still filled with tears. 'That's why I kept quiet about the money. I was tempted, you see, to take her away but I could not do it. In the end I could not do it so she is still lying in bed most days. And now, I have made matters so much worse. I am now facing a jail sentence, no doubt.' Harold was finding it difficult to get the words out. 'What will happen to Jessie then?'

'Harold, if you fetch me the money that is the end of the matter as far as I am concerned. But if you are agreeable I would like to send my friend round to see you. I think he might be able to help you both. Does your wife get up in the afternoons at all?'

'Yes, briefly, but if I was expecting a visitor, I would be quite strict and insist she does get up and I know she still has some pride left and would dress and get up.' Harold seemed to have gained some control and was somewhat less emotional.

'I'll fetch the money,' and he hurriedly left the room. Matthew heard him rummaging about in the room next door, which was probably their dining room and then he appeared with Arnold's money.

'You will find the money untouched, Inspector. I have not touched it since that day, that horrible day, since I saw the case sitting against the tree and I brought it home and looked at the contents. It was mostly squares of paper, Sir, wrapped up in fifty pound notes, very cleverly done, Sir, and would have fooled anyone, whoever did it,' Harold Davis looked over at Matthew, as if expecting some comment and when there was none forthcoming, he went on.' I just put it in a cupboard in the dining room.' He indicated the room next door.

'I'll take it from you now.' And Matthew gently took the money from the man's hands. 'I want to reassure you that I don't intend to make any charges here. I'll simply make out a report to say that the money was handed in and that all was well.'

The expression on Harold Davis's face when Matthew spoke, was reward enough for Matthew. His whole demeanour changed and he looked as if some awful burden had been lifted from him.

'I'll ask my friend to call round to see you tomorrow afternoon, around two o'clock, say. His name is Arnold Simpson – he will be driving a disabled car so you can look out for his arrival.' Matthew sounded confident enough, even though, he thought he had not as much as waited to contact Arnold in order to ask him. But knowing Arnold, he did think he would do his best to be here.

'I do believe my friend will do everything he can to help you. You have my card, Harold, and you may wish to be in touch. Do ring me at any time.' And then Matthew said his goodbyes and, money in hand, left Harold Davis's sad home to begin his drive back to his office.

Chapter 67

'Certainly, it is a very sad story and I am so glad you told me about it, Matthew.' Arnold had rang Matthew the following evening after Matthew had told him about his initial visit to the Davis's and the story of the attaché case and had arranged to drive round to Matthew's cottage, explaining that he had quite a lot to tell him and it would take much too long over the telephone. Now, sitting in Matthew's living room with a cup of coffee, Arnold began to tell Matthew about his visit.

'Did you know he is currently off work looking after his wife and has been given a warning that if he does not return to his work in the ambulance service he will lose his job forth with.'

'No, Arnold, I did not know any of that. I did wonder, mind you, how he could possibly leave his wife in the mental state she appears to be in, to go out to work as usual.' Matthew replied.

'Well, he did go on occasions when his wife's mother could relieve him and come and stay with her daughter. But it seems she does some part-time work, too, so she was limited in how she could help.'

Arnold hesitated in his narrative and then went on. 'But that is not all, Matthew. Harold's mother-in-law lives on the other side of the street from them and during the traumatic days and nights when their son was so ill, they spent all their time at the hospital. But you see they had a cat, a beautiful black cat who they had acquired as a kitten and since then, they had been inseparable from him. When their son became ill, Maud, that is Mrs. Davis's mother, took it upon herself to feed the cat. She did her best for him but no doubt out of loneliness, he began to follow her home to her house and would have spent time there with her. But then, no doubt anxious to see his owners and to get back to his own territory, he would go back home. It was on one of his trips when returning home that he was knocked down and killed instantly. That in itself has been very traumatic for them both – he was just like one of the family. They are suffering another loss here and then Mrs. Davis's mother-in-law is wracked with guilt, Matthew.' Arnold paused for breath. He had seemed to Matthew, to be anxious to unburden himself.

'So how did you leave them, Arnold?' Matthew was quite taken aback how involved already Arnold seemed to be in this young couple's plight. He had discovered so much more about them in the time he had been there than Matthew had during his.

'How did I leave them, Matthew? I told them I was going home to think about ways that I might be able to help them. I don't think just handing them money is a very good idea. They need some new focus I believe, Matthew, to enable them to attempt to move on. Perhaps some alternative employment that they would get paid for. So that's what I'm thinking, but in terms of exactly what or how to proceed, I just don't know' Arnold seemed to ponder over his next words. 'But did you know Jessica Davis was a domestic science teacher? So that might be something to latch on to.'

'Jessie, love, Mr. Simpson says he is going to help us. What do you think, love? Do you think the man's genuine?' Harold was trying his best to rouse his wife to show some sort of interest in the man who had just left their house. A man so obviously disabled and who had told them all about his wife having been shot dead, yet there he was, prepared to help and support them, and him a total stranger.

'I don't know why he would bother with us,' was his wife's only comment.

'Love, I don't know why, but I do believe he means it. I really do.'

Jessie Davis did not say anything more to her husband. But she knew this man, Simpson, could not help her in her sorrow, of that she was convinced. No one could. It just sucked her into this huge, black hole from which no one, she believed, would ever be able to lift her out of.

The very next day however, Arnold Simpson appeared on Harold and Jessie's doorstep in Ridgeway Street, a visit which shocked them both. Jessie had thought it unlikely they would ever see him again, and although Harold had known the man would be back, he had never imagined it would be so soon. He carried a cardboard box under one arm and what appeared to be a bag with groceries in the other. He was obviously struggling to maintain his hold on the box and when Harold opened the door he immediately gave the box to him. It was only then that Harold noticed the prosthesis on his arm and was shocked to think how this man must cope with his disability. He had noted his prosthesis on his leg yesterday when he sat down but he had never noticed the fact he had another. Then, when they were in the sitting room, Arnold asked Jessie to take the cardboard box from Harold and open it.

When Jessie did as Arnold asked, she was greeted immediately by the purrs of a beautiful Persian kitten, which looked up at her with such appeal in its eyes, that Jessie lifted it up at once and hugged it to her without thinking. Meanwhile Arnold, as he watched her, was relieved at such an almost automatic response the girl gave to such a lovely bundle. Then he turned to Harold and asked him to open the bag and when Harold did, it was to see that the bag contained cat food, a litter tray and litter.

'I thought I might bring you a pet to love and cherish. It won't replace your other one, I know, Jessie, but it will be of some comfort I believe, to you. And it is an indoor cat, so it will be safe here in the house with you.'

Arnold felt he had to acknowledge that this little kitten was not a replacement, because he was so very aware that whether it is an animal or a human that someone loses, nothing can ever replace them. Anything, he knew, that had been loved and lost was irreplaceable. All Arnold Simpson was simply trying to do today, was to give this young, lovely woman something to look after and hug and cherish. Such a beautiful animal might, just might, help lift her out of the black pit she found herself in.

Yes, he knew only too well it was beyond anyone's ability to replace the terrible loss these two young people had endured, but somewhere perhaps, this little bundle, which Jessie was still holding on to, would be of some comfort and company to her and her husband in their darkest days.

'Julie, I do hope I'm not interrupting your peaceful evening with Matthew but I would like a quick word or two with him.'

Arnold had appeared at their front door just after Julie and Matthew had cleared up the kitchen and were in the process of settling into their living room for the evening. Now Julie replied to Arnold, as she indicated a seat beside the window for him.

'He's just gone into the bathroom, he'll be back shortly. Is it confidential, Arnold? Do you want me to leave you and him alone?' Julie asked him.

'No, not at all, Julie. Oh, there you are Matthew.' Arnold addressed Matthew as he entered the living room. 'I wondered if you had any free time tomorrow, I know it's Saturday and you usually try to spend it with Julie here and Emily, but I would really like you to come and view a property with me tomorrow. Jason is coming, so if it doesn't suit, no harm is done, but I do value your opinion.'

Matthew looked over at Julie who immediately responded. 'Of course you must go, love. Besides I'm feeling rather tired at present so I wouldn't mind a day in the house.'

'Thanks, Julie. Actually it's a public house I want to go and see.'

'A public house? Whatever for, Arnold? Whatever next?' Matthew exclaimed.

'Actually, I'm thinking of the Davis's, to be honest. And I'm sure you must think I'm some sort of old, simple fool, with bags of money to throw around me, and maybe I am. But I do want to help and if it gives me an interest, sure that's good too. Harold Davis has now been officially suspended from his job because of his time-keeping, so he more than likely is going to lose his position. So I wondered.' Arnold hesitated 'It's only a thought, mind you.' he seemed reluctant to elaborate. 'I thought, as Jessie Davis has a domestic science background, between her and Harold, they might help to run it. The one I hope to look at with you, Matthew, has accommodation upstairs, quite a large apartment, in fact' Arnold looked at Matthew and Julie in turn. 'Do you think I'm mad?'

Matthew just shook his head and it was Julie who answered him. 'I think you are the most compassionate, generous man I have ever met. Imagine you even contemplating helping that young couple.' Julie went on, 'Matthew told me their very sad story and I must admit, if I had the money, I too, would try to ease their agony and despair. But you, Arnold, have acted on how you genuinely feel for them. Such kindness.' And Julie seemed quite overcome and fell silent.

'That's settled then, Arnold.' Matthew too, was overcome by the man's generosity but was trying to sound as matter of fact as he possibly could. 'What time to-morrow, then?'

'I did tell Jason we would leave home around ten o'clock in the morning.' Arnold answered.

'Look, Arnold, I'll drive you wherever you want to go, my car has slightly more room in it, I think.'

At this, Arnold smiled happily at Matthew.

'I do believe it has, Matthew. 'Pick your son and myself up around ten o'clock in the morning.'

Later that evening Matthew and Julie talked over everything they had learned in the last couple of days about the young couple from Ridgeway Street and how an angel in the form of Arnold Simpson had entered their lives in the most unforeseen manner. And much later as they prepared for bed, – they had talked at great length – Julie decided that her decision about those damning notes she had discovered could wait until the 'Attaché Case situation' as she liked to call it, had all been sorted out. It was so interesting to hear about this young couple and what Arnold meant to do to help them, that Julie felt her predicament could take a back seat in the meantime.

Chapter 68

'What do you think of all this, Matthew? I need your honest opinion, so do please tell me truthfully. Has this place potential?' Arnold looked at his two friends who had been so ready to accompany him this morning to this public house with its apartment above which he already envisaged the two young couple, whom he had lost his heart to three days ago, living here. Even though he was asking Matthew and Jason's opinion, he had more or less made up his mind that he was going to buy this place.

'I think it's in an excellent situation, Arnold,' was Jason's first comment after very quietly walking round the whole premises with his father and Arnold, 'So close to a sprawling housing estate, plus at least three streets of terrace houses, all within walking distance. How could it not do well?' Jason was becoming more enthusiastic by the minute. 'I know if I lived here I would be delighted to have a public house, plus an eating house within walking distance of my home. It has to be a winner, Arnold.'

Arnold was delighted with Jason's obvious interest in the place but he knew he valued Matthew's opinion, and his comments, Arnold felt, would be worthwhile. Now he turned to him. 'What do you think, Matthew?'

Matthew was silent for a moment, obviously trying to find suitable words and then he said very simply. 'I agree with everything Jason has said, Arnold, and not because he is my son, I hope you know that' Matthew smiled and then went on. 'There is one thing Jason has not thought of and it is the whole area the place is in, and I'm so glad to say that this part of Belfast, the Belmont Road area, has reported no violence of any kind over the years in any of its streets or indeed any of its public houses. So that to me, Arnold,' Matthew stressed, 'is more important than anything.'

'I'm delighted to hear your opinions, especially yours, Matthew, about the whole area. I must say I spent all day yesterday scouting around the whole place and came to exactly the same conclusions as you both have. Although I did not know of any history of fights or trouble, the whole place looked so clean and calm that I loved it all from the very beginning.' Now Arnold beamed at his friends before adding, 'And I have to say the owners, who are retiring to the seaside, have accepted the offer I put on yesterday, pending both my good friends' approval, which I have now had, and thank you both for that, but your day is not over yet. I would like you, Matthew, to drive me now to Ridgeway Street and you must come along too, Jason. I need to see how these young people will feel about my suggestion. They may well think I am an interfering old so and so, and wish I had never entered their lives. Ridgeway Street is what they have known and loved you know. I don't know how they might feel about moving from it, even though they already facing the threat of eviction through non-payment of their mortgage. But,' and here Arnold hesitated in his somewhat prolonged narration. 'If they give me a resounding rebuff, I will need you both with me to pick up the pieces. Besides, I am committed now to these owners here and who else will I get to look after the pub.'

Matthew and Jason had no answer to any of this and just followed Arnold quietly out to the car with Matthew then at the wheel, heading back to Ridgeway Street and Matthew marvelling at how people's lives and time can become so quickly entrapped in other people's troubles.

And how some people have the capacity and ease to walk away from such troubles, while others find it impossible to do so. Now Matthew prayed that all Arnold's kindness and generosity would not be turned down and that he would not indeed be rebuffed in his efforts to show kindness to others.

'Oh, Julie, it was a delight to witness it all, if only you had been there. Harold Davis's whole demeanour was transformed when he heard Arnold's proposal. It seems that before he became a full time ambulance driver, he did a bit of work as a bar man at night. So it's not new to him and it seems he rather liked it.'

'And what about his wife, love, how was she?' Although Julie had not met Jessie Davis she could only think of her as a sad, depressed woman struggling to come to terms with the loss of her son.

'She was most reluctant at first,' Matthew told her. 'And I was beginning to fear that Arnold was going to be rebuffed as he had dreaded he would be. But then, it transpired she was only worried about leaving her mother in Ridgeway Street after she had been so very good to her. So when Arnold described the large apartment and explained they would have plenty of room for her mother, if she was agreeable to going, Jessie's face lit up and she actually clapped her hands.' Matthew said. 'That's when I knew everything was going to be alright for Arnold.'

'And what happens next?'

'Well, Arnold told them to put their house on the market, he hopes they will get enough to cover their mortgage. It seems Jessie's mother's mortgage is paid out, so at least Mrs. Stevenson has no worries there. According to Arnold, she will have a bit of a nest egg when she sells her house.'

'Matthew, it does sound like a wonderful solution for that poor family. Just like something out of a fairy tale, so I do hope it all works out for them and that they are happy in a new job and a new home, it is quite a big change for them all, I think.' And Julie sounded quite sceptical.

'Well, if Arnold has anything to do with it, he'll make sure it works, Julie, and I just hope his health can stick it all. Sometimes I think he forgets about the prosthesis he has on his leg and his arm, so I think I'll tell him to try to take it a bit easier, although I think since Iris's death he likes to really fill his days. It is his way of coping, I know.' Now Matthew was reflecting on the last few days. 'To think this has all come about because we tracked down Arnold's attaché case and I told him, very briefly, about the man who had it and why he had it.'

'I'm sure it was meant to be, Matthew. You being the one to go there. I'm quite sure if any other officer had gone, Harold Davis would be facing a charge of theft, and how awful would that have been for his wife and himself and indeed for his mother-in-law.' Julie sounded quite cheerful as she went on. 'It was fate I'm sure, Matthew. It had to be fate that decried that you would be the one to go to that house and retrieve that case for Arnold.'

Even as she spoke to her husband, Julie was likening the fate that took Matthew to the house that day and the fate that ordered that she be the one to find the notes in the box in the study about Patrick Mullan, notes so very incriminating for a family member. She still found it difficult to believe that it was all because Matthew had asked her on that particular day to help him sort out those particular notes. If fate had decreed that she was to be the one to find them rather than Matthew, she firmly believed they were never meant to be produced in a court of law. Now that she firmly believed that she was right in her way of thinking, surely by destroying them, she would be bringing the greater joy to the greater number of people. But before she destroyed them, she had one very daunting task she must do. But she would really like to wait until she

332

had seen Arnold's latest project, the public house he had bought with its apartment above it. Now, as she sat with Matthew in the cosy sitting room of their cottage in companionable silence, she had to talk to herself about how she really was procrastinating and putting off that task which she knew she must eventually do. Surely it would be such a relief to her to talk to someone, no matter who, indeed anyone who would listen and she had no doubt the guilty party would be very prepared to listen to what Julie was saying.

Chapter 69

February 1986.

Julie entered the coffee shop and rather nervously looked around her, viewing the tables in their usual places and any occupants who were there. She had been meeting her friends and relatives here on a very regular basis and she was well known to both staff and customers, so usually, she felt very comfortable coming here. But this morning was so very different and she was relieved to see only one other couple who were strangers to her, sitting at a table by the window, no doubt because it had just gone nine-thirty in the morning, regular customers had not made their way there yet. Somewhat more relaxed now, Julie made her way over to a vacant table in a rather dark, secluded area of the shop. The waitress approached her almost immediately and greeted her warmly 'Good morning, Mrs. Hampton, are you waiting for some of your friends to arrive, or would you like me to bring you something while you wait?'

'A black coffee would be lovely in the meantime, thank you, Marie. There will only be one friend this morning and when she comes, she will no doubt have a coffee and we will have our usual scones, Maria.'

And then Maria, just as she always did, took a note of her order on her dog-eared notepad which she kept in the pocket of her uniform. In spite of her tension, Julie smiled at the routine of the place, obviously everything must be recorded even down to a couple of coffees and scones. Certainly, she was the only customer who was ordering at that moment, the couple by the window had already been served.

'Julie, how are you? I'm so sorry I'm late but we are meeting up somewhat earlier than our usual time, are we not?' Where's Jenny this morning?'

'Jenny won't be coming this morning. There is just you and I, Sheila. I've just ordered some coffee. Shall I order some for you? And shall we have our usual scones?' and Julie smiled at her sister-in-law as she spoke.

'That would be nice, Julie.' Sheila replied as she set her bag on the floor and pulled her seat in closer to the table. 'Why did Jenny not come this morning? She usually loves to meet up with us at every opportunity, doesn't she, Julie?'

'After the coffee and scones arrive, Sheila, I'll explain everything.' Julie answered. 'Oh, here is Maria with our coffee and scones just as I speak.' And Julie distributed the scones and butter and jam between them as Sheila thanked the waitress for her coffee.

'This is really nice, even just the two of us, Julie.' Sheila remarked as she buttered her fruit scone.

'You were wondering about Jenny not being here this morning. I did not ask her because I needed to see you alone.' Then Julie began to go through the contents of her handbag while Sheila watched, obviously quite intrigued by her sister-in-law's behaviour. Then Julie brought out two somewhat wrinkled notes and after smoothing them out thoroughly, she set them very discreetly on the table in front of Sheila.

'I believe these are yours, Sheila.' It was a statement, not a question.

Sheila lifted the two pages slowly from the table and it seemed to Julie, she was doing her best to come to terms with the fact they were her notes, it was her handwriting and the evidence before her was overwhelming. As Julie continued to observe her, Sheila's face went ashen but then in quite a controlled voice and out of context with her pallor and obvious shock, she nodded slowly, looked at Julie very directly and said, 'Yes, Julie, those are my notes. How did you come by them? Where were they?'

'They came from a house outside Hailsham, a house you posted them to when you posted the photographs of Patrick Mullan, Sheila. I have them since I found them one morning and have kept them safe ever since.'

'Why did you not give them to Matthew? Does he not know anything about them?' Now Sheila sounded incredulous. 'I mean how did he not possibly know? Was it not him who searched the house in Hailsham? How on earth did you come by them?'

'Sheila, I need to try to understand why you did such a dastardly thing as to identify Patrick Mullan's whereabouts to those who wished him harm. So before I start to explain my motives by coming to you with both these damning letters, before I even thought of showing them to Matthew, I need to know your motives.'

'You want to know Julie, why I identified Patrick Mullan's whereabouts to those who had the means to hurt him, I'll tell you, Julie, and I'll also tell you – which one of those letters states quite clearly – that I never wanted him dead. I just wanted someone to hurt him as he had hurt my dear friend and later, my sister-in-law all those years ago, when she was married to him. You must remember surely, Julie, that it was me Lucie came to, often in the middle of the night, after her husband, Patrick Mullan, had beaten her up and that was quite often, Julie. It was my bed Lucie Mullan lay down in quaking and bruised and battered. I suppose you could say he could have been forgiven for all that, but then later, the horror of what he did. He plunged the entire Hampton family into such despair and grief with the murder of Rob. I had to watch my darling husband,

Charles, go to pieces over his father's death, and I held Lucie tightly in my arms many, many times while she grieved for the death of her father. Have you forgotten about all that, Julie and the awful time your Matthew had, having been the one to witness the violent death of his father?' Sheila paused and looked at Julie expectantly, and then took a bite of her scone and a sip of her coffee.

'Of course I remember everything in great detail and always will, Sheila, but it was not our place to seek revenge. The courts punished Patrick Mullan for what he did. We should never try to take the law into our own hands. It is obvious to me this morning, you think quite differently to me on that subject.'

'I think the law was very lenient to him, not during his time in prison but when he got out and they actually gave him a new identity, a new job and eventually moved him to one of the most beautiful places in England, County Sussex. Well, I must say I became more and more bitter towards him the more I heard about his new wife, his new baby and a wonderful new way of life ahead of him.' Again Sheila hesitated, looking over at Julie for some reaction or some comment, but Julie seemed incapable of commenting on anything Sheila was trying to explain about her actions. Instead she just sat looking at her sister-in-law with a look akin to distain on her face.

Julie had great difficulty now adjusting to this new side to Sheila Hampton, Charles' loving wife and mother of his two children. This girl sitting before her, explaining away her evil act, was not her dear beautiful sister-in-law, this girl was a stranger who seemed quite justified that she was right in what she had done. Eventually, she found her voice and began to speak because there were things she was desperate to know, needed to know this morning.

'How did you manage to trace him? I believe these secret identities are all just that – secret identities, Sheila.' Julie could not understand how her sister-in-law had seemed to find it so easy to trace Patrick Mullan, when top security men went out of their way to give these special cases – just out of prison – new identities and new lives well away from those who wanted to exact revenge. Now Sheila was confirming which Julie had just begun to realise.

'It was really easy, Julie. You would never believe it. I placed an advertisement in the daily newspaper asking for help in tracing someone. I also said I was prepared to pay out excellent money to whoever was willing to help. I had one answer the very next day as it happened, but it was a very worthwhile answer. The man said he would be prepared to help me for a tidy sum. That was how he put it.'

'Sheila.' and here Julie felt compelled to interrupt her explanation of what she had done. 'Did you ever once stop to think that if you were caught, what it would be like for all of us? For all the Hampton family? Did you ever once think of Charles and your own children? Of Matthew and his career? Did you think of me and how it would be for me when I heard you had committed such a cowardly act? You, who were always so kind and attentive to me both during my stay in hospital and when I got home. How do you think I felt when I found these notes and knew, without a doubt, it was your writing? Did you think of any one of us? Or were you just intent on revenge rather like my assailant and Lewis's abductor was?'

While Julie had been speaking, Sheila had been sitting very still, her face ashen, and her eyes riveted on Julie, while she listened to her. But now Julie was relentless in her condemnation of her sister-in-law. 'Did you ever once think how it would be for all of us if you were found guilty of being an accomplice in Patrick Mullan's murder?'

Sheila was sitting staring at Julie and it seemed to Julie as if she had been struck dumb. Her mouth trembled but no words came and her eyes became larger and darker to

338

become deep pools within her white face as Julie waited for an answer to her questions.

Finally, in a low, trembling voice and a vehement shaking of her head, she replied. 'Never once did I stop to think about any of that, Julie, never once. I thought that if any of the family heard he had been hurt they might be glad to hear it but never once did I think how they might feel if they knew that I had been involved.' And suddenly, Sheila bent over the table, her head in her hands and began to sob.

Quietly, Julie reached over and handed her a napkin from the table. 'Well, Sheila, you may well cry now that you seem to realise the repercussions of your actions, how it would be for the family. You should be very thankful it was me who found those notes you now have in your hand and not Matthew.'

'Does that mean you don't intend..?' Sheila began, but Julie cut her sentence short.

'I haven't decided yet what exactly I am going to do. I think that depends on all you have to tell me.' Julie replied quietly. Then reaching towards her sister-in-law once more, she carefully retrieved the notes from the table where Sheila had just laid them. 'I need to know more, you see, Sheila. Tell me who the man was here who put you in touch with the man in Hailsham.' Julie settled down in her chair and waited patiently for Sheila to tell her all she knew.

Chapter 70

Sheila began to tell her story in a stilted, slow way, reluctant now it seemed, to verify that she had participated in such a scheme.

'The man who initially contacted me said he had a good contact. This contact often went to England and he in turn would soon find somebody who would do the job providing the money was alright.'

'Who was this man who answered your advertisement?' Julie asked, simply because she felt Sheila was struggling to know what to say that would be most important. But at the same time Julie was amazed at her sister-in-law's tenacity in pursuing her quarry.

'He only told me his first name. He said his name was Alfie.'

Julie just nodded, knowing at once it was the same Alfie Reid who had died in prison and whose notes Matthew had brought home. She was tempted to tell Sheila that her informant had died in Crumlin Road Gaol but decided to let her continue to talk.

'A few weeks after Alfie first contacted me he rang me one morning around ten thirty a.m., he knew not to ring me until Charles had gone to work and the children to school. He was very excited and said he had found out where Patrick Mullan was living and he told me it was Hailsham. He did say that he almost had him but he had managed to elude him. He then said he needed some money from me to find somebody to do the job I wanted done.' Sheila seemed to be finding it easier to talk and even anxious to tell all she knew. 'I met him one morning and handed over the photographs and £400 and promised him more when Patrick Mullan had been given the beating up he deserved. I told him I would need evidence that it had all actually happened.'

'What happened next? Julie asked, then added, 'Did you know that your friend, Alfie, Alfie Reid his full name was, was found dead in prison?' and immediately Julie had said it, she knew that Sheila had been totally in the dark about what had happened to Alfie Reid. Now she had such a look of shock on her face that Julie thought she might faint. She called the waitress back to their table.

'Could we have another pot of coffee, please, Marie? Nothing to eat and thank you.' Julie managed to smile openly at the young girl. When the coffee was brought, Julie insisted that Sheila drink some and was rewarded to see some colour return to her cheeks. Then Julie continued.

'I think Matthew told me he was poisoned.'

'Oh, my God. I did not know,' Sheila whispered but now, as if anxious to have this liaison with Julie over and done with, she hurried on. 'Do they know who did it, poisoned Alfie, I mean?'

'They reckon it was someone who visited him in prison the evening before, but they have no leads on him, as far as I know.'

'You see, I had another couple of phone calls but they were from a different man. He said Alfie was sick and had asked him to contact me. He told me he was the contact who often went to England and because Alfie had told me all about him, I felt it was all right. He also told me that his other contact in England had managed to take photographs of Patrick Mullan and he wanted to show them to me. He stressed that Alfie said he wanted the rest of his money as he had traced Patrick Mullan for me, so his job was done. He said Alfie had asked him to collect it for him.' Sheila now seemed exhausted as she finished her narrative but Julie still had some more questions for her.

'Did you not suspect this man at any point?'

Sheila just shook her head, obviously incapable of saying much more.

'Did you go and meet up with him as he asked you to? Did he show you Patrick Mullan's photographs?'

'Yes, I did meet him and yes he did show me photographs of Patrick Mullan. They had obviously been taken when he was going to his place of work and that was when I gave him the money to give to Alfie. No doubt, he kept the money and Alfie was killed so that he could tell none of this story. I heard nothing after I handed over the money until I heard Patrick Mullan had been killed – killed by a hit and run driver, I believe.' Now Sheila broke down and sat sobbing quietly, her head in her hands at the table.

'Sheila, I think we need to get out of here, the place is beginning to fill up even though it's still quite early. I'll go and pay for the coffees, so sit tight for a moment, then we'll leave together and don't mind if people are looking, it's not important.'

After paying the bill, Julie re-joined Sheila and then they both made their way out to the car park.

'Come and sit in my car for a little while, Sheila, you don't want to go home like that. Indeed, you could not go anywhere like that' Julie said at the same time, guiding Sheila by the arm to her car.

Once they were in the car, Julie in the driver's seat and Sheila in the passenger seat, Julie sat silently waiting for some sign that Sheila was more composed. Then as the silence lengthened and just as Julie thought she must say something to her sister-in-law, Sheila spoke.

'How am I ever going to live with what I have done, Julie? I just want to end everything, I really do. Will you promise me you will care for my girls and don't let them know the awful thing I did, please promise me that, Julie.'

'You what, Sheila? Do you think I have kept this secret from everyone for these last months, especially from my loving husband, for you to now crack up and threaten to end everything?' Julie felt incensed by what Sheila had just said to her. 'I could have sunk you months ago but I chose not to. Not really for your sake, mind, Sheila. I was not thinking about any regrets you might have. I kept this horror secret because of everything else our family has had to endure in the last few months. But I believe that learning this now about you, after knowing and loving you all these years, would probably be the worst thing of all, a criminal in the family. For us who have all suffered at the hands of criminals, it would be very hard to digest and move forward from if you were to be branded one.' Julie paused, 'I want one promise from you, Sheila and I shall make you one in return. I want you to promise me that for the sake of your children and Charles, you will never attempt to do anything stupid to yourself. In return, I promise that while you and your family are in this country I will never tell anyone, not even Matthew, no, especially Matthew. If you ever left here to live elsewhere, and who knows, people do up sticks and go somewhere new, especially if their children find themselves in another country, I might well change my mind. So that is my offer, Sheila. Are you going to agree to it?'

In answer Sheila reached over and hugged and kissed her sister-in-law and then Julie said, 'I do understand why you did it, you know, Sheila. Love for your friend, Lucie, and for your husband. And you might get a judge who would understand but then again you might not. So let's not take that chance.'

Julie hugged her sister-in-law, glad at last to have had someone to talk to about it all and also thankful to hear exactly why Sheila had acted as she did.

'There is one thing I don't understand, Sheila. The letters MH, what did they stand for?'

'Why Mrs. Hampton, of course, Julie. Not very innovative I know, but it was all I could think of and Alfie wanted some reference to jot down he said. Nothing very high powered I'm afraid, Julie.'

'I did wrack my brains you know, Sheila, to try and decide what they meant but I never would have come up with such a simple explanation. I was looking for something much more complicated, but that's it then.' Julie paused then and looked at Sheila directly, 'You and I have this burden to live with now, and I hope that knowing now that it is a burden halved we will be better able to cope. We have no choice, we will have to cope.' Then Julie remembered the notes in her handbag. 'I will keep the evidence Sheila. At the present time I need to look on them as my insurance. I hope you understand.'

Sheila just nodded her head – she was coming to the stage where she did not care if Matthew Hampton did find out. Who knows, perhaps he too, would find it very difficult to have her arrested and branded a criminal.

Chapter 71

'How are Harold and Jessie doing? Has Arnold said anything about when they hope to move in?' Julie had found Arnold's latest project so interesting and was very keen to meet the young couple he had taken under his wing. She knew too, that Arnold was in constant touch with Matthew regarding everything.

'Julie, the good news is that they have had a firm offer on their house, an offer which will just about cover their mortgage, according to Arnold. But the young couple who have put this offer on, are themselves trying to raise the necessary deposit. So there may well be a delay before they know for certain what their financial situation is like.' Matthew said. 'This is all related straight from Arnold, love, and he also tells me he would like them to move in to the apartment. He has had the painters and decorators into the place and he has also had a new bathroom installed in one of the bedrooms for Jessie's mother's private use. He is keen to get everything up and running and although Harold is there serving drinks during the day, he is always anxious to get back home to Jessie. So the pub has to close early at night and Arnold doesn't like that, he believes they are missing out on a lot of business.

'I would really love to meet them, I have heard so much about them. Perhaps when they do move in, you will take me for lunch in Arnold's new pub, wouldn't that be so good?' And Julie sounded very enthusiastic.

'Sounds like a great idea, Julie, but I would really like our first visit there to be as a family gathering and ask Jason, Lynn and the children. Indeed any of the rest of the family who would like to join us would be very welcome, don't you agree?' Matthew hesitated, 'Or if you just want you and I to have lunch together that would be perfect, too.'

'I think a family outing for our first visit would be lovely, Matthew, so let's hope Jessie decides to move in very soon and begin to show us all her culinary skills.'

'Well, I'll certainly be telling Arnold when I meet with him tomorrow, how much you are looking forward to dining in his new premises and sampling his wine.'

Matthew was delighted that Julie seemed to be taking an active interest once again in everything that was going on in the family circle and especially in this latest project of Arnold's. Indeed, all the family were quite amazed at Arnold's energy and enthusiasm for this new venture and Matthew realised that the man just loved helping other people on their steps to success. Matthew's own son and his wife and children bore witness to Arnold Simpson's generosity of spirit. Jason and his family now lived in a most lavish mansion, a truly beautiful place, which must be a real source of joy to them both. And now this young couple, Harold, Jessie and Jessie's mother, none of whom were related to anyone in the family, were being given the opportunity of a lifetime. It was all so generous of the man, but out of everything Arnold had done, one gesture above all the others had stood out as being the most understanding gesture of all. And that had been the purchase and the present of the beautiful, playful Persian cat to Jessie. That gift, to Matthew, personified more than anything how sensitive Arnold really was, and how he had recognised what the young couple were going through. He had known, in some small way how a small, so dependent living creature might help them live again. Again, Matthew felt, as he had so often over the last few months, how enriched his families' lives had become since Arnold Simpson had entered them.

As for Julie, he knew she too was astounded at the scope of his generosity and she was so very interested now in all that was going on in the new family Arnold had embraced. He knew it accounted for Julie's renewed interest in everything round her, that, and the fact that he had reduced his working hours considerably and he no longer brought any of his work home. His desk now was an empty one and only contained some new envelopes sitting waiting to be used, his paper weight which he had rarely used, but did look ornamental, and a couple of pens in their holdall. He had no regrets whatsoever about his decision to bring nothing remotely related to work home. That was exclusive to his office in the barracks, something he realised now he should have done long ago. It seemed to have made such a difference to Julie, and to their whole relationship.

A few days later, Arnold rang Matthew to let him know that Jessie, her mother Maud, and Harold would be moving to the apartment over the public house the next weekend and they would be open for lunches from the beginning of the following week. He explained to Matthew that Mrs. Stevenson had had a cash offer on her house and that would be one deal at least, clinched, and even though Jessie and Harold's was not settled yet, they were happy enough to move. In the meantime, Jessie felt that they ought to leave some of their furniture, in case this potential sale fell through. The place would look so much better, she believed, if there were some bits and pieces of furniture.

Arnold sounded in very good form as he talked. 'I just felt so good, Matthew, when I heard Jessie talk. She is really beginning to show a bit of interest, and do you know, I believe her new cat has a lot to do with it. She just loves that animal and spends so much time with it. And do you know, Matthew, I'm rather pleased with myself that I ever thought of it. It was such a simple thing to do, you know, and I must say I did it on impulse.'

'So you should be pleased with yourself, Arnold. It was a wonderful, sensitive gesture from you and you should feel very proud of yourself.'

Arnold thanked Matthew very modestly and promised to be in touch again very soon.

The Davis's move from their house in Ridgeway Street to the apartment above the public house was a smooth transition for them all. And Jessie knew it was simply because Arnold had organised so much help for them that they had precious little to do. He had enlisted Lynn and Jason's help, and Jason's young sister, Emily was there too, very keen to help Jessie put everything into their appropriate cupboards and drawers. Two of Jason Hampton's uncles, Charles and Thomas, were there to help lift any heavy furniture they were bringing with them. Jessie had never met any of them before but they soon put her at ease. Then of course her mother helped break the ice by making tea and distributing buns she had baked the previous day, to them all. Out of the proceeds from the sale of her house, Maud Stevenson had purchased two new sofas for her daughter's sitting room. They were in a pale green colour, a colour she knew her daughter loved. She also bought them a new fridge and washing machine, having suggested they leave the ones they had in the house. Secretly Maud thought, because her daughter had bought them second hand when she got married, that they would never survive the change.

It was four weeks later before Julie got her wish to dine in the restaurant of the public house, which had, by unanimous decision, been named simply 'Arnold's'.

Several members of the family came along too, as Matthew had originally wanted, and Julie was relieved to see Sheila was there along with Charles and Jenny and Thomas. Lucie and Paul had their two children with them for the occasion and everyone seemed in a more relaxed, contented manner than they had been for some time. But the highlight of Julie's day was when lunch, which had been delicious and a real tribute to Jessie's culinary skills, was over and Jessie took her up to view the apartment and show her the beautiful Persian cat she was now the proud owner of. On seeing the beautiful animal fast asleep on one of Jessie's brand new sofas, she fell in love instantly and decided that she would ask Matthew if they might purchase one. She knew it would help comfort her and help lift her out of her depression she still suffered from when she thought about the decision she had made about Patrick Mullan. According to Harold, the change in his wife since Arnold had presented her with the cat had been just wonderful and Harold told Julie he would recommend such a wonderful animal to anyone who was finding life difficult.

Chapter 72

August 1986.

After meeting her daughter and son-in-law's benefactor, Maud Stevenson had been overcome with the man's generosity of spirit, and his understanding and compassion for her beautiful daughter and her husband who had endured so much, She had felt so totally helpless and hopeless in the face of her daughter's trauma and grief over her darling son. Then this man, who had obviously been through so much himself, had come into their lives as the most wonderful benefactor they had ever met. Maud knew she would be indebted to him for the rest of her life, he had achieved what neither she or anyone else would have been able to achieve and that was her daughter's recovery from her deep depression and the real threat of a nervous breakdown. And to think that he had done so in a very simple way – he had done it by giving her the present of the cat. Something she, Maud, had considered doing on more than one occasion but lacked the courage to do, fearful of her daughter's heartbroken reaction. But Arnold Simpson, with some powerful instinct, had just forged ahead and bought the most beautiful animal for her daughter to love and cherish.

Indeed, Maud had to admit that she revered Arnold Simpson and despite his obvious disabilities, she found him very attractive and knew she was vulnerable to his attention to her and her family. And that, she knew, was in spite of the fact that her husband Jack had been dead for barely two years and she felt annoyed with herself many times for thinking of Arnold Simpson in that way.

'Where is Maud today, then?' Arnold had called at his public house to oversee how everything was going. He believed that the owner of any establishment such as this ought to show a healthy interest in everything. He depended on Jessie and Harold so much here but they did seem to be well able to handle most of the work and any problems that arose. And now today, after enquiring how everything was going, he realised Maud had not, as yet, appeared.

'Maud will be here shortly, Arnold.' It was Harold who answered. 'She has gone to some furniture shop or other because she says there is a good sale on. She has a real weakness for sales, you know. But she did ask me to specifically ask you if you have time, would you mind waiting until she returns.'

'Of course I've time. I have nowhere to go at present.' And Arnold smiled at Harold as he spoke, inordinately pleased that Maud had asked him to wait. 'I am not planning any more ventures, believe me. I have so much here, Harold, and so much at my home and on the Malone Road, what more could I ask for?'

Here, Arnold hesitated, reluctant to go on, reluctant to reveal his thoughts and all his memories of his love for his late wife, Iris and his loneliness without her company. He knew he craved some female company. The touch of a female hand on his arm or a female arm around his shoulder and an understanding look from a pair of beautiful eyes. But how could he, such a disabled example of manhood be, in any way, attractive to the opposite sex. He recalled many times, his conversation with Gavin Finlay, Rachel's husband, how he had expounded to Gavin, how in spite of his disabilities he was still attractive to the opposite sex. He knew now, as he had really known then, that it was all bravado on his part, and in truth he believed the opposite to be true. How he longed to be attractive but he thought that women might actually find him quite repulsive and not be remotely interested in him, wealthy though he might be.

Just as Arnold began to become impatient over Maud's non-appearance and he began to wonder why she had asked him to wait when she was obviously in no hurry to come back and his whole confidence was beginning to dissipate, the door of the lounge bar opened and Maud walked in. She was laden down with parcels and smiling broadly at Arnold. Setting her bags down, which seemed to Arnold to be bursting at the seams, she headed straight for him. 'Oh, Arnold, I'm so sorry if I've kept you waiting. I was held up in so many ways and in different places, that I thought you might not be able to wait, but here you are.' And Maud smiled brightly again at him, rewarding his patience so that he did not mind about anything else.

'Matthew, I would like to meet up with Julie and yourself sometime soon. I have been so involved in my new pub and how it is trading, that I feel rather guilty that I might have neglected all my good friends,' Arnold paused for a second. 'I do hope you understand how any new business venture is hard work, Matthew. I'm not making excuses but just a very valid reason for my neglect of you in the past few weeks.'

'Look, it's just so good to hear from you, Arnold. To be honest, Julie and I have not heard very much from any of the family circle lately, and I'm beginning to think that that is a good sign. A sign of normality returning to all our lives.' Matthew sounded so happy that Arnold too, was infected with his elation.

'What do you say, Matthew, we have lunch, courtesy of Jessie and Harold, say tomorrow around 12.30. p.m.?'

'Sounds good to me, Arnold, I'll just check with Julie that that's all right with her. Just hold a minute, she's in the kitchen.' Arnold could hear Matthew's step crossing the living room of his cottage, and then shortly. 'Hello, Arnold, Julie would just love to go tomorrow', Matthew said, then added. 'She says to tell you she just loves the place and she's quite sure a lot of people must feel the same.'

'Well, it does seem to be doing well.' Arnold said modestly, 'but I'll tell you all about it tomorrow and I'll see you then around 12.30. Bye, meantime.'

Julie was surprised to see so many of the family in Arnold's restaurant where Jessie now was fairly well established and able to produce the most delicious meals with the help of Maud.

'I thought it was only ourselves who were invited, Matthew.' Julie whispered as they walked along the long hallway with its beautiful windows, which showed the restaurant so clearly. 'That was silly of me' she said and smiled ruefully at her assumption that they might, in some way, be Arnold's special guests.

'You know what Arnold's like love. He loves to include everyone, but I think something else is going on here today rather than just a simple lunch for old time's sake, but we will have to wait and see,' Matthew replied.

Julie was surprised to hear Matthew say this, he was usually so circumspect but now she began to look at the gathering in quite a different light and she found she had to agree with Matthew. It did look like an extra special gathering, as if everyone was waiting in expectation for something or other. Julie was just about to try to speculate what it might mean but the opportunity was lost when, much to their surprise Harold Davis, in a most professional manner, announced their arrival to everyone who was already there. And Julie, for the first time in months felt truly relaxed and happy as she followed Harold to her seat.

It was Maud, Jessie's mother, who approached Matthew and her with the menus, explaining to them the dishes Jessie had cooked and ones which Maud would recommend. Then Harold brought the wine list to their table, explaining there would also be champagne at Arnold's request. Matthew declined any wine or champagne regretfully as he was driving and also needed to return to work in a couple of hours. Harold nodded in understanding and then brought the champagne bottle to Julie and poured her a glassful there and then. Julie loved champagne and had recently acquired a taste for it at Rachel's and Arnold's housewarming parties, not to mention their own party. It was hard to believe that nine months had passed since those days. There had, at least, been some healing since then, Julie thought as she sipped her champagne and gazed round the room, seeing all the individual family members who were here today. It was so obvious today that Arnold was held in very high esteem by each and every one of them. He had turned out to be such an honourable man, after all, and such an asset to their family. Who could ever have imagined that Arnold would have managed to live both with the grief of losing Iris and the awful knowledge of how she had died. Yet here he was today, everyone's hero, Julie reckoned, and still looked well for a man in his early fifties, considering his disabilities. And she hoped that someday he might meet someone who would understand him and be prepared to give him some happiness.

Harold was now pouring a soft drink into Matthew's glass on the table. 'There's to be a short toast, you see, Matthew. So you will need this. You must have something in your hand.'

'Thank you, Harold.'

354

'No, thank you, Matthew for everything. Without you, well, I don't know where Jessie and I would be today. It was you who sent Arnold to us, so we owe you so much.' And Harold smiled happily as he left their table and made his way now to the front of the restaurant.

'I have been asked by Mr. Arnold Simpson, proprietor of Arnold's public house, bistro and restaurant, to please be upstanding to raise a toast for Mr. Simpson's engagement to Mrs. Maud Stevenson.' Harold was at his most professional as he spoke. Then, before anyone had thought to lift their glass from the table, probably because they were so shocked by what they had just heard, Harold reverted to his own modest, ordinary self. 'Please join me in wishing my wonderful benefactor and a wonderful mother-in-law great happiness in their marriage. They both deserve it.'

Everyone immediately lifted their glasses in celebration of this wonderful news, and everyone there commented later, how surprised they were that Arnold had managed to keep it all so dark. Obviously he was anxious not to appear to be rushing anything after Iris's death. Even as they lifted their glasses, everyone realised that Maud was missing. Where was she? It transpired she was in the kitchen helping with the chores as she usually did. It was only after considerable pressure from Harold that she appeared, very rosy cheeked, whether from the ovens in the kitchen or from embarrassment at everyone's good wishes, it was hard to tell. Then it also needed a lot of encouragement from everyone for Maud, accompanied by her daughter, Jessie, to go round all the tables and show off her engagement ring, emblazoned with diamonds, which knowing Arnold, no one was too surprised about.

It was a wonderful couple of hours with Arnold responding to Harold's request for a speech; a speech, which was so sensitive to all who had lost loved ones over the years. He stressed that it was important to try to move on in life but also movingly said, that in no way, did that

355

mean loved ones were forgotten about. Quite the contrary, he insisted as he spoke so eloquently to them all of their individual losses and he did it all in such a sensitive manner that not one person there doubted the sincerity of what he was saying.

Arnold sat down to thunderous applause and then insisted that there were aperitifs and cocktails available for everyone before going home. Julie opted for an interesting looking cocktail Harold said he had just read up about, and would really like someone to try it.

On the way out of the restaurant with Matthew, Julie sought out her sisters-in-laws, Sheila and Jenny, and their husbands, Charles and Thomas. They had been seated at the other end of the restaurant during lunch and Julie was keen to speak to them all.

'I would love to meet up again soon for coffee, Sheila.' Julie was anxious to try to convince Sheila of the normality of everything.

'I was just saying the same to Jenny, Julie.' It was Sheila who spoke first. 'I would love to meet up. What about some morning next week? What would suit you, Julie?'

'Any day really suits me. Sheila.'

Will we say next Wednesday then, usual venue and usual time?' Sheila smiled as she spoke. 'Does that suit you, Jenny? I might have some interesting news to tell you both by then.'

'Wednesday's fine by me,' Jenny answered. 'I'll definitely look forward to that. I hope it's nothing too dramatic, we have had more than our fair share of drama, one way or another, to deal with over the past few months. I am very intrigued to know what your news might be'. Now Jenny smiled, easing the tension over any of the dramas that had occurred.

'Oh, Jenny, it's nothing like that. It might be good news, but we simply don't know if we have anything to tell you at all or not. I'm sorry to have said anything. It was just after hearing Arnold's good news I suppose I was carried away. But won't it be lovely just to meet up for our usual coffees anyway?'

Everyone then said their goodbyes, confirming once more the day and time to meet. On the way home however, Julie felt somewhat uneasy at Sheila's statement. Did she mean to confess all to someone or other? If Sheila did decide to do so, what would become of Julie? What would happen to this secure, happy family unit who were only now starting to come to terms with everything that had been going on in their lives during the last nine months?

But then as Julie thought about Sheila and her statement that it was probably good news she would have for them, she thought back to that day when she had taken the damning notes to Sheila, she realised her sister-in-law had no intention of confessing to anyone her involvement in Patrick Mullan's accident. So, whatever Sheila's news might be, Julie reckoned it had absolutely nothing to do with that.

Chapter 73

Sheila had not intended to say anything to either Jenny or Julie about what she was planning to do, she hoped, in the not too distant future. It had been an impulsive thing to say, considering she did not know if it would ever materialise or not. But she fervently hoped that it would because during the last few weeks, she had been fraught with anxiety and remorse. The first thing she had thought of each evening before she went to sleep and the first thing she thought of when she wakened in the morning was what on earth had ever possessed her to seek revenge on Patrick Mullan? What madness had possessed her to do such a thing when no one else in the family circle had ever thought to do so? But she did know the answer to her own question very well. She knew it was not really revenge for Lucie's beatings from Patrick Mullan, although they were very traumatic for both Lucie and herself. For herself, because she had to witness them on innumerable occasions when Lucie arrived at her door, hurt and bleeding, and for Lucie, who apart from her physical injuries, would always feel so humiliated because it was her husband who had inflicted them.

No, she knew that it was simply because of Charles, her much loved husband, who had been brought so low by his father's murder and she had never forgiven Patrick Mullan for his involvement in his death. She had loved Charles so passionately since she had first met him when Lucie was staying with her. She had never expected in those early days that Charles Hampton would have any interest in her and she was overjoyed when he told her he loved her. Since then, Sheila had sworn she would always be a loyal, faithful wife to him, which she knew she had been. But when his father was murdered and Charles was in such despair, Sheila found it a very difficult time in their marriage and it was then that the seed was sown to wreck vengeance on Patrick Mullan. This feeling was further fuelled by hearing of his new-found happiness with some other woman, his new identity and career, after the horrendous time she had endured watching Charles strive to recover both physically and mentally. At times, she had feared she would never get back the husband she had once known and that he would end his days in the psychiatric unit that he had been admitted to on several occasions. But gradually, through their love for one another, and his innate desire to be well, Charles did recover. Of course, she had never confided any of Charles' problems to anyone else in the family. They too were going through such a tormented time in their lives, she knew she could not turn to any of them and Charles, when he was in their presence, always tried to overcome his distress and make some semblance of trying to live again.

In her interview with Julie, and that is what Sheila had seen that fateful coffee morning with her sister-in-law to be – as an interview, she had confided very little of Charles and her ordeal to Julie but instead just gave her the bare facts of why she had sought revenge. It did not matter anymore what Julie thought, indeed, Sheila felt it did not matter anymore what anyone thought. She longed to end all this agony and despair she was in. But how could she? She had so faithfully promised Julie that she would never do such a thing. She must instead think of her husband and her two daughters, and, Julie reminded her, think of how Julie had kept her safe from the law by not revealing those notes.

Over the coming weeks, Sheila began to appreciate Julie's insistence on her promise not to do anything silly and to hold on tight to her thoughts of her family. Sheila knew that only for Julie, she would have contemplated ending it all.

Gradually, as Sheila began to come to terms with the enormity of what she had done, she did wonder if there was any way she might make some recompense for the wrong she had done. One morning, approximately three weeks after her meeting with Julie, Sheila had wakened suddenly, very alert and focused as to what she must do to try to atone for all her wrongdoings. Inspiration had really hit her as she climbed out of bed and made her way downstairs for some coffee, she suddenly could remember so much that was in some way or other connected to her association with Patrick Mullan.

She could remember Alfie so well, Alfie Reid, as his name turned out to be. Then she could see the black haired man so clearly who had met with her, in Alfie's place, to collect Alfie's money from her. At first, she had thought there was something remarkable about him but she could not remember what it was. No doubt, at the time she would have been really anxious to get away from him after handing over the money.

But now she remembered so vividly what there was that was so different about him and there was no doubt it would mark him out in any crowd. The instant Sheila had seen the man stepping out of his car she recognised immediately that he must have had a harelip as a child, for certainly, he had had not very successful surgery to repair it and the scar unfortunately was quite remarkable. It would distinguish him in any crowd. And that was another thing about that morning – he had made no effort to hide his car from her. No doubt he knew she was equally culpable in this crime as he was so he had reckoned he had nothing to fear. But Sheila had a weakness for some makes of cars and their number plates and this was a blue Audi he was driving and she mentally took a note of the number plate.

Over the next couple of weeks, Sheila thought very deeply about how she might have this man identified without bringing any suspicion on her. She would not wish anyone to suspect her at this stage, especially after Julie's attempts to keep it all under wraps. She would hope that by helping the police to bring him to justice, it might go some way to help her atone for her role in Patrick Mullan's murder. Not only would it help atone for Patrick Mullan's murder but also for Alfie Reid's, her original contact in all this. She had no doubt in her mind that the man with the disfigurement had been the one to take Alfie the cake, instead of Sheila's money to the prison. A cake, which according to her sister-in-law had contained poison. So she intended somehow to make some contribution to finding Alfie Reid's murderer. But the question was, how was she to get any information to the police? A telephone call was totally out of the question, as according to Julie, Matthew was still in charge of the case. So the very thought of ringing and asking to speak to whoever was in charge of the Alfie Reid murder case, made her blood run cold. She knew she could never take the risk of Matthew Hampton recognising her voice. She had had no choice only to send the information by letter. But this time she would not be writing anything in her own handwriting. She would have to type it and then send it anonymously to whoever was in charge so that no one would be able to trace it back to her.

She thought everything over very well before attempting to type anything and the letter was worded in such a way as to suggest the writer had been a visitor in the prison when the person with the cake had been there. Then the writer had seen the same man get into his car just outside the prison and because of the writer's interest in cars and the writer's photographic memory for numbers, the car's number was noted mentally. She was happy with what she had typed – it would appear from the words that the suspect had been seen at the prison. She must make absolutely certain that this was not traced to her because Julie's hard work in keeping everything secret would all have been for nothing.

She knew she was pinning her hopes on this information she was sending to the police going some way to making her feel somewhat forgiven for all her wrong doing. She believed that in some small way, if the person who had poisoned Alfie Reid was apprehended because of her information, it would help relieve her guilt. She could not do anything about Patrick Mullan but she was convinced that she could help in the search for Alfie Reid's killer.

Chapter 74

'Julie, I know I haven't brought any of my office work home with me for such a long time but today- well to-day – was different. I got a letter in the post, a typewritten letter, and would you believe it, the person who typed it seemed to have quite a vivid description of the person who must have visited Alfie Reid in his cell and had taken him the cake. The writer of this letter said that they themselves had seen the man concerned in the prison that evening and they were carrying what was obviously a cake box.' Matthew paused, 'I did not bring the letter home, Julie, I want to stick to my decision to bring no work home – but I felt I wanted to talk to you about it. I am thrilled with this breakthrough. Patrick Mullan's go-between might still elude me but if we have the man who poisoned Alfie Reid, it would go part of the way to solving things for me.' Matthew paused and he could see Julie was very alert and interested in what he was saying, and that was good, she had such an interest in everything now, it was quite remarkable.

'The letter described this man as being very distinctive due to the fact that he had obviously had an operation for a harelip which had not been very successful and had left him quite disfigured. But the best news, Julie, is that they were able to quote the make of the car and, wait for it, the registration number. And the writer said they hoped it was all accurate, because the number was quoted from memory, because the writer had always had an interest in numbers, particularly car numbers. Matthew waited for Julie to respond to this, what he considered was quite a phenomenon, the ability to remember numbers from way back, but Julie simply nodded, waiting for him to finish.

'So now we know so much and already my officers are out there looking for the man who poisoned Alfie Reid.'

July was quite speechless for a moment or two by everything Matthew was telling her, but then she quickly pulled herself together to talk to Matthew. She must bury her worrying thoughts of everything Matthew was telling her until later.

'I am delighted for you, love, and I am sure your men will pick him up in no time if the letter's information is all correct. I hope so, anyway.' But although Julie spoke very calmly, her mind was racing on, on to Sheila, her sister-in-law. It had to be Sheila who had typed this letter – Julie did not think it could be anyone else. It had to be Sheila who had been able to describe this man so well. Yet during that coffee morning when Julie had shown her the notes, Sheila had not described the man in any way. But then of course, Julie had not asked. She had not been interested in what he looked like, only that he had been given money by her sister-in-law. But now she could not begin to understand why Sheila had thought to type this letter anonymously to security. At least, Julie quickly realised, she had never mentioned money, which might immediately have made the killer realise who had grassed on him.

'I do believe it might be one of this man's own cronies who sent this, if they were in the prison at the same time as him.'

'More than likely it was, love.'

Now Julie realised that there really was nothing in the letter which might incriminate Sheila and really, the more

364

she thought about it, the more she began to think that it could have been someone else entirely who had genuinely seen the suspect in the prison, someone who was actually there at the same time as Alfie's visitor. Or even perhaps, a particularly observant prison officer. But still, in her heart, Julie felt that it had been Sheila, in an attempt to atone for some of her wrong-doing, had been the sender. Also there was one worrying factor in the letter which made Julie believe it was Sheila, a factor which very few people knew about, and that was Sheila's phenomenal memory for numbers. Now, Julie found herself hoping desperately that Sheila had covered her tracks well enough not to be suspected by the culprit of having identified him to the police. Sheila and she had come too far now for anything to be uncovered and Julie believed if Matthew knew how she had deceived him, he would find it hard to forgive her, he was such a consummate professional. But even now as she sat with Matthew, she could not find it in her heart to have any real regrets for what she had done. She believed that Matthew's inability to close the case on Patrick Mullan was nowhere near as important as their family and their happiness. So she could only hope and pray that Sheila, out of some act of conscience, would not betray either of them.

'I think it's all wonderful news, Matthew, and the description of this man does seem quite specific, doesn't it?'

'I just hope so, Julie, and I just hope it was his own car he was driving and not one he had borrowed to go to the gaol in.'

'Would that be a big setback for you, then?'

'Maybe, maybe not, but I still think we have a good strong link. The description is excellent and then of course we have a set of fingerprints from the box the cake was in, you know, Julie. So if we find this man and fingerprint him and the prints match, it will just be great to have Alfie Reid's killer charged with his death. It will go a long way to compensate for my failure to find the contact here with Patrick Mullan. Besides, the man who actually ran Patrick down is dead, so in a way that does close that case.' Matthew went on, 'I have more or less reconciled myself to that being how it is, Julie.'

'Matthew, I am glad to hear you say that, because the driver of the car who ran Patrick down at the end of it all, is the guilty party, and I'm glad you see it that way, Matthew because I think you were just torturing yourself.'

'I do know I was, indeed I do know that.' Then Matthew smiled at Julie. 'Enough of shop talk for today. Let's have a nice nightcap or two before we retire for the night.'

And Julie, in total agreement, said she would be the one to make them, made her way into the kitchen and began to pour the drinks. Now after talking once more to Matthew about Patrick Mullan, she felt more confident about their future together.

Chapter 75

February 1987

The day of Arnold and Maud's wedding was a wonderful warm one in spite of the time of year and the sun shone brightly for the entire day giving added brightness to altogether wonderful celebrations. Theirs had been a simple, quiet ceremony and at Arnold's and Maud's request, only Harold and Jessie from Maud's side of the family and Lynn, Jason and their children and Matthew and Julie only present at the service in the local Methodist Church on Malone Road. But afterwards, Arnold had invited the entire family circle to a garden party in his and Lynn and Jason's house. The same caterers who had supplied such beautiful food at his original house warming were there again to ensure Maud and he had a very successful wedding reception.

Arnold had specified that he did not want any stuffy speeches but it was very difficult to control this as many of his friends wished to say something and believed that Arnold and Maud's wedding reception was the perfect venue to do this. Matthew was the first to speak and his poignant words brought tears to many eyes. His main theme was how bravely Arnold had coped with Iris's death and how so willingly, he had handed over the ransom money in a bid to get Rachel home safely. Then, he reminded everyone there of his generosity towards Jessie and Harold and the wonderful opportunity he had given this young couple.

Everyone was surprised when Gavin, Rachel's husband, quickly sprang to his feet just as Matthew sat down. He began his speech by thanking Arnold profusely for firstly giving the ransom money so readily to save his wife's life. Then, he intrigued everyone, including Rachel, when he went on to say enigmatically that, thanks to Arnold Simpson's sensitivity and ability to be outspoken, and tell Gavin how things really were, he and Rachel had attained great happiness.

Matthew smiled to himself when Gavin sat down to thunderous applause, but Matthew knew Gavin would be asked a few questions before the day was out, by what exactly he had meant when he had referred to Arnold as outspoken. But Matthew knew Gavin would never divulge to anyone, not even Rachel, what he had meant. He would always keep Arnold's words to himself because Gavin probably believed that, as he watched Maud and Arnold together now, it could well have been Rachel and Arnold standing there. But thanks to Arnold's advice that had not happened.

There were others who insisted on having their say, so Arnold's hopes for only having a few speeches was futile, because so many guests wanted to say something. Jason spoke on behalf on Lynn and himself, thanking him once again for his generosity, his company and his advice. But mostly, Jason insisted, Lynn and him wished to thank him for his support and participation in Lewis's life and maintained it would have been so easy for Arnold to have walked away from his responsibilities but he had done the opposite, involving himself and Iris in his son's life. Now they wanted to wish him so much happiness with Maud.

The day and the celebrations wore on and as the evening drew to a close, it was Harold who once again, called everyone to order, stating that they had just one more announcement to make before the evening ended. He stressed that before he would go any further with this announcement he wanted everyone to know that Jessie and he were reluctant to say anything which might in any way detract from Arnold and Maud's day, but Arnold had insisted they should not let the day pass without letting everyone know that they were expecting a baby in four months' time. This statement from Harold was greeted with so much enthusiasm and delight by all the guests, that the young couple knew they would never forget this day.

Before Julie and Matthew went home that evening, Julie made a point of seeking Sheila out. She felt that her sister-in-law had been avoiding her for most of the day. But now, when Julie approached her, Sheila greeted her warmly, her smile genuine enough as she spoke. 'I've had a wonderful day, Julie and I do hope you have had too.'

'I have indeed, very much, Sheila.' Julie replied.

Then in a whisper Sheila said, 'Have you any regrets Julie? Do you wish you had told someone about me?'

'Absolutely not, Sheila. I must live with my deceit, Sheila,' Julie whispered in return. 'But look around here and just think if I had told how different it might all have been. Have you thought of that?'

'To be honest, Julie, I have thought about little else all day. Not that it spoiled anything – but it is just there, you know. I have had it all very well illustrated to me today, exactly what you meant Julie, when you said it would destroy everything.'

'I'm glad you understand why I did what I did.' Julie was relieved to be talking to her sister-in-law and knew she had finally begun to realise all the implications for Julie and what she had discovered all those months ago.

'By the way, Sheila, you did tell us you might have some news of you and your family. We are still in the dark.' Julie added.

'So are we, to be honest, Julie. But I can say nothing until we are clearer about what is happening in our lives.'

Chapter 76

Julie parked her car in the car park of the complex, which housed the coffee shop that Sheila and Jenny and she had been meeting in so regularly for some years with Lucie, also being there when her work commitments permitted her. This morning was however somewhat different, Julie felt, from all those happy, carefree times when they met. This morning was the first morning the sisters-in-law had met since the morning only Julie and Sheila had been there and Julie had had the damning notes with her.

Since that morning, they had all made provisional dates to meet but always Sheila had called them off, pleading other commitments. But Julie suspected that Sheila's frame of mind was such that she could not bear to meet up with any of them and try to act normally. She must have had a lot on her mind and Julie wondered what torment her sister-in-law had gone through before deciding to point the finger at the man she believed had murdered Alfie Reid. Especially, she must point the finger without incriminating herself in any way. But now this morning, they were at last meeting up and Julie hoped it would be as carefree as possible, given the situation between Sheila and herself. As she made her way through the doors of the coffee shop, she was glad Matthew had told her about the anonymous letter. If indeed, Sheila had sent it, as Julie believed she had, at least now she might have a freer conscience. Now, it was good to see that Sheila was already there with Lucie – who must have managed to get a couple of hours off work – and they were talking very animatedly to one another. As Julie approached she was rewarded by a warm smile from them both.

'We've just arrived, Julie. How are you?' Lucie asked her then went on, 'I am never ceased to be amazed how you manage to walk so perfectly. No one would ever dream you have an artificial limb. It is quite amazing.' Lucie smiled broadly as she spoke.

'Thank you, Lucie. You must remember I had a very good teacher in yourself. Your determination and encouragement went a long way towards getting me like this,' Julie answered. 'It is lovely you could join us this morning – it's quite a while since we met up.' Julie was pleased to hear that Lucie, with all her medical experience, was so positive about Julie's walking and posture.

Just then, Jenny joined them and they settled down to order their usual coffee and scones and bring one another up to date with what was happening in their lives. Initially, the talk centred mostly on their children and what was happening with them all and everyone was interested in all their activities. In particular, Julie's sisters-in-law were keen to know how Lynn and Jason were, now that Arnold had brought Maud to his apartment in the grand house. Julie was able to reassure them that everything was working out exceptionally well for them all, although she did tell them that Harold and Jessie said they missed Maud's presence in their apartment. But they were quite light hearted about it, knowing Maud Stevenson loved where she was living now.

'Girls, I did say at Arnold's engagement party that I might have some news for you in the near future.' Sheila hesitated, and then looking steadfastly at Julie, continued. 'As you know Evelyn has obtained good grades in her examinations for entry to University. Well, she applied to Trinity College in Dublin to study law and has just heard back from them that she has been accepted. But that's not all – wait for it. Charles has been offered a post in one of Dublin's Survey offices, assessing Ordnance Survey work. So when we heard that Evelyn had gained entrance to Trinity, Charles decided to accept the post. He is very keen to accept it in any case, as the money is very good and he says he would find it hard to refuse. That means – girls - that we will be moving in the next couple of months to live in Dublin. It is a bit daunting I know, new job, new country, new house, but I am looking forward to going, I must say.' And Sheila seemed to direct her last few words directly to Julie.

Julie's mind was in a whirl as she listened to her sister-in-law and she realised what exactly Sheila was trying to tell her. Sheila was trying to tell her that once she was down in Dublin she would be safe from any prosecution for anything she had done wrong in the North. Did that mean that she was actually trying to tell Julie that she could now let Matthew know who the contact here was and who had been indirectly responsible for the death of Patrick Mullan. Yes, Julie had no doubt that Sheila was trying to say that if it would ease her conscience regarding Matthew, she had Sheila's consent to do so.

Now, Sheila was speaking again. 'As soon as we know the exact date and the address and telephone number of our new home, which at the minute we haven't even thought about, I promise to let you all know. And you must promise me,' and here Sheila's voice broke, 'you must promise to keep in touch and visit me often. I shall miss you all so much.'

Now, as they all sat finishing their coffee and trying to digest this latest piece of news and the knowledge that their close knit group of sisters-in-law would never be the same again, simply because one of them would be living a hundred miles away.

Julie firmly believed that Sheila had probably encouraged Charles to apply for this post, especially once she had confirmation that Evelyn would be going to Trinity. Julie believed it was highly likely that she had, and now Julie sincerely hoped that everything would work out for her and Charles and their family. She felt Sheila may well have decided to move outside the jurisdiction of the law, in order to help Julie decide what to do about Matthew. But obviously, Sheila had not given much thought to how things might be for Matthew and she, when he found out she had deceived him. Julie could never foresee a time when Matthew might find such deceit easy to forgive. He was such an upright, honest citizen himself and had a low tolerance for anyone who stepped outside the law.

As all four women said their goodbyes and hugged and kissed Sheila, promising faithfully to always keep in touch, Julie was deeply troubled about the whole thing and knew that if Sheila was doing it to help Julie, she was very mistaken. After all, her sister-in-law had done something to help ease her conscience when she had provided police with so much evidence to help try to trace Alfie Reid's killer. Why on earth could she not have left things at that? Was she now convinced she must be a martyr? She had only added to Julie's guilty conscience by believing she had left the path open for Julie to confess.

Chapter 77

'Yes, Sir, we have managed to pick our suspect up. The registration number and the type of car led us to a flat in Carrickfergus – an unlikely place I would have thought, but the man who answered the door fitted the description in the anonymous letter just perfectly. I have not much doubt he is our man. We will fingerprint him and see if his prints match those found on the cake box in Alfie Reid's cell.'

Ernest McAllister smiled at Matthew, now in appreciation. 'I hope so, Detective, I really hope so. I do know how important it is to you to get some of the mysteries surrounding Patrick Mullan cleared up. So let me know as soon as you have the results and we'll take it from there.'

'Thanks, Sir. I'm going on home now but I have left firm instructions with everyone regarding what has to be done.' Matthew returned his superior's smile, it was a good feeling to think that he might soon solve another case. 'I won't hang around. I do like to stick now to my scheduled hours and as you know I no longer do very much in the way of overtime. I think I was on the verge of burning myself out, certainly that's what my wife thought.'

'Well, you are certainly managing very well indeed Detective, I do believe you are even more focused.'

'Thank you, Sir.' And Matthew left his superior's office feeling quite good about everything.

Matthew knew that he was indeed more focused than he had been and he knew that was because Julie now seemed so much better and much more relaxed and their relationship impinged directly on how he concentrated on his work. He wondered if he should tell her this latest development in the Patrick Mullan case, as he still thought of it as. If the fingerprints identified him as the man who handled the cake, it would be another case solved. Only for that mystery witness, at or in the prison at the same time as this suspect, writing the anonymous letter they would still be in the dark. Matthew thought the most amazing aspect of the letter had been the fact that the writer had remembered the registration number of the car so well, and after such a lapse of time. Whoever the writer was they certainly had a most photographic, retentive memory, there was no doubt about it.

When he did arrive home a bit later than usual, the traffic had been a bit heavy due to another bomb scare. Although the threat had been lifted, it had left a backlog of traffic, which took some time to clear.

He noticed Julie had opened a bottle of wine and had consumed almost half of it, something she had not been prone to doing recently. But this time he knew exactly what was bothering her. She had told him yesterday evening about Charles and Sheila moving to Dublin because Charles had obtained work there. She had been upset when she had been telling him, and although he was shocked and surprised that Charles had not thought to tell him – his own brother – but then Matthew realised that the women had met up as they usually did, and as always, were prone to confide everything to one another. So no doubt Charles – cautious, deep thinking Charles – would tell his brothers and his sister, Lucie, in his own good time.

'Julie, love.' Matthew greeted his wife lovingly, 'Are you still pining for what you see as the loss of your sister-in-law's company.' And Matt hugged Julie as he spoke. 'Remember, I won't see much of Charles either and he is my brother. But I will guarantee to you that you and I and young Emily too, of course, will visit Sheila and Charles on a very regular basis in Dublin.'

'I do sincerely hope so, especially as Charles is your brother and this will be the first time in a long time you will not see so much of one another. And now that your hours are so much less we have no excuse.'

Then Julie went on, 'Any developments in your work, love?'

Matthew said there was nothing more conclusive to tell her. His news about the arrest of Alfie Reid's suspected killer would keep. It was always best not to assume anything in these cases and wait to get the ultimate proof. He would feel better telling her conclusively, they now had Alfie Reid's killer in custody.

However, as the evening wore on and Julie seemed to lift herself out of her despondency Matthew was tempted to talk again about the phenomena of anyone being able to memorise numbers to such an extent. He wondered if they had been totally honest when they had told him in the letter that it was as they were typing the letter that the registration number came back to them so easily. Who was able to do that? Certainly, even after years of experience and trying to memorise things, Matthew knew he still had to write everything down to make sure he had it right.

'I am delighted, Sir, to tell you that we have arrested Paul Woodside for the murder of Alfie Reid in Crumlin Road Gaol.' Matthew had made his way to the Superintendent as soon as he had received notification that the man they had arrested had now been charged.

'And have you obtained all the forensic evidence you needed in order to charge him?'

'Yes, Sir, the fingerprints on the cake box matched that of our suspect's. I must say, Sir, we owe a lot to the prison officer who retrieved the empty cake box from the man's room after he read his note and had it analysed. It was very good thinking on his part and I do hope someone commends him for it.'

'Yes indeed, do contact the Governor and tell him that we are indebted to the officer. Will you do that Matthew? The Superintendent said and then went on, 'Congratulations again, and I am delighted to say that I am glad the anonymous letter turned out to be so genuine. As you and I both know it is not always the case and can be just the product of a very imaginative, overwrought mind with no substance to it. But this information was worded in such a way as to be very well informed and substantial. I can't help feeling Matthew, that they were someone of good standing who was at the prison that same evening as our prisoner.'

Chapter 78

'Julie, I have some good news this evening, mind you it has all to do with my work.' And Matthew hesitated. 'I know I no longer bring it home, page after page, but I do still like to bring you up to date about everything.' Matthew had just returned from work and had sought Julie out in the kitchen.

Julie paused in the middle of stirring the stew she had just made. 'Well, what is the latest, Matthew? I do like to hear how your day went and I do hope you know that anything you do tell me I don't go round the streets and our family talking about it. Well at least I hope you know.'

'Of course I know that. I wouldn't be daft enough to tell you anything if I thought you would go and talk about it.'

'Right, Julie, the anonymous letter I received some time ago proved to be accurate in so many ways. We have charged a man with Alfie Reid's murder thanks to our anonymous writer and of course the prison officer who kept the cardboard cake box.' Matthew paused while he took the plates out of the oven and placed them on the table in readiness for the stew Julie had made. 'But I have to say that without the letter describing the suspect, the car and the number plate, we would never have traced him in the first place. Do you not admire anyone who is so good with numbers that they can just reel them off from memory? I know I do. Julie. As for me, I tried to avoid even the simplest sums in school, I was so hopeless. I don't foresee a time when that might change, I won't ever change.'

'Matthew, you are dwelling on that registration number far too much and I wish you would stop.' Julie sounded very short with him suddenly and then she went on in a softer tone. 'I think you have so many other attributes that having no recall for numbers is not what I would call a failing you have. Do you not agree?'

In answer, Matthew just shrugged his shoulders and Julie knew he was still thinking about this anonymous person with this gift for numbers.

'Right, Matthew, now that that case is closed, what about Dublin?' Julie asked, anxious to distract him.

'I have been thinking about that, Charles forwarded me his new address a couple of days ago as you know, Julie' Matthew brightened up suddenly. 'I would love to see how they are settling in, and I would love Emily to come with us but I know she would much prefer to spend her weekend with her older brother Jason and his children. And of course she is very keen to stay there since Lewis was kidnapped – she probably thinks she could, in some way, have prevented that happening had she been out playing in the garden with him.'

'Well, I don't think we should try and coerce her into coming with us if she would rather be here, although I did think she would be keen to see Evelyn and Ethel and hear how they like living in Dublin. But I will ask her to come with us and then we'll see what she thinks.' Julie answered. 'It's hard to believe they have been gone from here over a month ago already.'

Matthew knew Julie was anxious to go as soon as they could, so after phoning Charles to his new work place – he did not as yet have his home telephone number – the two men organised that Matthew and Julie would be down to see them in two weeks' time. Emily was in two minds as to whether to go or not but in the end decided to stay with Lewis, Eva and their parents. But she did stress to her mother that she would go down and see her cousins the next time her parents were going. So, Matthew and Julie made the journey down to Dublin without their daughter but knowing that her brother and his wife would look after her well.

The weekend turned out to be a success, which Julie, in particular, was very relieved about. There was no noticeable tension between Sheila and her, and the two brothers seemed very happy to spend some time in one another's company. They were living in a rented house but Charles explained to them that if everything worked out for them, they would hope to buy it in the near future. It was a beautiful Georgian terrace house spread over four floors with high ceilings and large rooms with windows which seemed to flood wonderful light into all the corners and crevices in a most comforting way so that the place all felt so homely and welcoming. Charles talked at length about his new line of work, emphasising that he now only mainly oversaw the surveying work that was going on. In the meantime, Sheila showed Julie through her new home explaining how – if they were fortunate to buy it – how they would change the colour scheme in some of the rooms but in the meantime they were happy enough to live in it as it was.

They were in one of the bedrooms upstairs when Julie decided that it was as good a place as any to confide to Sheila the latest developments in the Alfie Reid case.

'Sheila, you are probably not aware that they have arrested and charged a man with the murder of Alfie Reid.' Julie spoke in a low voice because even though there was only the two of them in the room she could not run any risks of being overheard. 'Matthew tells me it is an open and shut case now because the man's fingerprints match those found on the cake box which was given to Alfie Reid.'

Now when Sheila turned to Julie, Julie could see that her face was alight with something akin to relief and Julie was suddenly glad she had told her sister-in-law this.

Then Sheila clapped her hands softly and just for a moment. 'Why, Julie, that is wonderful, you know.' She hesitated for as moment as if she was about to say something more but she suddenly went quiet and seemed at a loss for words. So it was Julie then who relieved the tension. 'It was all thanks to the anonymous letter that Matthew received, you know. He says he would never have traced Alfie Reid's killer only for the letter.'

Sheila seemed to have recovered her composure now, just briefly saying how glad she was he had been apprehended. Then she surprised Julie by her next statement.

'Now that I am down in Dublin, I am safe here. I haven't been convicted of anything so no one could force me back to the North on a charge. It is only if I have already been convicted, they could bring me back to the North. But I won't be taking any risks by going up to visit any relatives in the North because I do recall you saying, Julie, that if I left the country you might consider confessing everything to Matthew. So in order to salve my conscience, I want to give you that choice. I shall miss going to visit up North and although it is lovely here and the children and Charles seem happy, I am beginning to miss the place already.' Sheila gave Julie a wan smile as she spoke.

'Oh, Sheila, did you engineer this whole move in order to pave the way for me to tell Matthew everything.' Julie felt uneasy now by what her sister-in-law was telling her.

'Oh, no – well, partially, perhaps. Charles was offered the post and Evelyn was offered a place in Trinity so I did encourage them both to accept the offers. I suppose it slowly evolved in my mind that it would be the answer for you, Julie.'

'You did not need to think about what might suit me in all this, Sheila. I am still faced with making the most formidable decision of my life. When or indeed if, I tell Matthew anything.'

'I'm afraid I can't help you there, Julie. This is how it is for me here now.' Sheila replied and then added, 'We best get back downstairs or the men will wonder what on earth we are gossiping about up here.'

Julie agreed and the two women made their way back down to the sitting room where the two men seemed very relaxed indeed, watching television. Charles was very interested to know what Julie thought of the house and its surrounding area. Julie was quick to say that she thought the house was lovely with its four floors and the whole spaciousness of the place.

'I daresay we don't have much use for four floors but Sheila and I both loved the place and its setting and its most welcoming feel. As you know, the fact that it is just rented means of course we can move if anything changes for us, and we need to see how both girls settle down before we make any decision to buy.' Charles paused, then added, 'My firm in Northern Ireland say they are more than happy to keep my job open for a time in case we are disappointed with life down here and how it all goes for the girls. Evelyn seems fine, I suppose any University would be new to her no matter where she was. So she seems very philosophical about it. Isn't that so, Sheila?'

'Yes, Julie, we have no concerns about Evelyn but Ethel, I suppose because she is that little bit younger, feels at a loss and seems to be missing her friends, but hopefully, she too will settle. Charles maintains that if either of the girls or I are unhappy we'll all just up sticks and come back to the North.'

'Well, there would be no shame in that you know, Charles – Sheila. None at all, No one should stay anywhere they are unhappy no matter what the circumstances.' It was Matthew who spoke, obviously concerned about his brother's line of thinking. 'I know you have given up your home in the North, Charles, but I hope you would not let that have any bearing on your decision.'

'I'm sure we'll all settle down, Matthew, and Charles loves his new job and that means a lot and here we will be very comfortable.' Sheila intervened, then added 'Let us have a drink before we retire for the night and please don't be going home tomorrow thinking we will soon be up the road after you. These things take time.'

And Matthew totally agreed with his sister-in-law that indeed they did.

Matthew and Julie left the next morning after breakfast with sincere promises to keep in touch. In particular, Sheila said she wanted to hear as soon as Jessie Davis had her baby. Charles and her would be sure to send an extra special present. Then, as they were getting into the car Charles said that indeed, if he could spare the time, they would come up some weekend to visit them and go and see this new baby. On the way home, Julie marvelled at how normal things were, or appeared to be, between Sheila and herself. No one would ever guess at the awful secret that lay between them.

Chapter 79

Julie was looking forward to meeting up with Jenny and Lucie this morning in their usual venue. It was not lost on Julie than when she suggested a coffee morning, Lucie seemed to go out of her way to make herself available. Certainly, Julie appreciated it and although she never mentioned it to Jenny, she wondered had she too, noticed it. No doubt, Lucie was sensitive to the absence of Sheila on these occasions and thought that her more constant presence might somehow fill the gap. Besides, this particular coffee morning was by way of celebrating the safe arrival of a baby daughter for Jessie and Harold. A little girl who, they had said, would be named Iris. Everyone agreed that it was wonderful news and as Julie sat down at the table beside her sisters-in-law she could see they were both delighted and anxious to share the good news with one another.

'I rang Sheila first thing this morning to tell her about the baby.' These were Jenny's first words to Julie, meanwhile, Lucie was nodding and smiling broadly. 'So did I, Jenny, but Sheila never told me that you had already rang her.'

'I rang her too, Lucie,' Julie said, 'but she did say both of you had beaten me to it. In fact by the time I rang she had herself organised to go shopping to buy this new baby a present. She did seem truly delighted to hear all was well, I must say.' Julie did not add that Sheila had said, in rather a wistful voice how much she would love to take a train and come up to see this new baby who must mean so much to Jessie and Harold. Obviously Sheila had not expressed those thoughts to either Lucie or Jenny and Julie understood why she could not. They would both have been organising Sheila on the next train, if that was what she wanted.

The three sisters-in-law were discussing the shopping for presents for this so precious baby, when Julie noticed Lucie's attention had been diverted by some other customers entering the shop. As the newcomers moved towards a table in the corner, the elderly lady who had a little girl by the hand, noticed Lucie who had just got to her feet, looking uncertain, Julie thought, as to whether to go and meet the lady who was smiling at her now and obviously knew her. The elderly lady looked quite familiar to Julie too, but she could not place her. Then she heard Lucie say, quite distinctly, 'Mrs. Mullan, How are you? And is this Alice whom you told me about?'

And Julie realised as she watched Lucie being greeted by the elderly woman, who exactly she was looking at and who it was Lucie was now talking to. It was Patrick Mullan's family, his bereaved mother, his widow and his fatherless child. As Julie waited to see if Lucie would extend the introductions to Jenny and herself, she wondered how anyone could ever have done anything to leave this family so bereft and desolate and who had any right to do such a thing.

Now, as Lucie urged Mrs. Mullan and her daughter-in-law over to Jennie and her she was struck by the resolve and pride which emanated from Patrick Mullan's widow. Julie sensed some determination about her, no doubt that determination must stem from the basic need just to cope, if only for the sake of her precious daughter, who now stood smiling shyly at Lucie. Such a beautiful child, Julie thought, with her dark hair and eyes, so like her father. She must surely be a daily reminder to her mother and grandmother of their loss, and guilt and remorse swept over Julie as she smiled at the family and pulled chairs out from the table, indicating they should join them. The two women and the little girl sat down, Julie thought, with some reluctance. But then the younger woman spoke. 'I am Helena,' she said, 'and although I have never met you, I do know you have suffered just as we have done.' Just a few words, was all Helena Mullan said, but they were so apt and touching that any awkwardness about sitting together dissipated and they all enjoyed their coffee and scones together. Alice, as Julie learned the little girl's name was, was treated to a cream bun followed by a lovely ice cream cone, which Julie insisted on paying for with the coffees. Then, Lucie said she must get back to work and everyone beginning to gather their belongings in order to leave, with Lucie and Mrs. Mullan exchanging telephone numbers before they left.

On the journey back home, Julie's mind was filled with the images of the two Mrs. Mullans and of Alice. Especially of Alice, and the child so graciously accepting the cream bun from her and then the ice cream. How endearing but also how vulnerable the little girl had looked even when she was so obviously enjoying what she was eating. When Julie reached home and made her way into the cottage she was glad no one was at home, she was glad of the peace and utter stillness of the house. Not that she had expected anyone to be there at that time of the day, Matthew was at work and Emily at school, but there were occasions when Matthew would pop in if he was out and about. So hopefully she would not have to face him until this evening, when hopefully she would be more focused on what she must do.

As the day wore on, Julie even contemplated ringing Sheila to Dublin, to let her know who they had coffee with and that arrangements had been made to meet up again in the near future and to let her sister-in-law know the pleasant time they all had together. But then, Julie realised it would be a most spiteful thing to do and it would really upset Sheila to learn anything about Patrick Mullan's relatives. She knew she must do nothing in the meantime, Julie decided. She knew a good rest was what she needed but most of all she knew she needed to think.

Chapter 80

The hours seemed to drag past all day while Julie waited to hear Matthew's key in the door, even though earlier that day she had simply wanted to be alone. Emily had been home from school and was now away to her cousin, Jayne's house, she had said, for a bit of company and Jayne wanted her to stay overnight with her. They were both missing Evelyn and Ethel so much she told her mother, that they wondered what on earth had made the whole family move down to Dublin. It was a Friday evening and usually Julie insisted that Emily did not stay overnight because Matthew liked to go out as a family on a Saturday, but after some disagreement, Julie finally agreed to Emily staying over at Jayne's house. Julie insisted that she must be ready to be collected first thing in the morning by either Matthew or herself. Sometimes, Julie had felt in recent months that Emily could not relate to either of her parents. Indeed, Julie had the strong impression that their daughter could barely tolerate either of them but more especially her mother. Julie realised that the fault must lie with her, she had been constantly preoccupied with what she had discovered and the weight of the guilt she carried around with her. Now though, she just smiled at her daughter and told her to give her Aunt Jenny her love and it would probably be Julie who would collect her in the morning.

She must have fallen asleep in the chair after Emily had left the house because she was awakened by the sound of Matthew's key in the door. She had not heard the sound of his car engine and to think she had been listening out for it for some time. Then, even as the door opened and Matthew appeared, the telephone rang in the kitchen. It was a strange voice that addressed her. 'Mrs. Hampton. Are you Mrs. Hampton?' the caller asked.

'Yes, I am Mrs. Hampton,' Julie said expectantly.

'Sorry to trouble you, Mrs. Hampton, but it is the police here. We are at a pharmacy on the Lisburn Road, a pharmacy by the name of Stewarts. We have your daughter here, she has been charged with theft.' Julie felt for a moment that she must faint with the shock of what the police had just said. 'Theft?' she repeated.

'I'm afraid so, Mrs. Hampton.'

'I'll let you speak to my husband.' And Julie, white faced, handed the phone to Matthew. 'It's Emily, she has stolen something. I think that's what the policeman said.'

Then Matthew spoke clearly and calmly to the caller. 'This is Matthew Hampton, Emily Hampton's father'. Now Matthew was listening intently to what was being said, then he replied. 'We will be along to the pharmacy very shortly.' Then turning to Julie. 'Let's go, dear and try to sort this all out.'

The pharmacist in charge of the store must have been looking out for them arriving because the door was unlocked as they approached and then opened by him. He ushered them into a room where Emily and Jayne, and Jayne's parents, Thomas and Jenny and two uniformed policemen were. The two girls were in floods of tears. The pharmacist told Matthew and Julie, as he had told Jayne's parents – the girls had stolen lipsticks and eyebrow pencils from the store.

Much later and after statements had been taken and signed by the two girls and their parents, and the lipstick and eyebrow pencils were paid for, Matthew, Julie and Emily drove home in comparative silence, with Matthew addressing his daughter only once. 'Emily, you will not be charged with theft on this occasion, simply, I think, because of my standing in the police force. But never expect, not ever, that I will help you out on any other occasion.' Matthew was finding it extremely difficult not to feel sorry for his daughter at this time in her life, he believed that during the awful time of Lewis's kidnap, and Rachel then suffering such injuries, Emily had been sorely neglected by her parents. True, she had always insisted she wanted to go to stay with Lewis, but was that because she got no attention whatsoever from her parents? And was this escapade with her cousin Jayne, simply attention-seeking behaviour?

Emily, still in floods of tears, which she seemed unable to control, just kept repeating how sorry she was.

Meantime, Julie, as they drove along towards home blamed herself and only herself for what had happened. Emily had done this tonight, Julie believed, because her mother had been too preoccupied in the last months to talk to her, to show any interest in her and what she might be doing. Julie had been too engrossed with her own deceit and the problems it had brought, that she had paid little attention to anything else. Now as the three of them entered the cottage and Emily made her way straight to her bedroom, Julie knew what she must do and she must do it tonight.

'Matthew, let us go into the sitting room with our dinner just on our knees and a nice glass of wine with it.'

'That sounds like a good idea, love. I'll go and turn on the gas fire as it is beginning to get rather chilly in the evenings, now. I think we need to have a good talk about Emily.'

Julie knew they did need to talk about Emily and what to do for the best, but first she must speak to Matthew about another equally important problem.

Later, after they had eaten their rather belated dinner and a glass of wine each, Julie suggested that should have another wine in order to try to relax after their ordeal in the chemist's shop. Then, Julie checked on Emily on two or three occasions and was rather surprised to discover that her daughter was fast asleep, obviously unperturbed by her behaviour and the result of it earlier in the evening. Perhaps that was how it was with young people Julie reflected, as she went to re-join Matthew, they seemed to be able to shrug things off so easily and see them as relatively unimportant in their young lives.

'Here is another glass of wine,' Julie said softly but instead of sitting down beside Matthew on the couch, as she always did, she sat down in the chair facing him.

'Matthew,' she began. 'I have something very important and very serious to tell you.' Julie's voice was low and hesitant. 'I will understand, my love, if you never want to have anything more to do with me, ever again.' Julie found it very difficult to speak, she was so overcome but at the same time she was thankful that, at last, after all this time, she had found the courage to tell her husband of her deceit.

'I really have to tell you, Matthew,' and now there was a note of desperation in her voice.

Matthew sat, so very quiet, watching his wife as she spoke to him and then he spoke to her in his even, well-modulated voice, quite passionless and measured. 'Yes, Julie, I know you have, my dear. You have indeed something to tell me. I know, you see.'

Julie was lost now by what Matthew was telling her, they seemed to be at cross purposes here in this sitting room and Julie began to feel exasperated, just when she had decided to confess to him, Matthew was off on another wave length altogether.

'No, please, Matthew, you must listen to me. You could not know what I have done, I know you couldn't.' He could not possibly know anything, so what was he talking about? This was not going the way she wanted to, and she felt thwarted by Matthew's attitude.

'But I do, my dear, I am sure we are talking about the same thing. It's all about Sheila isn't it?' Matthew said this now in a matter of fact way.

Now Julie just nodded dumbly, stunned into silence for a moment. Then she found her voice. 'What do you mean, Matthew? What do you mean, it is Sheila?'

'Sheila is the contact I was so keen to identify as being the person who wrote those two notes.' Matthew's voice was still even and matter of fact.

'So you do know?' Julie just whispered and then, after a long moment. 'How long have you known? Please, Matthew, tell me. Why didn't you say something?'

'But don't you see, Julie. I have been waiting for you to tell me, and I do think I have been very patient over these long months. It was you who had the notes, after all. The notes, which were found in the house in England. Sent there, I presume, by Alfie Reid.'

'And you found the notes that I had hidden, Matthew.' Julie was now almost incapable of thinking, she was so shocked by the revelation that her husband had known for some time and all the time she had been torturing herself by trying to keep the notes from him.

'Yes, Julie, I found the notes one day as we were moving from the annexe to the cottage. They just slipped from the back of one of the drawers in your dressing table.'

Oh, my goodness, Julie thought to herself, I forgot, after all, to transfer them from the dressing table to my handbag before we moved house. She had meant to do it as a priority on two or three different occasions but had been waylaid by something, or someone else. Matthew was now talking again.

'But it was you, Julie, who originally found the notes, not me. So you deceived me here, Julie, you led me to believe there was nothing of significance in those boxes and yet you had indeed found something. I am glad it was you who found them, Julie, because obviously you recognised the writing, whereas the writing would have meant nothing to me. So you have done a real cover up of evidence here, Julie. So that is a crime, perverting the court of justice. Yes, Julie, I knew those notes meant a lot to you, otherwise why had you held on to them? So I waited for you to tell me, and here you are telling me now.' And Matthew threw out his arms in an all-encompassing gesture.

Julie could no longer sit just nodding dumbly as Matthew spoke, and now she said quite clearly to him. 'Yes, I am guilty of all you accuse me of but I recognised the writing from Charles and Sheila's Christmas card and checked the notes against the card for conclusive proof and of course the writing was a perfect match.' Julie broke down completely now and began to sob.

'I did not know what to do, believe me, Matthew, I didn't. But I knew you were so upright you would have had Sheila arrested and I could not bear to plunge the family into more despair than they have already gone through. I did fervently believe that everyone had suffered enough in the past year.' Between her sobs Julie tried to explain why she had incriminated herself.

'Of course, Julie, when I first discovered the notes I had no idea who had written them and why you were withholding them from me. I would not have thought of checking them against any Christmas card. I suppose it never entered my head it might be one of the family or one of our friends. That was a stupid assumption I made, no doubt about it.' Matthew was intent now on telling Julie all he knew about the cover up. 'And do you know when and how I realised that it was Charles's wife who was the culprit. It was when I received the anonymous letter from her. Of course I did not know then, who it was from, but then the writer said about their unique ability to remember numbers and how they became logged into their brain. At the beginning I could not think who I knew had that ability, then I began to remember how Sheila used to be able to rattle off people's telephone numbers and car registration numbers of some of her friends and family.' Matthew waited to see if Julie would say anything about this. Then he asked her. 'Do you not remember that, Julie?'

'No, Matthew, it probably would not have meant anything to me anyway at that time in our lives. But I can see now how significant it was to you when you remembered. But Sheila rhyming off numbers, while I might have thought she was very talented, it did not mean that much to me.'

Matthew nodded, anxious to go on.' So I began to think then that somehow those two notes – one enclosing the picture of Patrick Mullan, the other specifically stating he was not to be killed, but just hurt – might have some connection to Sheila. Then I also thought there might well be an ulterior motive for Sheila wanting to go and live in Dublin, but then of course Charles having a job down there was genuine enough. So I still waited for you to tell me.' Then Matthew asked her. 'Does Charles know anything about any of this, Julie?'

'No, I showed the notes to Sheila and she immediately owned up to what she had done. Charles knows nothing whatsoever about it.'

'God, I am so glad to hear that. I do believe it would tip him over the edge, my dear. You see I do know what Charles and Sheila came through after dad's murder. We all, every one of us, had a bad time but I can tell you, Charles and Sheila had a horrendous one.'

Julie was quite surprised to hear this. She had known very little about Charles and Sheila, she had been so intent on trying to make her husband well again. After all, he had been with his father that awful day and had witnessed everything. So Julie had thought that the rest of the family got off lightly compared to Matthew.

'What exactly do you mean to do now, Matthew?' Julie asked him, so tense and concerned she was now, for Sheila and Charles and certainly for herself and her marriage.

'Well, first of all, Julie – and I have given this a lot of thought – hoping that sooner or later you would tell me what you knew. First of all, I want to ask you for the notes. I must have them, Julie.'

'Oh, Matthew,' was all Julie could say.

There was a silence then between them before Julie could find any courage to speak.

'What are you going to do with them Matthew?'

'I am going to file them away with all the other notes and pieces of paper relating to Patrick Mullan's file. That is what I am going to do. After all, I did not identify the writing on those notes, that's for sure.'

'Matthew, do you mean? Do you mean to keep the case closed then? Is Sheila safe?'

'Julie, certainly I mean to close the case. I fear for my brother, I fear for Sheila but I also fear for you and Emily.'

Julie made to move over closer to Mathew but he held up his hand.

'And no doubt that when the jury see Sheila's note requesting that she only wanted Patrick to be hurt but not killed, when they would hear all about what she and her husband suffered after dad's death, she would probably be acquitted of murder. But still at this moment in time, I do not want to take the risk that it might all go wrong for her and for you. She might still be charged with manslaughter, that is of course, if you were prepared to give evidence in court against her.' Matthew looked earnestly at Julie and pointed to the sofa beside him.

'So you see Julie, I am not the upright, honest man you have been thinking all these months that I am. No,' and Matthew sounded almost disappointed.

'In fact the truth is Julie, had I recognised the writing on those notes, I probably would not have reacted any differently to how you did.' Matthew said, and Julie just hugged her husband repeatedly as they sat together, she was too choked with tears to answer him.

'Do hold on to the fact, Julie, that Sheila only wanted him to have a bit of a beating, nothing else. So really she is innocent of murder.'

'Matthew, if you only knew what this means to me. I still can't come to terms with the fact that you have known since you received the anonymous letter.'

'And I could hardly believe you harboured those notes without relying on me to make what I would like to think would have been a balanced decision.' Matthew returned Julie's hug in a distracted manner, not his usual loving embrace, but Julie appreciated that, at least, her husband was hugging her.

'We must move forward from this Julie. I am concerned for Emily, obviously all the trauma of the past year has told a tale on her. I believe the pharmacy staff were so understanding about what had happened because they knew exactly who we were and what we have gone through. So let's concentrate on keeping a close family unit from now on, Julie. Just the three of us.' And then Matthew smiled. 'But then of course, we have grandparents, great grandparents, uncles, aunts, brothers, sisters in law all to concentrate on keeping close to us. But let's spend a lot of time with Emily, she needs it and she deserves it and then we will keep in close contact with Sheila and Charles, and if they are unhappy in Dublin, we must make it clear they are at liberty to come back up here. As for ourselves, we must promise never, ever again to keep anything, no matter what, from one another. And Julie was only too anxious to agree with him.